Honor, duty, courage, passion . . . the men of the Navy SEALs are a special breed of hero, and in these stories by eighteen top romance authors these heroes are celebrated not only as symbols of devoted service to their country but as the kind of man every woman wants to love. They'll rescue a damsel in distress and her lap dog, too. They'll battle hometown dramas and international bad guys. When it comes to giving away their hearts, they'll risk everything.

All proceeds from sales of *SEAL of My Dreams* goes to the Veterans Research Corporation, a non-profit fundraiser for veterans' medical research.

Among them, the authors of *SEAL of My Dreams* have won dozens of writing awards including multiple RITAs from Romance Writers of America. Their nearly 600 published novels have sold at least 25 million copies worldwide. The *SEAL of My Dreams* roster includes many of the best-known authors in modern romance fiction. In addition, many have strong family connections to the servicemen and women of our nation's military, and many specialize in novels featuring heroes and heroines from all branches of service.

Visit the authors at their websites and at http://sealofmydreams.com.

SEAL of My Dreams

An Anthology with Stories by

Robyn Carr
Jami Alden
Stephanie Bond
Kylie Brant
Helen Brenna
HelenKay Dimon
Cindy Gerard
Tara Janzen
Leslie Kelly
Elle Kennedy
Alison Kent
Jo Leigh
Gennita Low
Marliss Melton
Christie Ridgway
Barbara Samuel
Roxanne St. Claire
Stephanie Tyler
Loreth Anne White

Bell Bridge Books * Memphis, TN

Bell Bridge Books
PO BOX 300921
Memphis, TN 38130
ISBN: 978-1-61194-051-0

Bell Bridge Books is an Imprint of BelleBooks, Inc.

Cover Design: Croco Designs
Interior design: Hank Smith
Photo credit: © John Moore @ Getty Images

:Lmsd:01:

Acknowledgements

Many thanks to Croco Designs, who donated the design work for the fabulous cover of the book, and Getty Images, who discounted the licensing fee. Also to Sharyn Cerniglia at Bell Bridge Books, who donated her copyediting tasks.

The cover model is the real deal, an active-duty SEAL at the time this picture was taken by photographer John Moore. We offer our heartfelt respect and thanks to him—his identity is classified, but we hope he sees this note. The photo is titled "U.S. Navy SEALS Prepare For Night Mission In Fallujah," and captioned: "FALLUJAH, IRAQ - JULY 27: A U.S. Navy SEAL prepares for a night mission to capture Iraqi insurgent leaders July 27, 2007 near Fallujah, Iraq. American Special Forces operate throughout Iraq, targeting 'high-value targets' in commando raids, often at night to take advantage of their night vision superiority."

Table of Contents

FOREWORD

Robyn Carr

America is in love with the Navy SEALs.

We stood witness as a nation, as a world, to acts of bravery and mastery driven by patriotism as they took down one of the world's most dangerous villains. When the highest level of competence and fealty was required, the SEALs were called. And they did not take a bow.

Here's what they are not—they are not celebrities, movie stars or sports idols. They are flesh-and-blood men who have volunteered for the highest level of military training available and taken an oath to perform heroic acts at great personal risk in the defense of a country that will not put their pictures on magazine covers or pay them a multi-million dollar contract. Indeed, their 'bonus' will come in the form of hazardous duty pay. They are compensated by their rank and could choose far less dangerous or frightening roles. And their success as SEALs depends, at least as long as they serve in this capacity, on anonymity.

Who is better equipped to honor the image of our greatest warrior heroes than the gifted pens of some of the romance industry's finest authors of romantic fiction. In this volume, the visage of some of the world's most revered heroes is captured in scenes of love, bravery, laughter and passion, all created to bring into focus the SEALs of our dreams, those men we hold in such high esteem.

While the SEALs have the distinction of recently compromising the world's most insidious criminal and as a team are recognized and honored for their astonishing success in that mission, it brings into specific relief the number of units and teams in the Armed Forces who we, as a nation, rely on to defend our freedom. From Green Berets to Rangers, every branch of service is renowned for their Special Forces' Olympian skills and almost mystical abilities. And always, they anonymously perform these duties for the safety of their comrades and the citizens they protect.

I seem to be spending a lot of time in airports lately, and I use much of that time approaching military men and women traveling in battle dress uniform and wearing suspiciously dusty, beat up boots. With mist clouding my vision and a lump in my throat, I thank them for their service and, when I do so, because I'm not intimate with unit insignias, I have no way of knowing if their job has been to take out the free world's worst enemy or count paper clips. And in point of fact, what is important to all of us is that our faithful men and woman who serve are there for us, defending our freedom and liberty, in whatever capacity they are able. What matters is this—every single job in the Armed Forces is essential, is honorable, is worthy of the highest praise and deepest gratitude. Every raised voice is needed, every hand lent to the task and every heart committed.

Which brings me to this—while the volume you hold pays tribute to the Navy SEALs, the proceeds from these works of the heart will benefit all military men and women. No one involved in this project will profit except the Veteran's Research Corporation, a non-profit foundation supporting medical research for veterans. The money this project earns will directly benefit our veterans from all branches, all units, all missions. God bless and keep them, one and all.

COMING HOME

Jami Alden

Chapter One

Nick DeMarco had been to the most hellish corners of the earth, had witnessed the horrors people could inflict on one another. He'd seen his closest friends fall in a battle, had held their hands as they bled out.

He'd gladly relive any of those moments to not have to be here right now.

Standing next to a fresh grave at St. Mary's cemetery, listening to Father Fiore deliver the final sacrament before his mother was lowered into the ground. At the priest's direction, Nick picked up a handful of dirt and tossed it on top of the casket.

The finality of the gesture hit him like a kick in the chest, breaking through the cloak of numbness that had settled over him since he'd received the news three days ago. Joan DeMarco was really gone.

He endured what felt like a thousand kisses on the cheek, shoulder squeezes and murmured "I'm so sorry." There had been over five hundred people at both last night's rosary and this morning's mass. Many of them had joined the procession to the cemetery. In her forty-year career teaching freshman English at Greenwich High School, Mrs. DeMarco was a favorite with students, parents, and her colleagues.

Many of them had shown up today, taken the opportunity to tell him how his mother touched their lives, how much they loved her. Nick might have been touched, had he been able to get past the feeling that he'd taken an RPG to the chest and been blown wide open.

"Hey, nice threads," the familiar voice shook away a bit of the fog, and Nick looked into the sympathetic face of Robby Girardi. Though Robby was thirty-two, like Nick, Robby's face was still round, almost childish on top of his wide neck, and his black hair was still so thick it stood up like a brush on top of his head.

Nick and Robby met on the first day of kindergarten and were inseparable through elementary and middle school. Joan started calling them Mutt and Jeff after Robby's height topped out at five four in ninth grade and Nick had shot up another foot to tower over him.

Nick gave his old friend a feeble smile and returned Robby's hearty, back slapping hug. "I hate wearing the damn thing," Nick said, tugging at the collar of what he and his SEAL teammates referred to as the ice cream suit, blinding white from head to toe. "But Mama always liked me in it."

"When did Mama Joan get to see you in it?" Robby asked, the accusation evident in his voice. "Last I checked you haven't been home in what, ten years?" He saw, along with accusation, hurt in Robby's eyes. When Nick had left that last time, he'd left for good. Turned his back on the town he grew up in and everyone in it so he wouldn't have to be reminded of what he'd lost when he'd chosen a different path.

"More like nine and a half," Nick said lamely. "She came to see me a few times." But not enough, and not at all for the past year and half, because she'd been too sick. And Nick hadn't managed to get his ass on an airplane to the east coast to see her.

Because for all that he was a Navy SEAL, had made it through the most rigorous training program on the planet, and regularly carried out dangerous combat missions, deep down Nick was weak. A coward.

Even though he'd known better to believe her false assurances that she was feeling well and she was having no problem with the chemo, Nick had planned to visit three times in the past six months, only to postpone it at the last minute. All because he was afraid of coming face to face with the reason why he'd left.

Now it was too late, and Joan was dead. Not because of the breast cancer that the doctors had been treating aggressively, but so far successfully, but because of an infection. Any normal healthy person would have been able to fight it off, but with her immune system depressed by the chemo, her body hadn't stood a chance against the virulent bacteria.

And Nick, her only son, the only close family she had left, hadn't dragged his sorry ass home to say goodbye.

"I'm sorry," Nick said, as much to his mother as to Robby. "I should have come home more often."

Robby's mouth pulled down at the corners, his eyes dark with sympathy. "I get it. I remember how everything went down. Speaking of, have you seen—" Robby's voice cut off abruptly. "Never mind. Here she comes."

Nick followed Robby's gaze into the crowd. His entire body went hot, then cold when he spotted her. Sarah Decker, the reason he'd never returned to Greenwich after that last, ill-fated visit nine years ago.

Just like the first time he'd spotted her the first day of seventh grade homeroom, Nick was unable to take his eyes off her as she moved through the crowd. She stopped to talk to several mourners on the way over, her light blonde hair falling over her shoulder, obscuring her face as she leaned in to listen to Dr. Hicks, the superintendent of the schools.

Nick braced himself as though for impact, summoning up all of his hard earned discipline as he threw his shoulders back and lifted his chin in full (military) stance. Gaze forward, unseeing. Impervious, impenetrable.

Then she was there, and he felt his meager defenses strain under the force of her tentative smile, her teary, "Hi, Nick."

"Sarah," he said, hoping she didn't notice how he was drinking in the sight of her. Other than a few fine lines around her blue eyes, she looked exactly the same as she had nine years ago. Her body was still slim and modestly curved beneath a form fitting, sleeveless black dress.

With her big blue eyes and fine, almost delicate features, fair skin with its dusting of freckles, and slender frame, her beauty was in stark contrast to Nick's dark good looks and tall, muscled frame.

They used to joke about how when they had kids their features would cancel each other out.

The memory hit him out of nowhere like a knife in his gut, and it took every ounce of strength he had not to double over.

They'd had so many dreams, so many plans for the life they were going to build together. Then on September 11 the towers had come crashing down. Killing a half dozen of their close friends. Killing Sarah's father, who had been on flight 93, on his way to a board meeting.

Nick had known, with every fiber of his being, he needed to do something meaningful with his life. Something that would have a bigger impact on the world than working at some investment bank trying to spin money into more money by moving it around.

The attack had come just one month into their senior year of college, throwing their lives into turmoil along with the rest of the country. Sarah had pushed through her grief, insisting that her father would want her to finish school and go on with their lives.

Though Nick had broached the subject of joining the military after graduation, Sarah would always immediately change the subject, determined that their lives would go on exactly as before. Frustrated, Nick had stopped trying to win her over, thinking he'd make a move and leave her no choice but to deal with it.

So in July of 2002, two weeks after they had graduated from college—him from Boston College where he'd gone on a football scholarship, her from Harvard—Nick had canceled the interview one of Marcus Decker's former colleagues had set up for him at Goldman Sachs. Instead, Nick headed to the local recruitment office to enlist in the Navy.

Sure, he'd known Sarah would be furious at him. In her mind, their plan had been set for nearly a decade: after graduation, they'd get married and get jobs and an apartment in Manhattan. Once they'd had enough of city life they'd move back out to Greenwich to raise their family.

While it hadn't been Nick's dream to follow in his to be father-in-law's footsteps, he knew he had to do something to support Sarah in something close to what she was accustomed. Not that she was a snob, at least Nick had never seen that side until it was too late—it was that, unlike Nick who was raised by a single mother living on a teacher's salary, Sarah had never been told she couldn't go to the movies because they needed to save every spare penny to pay the property taxes on their small house on the water.

While Sarah had received a brand new white BMW on her sixteenth birthday, Nick saved for two years, mowing lawns, cleaning pools, and waiting tables at the pizza place down town once football season was over, all so he could buy a ten year old pickup with tricky starter.

Sarah had never cared about the differences, and neither had Nick. He knew he was smart and capable enough to make his way in the world. He might not end up like Sarah's father, who had been one of the richest men in one of the country's richest towns, but he'd do all right by her. They loved each other, that was all that really mattered.

At least, that's what Nick thought. But when it came down to it, she hadn't loved him nearly enough to stick by him when he realized he'd never forgive himself if he didn't do what was right. Do something bigger than himself and the privileged little world they'd grown up in. But he'd seriously overestimated Sarah's devotion to him. And when push came to shove, her privileged little world had won over him, hands down.

"I'm glad you could make it today," she said, snapping him back to the present.

"I should have made it sooner," he said bitterly. But he hadn't, because of her. On some level he knew it wasn't fair to blame her. He was a grown man and made his own choices, but right now it felt good to direct some of the soul crushing guilt in her direction.

"It happened so fast. On day she was fine and the next . . . ." Sarah broke off and squeezed her eyes shut, but couldn't stop the tears rolling down her cheeks.

In spite of everything Nick had a sudden, overwhelming urge to pull her into his arms, comfort her and protect her like always. *Yeah, you were her devoted lapdog for years and look what it got you,* he thought, steeling himself.

Sarah sniffed delicately and gave him a quick scan up and down. "You look really good in your uniform," she said with a watery smile.

The uniform, and all it represented, to him, to her, to them, suddenly felt about two sizes too small. Nick felt his lip curl as he said, "Navy comes through with the cool clothes, even though they don't pay enough to keep you in high style." He gave her the once over as well. He didn't know jack crap about fashion, but he knew enough about Sarah and her taste to know the simple black dress probably cost more than a month of his military salary, and the black heels would cover his car payments for at least two months.

"Speaking of which," he said, trying to ignore her stricken look as he scanned the crowd, "don't you need to go find your banker? Get yourself back to the estate and count your money?"

Sarah laughed softly, though she couldn't disguise the hurt in her eyes. "There's no banker," She held up her left hand to prove the absence of the gigantic rock she'd sported the last time he'd seen her, and the absence of any ring at all, for that matter. "No estate either, other than my parents' anyway. Steven and I broke up a long time ago."

Nick digested that bit of information, surprised his mother hadn't ever mentioned anything. He knew his mother had kept in touch with Sarah after the split. She had to have known Sarah had never made it to the altar with the pompous douchebag Nick had met on his one and only visit back to Greenwich after he'd joined up.

But Joan had never said anything. *Probably because the one time she tried to mention Sarah, you told her you didn't want to hear another word about that faithless bitch.*

All this time, when his defenses had weakened enough to let Sarah creep back into his thoughts, he'd imagined her living in some big house, another man's wife, having another man's children. Nick seized on the pain it caused, using it to remind himself that she had moved on. That part of his life, their relationship, was over, nailed shut.

She'd chosen a different life, a different man.

Now she was telling him none of that was true. *It doesn't matter,* he told himself. "Sorry to hear that. If you haven't already, I'm sure you'll land some other schmuck who can give you the life you think you deserve."

Her eyes narrowed and got a feisty glint and Nick felt an answering heat. He'd always loved getting a rise out of her. She was always so cool, so composed, but every so often he was able to push her over the edge. He'd always loved being one of the few people who was able to get her to lose control, whether it was her temper, her laughter, or in bed. Especially in bed.

"I'm taking pretty good care of myself these days, thank you very much."

His eyes raked her from the top of her blonde head to the tips of her heel clad toes. "I can tell—all the hours at the gym must be paying off. And the tight dress and the do-me shoes make sure every single guy here knows it."

Her cheeks flushed red and her fists clenched at her side. In spite of the gloom of the day Nick bit back a smile at the signs of her struggling to control her temper. "That's not what I'm talking about and you know it." She shook her head, closed her eyes. When she opened them, the anger was gone. In its place was a look so bleak it made his breath catch in his throat. "I was hoping when I saw you today . . . "

"What?" he asked in spite of his common sense screaming at him to keep this encounter as brief as possible.

She started to open her mouth, but they were interrupted by a short, stout woman who he recognized as Mrs. Morelli, his mother's best friend who'd worked with Joan at the high school for the last thirty years. She grabbed Nick in a fierce hug which he returned, struggling not to choke on the fumes of her heavy perfume.

"Thanks for all your help, Mrs. Morelli," he said. In his absence, she'd taken the reins with all of the funeral preparations.

"Of course," she said with a wet sniff. "Anything for Joan. But it's really Sarah you need to thank," she said, nodding in Sarah's direction.

"I do?" He looked at Sarah, whose gaze was fixed on the thick grass under her feet.

"Yes," Mrs. Morelli said emphatically. "If it weren't for her, we never would have been able to have mass here. And you know how much it meant to your mother."

Sarah shrugged. "I just made a couple phone calls. It wasn't that big of a deal. Now if you'll excuse me," she started to slip into the crowd.

"Wait." Nick caught her upper arm in his hand to stop her. His palm sizzled at the first contact with her skin, and it took every ounce of willpower for him to let her go, to not slide his fingers up and down and explore the silky smoothness. For a moment he was so stunned he couldn't remember what he was going to say.

"What is it?" Sarah prodded gently.

"Thank you," he finally blurted out. "For helping us reserve the church."

Her pink lips curved into a sad smile. "You know how much I loved your mother. And honestly, it really was just a phone call."

Nick felt a pinch of shame for giving her a hard time before. Their past aside, Sarah was a genuinely caring and compassionate person. It had been one of the many things he'd loved about her. "It might not seem like a big deal to you. But it meant a lot to my mother. And to me."

He watched as her eyes welled with tears, staring into the blue depths, and felt a twisting, falling sensation that set off warning bells. He knew he had to get away, and was relieved when Robby called out to him from the crowd.

He murmured his good-byes and went to join his friend.

"Any old flames rekindled?" Robby asked, giving him an elbow to the ribs.

"Hell, no," Nick snapped. But as he joined the conversation with a few of his old high school football buddies, he found himself tracking her blonde hair and slim form through the crowd. And when he saw her headed to the parking lot he had to clamp down on the urge to go after her.

Chapter Two

By the time he got back to his mother's house, Nick felt as exhausted as he'd been at the end of Hell Week. But unlike then, when he'd been able to collapse into a deep, dreamless sleep for the next twenty hours, now he was too keyed up by the emotions churning inside of him.

He changed out of his dress whites into a pair of cargo shorts. August in Connecticut was hot and humid, even at seven in the evening, so he skipped the shirt. Despite the heat, he felt a chill settle into his bones at the profound silence of the house he'd grown up in.

Though there were only two of them, their small house had always seemed a flurry of noise and activity. There was always a group of Nick's friends, including Sarah, who would wander in at various points after school, usually staying for dinner. The house would fill with the sound of laughter and his mother's beloved opera playing on the boom box she kept in the kitchen.

He wandered aimlessly through the house, his chest tight. Though the house was still full of her stuff and the things Nick had left behind, it seemed desolate, empty.

He went to the end of the hall and pushed open the door to his childhood bedroom. Nothing had changed since the last time he'd been here, or since he'd left for college for that matter. His double bed was still there, with its dark green quilt and pillows piled haphazardly at the top. The dresser that still contained the clothes he hadn't needed at school. A handful of books on the shelves.

The small desk where he and Sarah had crowded together to do homework, only to end up getting distracted by each other sometime around the third study question. He swallowed hard, remembering the first time he'd kissed her right there at that desk.

His gaze flicked to the bed. There had been a lot of firsts there, too.

The tightness in his chest got worse, threatened to cut off his breathing. This house, once so full of happiness and love, now seemed to exist only to remind him of what he'd lost.

On that morbid thought he headed back down the hall to the kitchen, where he was grateful to find a bottle of single malt, three quarters full. His mom's only vice had been a glass before bed each night.

He filled a tumbler with ice, tucked the bottle under his arm and headed out onto the patio outside the kitchen where he settled into one of the pair of Adirondack chairs looking out over the water.

Their house, though modest, stood on one of the most spectacular pieces of waterfront property in all of Greenwich. Overlooking Long Island Sound, it had once been the carriage house of a much grander estate which had been broken up and subdivided back in the sixties when the owner went bankrupt.

Knowing how much his wife loved being near the water, Nick's father had bought it and fixed it up himself. Over the years, Nick's mother had been offered millions for the property alone, but she'd refused to sell, not willing to leave the house and its memories of her all-too-brief marriage.

Nick settled into a deck chair and poured himself a stiff drink as he wondered if his father realized how much Joan had loved him, enough to sacrifice millions of dollars to hold onto his memory.

The scotch burned its way down to his stomach and his mouth pulled into a tight line. Once he'd thought he and Sarah had shared that kind of bond. Apparently not.

His eyes started to burn, and he told himself it was the scotch. It wasn't like him to get so maudlin, even over her. That was an advantage of being in his line of work—there wasn't a whole lot of time to moon over the girl who broke your heart.

But seeing her today . . . it had been as awful and wonderful as he'd always feared, and he knew it was going to be a long time before he could go to sleep without seeing those big, teary eyes, the sad smile on her soft pink lips.

"I see you found her stash."

Nick shot straight up in his chair as he looked up to see Sarah standing next to him. She held a foil covered plate in her hand and wore a tentative smile on her lips. Her eyes widened as she took in his shirtless state. "Wow, you've, um, really filled out."

Nick tried to ignore the flare of heat in her eyes and the answering flare in his gut. "What's that?" he asked, gesturing to the plate in her hand.

She looked at the plate, starting a little as if she just remembered it. "A peace offering." She set the plate down and removed the foil with a little flourish.

"Lasagna," Nick said, smiling a little as the aroma of tomato sauce and oregano hit his nostrils.

"When you didn't show up at Mrs. Morelli's I thought I'd bring you some. I know it's your favorite." She pulled a fork out of thin air and set it next to the plate.

Nick hadn't been able to handle the prospect of more pats on the back, more somber "I'm sorrys." Not to mention he didn't need any more encounters with Sarah messing with his already screwed up equilibrium.

He knew he should ask her to leave. Yet when she nodded at the bottle of scotch and asked, "Mind if I get myself a glass?" he found himself saying, "Go right ahead," around a mouthful of lasagna.

Sarah came back out, ice filled tumbler in her hand. She sat down in the Adirondack chair next to him and poured herself a drink.

He hadn't even realized he was hungry until the first bite hit his stomach. He counted back and realized he hadn't had anything to eat since he'd left San Diego the day before, his hunger drowned out by grief and guilt. "Thanks," he said. "This is really good."

"It should be. It's your mother's recipe."

His fork froze halfway to his mouth. "My mother gave Mrs. Morelli her lasagna recipe?" he asked, stunned. His mother had one of the biggest hearts and the most generous spirits on the planet, but she was downright stingy when it came to sharing her recipe secrets.

"No, she gave me her recipe," she said, cocking and eyebrow as she took a sip of her scotch.

"No way. When?"

She sat back in her chair, cradling the tumbler in one hand, and gazed out over the water. Her mouth pulled into a sad, wistful smile. "Right after we graduated from college. She told me she wouldn't be around forever, and I would need it so I could make it for you on your birthday and Christmas."

Nick's throat went tight and the lasagna congealed into a cold lump in his stomach. He put the fork down with a clink. "It's good," he said tightly. "I'm just not as hungry as I thought I was."

Wordlessly, she reached out and covered his hand with hers. "I'm not going to tell you it gets any better," she said softly. "But there will be a day when you wake up and it will hurt a little less."

He turned his palm up and entwined his fingers with hers. He knew the smart thing would be to pull away, but the soft warmth of her hand, the feel of her slender fingers laced with his, felt so good, so familiar, sending a ray of heat through the cold that seemed to have settled into his bones.

He studied her profile, light of the setting sun highlighting her high forehead, small, straight nose and firm chin. She still wore the dress from the funeral, and up close he could see it had wrinkled in the heat. Her scent drifted over to him on the salty breeze, fresh, floral, as delicious and irresistible as ever. He took a sip of his scotch, but even the smoky, peaty aroma couldn't get her scent out of his head.

Sarah took her own glass and raised it to the sky. "To you, Joan. I hope they serve scotch in heaven."

Nick raised his own glass with a little smile. They were quiet for several minutes, staring out at the last of the sun playing off the water. How many times had they sat out here, talking or sitting in comfortable silence? It felt so perfect, so right.

But nothing was right, he reminded himself. Hadn't been for a long time.

He pulled his hand from hers, drained his glass and poured himself another. He blamed it on the scotch when, after a few minutes he asked, "So what did happen with the banker?"

She sighed heavily and took a substantial swallow of scotch, shuddering a little as it went down. "Remember when you ran into us at MacKenzie's?"

Like he'd forget the day his heart had been ripped out of his chest. All that first year, despite Sarah's refusal to communicate at all, somehow he'd been convinced that if he could just see her in person, get her to talk to him, he could convince her to give them another shot. Robby had tried to warn him that she'd moved on, but he'd refused to believe it.

Until he'd walked into their regular hangout and seen her with him. Steven, the banker. She'd introduced him almost defiantly as her fiancé, and informed him that he was a senior director at her father's former firm.

When Nick had taken off for the Navy, Sarah had replaced him with exactly the kind of guy she wanted.

"I remember," he said tightly, immediately regretting that he'd asked. He knew if he traveled down this path he risked reopening wounds that might not heal this time around.

"You accused me of being a cold, shallow bitch who didn't care about anything but landing a rich banker husband."

Nick took another swallow of scotch. "Nothing to dispute there. You wanted our life to go down a certain path, and when I wanted to change course, you cut me off and found someone else."

She drained her drink and refilled. "It was never that simple, and you know it," she snapped. "I admit, I was acting spoiled and immature." She paused a moment, squeezed her eyes shut. "So much had happened. And Daddy," her breath caught in her throat. "It was still so soon after he died, and I felt like everything was falling apart. I just wanted something to stay the same, to pull everything back under control. I didn't know how else to handle it."

Nick closed his eyes and felt a wave of fresh guilt that he hadn't realized how vulnerable she'd been. He'd known she was grieving, of course. But his own immaturity and, hell, plain cluelessness had blinded him to the fact that he'd pulled another rug out from under her and then basically told her to suck it up and deal with it.

He found himself uttering something he'd never admitted out loud. "It was my fault, too. I should have made you understand how important it was to me so we could make a plan together."

She reached for the glass and took two deep swallows. "No, I should have listened to you when you tried to talk to me about why you wanted to join up. I should have tried to figure out a way for it to work." She shook her head. "I just couldn't get it out of my head that you would die. That you would go away and never come back. So many people we knew had died, and I couldn't stand the idea of being left behind."

His hand reached out to cover hers. "So you pushed me away and thought you'd be safe with Steven." He'd never forget the pain of seeing her with someone else, but with nearly a decade of hindsight and maturity on both their parts, it was easier now for him to understand why she'd acted the way she did.

She clutched his hand and nodded miserably. "On paper, he was everything I thought I needed. He wanted everything I thought I wanted. Then we saw you in that bar, and I knew I didn't want any kind of life without you in it." She released a wobbly sigh.

But by then it was too late, and when she'd reached out to him, Nick, heartbroken and bitter, had cut off communications. Given her a taste of her own medicine. "God, we both really screwed up, didn't we?"

He reached out, stroked his hand over the thick silk of her hair, traced his fingers over the line of her cheek bone. The sadness in her eyes faded, replaced by something else, memories of how they used to touch each other, how he'd spent years memorizing every inch of her until he knew exactly how and where to touch and taste.

He wasn't sure who moved first, but suddenly she was in his lap, arms wrapped around his bare shoulders as his mouth came down over hers. At the first taste, all the anger, hurt, and grief fell away. Nothing mattered but the taste of her on his tongue, her hands hot against his bare skin, her soft curves as she arched her body closer to his.

He scooped her up into his arms, carried her into the house, and laid her across the bed where they'd given each other their virginity so many years ago. Then he'd been nervous, so eager to finally have her but terrified of hurting her. After it was over they'd laid in the dark and whispered how much they loved each other.

Tonight there was nothing tentative in the way he took her. He stripped off her clothes and his, used his hands and mouth to find all the remembered secret spots guaranteed to drive her wild. By the time he slid inside her she was gasping with need, her hand clutching at his shoulders as she cried his name.

God, it was all so good, so much better than his memories. So good it made his heart feel like it was going to explode in his chest.

He knew there was no going back, there would be no whispered words of love tonight. But as he felt her body clutch around him, triggering his own pleasure, he finally felt like he was home.

Chapter Three

"Crap!" The soft curse and the sound of a shoe thumping to the floor pulled Nick from sleep. His years as a SEAL had conditioned him to go from dead asleep to fully alert in a split second, and he quickly became aware of several things. One, it was early, the sun not yet fully up outside. A glance at his watch confirmed it was just after six.

Two, he was naked under the sheets. Because he'd spent several hours reacquainting himself with every inch of Sarah Decker's body. And found it as delectable as it had been the last time he'd gotten his hands on it.

And three, Sarah herself was *not* naked, he noted with irritation. Not only was she not naked, she was tiptoeing around the room like she didn't want to wake him so she could make a clean getaway.

The thought that she could just take off without a word hit him like a fist in the gut. Not that he had any expectation of them starting up where they'd left off. Clearly they still had feelings for each other—strong ones—but too much time had passed, their lives were too different. And despite what she'd said, he didn't expect she was any more ready to deal with his reality today than she'd been ten years ago.

He watched her pad silently from the room, forcing himself not to call out to her. He braced himself for the sound of the front door opening and closing, signaling her departure from his life for the last time. It was good, he told himself. They finally had closure, and now he could finally let go and remember his first love without bitterness.

If that's true, why do you feel like someone drove a truck over your chest?

He'd barely completed the thought before he heard her footsteps, not headed for the door, but back down to his room. He kept his breathing steady, his eyes narrowed into slits as she approached his side of the bed. The aroma of coffee hit his nostrils and he heard a soft *thunk* as she sat a ceramic mug on the bedside table.

He felt her weight settle on the bed. Soft strands of hair tickled his chest as she bent her head and pressed her lips to his in a kiss that sizzled all the way down to his toes.

"Good morning," she whispered as he opened his eyes.

"Good morning, beautiful." He slid his hand up to cup the back of her head and pulled her mouth back to his. His other hand slid up the outside of her thigh to rest against the soft curve of her backside. "How about you get back in here and keep me company?"

She rested her forehead against his. "I so wish I could." She sat up and reached for the mug on the side table. "But I have a flight to catch and I'm already running late."

He pushed himself up against the pillows. Right. It was August, and Sarah's family always spent the summers jetting all over the place. "Where to? Jackson Hole? Martha's Vineyard?"

She laughed softly. The sound curled around him but couldn't banish the cold lump in his stomach at the thought of her leaving. "Not exactly. Try Bucharest." She stood from the bed and tugged at his hand. "Come on, walk me to the door like a gentleman."

Stunned, Nick let himself be pulled from the bed, forgetting he was naked until he caught Sarah staring at him with a frankly covetous look on her face. "God, I wish I could stay. Here, put these on," she grabbed his shorts from the floor and tossed them to him, "or I'll never get out of here."

"What the hell are you going to Bucharest for?" he said as he trailed her down the hall to the front door.

"Let's just say you weren't the only one who realized you needed to take a different path."

As Nick tried to figure out what that meant, she picked up her purse off the chair by the front door and reached in to pull out a flat silver case. She popped it open and extracted a white card.

She tucked it into his hand and looped her arms around his neck. "For the next six months or so, email is going to be the easiest way to get in touch with me. It's on that card, and I really hope you use it."

He looked down into her eyes, saw them fill with tears and felt an answering sting in his own as he wrapped his arms around her waist. "I will, I promise." He didn't know where this was going, if it could go anywhere, but after losing ten years to their immaturity and stubbornness, he couldn't let this be the last contact he had with her.

He bent his head, drinking in the taste of her, his heart aching as he wondered when he would get the chance again.

She cradled his face, the desperation in her kiss matching his own. "I hate the reason for it, but I'm so glad I got to see you, Nick. No matter what happens, last night meant everything to me."

His throat was so tight he could barely choke out, "Me, too."

One last kiss, a whispered goodbye, and she was gone.

He stared at the door for several long moments. Even as the ache of her absence settled into in his bones, he felt something else, something he hadn't felt in a very long time, especially when he thought of Sarah.

Something warm and bright and good. Hope.

Three months later

Nick watched out the window of the cab as the beautiful historic buildings of downtown Bucharest gave way to communist era developments. The squat, grey skyline wasn't improved by November's cold grey weather. But nothing—not the dreary setting or crappy weather—could dampen Nick's spirits as he paid the driver who'd taken him from the airport to the group home where Sarah was helping women and girls rescued from sex traffickers get back on their feet through education and work experience.

He spotted her easily, her tall, slender frame and blond hair pulling his gaze like a beacon. Her hair was scraped back into a pony tail, she wasn't wearing a speck of makeup, and she was wearing a bulky sweater and baggy pants. She was still so beautiful it hurt to look at her.

He took a moment to watch her, unnoticed, as she spoke to the man who approached her. There was a quiet confidence about her that he couldn't help but admire.

This would have been the last place he would have guessed Sarah would have found her calling.

He'd been shocked, when he'd looked at her business card that morning after his mother's funeral, to realize Sarah worked for a global nonprofit that helped rescue girls and women sold into the sex trade.

Over the last few months he'd learned through her emails that after they'd split, she'd landed a job in Manhattan thanks to her father's connections. *I thought I had everything I wanted,* she'd written, *but I woke up one day and realized my life had become so empty. I didn't care about anything, and I'd become another useless cog. Our family has all this money and all this influence, and we weren't doing anything meaningful with it.*

When a former Harvard classmate involved in the organization had hit her up for the annual fundraising campaign, Sarah had done more than open her wallet. Not only had she made a substantial donation, she'd quit her job in Manhattan and signed on as a corporate liaison, and used her family's influence to land corporate donations of cash, medical supplies, building materials, and international business contacts to help working-age victims get stable, well-paying jobs.

It took me awhile, but I finally got what you meant about being part of something bigger than ourselves.

Even though he hadn't even been able to hear her voice, Nick felt closer to Sarah after these last three months than he ever had before.

Never loved her more than he did right now.

He damn well hoped she felt the same. He called her name, and took it as a good sign that she shrieked in delight and shoved the clipboard she was holding into the hands of the woman next to her. Ignoring the questioning gazes of her coworkers, she ran across the room at a full sprint and flung herself at him so fast he barely had time to drop his duffel and catch her.

"Oh, my God, what are you doing here?" she asked, her face muffled against his neck.

Any doubts he'd had about surprising her fled as her arms locked around him in a vice grip as though she was afraid he was going to disappear any second.

"I had a couple weeks of leave after our last op, and I heard Bucharest is beautiful this time of year," he managed to get out between kisses.

"Right, especially in November, when it's cold and gray and the sun never shines. Seriously, I can't believe you came here, of all places to spend your vacation."

He pulled back, cupped her cheek, loving the lovestruck grin on her face. He knew it mirrored his own. "Why would I want to spend my time off with anyone but the woman I love?"

Her breath caught, and her blue eyes widened along with her smile. "You do?"

"Yeah, I do. I love you, Sarah."

She buried her head against his chest and Nick waited an agonized eternity for her to whisper, "I love you too. It's always been you."

"It's always been *us*," he corrected, his arms tightening around her. It had taken ten years of heartbreak and shared tragedies to bring her back to his side, and no way was he ever letting her go.

BABY I'M BACK

Stephanie Bond

Chapter One

Beneath his U.S. Navy SEALs T-shirt, Seaman Barry Ballantine's heart thudded against his breastbone. He wondered if he would recognize anything about his mountain hometown of Sweetness, Georgia. The last time he'd seen it, the entire town had been reduced to matchsticks. He'd been fifteen when the F-5 tornado had landed like a giant mixer in the bowl created by the surrounding mountain range, ravaging the small downtown and outlying homes. No human lives had been lost—the disaster had been dubbed The Sweetness Miracle—but the devastation had been the death knell for the small isolated community.

When the tornado descended, he'd been inside Moon's Grocery, grabbing a soda and making plans with friends to meet later at the Timber Creek swimming hole. The power had gone out—not uncommon when a summer thunderstorm blew through. But when the wail of an unfamiliar siren had sounded, Mr. Moon had herded everyone into the basement. Twelve years had passed, but Barry still remembered the roar of the monster twister rolling over them like a hundred freight trains. The relief of surviving the storm had given way to the terror of being trapped—more than fifty people had been buried alive in that basement, with no idea if anyone had even survived to rescue them.

And then someone had broken through—Emory Maxwell, the boyfriend of Shelby Moon, who was among those trapped in the basement, and his buddy Porter Armstrong, who were both in Sweetness on leave from the Army. Emory was the person who'd sounded the alarm from the water tower and was credited with saving the townspeople. Barry had been full of himself at that age and few things had impressed him . . . but when he'd been pulled out of that dark, dusty hole by the hands of two uniformed soldiers, he'd been awestruck by their bravery. On the spot he had silently committed to joining the Armed Forces when he was old enough.

Barry glanced to the wooden box sitting in the passenger seat and wished he could recapture the enthusiasm of that moment . . . perhaps it was that hope pulling him back to the only home he'd ever known. He passed a new sign announcing *Sweetness 3 Miles*, and geared down his Jeep for the steep, steady climb that would eventually take him into what used to be the center of town.

In the aftermath of the tornado he'd thought the place had resembled a war zone. He'd been right—since joining the SEALs, he'd seen plenty of war zones firsthand, except unlike The Sweetness Miracle, they'd all come with casualties. He wasn't naïve, he'd known what he was signing up for, that loss would be part of the job. But knowing it intellectually was one thing, and washing a comrade's blood out of your clothes was something else entirely.

A pain shot through his left foot. He inhaled sharply and tightened his grip on the steering wheel until it subsided.

The landscape on either side of the newly paved road began to look familiar. It had rained earlier, turning up the brightness on the remaining fall foliage, brilliant orange and yellow and bronze. Clear puddles on the shoulders reflected a crisp October sky. His open Jeep allowed the sounds and scents of autumn to filter in—buzzing insects and pungent fallen leaves. Ahead on the left was a new metal bridge that spanned Timber Creek. At its base was a sign pointing the way to a recycling plant. According to the town's website, the Armstrong brothers, all of whom had grown up in Sweetness and served in different branches of the military, were rebuilding the town on green industries.

He wondered if any other former residents had moved back to Sweetness, if he would know anyone, or if anyone would know him. His friends from high school had scattered after the twister, some of them landing in Atlanta, like his family, but not in the same neighborhoods or the same schools. Everyone had started over somewhere else, but he'd never felt like he belonged anywhere but Sweetness.

Farther ahead on the left was the old Evermore covered bridge—

no, the original had blown away. This had to be a replica, but the sight of a familiar landmark tucked into the picturesque curve lifted his spirits.

But when he rounded the curve and looked up, a bona fide grin spread over his face. The white water tower, the only structure spared by the twister, still stood on the top of a ridge heralding "Welcome to Sweetness" in black letters. Its surface was marred with bits of graffiti—apparently climbing the tower and proclaiming love with a spray can was still a popular activity. He'd always thought he'd do the same someday, but hadn't yet been inspired before the tornado had struck and his family had left town.

Oh, there'd been plenty of pretty girls around when he'd lived in Sweetness, and because he was a jock, they'd seemed eager enough to spend time with him, but there had never been anyone particularly special then . . . or since. He'd joined the Navy after high school and the transient lifestyle had been exciting, but solitary. Becoming a SEAL had been a professional and personal pinnacle, but the deployment and covert missions didn't lend themselves to a long-term relationship. He'd never let his mind go there.

And now—

He saw a flash of color out of the corner of his right eye, on the shoulder of the road. Too late, he realized it was a runner—a female runner—just as he plowed through a puddle of water, drenching her head to toe.

Chapter Two

In the side mirror of the Jeep, Barry saw the runner stop and lift her arms helplessly as water sluiced off her. She shouted something he was relatively sure was meant for him. He winced and slowed, then checked his rear view mirror and backed up until the Jeep was next to her.

"You okay?"

She was wearing orange running shorts and a white T-shirt, which were now plastered to her slender curves, he noticed appreciably. Water dripped from her dark ponytail, and wet bangs hung in her eyes—eyes that were shooting lasers at him. "Do I look like I'm okay?"

"Actually," he ventured, "you look pretty good from here." He gave her his most charming smile. "Sorry about that—I didn't see you."

"Really?" She indicated her neon-colored running clothes. "Are you blind?"

"No," he said cheerfully. "Hop in, I'll give you a ride."

Her eyes narrowed. "You don't know where I'm going."

"I grew up here—wherever you're going, it can't be far."

She angled her head and stepped closer. "You're Barry Ballantine."

He grinned. "That's right. Do I know you?"

"No," she said, then took off on a jog in the direction she'd been running.

Barry frowned, then backed up the Jeep to keep pace with her. She ignored him and slung water from her long arms. His mind raced to place her, but he felt sure if he'd seen this dark-haired beauty before, he'd remember it. Porter Armstrong knew he was coming—maybe word had gotten around town to be on the lookout for a stranger. Sweetness was like that . . . or at least it used to be.

"C'mon, jump in," he cajoled. "I'm sorry—let me make it up to you."

"You can't," she yelled.

"Hey, that's not fair, I'm trying here." A horn blared behind him. He slammed on the brakes and the car went around him.

The woman had stopped, her hands up, as if bracing to see a collision.

"You're going to cause an accident," he said pointedly, then leaned over and opened his passenger side door. "C'mon, get in. You're shivering."

The woman looked at the door, then down to her soaked clothes and relented with a drop of her shoulders. She strode to the Jeep wordlessly. Barry scrambled to move the wooden box in the seat to the floorboard. She swung into the seat and banged the door closed, but sat as close to it as possible, as if she might dive through the open window if he made a wrong move. Her shoes squished and water dripped from the end of a very pretty nose . . . and chin.

Barry stared at her profile, searching his memory banks and coming up empty. He reached into the backseat and pulled a sweatshirt from his duffel bag. "Here, put this on."

"Thanks," she mumbled, pulling the sweatshirt over her head. It swallowed her, but the shivering subsided.

"Where to?" he asked.

She didn't look at him. "I'm staying at the boarding house, straight ahead."

He put the Jeep into gear and drove slowly. "You'll have to show me when we get there. I've been away for a while."

"I know."

He frowned. "So how do you know who I am?"

Her mouth tightened. "We went to school together . . . here."

Surprise shot through him. "Here in Sweetness? I'm sorry, I don't remember. What's your name?"

She finally turned to look at him. "Lora Jansen."

The last name rang a bell because there had been several families named Jansen in the area, but he couldn't place the sweet, heart-shaped face of the girl next to him. Her eyes were as green as grass, framed with a dark fringe of lashes. Her mouth was wide and curvy, and he had the feeling if he could coax a smile out of her, dimples would appear under those high cheekbones. How could he forget such a face?

"Were you behind me?" he asked. Their high school had been small, a couple hundred kids at most.

"Actually, I sat directly behind you in sophomore English."

He squinted. "We were in the same grade?"

She nodded and pulled at the hem of her wet shorts. "What brings you back to Sweetness?"

He took in her fresh face and wide-eyed innocence, and felt a surge of gratitude that she would never have to see the things he'd seen. "A favor for a friend."

She pointed as they approached the downtown area. "The boardinghouse is the large building with the porches."

Barry looked around at the collection of structures that were so different from the original downtown area—in addition to the boardinghouse was a diner, a general store, a city hall building, a medical clinic, and a strip of storefronts that housed a hair salon and other businesses. Pedestrians bustled around on new sidewalks. In the distance, he saw a new school. "I can't believe it," he murmured. "They really have rebuilt the town."

She nodded. "The Armstrong brothers are the driving force for pretty much everything around here. The town's expanding every day. You can let me out here."

He pulled into the parking lot of the diner that sat across from the boardinghouse. She'd jumped out before the Jeep stopped. When she banged the door closed she chirped, "Thanks," and turned to go.

"Wait," he called. "Can you tell me where I can find Porter Armstrong?"

She gestured toward a narrow side road. "He's usually at the construction office. You can park here and walk—it's not too far."

"Thanks . . . Lora. Sorry I got you wet." He scratched his temple. "And I'm sorry I don't remember you from school—I guess it's been too long."

She gave him a flat smile. "I went by another name back then."

"What was it?"

"Metal Face." She lifted her hand in a wave, then looked both ways before jogging across the road.

Her words resonated in his head like a gong. Metal Face—the name he and his buddies had given to a gangly dark-haired girl in their class who had a mouthful of braces and big, wire-framed glasses. They had teased her mercilessly . . . how miserable she must've been, and how much she must've hated him. He didn't remember directly taunting her, but he certainly hadn't done anything to stop it. And what did it say about him that he couldn't even remember her real name?

Well, if it was any consolation, Lora Jansen had shown them . . .

Metal Face had grown up to be a knockout. Good for her.

Shoulda, coulda, wouldas flitted through his head as he parked the Jeep. Barry reached for the wood box in the floorboard and hopped out. After collecting a cane from the rear seat, he turned in the direction of the construction office. It would be nice to see Porter Armstrong again after all these years.

"Ooh!" Lora closed the door to her room with more force than necessary. It was so like Barry Ballantine to breeze back into town and humiliate her all over again, as if he was still the most popular jock in school and she were still Metal Face. She yanked off the sweatshirt he'd given her, along with her wet T-shirt, then grabbed a towel to dry her arms and squeeze more water out of her hair. Her hands shook, more from anger than cold.

Of course he would have matured into a gorgeous man, his sandy hair still sun-kissed, his blue eyes even more arresting, his chiseled jaw even more . . . *chiseled*, darn it. She hated how she could look into his eyes and revert back to her fifteen-year-old self, clumsy and tongue-tied. She'd heard through the grapevine that Barry had joined the military, which the Naval insignia on the sweatshirt he'd lent her seemed to bear out.

She released her ponytail and walked to the window while she towel-dried her hair. Barry had parked his Jeep and emerged, taking her advice, she presumed, to walk to the construction office. It came as no surprise that he was tall and wide-shouldered, but she was shocked to see him using a cane and favoring his left leg. As she watched his awkward gait, she zoned in on the injured leg with a practiced eye. The top part of his jeans leg was filled out with a powerful thigh, but the bottom part of his pants billowed loosely around a stiff core. Lora covered her mouth with stunning realization.

Barry Ballantine was walking on a prosthetic lower leg.

Chapter Three

Lora couldn't get her mind off him, not even after she started her afternoon shift at the Sweetness Family Medical Center. When Dr. Nikki Salinger had brought her on board as a physical therapist, she'd had her doubts that a town the size of Sweetness—even if it was growing every day—would offer enough patients to keep her busy. But with the army of men and women the Armstrongs had employed to build the town, there was always a back, neck, limb, or joint that needed to be rehabilitated. Today between Mr. Tyler's trick knee and Ms. Jacoby's carpel tunnel, she found her mind going back to Barry again and again. She felt horrible for being so short with him—it wasn't as if he'd splashed her on purpose. And it seemed petty to hold him accountable for all the unkind teasing that had come her way in high school. That was, after all, more than a decade ago.

On the other hand, she didn't want to fall into the trap of feeling sorry for the man simply because he'd lost part of his leg—amputees were not to be pitied. But she was sensitive to the fact that it was likely he'd lost it defending his country, and to the fact that his life would always be harder than a person who had two healthy legs.

By mid-afternoon, the man had worn a rut in her mind. So when she walked a patient to the lobby and she spotted Barry coming into the clinic, she thought she'd conjured him up. She watched him move, took note of his alignment and how it threw off his gait. He stopped in front of the receptionist's desk and spoke briefly. When the woman gestured toward the waiting area, he headed toward a row of chairs. Before he could sit, he noticed her and stopped.

Lora felt obliged to move toward him. Her pulse clicked higher with every step. "Hello," she said simply.

He straightened and subtly moved the cane behind him. "You, again." He tried to smile, but she noticed the pinched look around his mouth.

"Me, again."

"Are you a doctor?"

"No, I'm a physical therapist."

His eyes clouded. "I've seen my share of those."

She inclined her head. "How long have you had the prosthesis?"

Surprise flickered over his face. "About three months."

"Is it trans-tibial?"

"Yeah, I got to keep my knee, thank goodness."

She nodded. "Do you mind if I ask what brings you in to the clinic?"

He gave her a tight smile. "I need a prescription."

"For pain killers?" When he didn't respond immediately, she added, "I can tell you're in pain."

"Damn foot still thinks it's down there."

"Have you tried massage?"

His mouth tightened. "No offense, but the pain meds work for me."

She kept her tone light. "No offense, but I can get you off that cane."

Anger flashed in his eyes. He brought the cane around front and leaned harder. "I'm okay with the cane—I think it adds character."

Lora inclined her head as she backed away. "Sorry to intrude. I'm sure Dr. Salinger will get you what you need."

"I think you need more physical therapy," Dr. Salinger said.

From the exam table where Barry sat, he tamped down his irritation. "I've had six months of physical therapy." He thumped the exposed metal prosthesis, then rolled down his jeans leg. "I've gotten as good with this thing as I'm going to get."

The doctor gave him a little smile. "Maybe."

"I'm not addicted to the painkillers," Barry said. "I take them only when I really need them."

She nodded. "I believe you. I completed my residency at a veterans' hospital, so unfortunately, I've treated many amputees. I think the right physical therapist would not only increase your mobility, but also decrease your pain. I don't know how long you're planning to stay in Sweetness, but we have an excellent therapist here at the clinic."

Barry set his jaw. Having one of the male physical therapists at Bethesda Naval Hospital work on his stump was one thing, but having Lora Jansen's hands on him and letting her see him stumble and fall around—no thanks. "I'm only going to be here for a few days."

Dr. Salinger studied him until he averted his gaze. When he looked back, she angled her head. "I'll make you a deal, Seaman Ballantine—I'll write you the script for the pain meds, *if* you agree to a one-hour session with our physical therapist before you leave today."

Barry pushed his tongue into his cheek—he didn't like being blackmailed. But he'd been trained to handle torture at the hand of the enemy . . . he could handle Lora Jansen for one measly hour.

"Again," Lora said.

Frustration ballooned in Barry's chest and he made a face.

She arched an eyebrow. "You have a problem with walking?"

"No," he said more vehemently than the situation warranted. "But I've walked across the room and back a dozen times." And he hated that each time she'd studied him as if he were a newly discovered species of animal.

She lifted a camera. "This time I'm going to record you."

"This isn't like any PT I've had," he grumbled as he once again traversed the floor of the long, narrow room furnished with equipment, sets of stairs, walking corrals, and massage tables.

"And now back, please."

He retraced his steps, feeling irritable and self-conscious. And the more self-conscious he felt, the more he leaned on the cane. "Do you get paid to watch people walk?"

She lifted her head from the camera. "Sort of. Okay, you can have a seat." She nodded toward a chair, then hooked up the camera to a television monitor in front of the chair where he sat. The video of him walking came on the screen. She stilled the picture, then picked up an erasable marker, drawing lines and circles on the screen as she talked. "Your alignment is off here and here. See how your hips are tilted?"

He scowled and rubbed his aching left knee. "Yeah, it's called walking on an artificial leg."

"You're actually relying way too much on your prosthesis," she offered. "If you improved your posture and balance with Pilates and weight belts, you could shift your center of gravity back to where it used to be."

He chewed on his tongue as anger churned in his stomach . . . anger at a violent world, anger at the randomness of life. If only he'd stepped right instead of left that day, he'd still be with his unit in

Afghanistan, instead of sitting here in la-la land with a slip of a girl who wanted to fix him with yoga. "I'll keep that in mind," he said through gritted teeth, pushing to his feet. "I think the requisite hour is up."

She glanced at her watch and nodded, then used a dry eraser to remove the marks she'd drawn over his figure. She walked to the door with him, then stuck out her hand. "It was nice to see you again, Barry. Good luck."

He shook her hand, startled at the bolt of awareness that traveled up his arm at the softness of her fingers wrapped in his. She smiled, flashing those dimples he'd suspected lay in hiding, then extracted her velvety hand. As she walked away from him toward the video equipment, remorse bled through him. Lora Jansen was a sweet woman who, despite having past and present reasons to dislike him, had only offered to help. It wasn't her fault he was angry at the world, or embarrassed for her to see him like this.

"Lora."

She turned back, her eyebrows raised in question. She was lovely, he thought, naturally pretty with fine-boned features and luminous eyes. Her shapeless white lab coat hid her figure, but after seeing her earlier in wet running clothes, her slender curves were emblazoned on his mind. His pulse pounded as he suddenly realized he was very much looking forward to spending more time with her—that is, if he hadn't blown it . . . again.

He cleared his throat. "I'll be in Sweetness for a few days. If you can work me into your schedule, I might as well try some of the things you suggested." He shrugged. "I don't have anything better to do."

She gave him a curt nod, as if it didn't matter to her one way or another. "Be here tomorrow morning at ten."

Chapter Four

"Fifty more, and more slowly please," Lora said to Barry, who lay on the floor of the PT room doing jackknife situps.

He fell back on the floor with a noisy exhale. "What is this, boot camp?" He reached down to massage his left knee, exposed in the gym shorts he wore. His metal prosthesis began just below his knee and ended in a lifelike foot wearing an athletic shoe.

The pain pinching his face tugged at her heart. "May I?" she offered, gesturing to his knee.

He looked wary, but nodded.

As a professional, she was trained to mentally remove herself from the intimate act of touching another person, but with Barry, it took all her concentration. The man was a beautiful specimen of male strength, with long, lean limbs, and a well-muscled torso. Steeling herself against his powerful appeal, Lora knelt to lever her weight over his knee and massaged the flesh with firm, deep pressure. He grimaced.

"I'm sorry," she murmured. "Are the phantom pains bad?"

"Better than they were in the beginning," he said through gritted teeth.

She cast about for conversation to take his mind—and hers—off his magnificent body. "Do you mind telling me how it happened?" She held her breath because she knew she could be treading on a touchy subject.

He was quiet for a while, wincing as she coaxed the muscles in his thigh to relax and the nerve endings to stop sending sensations to an absent limb. "Common story," he finally said with a shrug. "I was on reconnaissance patrol, an IED went off."

"That must have been horrifying."

He only grunted.

"Were there other injuries in your unit?"

She thought he wasn't going to answer, but after a long silence, he said, "Yeah," but in a way that let her know the topic was closed.

She released him and sat back. "Okay, break's over. Fifty more situps, please. Try to raise both feet at the same time and to the same level."

She put him through several series of exercises nonstop. He wasn't happy about some of the Pilates poses, especially when she made him lean on her to balance, but at the end of the session, he was sweating and tired, and she was satisfied with his effort, if not his progress.

"Good session today," she said. "Do you know yet how long you'll be in Sweetness?" She told herself it had everything to do with wanting to make the most of his PT and nothing to do with the fact that she was enjoying their time together.

"I'll know soon. Probably a week or so, then I have to get back to my life."

"Where is that?"

"Not here," he said with a bite to his voice. "Hopefully somewhere exotic and exciting."

He couldn't have made it more clear that nothing of interest was happening in Sweetness. "You said something about being in town to do a favor for a friend?"

"That's right." But he averted his glance and didn't offer details.

"Where are you staying?"

"Porter was good enough to let me stay in the bunkhouse with the workers while I'm here."

She nodded, recalling that all the Armstrong brothers had military backgrounds . . . of course they would extend themselves to a fellow soldier.

"Same time tomorrow?" he asked, already heading toward the door.

Lora was accustomed to her patients being happy to see an end their PT appointments, but a small part of her was disappointed that Barry seemed so eager to be out of her company. "Yes, same time tomorrow," she said.

But he was already gone.

As he closed the door behind him, Barry sagged with fatigue. Frustration crowded his chest—he didn't like appearing weak in front of Lora and he *really* didn't like the push-pull of attraction he was starting to feel for her in such a short time. He attributed it to the undercurrent of tension he felt concerning the way he and his friends had treated her when they were younger. There was so much in the news lately about peer pressure and bullying; he'd listened to the reports with a sanctimonious attitude, wondering how kids could be so thoughtless, with zero recollection that he'd done the same thing, and to someone who'd probably grown up to do better things with her life than most of the people who'd teased her.

She was obviously well thought of in town—that evening he spotted her running down the same road he'd driven in on and everyone she passed waved and honked. And the next morning when he arrived for his appointment, she was in the lobby giving parting instructions to another patient who hung on her every word.

"Thanks, Ms. Jansen," the man said, rotating his arm from the shoulder. "I haven't felt this good in years."

"The credit's all yours, Mr. Pennington," she returned. "You've been faithful to your exercises and put in a lot of hard work."

But the man beamed at her. "You're a godsend, Ms. Jansen."

She thanked him and winked. "I'll see you next week."

"Sure thing."

Barry squashed an unreasonable pang of jealousy and decided he needed to unburden himself before these feelings of guilt tricked his heart into thinking it felt something that wasn't real. So after Lora had put him through an arduous set of exercises with a weighted vest that forced his shoulders back, he stopped and blurted, "I'm sorry."

Lora looked confused. "But you're doing great."

Suddenly this didn't seem like a good idea. "I meant I'm sorry about . . . when we were kids."

Her eyes widened. "What?"

"The name calling . . . I'm sorry."

A flush climbed her face, and she grew flustered. "It wasn't your fault . . . it was just a stupid nickname."

"It was mean, and I'm sorry."

She searched his face, then gave a curt nod. "Apology accepted." Then she angled her head. "But if you think now I'm going to go easy on you, you're sadly mistaken."

Relieved at her good humored response, Barry laughed, then waited as the guilt drained away to take with it these confusing sensations were Lora Jansen was concerned.

A few seconds later, the guilt was gone . . . but to his dismay, the confusing feelings remained.

Chapter Five

A few days later, the feelings for Lora hadn't dissipated, but Barry had identified where he'd felt this sensation before—just before a free fall parachute jump over Kandahar.

"How's it going, Seaman?"

Barry looked up from the lunch counter in the diner to see Porter Armstrong standing there.

Barry smiled and extended his hand. "Fine. The accommodations make me feel right at home, although I have to say, the showers are nicer than what I'm accustomed to."

Porter grinned. "I remember . . . sometimes we got one a week. And the rest of the time—"

"—a giant baby wipe," Barry finished, and the men laughed in a moment of camaraderie. Then he sobered. "Listen, Porter . . . I don't mean to sound ungrateful, but I hadn't planned on spending this much time in Sweetness."

Porter looked rueful. "I guess we were hoping you'd decide to stick around."

Barry blinked. "In Sweetness? No, sir, I'm going back to the field."

Porter raised an eyebrow. "Surely that isn't possible."

"I'm relying less on my cane," Barry insisted. "I'll be back up to speed soon."

"Thanks to your physical therapy with Lora Jansen?"

Barry smirked. "I see word still travels fast in this town."

"Yes . . . but if the PT is working, all the more reason to stay."

Barry lifted his coffee cup for a drink. "I can continue PT at Bethesda. I'm sure Lora will forward my exercise plan."

Porter nodded. "I'm sure she will, but I have it on good authority that Lora might be sad to see you go."

Barry choked on his coffee.

Porter gave him a wry grin. "Nikki—Dr. Salinger—might've

mentioned that she noticed some chemistry between you two."

Barry had heard Porter and Nikki were a couple, had seen them together around town. "Dr. Salinger must've been seeing things," he said casually, "because I have too much on my plate right now to think about . . . chemistry. And while my SEAL days are over, I'm not ready to leave the Navy."

Porter looked dubious, but inclined his head. "I understand you're eager to get on the road, but we still need more time to make arrangements for the ceremony. How about Friday?"

Barry tried to hide his frustration. Two more days seemed interminable, but he nodded. "If you don't mind, though, I'd still like to keep this private."

"Sure thing." Porter clapped him on the shoulder, then said goodbye and walked away.

With Porter's comments churning in his brain, Barry paid his bill and pushed to his feet, noting with satisfaction he didn't need the cane to stand, and recalling with a start that he hadn't taken a pain pill today—he hadn't needed to. The realization cheered him immensely.

Several people spoke as he left the diner—the faces were becoming familiar, and he knew a few names, too. The men in the living facility they called the barracks were a congenial group, and many were ex-military. Everyone had made him feel welcome.

He borrowed a four-wheeler to explore the town. The area outside the city limits was still in disrepair, but progress was slowly extending to the valleys and ridges where most of the former townspeople had lived. Barry's family had lived on Clover Ridge, where the Armstrongs and many other families had made their homes before the twister changed the landscape and the trajectory of everyone's life. But even as nostalgia pulled at him, he was starting to feel confined and itchy from idleness. He needed to re-engage his mind and his body, and he couldn't do it in Sweetness.

No matter how tempting Lora Jansen had become.

He tightened his grip on the handles of the four-wheeler and descended from the ridge slowly in deference to the broken and weed-choked asphalt. About halfway down, a noise caught his attention. He cut the engine, ears piqued. It was the whine of a dog, in distress. Barry's pulse spiked. He glanced at the rugged terrain, then back to his cane—if he fell, he could injure himself further. But neither could he ignore the animal.

He pushed to his feet and gingerly picked his way through the tall grass, calling out soothing noises to the dog that was now barking. It took him several minutes to locate the animal, a male German Shepherd mix whose feet were caught in the remnants of a barbed-wire fence. He looked to be around six months old. He was scratched and bloody, but appeared to have no broken bones.

"How did you get up here, boy?" he murmured to the dog, which attempted a few intimidating barks as Barry drew closer, then submitted to his rescuer, too weak to fight. It took Barry several long moments to free the animal, and he got a few deep scratches of his own for his trouble. He hoped the dog wouldn't run away when it was freed because he had no illusions of being able to chase it down. Instead, the dog wobbled over and leaned against his prosthetic leg, turning trusting eyes up to Barry.

His gut tightened and he wanted to walk away, wanted not to get involved. But the dog clearly needed medical attention. So he leaned down and scooped it up with his right arm and slowly made his way back to the four-wheeler, relying heavily on his cane, but recognizing his overall balance had improved dramatically in just a few days. The dog didn't put up a fight, waiting patiently while Barry got them both settled on the all-terrain vehicle. He fired up the engine, held the trembling dog against his chest under his coat, and headed back to town.

He had to get out of Sweetness . . . the longer he stayed, the more complicated things became.

Chapter Six

Lora was walking out of the clinic with her lab coat folded over her arm when Barry rode up on a four-wheeler. Her heart cartwheeled at the sight of him, but she schooled her face into a professional smile. Until she saw the blood on his hands and coat.

She gasped. "You're hurt."

"Not me," he said, opening his coat. "My friend here was caught in a barb-wire fence. Can you help?"

At the sight of the scratched and bleeding fur ball, she melted. "How bad is it?"

"Superficial cuts, but he's weak."

"I can treat him in the utility room of the clinic." She gathered the whimpering dog in her arms. "Follow me."

"Unless you need a hand, I think I'll take off," he said.

She looked up, surprised. "I can handle him, but he's your dog."

He lifted his hands, stop-sign fashion. "He's not my dog. I found him, and I'm handing him off. See you later."

Barry drove away and Lora stared after him, perplexed over his abrupt demeanor. She'd selfishly hoped his unexpected apology over teasing her when they were young would pave the way for them to become friends. Instead as he'd progressed in his physical therapy, he'd withdrawn more personally.

"Let's get you patched up," she murmured to the dog.

Thankfully, the stray's wounds required no more than cleaning and a few stitches. The poor thing was dehydrated and malnourished, so she fed him and gave him water, then took his picture and printed flyers for Dog Found and posted them all over town. Even though Sweetness was off the beaten path, it wasn't unheard of for stray animals to be dropped off along the state road leading to the town and somehow finding their way to civilization. Until she found an owner, she received permission to keep the dog in her room at the boardinghouse.

The next morning at Barry's PT session, he was more pensive than normal. In fact, his overall mood seemed antsy and distracted.

"How is your pain level?" Lora probed.

"Fine," he said. "Better, even." He pursed his mouth. "How's the dog?"

"Healing. I'm trying to find him a home."

"I saw the flyer at the diner," he said, his tone clipped. Then he proceeded to throw himself into his exercises with more zeal than necessary.

Lora was gratified to see him walk the length of the room many times without his cane. "Your alignment is much improved. How does it feel?"

"Awkward," he admitted. "I have to concentrate."

"It'll be second nature soon," she assured him. "Why don't you give the steps a try?"

He walked to the set of four steps up and four steps down girdled by a handrail. Slowly, he maneuvered them, using the rail only occasionally. "Why did you come back?"

She looked up from where she was making notes on his file. "Pardon me?"

His expression was curious. "Why did you come back to Sweetness? You couldn't have great memories of living here."

He was referring to the bullying again. She gave a shrug. "School was tough, but otherwise my parents made sure I had a happy childhood."

"Where did you go after the tornado?"

"To Chattanooga. My father got a job there."

"Did you like it?"

If anything, the teasing at her new school had been even worse. "It seems that kids are the same everywhere."

His mouth tightened. "And after high school?"

"Classes at the University of Tennessee, then my PT training." She smiled. "A fairly uneventful life."

"Do you have a boyfriend?"

Lora's pulse picked up, but Barry's tone was casual. In fact, he was focused fiercely on descending the stairs.

"Uh . . . no," she offered, trying to match his tone.

"That must be by choice," he said, still not looking at her.

Lora frowned, not quite sure where the conversation was going. "What makes you say that?"

He shrugged. "There are a lot of single men in town."

He stumbled on the last step. Lora lunged forward and put her arms around his waist to stabilize him. He steadied, but it left their faces mere inches from each other. Lora blinked and before she could pull back, he had closed the space and captured her lips with his.

If she said she hadn't thought about what it would be like to be kissed by Barry Ballantine, she'd be lying. In truth, she'd thought about it a thousand times while sitting behind him in sophomore English, and a few hundred times this week alone while lying in bed. But in her wildest dreams, she hadn't imagined it would be this good, that his lips would be gentle, but firm, that his tongue would coax hers into a sensual dance, that—

He abruptly pulled back. "I'm sorry."

She released him and struggled to pull breath into her lungs. Her mind raced, trying to assemble an appropriate response when her body screamed for more.

"That was wrong of me," he said, descending the last step heavily.

Her throat convulsed and she glanced at her watch to regain her composure. "That's probably enough for today," she agreed.

But long after he'd made his escape, his kiss kept her occupied even as she went through the motions of therapy with other patients. That evening, the found dog was a welcome distraction because while his furry little body hadn't full recovered, his spirit certainly had. He was playful and congenial and bright, judging by the way he caught on to the game of fetch, and she was able to teach him to sit with only a few minutes of training and a few snacks. At first he wasn't crazy about the collar she put on him, nor the leash she attached to it, but he acclimated quickly.

Lora was nervous about seeing Barry the next day for his appointment, but as she watched the puppy play and run, an idea formed in her head. The next morning when Barry walked up to the entrance of the clinic, she was waiting for him in the parking lot with the dog on its leash.

"What's this?" he asked warily.

The memory of his kiss hit her full force, but she rallied. "I think you're ready to maneuver around obstacles outdoors. I thought we might take a walk up to the school and back."

He glanced up to mentally stake out the distance. "That looks easy enough. Is the mutt coming, too?"

Lora was surprised at the irritation in his voice. She had hoped the man and animal would bond—keeping up with a pet would be good for Barry's continued mobility. "I was hoping you'd take his leash."

An odd expression crossed his face, then he shrugged and reached for the leash, extending the cane to her in trade. "No one's claimed him yet?"

She took the cane, knowing Barry had just passed a mental hurdle by relinquishing it to her. "No. I think he might've been abandoned. It's a shame—he's energetic, but he obeys so well."

"German Shepherd mixes are usually smart," he offered, but he clasped the leash cautiously.

"Do you have pets?"

"No. And I don't want one."

The man apparently preferred to travel light, she presumed. His SEALs deployment probably had curtailed attachments . . . she wondered if that extended to women. "What are you going to do when you leave here?" she asked.

His jaw hardened. "I'm still in the Navy. I'm hoping they'll find a place for a cripple."

Lora frowned. "That's not a very nice term. You're far from being incapacitated. Did you have a specialty?"

He was quiet for a long time, staring at the leash he wound and unwound around his hand. "Actually, I was a dog handler for our platoon."

Her mouth opened in surprise. "A dog handler?"

He nodded. "Silky was our war dog for two years, a Belgian Shepherd . . . strong, smart, loyal. He could detect explosives or set remote cameras. He did whatever I told him, even if it meant running straight into danger."

She caught the past tense verb, remembered the wooden box in his Jeep that first day he'd come into town, and the favor he had to do for a friend.

"You mentioned there were other injuries when you lost your leg," she said. "Did Silky die?"

Barry nodded. "He alerted me to an explosive, then we came under sniper fire. In the confusion, he misinterpreted a signal and advanced instead of retreating."

"And you followed him?"

He nodded. "But he took the brunt of the explosion."

Suddenly, his aversion to the stray dog made sense. "I'm sorry, Barry."

A muscle worked in his jaw. "I brought Silky's ashes with me back to the States. Sweetness was the only place that ever felt like home to me. I contacted Porter Armstrong and he offered a plot in the cemetery on Clover Ridge to bury the ashes." He looked up at her. "You probably think that's silly."

She shook her head. "Not at all. Silky died in the service of this country, he should be honored."

"The ceremony is tomorrow."

"And then you're leaving?"

He nodded. "Your PT program has given me hope of returning to the field in some capacity. So . . . thank you, Lora."

She basked under his praise, but with mixed feelings. The progress he'd made had fueled his eagerness to leave Sweetness. She'd known from the beginning he was only visiting, but it struck her now that she'd grown alarmingly used to seeing him every day.

She was falling for Barry Ballantine.

Suddenly a squirrel darted across their path and the dog practically leapt into the air, barking frantically. The yank on the leash was enough to throw Barry off balance. He fell to his left knee hard on the concrete sidewalk. He grunted, but maintained his hold on the leash. "No," he yelled. The dog quieted with a little yelp, then came back to lick Barry's hand.

Lora had to hold herself back to keep from going to his aid. She tightened her grip on his cane and watched while he slowly pushed to his feet. His core muscles bunched as he levered his newfound sense of balance to straighten and lift his big body. When he was standing erect, he looked at her and beamed.

Lora smiled back, but she knew the swell of her heart was more than pride for a patient. It was love for a man . . . and sadness over her impending loss of that man.

Chapter Seven

Barry wore his dress uniform for the ceremony to bury Silky's ashes. Porter offered him a ride and Barry accepted. When he reached the door of the quad-cab pickup carrying the precious wood box, he was surprised to see Porter's brothers, Marcus and Kendall, in the backseat.

"I know you said you wanted a private ceremony," Porter said. "Hope you don't mind the extra company."

"Not at all," Barry said, knowing Marcus was a former Marine and Kendall, a former Airman. The men told him they'd all been around service dogs during their stints overseas, especially Kendall, who had aided in many disaster recovery efforts. Barry was proud to have them along to honor Silky . . . although he hadn't expected the crowd that had gathered at the Clover Ridge cemetery.

"Sorry," Porter offered with a rueful smile. "You know how word gets around in a small town."

Emotion clogged Barry's throat as he glanced over the faces of the men, women, and children who stood around the small square hole dug in the wet ground. His gaze stopped on Lora, whose bolstering smile gave his heart a workout as intense as any PT session.

Next to the grave sat a small concrete box with a lid—the crypt Porter had custom made for the ashes. Barry threaded his way through the crowd and knelt to lower the wooden box into the crypt, then placed the lid on top. He knew all eyes were on him as he slowly pushed himself to his feet, but for the first time in a long time, he felt strong and healthy. Porter and Kendall stepped forward to lift the crypt and lower it into the earth.

"Would you like to say a few words?" Porter asked.

"Yes," Barry said, then turned to face the crowd. "Thank you for being here. You didn't know my dog Silky, but he was a brave, loyal soldier who saved lives every day. I'm proud to have been his handler." He paused, then smiled. "Will Rogers once said 'I love a dog . . . he does nothing for political reasons,' and that was Silky. He just did his job because he wanted to please. He didn't know he was a hero, but I do, and I hope you think so, too."

Barry picked up a shovel and began to scoop dirt over the crypt. Porter picked up another shovel and helped him fill the small grave. Then Kendall stepped forward.

"The town of Sweetness wanted to make sure Silky is remembered." He revealed a flat headstone that read, "Silky . . . U.S. Navy SEAL War Dog" and the year. Barry's chest tightened with affection and gratitude toward the townspeople. He realized it was the memory of the fellowship of the small town that had pulled him back . . . and he was happy to know the sense of community flourished once again under the hands of the Armstrong brothers.

He accepted the headstone with a grateful nod, then stooped to settle it over the top of the small grave. When he straightened, he addressed the crowd. "Thank you all for coming. You'll never know how much it means to this hometown boy to have you all here."

The crowd filed by the grave for a glimpse of the headstone and shook Barry's hand, asking about his own health. He greeted everyone, but out of the corner of his eye, he looked for Lora, noticing she hung back. When the crowd dissipated, she finally stepped up.

"That was so nice," she said.

"Thanks for coming," he said. He was sure she could hear his heart pounding.

"You're leaving now?"

He swallowed hard and nodded.

She smiled. "If you'll contact the clinic when you get settled, someone will forward your exercise schedule to whatever facility you choose to continue your PT."

"Thank you."

From her bag she withdrew the sweatshirt he'd given her on the day he'd driven into town and handed it to him. "It's clean."

He wanted to tell her to keep it to remember him by, but he didn't have the right. He'd been nothing but trouble for Lora Jansen, from the teenage teasing to the day he'd returned to Sweetness, to his stubborn attitude about what her PT could do for him, to a hijacked kiss. She had plenty to remember him by . . . and none of it was good or appropriate.

"Barry," Porter said from a few feet away where he stood with his brothers. "Can we have a word?"

"Sure," Barry said, then turned back to Lora.

"I'm going," she said, gesturing vaguely to an area where cars had parked alongside the road.

"Thank you for everything," he said, although the words felt woefully inadequate.

"Just doing my job," she said breezily, then smiled. "But you're welcome. Goodbye."

"Goodbye."

He watched her go with a heavy heart, realizing for the first time how his fellow soldiers felt when they had to part from the women they cared about . . . *from the women they loved.*

The realization struck him like a thunderbolt, but he felt powerless to do anything about it. Sweetness was growing and expanding, but there was nothing here for him . . . except Lora. But if he stayed, he'd have nothing to offer her, no way to make a decent living, not with his disability.

"Earth to Barry," Porter called good-naturedly.

"Coming," Barry said, and grudgingly dragged his gaze away from Lora's retreating form.

Chapter Eight

Lora fought back tears as she ran along the shoulder of the road leading out of Sweetness. Barry was long gone, no doubt, on his way to some exciting place. After the ceremony she'd returned to her room to change and to collect the stray dog that still hadn't been claimed. She glanced down at him now, jogging happily next to her on his leash. She would have to advertise soon to find him a home. And he needed a name, although she guessed she should leave that privilege to whoever adopted him.

At the sound of a car coming up behind them, Lora tightened her hold on the leash. The car was on the opposite side of the road, but the dog might still be spooked, or tempted to chase the wheels. When the vehicle slowed, she turned her head. At the sight of Barry leaning out the driver side window of his Jeep, her heart thrashed wildly in her chest. He was unbearably handsome in his dress uniform. She slowed to a jog and the dog barked a greeting to Barry, straining at the leash.

"Hi," he called, driving slowly to match her pace.

"Don't you mean goodbye?" she asked, hoping desperately she didn't look as if she'd been crying.

"For now," he said.

She stopped. "What do you mean?"

He smiled. "I have to report to Norfolk to take care of some things. I've been offered the chance to set up a training facility for military dogs."

"Wow." She was truly happy for him, truly sad for herself. "That's nice—"

"Here in Sweetness."

Her eyes widened. "Here?"

He nodded. "The Armstrongs set it up—they have connections to every branch in the Armed Services, and donated the land."

Her pulse rocketed. "But . . . you've been all over the world, seen exotic places . . . are you sure you'll be happy here?"

He angled his head. "That depends . . . will you be here when I come back?"

Her heart fluttered with the hope that he cared about her the way she cared about him. "Yes."

"Then I'll be happy here," he said, and put the Jeep in park.

She looked both ways, then ran across the road and met his mouth for a kiss that resonated with promise and hope. How was it possible that life had changed so gloriously in only a few days? At her feet the dog barked excitedly. They laughed and parted.

"I hope you'll be here, too," he said, offering his hand out the window to the dog. "You'll be my first recruit."

"He'll be here," she said. "I was thinking of naming him Sealy."

He grinned. "Great name."

They kissed again, a slow, sweet pledge of their hearts. At the sound of a horn, she lifted her head to see a line of traffic had formed behind his Jeep. More horns blared and people cheered and hollered.

Lora blushed, then they exchanged another kiss for the crowd. "Go," she said, "so you can come back to me."

"Oh, I'll be back," Barry said, then he waved and pulled away.

Lora's heart overflowed. She knew he would.

SEALed FATES

Kylie Brant

Chapter One

Cort Ramsey was not having a good day.

He got down from his horse, landing gingerly on the prosthesis attached to his right knee. The chafing where the strap rubbed against his skin was a reminder that as far as shitty days went he'd had far worse recently. It said a lot about him that he'd rather be staging covert ops with his team seven thousand miles away than riding fence on his father's run-down Montana ranch.

But those days were behind him. He wasn't a SEAL anymore. Wasn't a soldier of any sort. He'd lost a leg in the mountains of Pakistan and a brother in Kabul a year earlier. Bad days had become the norm. Chasing a bat-shit crazy cow for three days across his father's property didn't even rank close.

The animal wasn't in sight, but it was obvious she'd been in the vicinity. The barbed wire was snapped on the fence before him. He'd found three other areas so far where the fencing was down, but not before the cow had. It had been a while since his father had had someone ride fence. Cort didn't know exactly how long the bunkhouse had been deserted. The old man wasn't saying. But since Gabe Ramsey didn't seem up to running the place these days that left Cort.

The pack mule he was leading carried the fencing supplies. But rather than unload them, he looped both sets of reins around a fence post and stepped over the downed wire to cross onto the next property. Boards in the newly constructed eight-foot high fence surrounding the back yard of the old Paulus place next door had been heaved in and posts were leaning inward at one section.

He blew out a sigh. The cow was nowhere in sight, but this was undoubtedly her handiwork. Which meant the repair was his responsibility. He turned to limp in the direction of his horse.

"See? I told you it was him."

Cort stopped. Looked around.

"Let me see."

The whispers were definitely not tricks of the breeze. And the voices came from kids. He narrowed his gaze in the direction of the damaged fence. Paulus's kids were around Cort and Colton's ages, and last he'd heard were long gone from Montana. Grandkids maybe?

"Just a minute." A boy's voice this time. Older than that of his companion. Cort walked closer, amused despite himself.

"I'm gonna tell Mom you're not sharing." A young girl's voice, with a definite pout in it.

"Don't be such a baby. Here." There was movement in the fence about five feet to Cort's left. Drawing closer, he saw something long and black extending between the slats.

"I can't see . . . wait!" The girl's next words were laced with disappointment. "That's not a seal, Matt. It's just a man."

"Is too a seal."

"Where's his ball, huh? A seal can sit a ball on his nose, and . . . and clap his flipper things. Where's his flippers?"

With a bit of maneuvering Cort went down on one knee and studied the thin tube of black plastic sticking out from the fence.

"Not that kind of seal, dummy. A seal is like a soldier. He can blow stuff up and jump out of helicopters."

Maybe once, Cort thought. *Not anymore.* That part of his life was over. And he still didn't know what the hell he was going to fill the emptiness with.

Chapter Two

"Let me look through it now," the boy said.

'It' appeared to be a sort of cheap plastic telescope, complete with bends and joints in the body with a lens at the end. He picked up the end of the device and put his eye to the lens. A muffled shriek sounded on the other side of the fence.

"That seal man is looking at me!"

"Give it . . . " A moment later the wide dark eye on the other end of the telescope was replaced by an unwavering blue stare. "You're the seal, aren't you?"

"Used to be." Not even to himself would Cort admit how much the words burned. "Not anymore."

"Did you ever blow stuff up?"

A smile pulled at the corner of his mouth. "Once or twice."

"And jump out of helicopters?"

"More times than I can count."

"And shoot people?"

Time to call an end to the conversation. He doubted Paulus would thank him for filling his grandkids' ears with *that* sort of information. "Your grandpa around?"

"We don't have a grandpa."

Cort paused. Not relatives of Ed's then. "Your dad?" Whoever was in the house, it'd be easier to deal with an adult than try to have a conversation with two little kids.

"Our daddy's in heaven." This from the little girl.

Okay, he was out of ideas regarding the identities of the kids. "Your mom?"

"She's inside. You can't come back here but you can knock on the front door. Don't tell her we talked to you, though, ok?"

The anxiety in the boy's voice had his doubts rising about the unseen woman but Cort assured him, "I won't."

Casting a backward glance to check on the bay and the mule, he followed the fence to the corner where it butted up against the house. Was nonplussed for an instant when he didn't find a gate that would allow entry to the back yard. Who built a fence that could only be accessed from the house?

Assuming it was on the other side, he continued along the steel sided home and rounded the wide front porch. He, his brother Colton and Tucker Paulus had spent many a fine hour terrorizing Tucker's two sisters as they played Barbies on the porch swing that still hung in the corner. The memory was accompanied by a tug of nostalgia.

But if the porch looked the same the front of the house didn't. His boots rang hollowly as he walked up the steps and across the worn tongue and groove plank floor. Instead of Bonnie Paulus's lace curtains, drawn blinds covered the two big front windows, and the other windows he'd passed. The screen door had been replaced with a study storm, and the carved oak door with the wavy glass pane was gone. In its place was a steel one with only a judas hole to punctuate the panels.

One thing was certain, Bonnie Paulus hadn't made these changes.

With that in mind he gave the storm door a hard rap and stood waiting for a stranger to answer it.

And the woman who answered the door *was* a stranger. For all of about three seconds. Then belated recognition filtered in. He tipped his hat back with a crooked finger and smiled with the first genuine pleasure he'd felt in four months. "Well, hey there, Emma."

Chapter Three

Emma Watkins Cunningham set down the pistol she'd grabbed on the table beside the door. Although her heart was still hammering double time, relief and pleasure had her opening the storm door. She walked into Cort Ramsey's arms and was immediately enveloped in a hard hug.

"Cort," she murmured, memories swamping her. He'd been two years behind her in school but Colton's younger brother had been impossible to ignore, even then. With his high spirits, infectious devil-may-care grin and streak of wildness, there had been many girls in town that had vied for his attention. She'd only had eyes for Colton at the time, but she'd been female enough to recognize his appeal.

"I'm still so sorry about your brother." She gave him a final squeeze, then stepped back enough to tilt her head up, meet his laser blue gaze. "I wish I could have made it back for his funeral."

He tucked the tips of his fingers in the front pockets of his jeans in a slouch that was striking in its familiarity. "We got your flowers. And the card. You had troubles of your own at the time."

She'd just buried her husband, Emma recalled with a pang. And with the blindness of grief had been clueless about what the next year would bring. She'd been clueless about a lot of things back then. But her education had been completed in the most vicious of ways.

"I had no idea that you were back." But she'd heard from Ed Paulus just what had ended Cort's career in the Navy. With effort, she kept her gaze from straying to his leg and fixed firmly on his face. Pain and tragedy would have carved those angles in it. The shaggy blond hair looked military-short now beneath his hat, but was as bright as it had been when he'd been a kid. He was too lean, but his shoulders still strained under the faded denim work shirt. He looked tougher than she remembered, with a faint sheen of danger that was vaguely unsettling.

But far more unsettling was the zing of attraction that shot through her when she'd been in his arms. Emma chalked it up to lack of sleep and weeks spent running on adrenaline alone.

She almost made herself believe it.

"So did you buy this place from Paulus?" He cocked his head, looked past her into the living room. In a belated move, she shifted position, trying to block his view, mentally damning herself for not pulling the door shut after her.

"Just rented it. Bonnie's hips are bothering her and they bought a place in town. Ed's completely retired. He leases his land to John Barnes."

Cort gave an absent nod then sidestepped to get a better view of the living room over the top of her head. "You opening up a technology store?"

For a moment Emma felt hunted. Of course he'd see the cameras and monitors still in their boxes on the floor. "I'm . . . it's a security system. A woman out here alone with small kids . . . "

He seemed to accept her explanation at face value. "Sounds smart. The fence looks new, too, which makes me feel even worse about telling you that one of our cows got loose and damaged it."

She knew her dismay showed in her expression. But the fence had taken her weeks to complete and she had far more to do before this place was ready.

"Nothing major," he hastened to assure her. "I just need to replace a couple boards and reset two of the posts."

Forcing a smile, Emma said, "Don't worry about it. I haven't returned the extra supplies. They're still in the barn."

His look sharpened and she was reminded then that secrets hadn't lasted long when Cort had been around. His fun-loving exterior had masked a sharp mind. People who didn't know him better had often underestimated him.

"*You* haven't returned . . . you didn't build it yourself."

The certainty in the words had her spine stiffening. "Didn't I?"

In answer he reached out and took one of her hands in his, turned it palm up. It was ridiculous to feel embarrassed about the calluses that had replaced the blisters that appeared that first week, in spite of the work gloves she'd worn.

"If I'd known you were that handy I'd have hauled you out of bed the last three days to ride fence with me."

Because he hadn't let go of her hand she gave a slight tug until he freed it. Then curled her fingers into her palm, trapping the heat that lingered there. "I'm afraid I'd slow you down with two kids in tow. Although Matthew would consider it quite the adventure, Molly isn't much into roughing it. They're five and three."

"All the more reason to let me do the repair. I'll be back tomorrow to fix that section." He gave a barely perceptible nod to the mess in the living room. "Looks like you've got enough to do, and it was Gabe's cow that did the damage."

She hesitated. It was on the tip of her tongue to argue with him. She didn't want anyone around the place; it made her nervous. But this wasn't just anyone, it was Cort. She'd once fancied herself in love with his brother. They'd gone to the same schools, haunted the same hangouts. He was as safe as any man could be.

"Suit yourself."

The slow smile that crossed his face sent tiny alarms shrilling through her. Because safe was no longer a word that fit Cort Ramsey, if it ever had.

"I usually do."

Chapter Four

Before returning to his horse Cort rounded the other side of the porch and checked the fence there. As he suspected, there was no gate accessing the back yard. He didn't have to examine the rest of the sections to know that he'd find none around its entire perimeter.

Pensively, he took his time walking back to where he'd left the horse, his mind only half on the nagging phantom pain in his injured leg. Emma looked good; she always had. Her long dark hair was cut in a way that framed her face. But her big dark eyes were clouded with worry that hadn't been there a decade earlier.

The fence was one thing. The elaborate security system, complete with outside cameras and inner monitors, if he didn't miss his guess, was an expensive one and likely the only one of its kind within fifty miles.

He'd seen the handgun on the table next to the door. Observed the canned goods and bottled water stacked neatly on the counter. Emma Watkins Cunningham wasn't just settling in to her new home.

She was preparing for a siege.

The five a.m. alarm released only two beeps before Emma rolled to the side of the bed and silenced it. She continued the momentum out of the bed and padded toward the shower.

Though she'd hated getting up before dawn when she'd been a teenager, she didn't mind it so much now. The kids would sleep for another two hours and it was the only time until after they went to bed that she had to herself. It would be a peaceful start to her day if it weren't packed with urgency.

How much time did she have?

She dragged the sleep tee over her head and adjusted the spray before stepping into the shower. When she was busy the constant nagging question was relegated to the back of her mind. But at times like these, without immediate distractions and duties, it moved front and center, instilling her with dread.

She'd figured a month. Hoped for more. As Emma shampooed her hair she flipped through her mental calendar and her stomach hollowed out. It'd been twenty-seven days since she'd packed up the kids and casually let it be known that she was heading down to the Palm Beach home. But once there, instead of giving the taxi driver the address to the beach house, she'd directed him to a car lot where she'd paid cash for a used Suburban.

The drive to Montana had taken three days. But every hour since she'd gotten here had been a blur of activity fueled by purpose.

The courts couldn't protect her children. Neither could law enforcement. It was up to her.

Powered by renewed sense of urgency, Emma toweled off and dragged a comb through her hair. Time was running out. And things weren't ready.

Striding back to her room, she dressed rapidly in jeans and another tee. She took a moment to tiptoe down the hallway to check on Matt and Molly before changing direction for the family room. Building a fence alone had been a snap compared to trying to decipher the complications of the security system specs. She was hoping that sleep would make her mind sharper.

Emma veered toward the kitchen for her morning jolt of caffeine and carried a mug of coffee back into the living room with her. Determinedly, she picked up the instruction manual and sank on the rented couch. Every stick of furniture in the place had been rented from the same company, which specialized in furnishing entire businesses and homes. She'd had it delivered from Butte, paying extra for the mileage required. One advantage to living out in the middle of nowhere was that deliveries didn't bring any comments from neighbors. The nearest ranch was Ramsey's, and that was five miles away.

That distance hadn't kept Cort from landing on her doorstep yesterday, however. Recalling the moments she'd spent in his arms, nerves fluttered in her stomach. She soothed them with another swallow of coffee.

Emma was deep into reading about photoelectric cells, sensors and closed circuit systems when a foreign sound reached her ears. Lunging from her seat, she ran to the hallway closet and reached for the top shelf where she'd stored the handgun, rifle and ammunition. Quickly loading the rifle, she moved swiftly to the side window and peered out between the slats of the blind.

She didn't recognize the pickup parked twenty yards beyond the fence. But the lumber piled into the back was familiar enough. She had more just like it in her barn.

Her *locked* barn.

Chapter Five

Cort had a renewed appreciation for what Emma had accomplished. Just resetting the posts and replacing a few boards had taken him a couple hours. Of course, these days everything took a little longer. Sometimes he still forgot he was wearing an artificial leg and expected it to respond like the limb of old.

More often than not when he made that mistake, he landed on his ass.

He piled his tools and the lumber scraps in the back of the truck and drove to the barn to unload them. Then, without conscious decision, he headed toward the house.

He couldn't deny the burn of anticipation he felt at the prospect of seeing Emma again. It was hard to imagine what had brought her back to these parts. Her dad had died when she'd been a kid and her mother hadn't lived around here for years.

The back of his neck prickled as he walked up the porch steps. Cort knew he was being watched out of the judas hole again even before the door swung open and she stood facing him, hands on her slim hips.

He tucked his fingertips into his jeans pockets and rocked back on his heels. "Pretty thirsty after all that labor. I work cheap, though. A cup of coffee should do it."

Though her lips looked like they wanted to smile, she kept them in a firm line. "Payment? I seem to recall that your cow did the damage."

"Gabe's cow, actually. And since there's absolutely no way you'd get him over here to repair the fence, I did you a favor."

"If breaking into my barn can be construed as a favor. It was locked."

His mouth quirked. "Ah . . . I circumvented."

"You circumvented." She narrowed her brown eyes at him. "I imagine you have some experience in that area."

The familiar pang occurred at the reference to his past, but it was milder this time. "Among other things."

An ear-piercing shriek interrupted whatever Emma had been about to say. She stepped inside the doorway and turned her gaze toward the kitchen. "Molly." Her voice was stern. "Use your inside voice."

Cort took advantage of her distraction and slipped inside the house, picking his way carefully through the cartons still in the living room. The kids he'd talked to yesterday were seated at the kitchen table, in their pajamas.

"Mom, you let the seal in," hissed the boy.

She tossed Cort a half-amused, half-irritated look. "He sort of let himself in. He seems to have a habit of that."

Cort walked past her to the kitchen, bee-lining for the automatic coffeemaker on the counter. He opened cupboards until he found a mug and poured himself a steaming cup. He caught Emma's eye then and nodded toward the littered living room. "You over your head in there?"

He knew in the next instant that it had been the wrong thing to say. The amusement vanished from her expression, to be replaced with a look of determination that was also familiar. "I can handle it."

Maybe she could. He brought the mug to his lips and drank reflectively. But for the life of him he couldn't figure out why she'd try. "Place you bought it from probably does installation."

"The waiting list was too long."

Her response was clipped, but it gave him something to contemplate while she herded the kids back to their bedrooms to get dressed.

He could imagine that her rich husband's death had left her pretty well heeled. So she could certainly afford state of the art security systems. She could also afford more than the used Suburban he'd seen in the barn. Hell, she could do better than renting the Paulus ranch house, which was homey enough but had to be a far cry from what she'd grown used to.

He settled comfortably onto the couch and picked up the instructions to the security specs. Sipped from the mug again as he perused them. But his mind wasn't on the directions.

He'd been to town a few times in the last three weeks since he'd been back, and he hadn't heard a word about her return from the usual mainstays of the local grapevine.

There had to be a reason for that.

A slight buzz sounded and habit had him reaching for his cell phone. In the next instant he realized the sound was coming from another direction. Saw Emma's phone sitting next to a lamp on the end table. Cort had half-risen from the couch when common sense had him retaking his seat.

He wasn't in the intel business anymore. Didn't take every advantage that presented to supply himself with facts. It was still hard to remember sometimes that he'd returned to the outside world, back to the manners and mores that hadn't applied to the life and death situations he was accustomed to.

Whatever Emma's secrets were, they weren't life and death. The most dangerous thing about the woman was the effect she had on him.

Staring down at the specs spread across his lap, the thought was immediately discounted. He'd just been too long without a woman. Hadn't been interested, to tell the truth.

But there'd been 'interest'—and a lot more—stirring the moment he'd seen Emma walk out on the porch yesterday.

The admission had him scowling, his mood darkening. So when Emma re-entered the room, preceded by two noisy kids, his tone was abrupt. "Your phone went off while you were gone."

Her reaction had his instincts heightening. Her face paled and he'd have had to be blind to miss the expression that flickered across her face before she deliberately blanked it.

Dread.

Chapter Six

She sat cross-legged on the floor in the middle of the clutter when Cort returned, visibly shaken, staring fixedly at the specs.

Something twisted in Cort's stomach at the sight of her. She was pale, deathly so. He immediately revised his earlier conclusion. Whatever had caused Emma to pack up her kids and return to Montana may not be life or death, but it sure as hell was serious.

And it was past time that he learned what it was.

"Bad news?"

"What?" She looked up distractedly, appeared confused for a minute. "Where are Matt and Molly?"

"I've got them hunting for the elusive but incredibly lucky four-leaf clover." He jerked a thumb in the direction of the back yard. "A search that could take hours, if done properly."

She didn't smile, just nodded distractedly. "They'll be safe in the yard."

He stared at her, but found no answers in her expression. "Safe from what, Emma?"

She rose with an ease that he would have envied if every thought, every instinct wasn't attuned to what she wasn't saying. "I appreciate the help with the fence. I'm sure you have more important things to do, so . . . "

The invitation to leave was issued and ignored. "What's this all for?" He waved a hand around the room. "A security system, a fence, a sturdier front door . . . exactly why have you holed up here? What are you running from?"

The coolness that settled in her eyes was new and it was a change he didn't like. "I'm not *running* from anything."

"No." He leaned a shoulder against the wall and surveyed her. "You're hunkering down to make a stand. I recognize the preparations. I just don't know from what or why."

When she made no answer he pushed away from the wall and

headed to where her phone still lay. Realizing his intent, she lunged for it. The fact that he got to it first had far more to do with his longer reach than superior agility.

Turning his back to her when she made another grab he quickly discovered the recent text and read it a second before the phone was snatched from his grasp.

"Dammit, Cort, we may be old friends but we aren't kids any . . . "

He reached out to catch her wrist. "'They know where you are?'" He repeated the message. "Who knows where you are, Emma?'"

If anything, her face went whiter at the question, but the tension riding in her shoulders sounded in her voice. "None of your business. You need to leave. Now."

In answer, he turned to riffle through the newly purchased contents in the room until he found a receipt stapled to the side of one of the boxes. Let out a low whistle. "That wasn't a cheap trip. Paid cash for all this?" When she didn't answer he straightened. Looked her in the eye. "Bet you paid cash for the used Suburban, too. And the fencing supplies. And the rent paid to Paulus. Because you didn't want to leave a trail, did you, Emma? But someone tracked you down despite your efforts."

"Cort." His name was rifle sharp and might have stopped him when they were kids. It had no effect now.

"Now you can lie or refuse to tell me what kind of trouble you're in. Then I'm going to have to retrace your path, look into what was going on in Manhattan before you left there. I'm good at that sort of thing, but if you make me go that route rather than telling me up front, it's going to piss me off and waste time." And he wanted, more than he was comfortable with, to have her share the information freely because she trusted him.

Her eyelids slid closed for a moment and she looked for the moment to be on the verge of exhaustion. "Just let it go. Please."

But when she looked at him again he just gave one slow shake of his head. "I won't do that. But if you don't want to tell me what's going on, maybe the sender of the text would be more willing to talk about it."

When she swayed a little, remorse stabbed through him. But it wasn't strong enough to deter him. If she was in trouble, she didn't have to face it alone. He might not be a SEAL anymore, but he knew enough about trouble, and how to avert it, to be useful here.

And God knew he needed to feel useful to someone.

Chapter Seven

"She'd lose her job. Probably be deported." Emma sank on the couch, the cell still tightly clenched in her hand. "Elena Sanchez is my former mother-in-law's housekeeper. She's been keeping me informed of Michelle Cunningham's intentions."

"Which are?"

She glared at him. Who was he to stride back into her life and start demanding explanations? She hadn't answered to anyone since Parker died, and didn't much care for the experience.

But as quickly as her ire rose, it dissipated. This was Cort. Like it or not there was a bond between them, forged by long-time friendship, shared experiences and shared loss.

And knowing him as she did, she didn't doubt for a moment that he'd start digging around on his own if she didn't tell him everything.

"Michelle Cunningham has hired someone to take the children away from me for good." Her voice was amazingly calm given the knots twisting inside her at the thought. "I assume she means to kidnap them, get them out of the country smuggled aboard her yacht. She has any number of homes in the world, and the resources to start a new life wherever she pleases."

He frowned. "So you go to the police."

"And tell them what? That Michelle's Honduran housekeeper, who is in the country illegally, is feeding me the information she gleans from spying on the woman who pays her minimum wage? Elena would be deported, but little else would happen. They'd question Michelle, *maybe*. She'd tearfully inform them her concerns for her grandchildren had played out in the courts, and being a law-abiding citizen, she was willing to live with the verdict."

"Wait a minute." Cort straightened and she was struck again by that aura of danger he carried with him. "She sued you in court for custody of Matt and Molly? On what grounds?"

Just the memory of that nightmare was enough to stir anger again.

"Grounds she made up. Tried to claim I was unfit, addicted to drugs, that I'd left the children alone." Memory of the lies she'd had to combat in a court of law could still ignite her temper. "My character witnesses were able to refute her allegations. The case was thrown out." Her smile was grim. "That pretty much ruined the pretense of a civil relationship between us. I cut off her access to the children after that and according to Elena, she turned her focus to winning another way."

His eyes had gone flat and hard. "This was your mother-in-law?"

The incredulity in his voice had dark humor rising. "She's not exactly the nurturing type. I was never good enough for Parker in her eyes and I couldn't be controlled like she was used to doing to her son. We never hit it off, but our feelings used to at least be disguised." The gloves had come off during Parker's illness, however. And while Emma wasn't totally surprised by the depth of Michelle's venom she'd totally underestimated the lengths the woman would go to get what she wanted.

And what she wanted in this case were Emma's children.

"I trust Elena. I helped her with her son once when he was in trouble and she feels indebted to me." Because her lips wanted to tremble then, she firmed them. "I don't know how recent her information is, though. I might only have a day left. Possibly two before an attempt is made."

It was impossible to know what Cort was thinking. His expression remained enigmatic. But there was a curious sort of relief experienced in the telling, as if weight had been lifted from her. She was nonplussed a moment later when he turned and walked back into the kitchen. A couple minutes later he returned and crossed to her, shoving a piece of paper in her hand. "You'll need to go to Butte. Any closer won't have the supplies we need."

"I'm not going shopping, Cort. I have to be with the kids at all times."

"I'll stay with them," he announced calmly. His bright blue gaze was alight with purpose. "Chances are we've got a little time to work with, but if an attempt is going to be made, they'll be safer with me here."

That sparked her temper. "I grew up handling guns. I can protect my children." A desperate mother was capable of going to great lengths to keep her kids safe. Michelle Cunningham was going to find that out.

He gave her a slow nod. "I expect you'd do your damnedest. What you've accomplished alone took brains and guts. But truth is, I've had training only a few in the country are given. I've used it in situations you can't imagine. If it comes down to you or me against whoever she's sending, who can do a better job protecting those kids in the back yard?"

His words struck her hard in the chest. Torn, she looked down at the paper he'd handed her, the jumble of words on them making no sense at the moment. It was anathema to her to give up even a fraction of control with her children in danger.

He waited silently, as if understanding her inner battle. With difficulty Emma swallowed around the boulder that had lodged in her throat. Sidestepping emotion, she reached for logic. Cort would make a valuable ally. He hadn't acquired that lethal air by fixing fence on his dad's ranch.

"I'll be back as quick as I can."

"Take the truck." She caught the keys he took from his jeans pocket to toss to her. "In case they somehow got your license plate."

The thought chilled, but shoving doubts aside, she strode to the door. As nervous as it made her to put her fate and that of her children in the hands of another, she'd be a fool not to recognize that Cort Ramsey was her best weapon in this desperate battle with her former mother-in-law.

Chapter Eight

"You've been busy."

Cort carefully made his way down the ladder that allowed him access to the back porch roof. The last thing he wanted to do was land on his ass at her feet, and he'd had some near misses that afternoon. "I've got half the cameras installed and hooked up to two of the monitors inside."

Her eyes were on the children, tearing around the back yard, each sporting a doo rag fashioned from some bandanas he'd found in a drawer in the kitchen and brandishing a length of foam packaging he'd taken from the monitor boxes. "They're pirates, and I have to say, pretty blood-thirsty ones. They've been demanding I walk the plank for the last hour. I can't guarantee your safety."

Emma flashed him a slow smile that had his gut clenching. "You were always the creative one."

"Believe me, it takes creativity to keep those two occupied." The work had probably taken hours longer than it should have since he had to keep stopping to tend to them. Which gave him a renewed respect for what she'd managed to accomplish with the fence. "I fed them lunch but they said they don't take naps anymore." The look she gave him said otherwise. "So they scammed me." His mouth curled. "They were pretty convincing."

"Con artists usually are." Hands on her hips, she tilted her head back to survey the camera he'd mounted. "Didn't take you long to figure out the system, I see."

"I have a bit of experience."

"Maybe with me helping we can get the others up by nightfall."

"These will provide enough security for now." The house set back from the road at least a quarter mile. If time allowed, he'd set something up for the barn and closer to the road, but it wasn't his highest priority. "You can take the two-sided tape you bought and run it along the top of the fencing."

Comprehension lit her face. "And then stick the thumb tacks sharp side up along the tape? I wouldn't have thought of that."

"I'm the idea guy for things you don't have the experience to think of." Which was probably why she hadn't considered the dark thoughts that had been haunting him all afternoon about her situation. Now, however, wasn't the time to share them with her.

"Mommy!" Molly had spotted her and was running across the yard at top speed, Matt hard at her heels.

Emma shot him a worried look. "I'm hoping in the rest of the supplies you had me pick up that you have an idea for the front of the house. I was planning an electric fence but chances are . . . "

Her voice trailed off as Molly reached her and was scooped up in her arms. But Cort knew what she'd been thinking.

Chances were they wouldn't get an opportunity to take that precaution.

Matt and Molly's voices rose in an attempt to drown each other out to be the first to tell their mom of their adventures that day. Cort winced a little at the look Emma sent him when they excitedly recounted the 'pirate grub' he'd made for lunch. "Scrambled eggs with cut up hotdogs," he said defensively, bending to scoop up the empty packaging on the porch. "It tastes okay with ketchup."

"It was awesome, mom!" Matt assured Emma.

Cort could tell that she remained unconvinced but she didn't say anything more about it. Which was good, because it he'd been uneasy enough realizing how comfortable he'd felt with the kids cooking them lunch and spinning tales of long ago pirates who'd eaten the same thing.

It shouldn't feel so natural to feel protective of her and her family.

The thought had something inside him rearing back. Emma had reluctantly accepted his help because she was in trouble, not signed on for anything more personal. He was here because she trusted him, that was all.

As the thought seared a path through his chest, he knew he was going to have a helluva time remembering that.

Chapter Nine

Emma shot Cort a look when she re-entered the living room. He was on the couch, his head bent, engrossed in his task.

"Kids in bed?"

She gave a wry smile. Barefoot, she would have sworn her approach had been soundless. "Yes. They crashed earlier than usual."

"Because they hadn't had a nap?"

"It's not the first time they've gone without." And he'd have been hard pressed to get them to lie down regardless, she thought, sinking onto the couch next to him. Both of her kids seemed to regard Cort as half man, half super-hero.

And maybe, in some respects, they were right.

She studied him surreptitiously. Other than a limp, his injury didn't slow him down much, although she could tell by the way he moved sometimes that he wasn't quite used to the prosthesis. If it caused him pain, that didn't show either. Emma had a feeling that Cort Ramsey had become used to keeping his emotions in check.

She'd be wise to do the same.

It had been a curious experience to cook supper for the four of them while he'd made some phone calls on the back porch, and then to call him in for the meal, as if he belonged there. Odd to listen to her children chatter endlessly about what he was doing, why he was doing it, and the purpose of the tools he'd been using.

It was especially strange, and not entirely welcome, to discover that the feelings he'd awakened in her with that brief hug on the porch the day before hadn't dissipated. And recognition of that fact made her edgy.

"What's that?" She indicated the contraption he was taping together with the duct tape she'd bought in town.

"It's going to be a transmitter and silent alarm." He held it up to show her how he'd secured the two-way radio with the alarm.

Comprehension registered. "So if someone stumbles over that

wire you ran across the front of the property . . . "

"If they set off the trip wire, they'll trigger the alarm which will be transmitted to the second radio we'll have in the house." He nodded toward the radio in question.

"You had me buy eight radios and four alarms."

"Tomorrow I'll run perimeter trip wires thirty five feet from the property line on all sides." At least he hoped he'd be given the opportunity. "The alarms will be set to different frequencies so I'll be able to tell which side is being breached." When he saw her jerk a little, he mentally damned his choice of words. This wasn't an op he was running, it was her life.

Reaching out, he took her hand. "We're going to be ready. Whether it's tonight, tomorrow or the next day . . . we'll be prepared. I won't let anyone hurt you or the kids."

Relief flickered across her face. "This isn't your fight. I feel guilty for making it seem like it is. But I'm also glad you're here and that makes me feel guilty again, so . . . "

"Guilt's a useless emotion." He made peace with that much in rehab. It was useless to feel guilty that he'd made it home alive from Pakistan when some of his team mates hadn't been so lucky. Equally worthless was his guilt over his sense of loss about his leg when Colton hadn't come home at all. "You need the kind of help I can provide. And I don't mind helping. I've always . . . "

Liked you, is what he meant to say. Maybe cared a little. But his throat stopped working and the words remained trapped in his brain. Which had become strangely disconnected with logic. Because instead of saying more, he leaned in slightly and kissed her.

Her lips were full and exquisitely soft. He half expected her to pull away, to show the good sense he was lacking and firmly remind him of why he was here. What he didn't expect was for her to lean into the kiss. To slip her arm around his neck and open her mouth beneath his.

Without conscious decision he hauled her closer, his free hand spearing through her fall of long dark hair. Heat spread in his belly, licked through his veins. For a moment, just an instant, he immersed himself in her. Scent, taste, touch. Let the sensations zap and sing through his system. Emma Watkins wouldn't be a woman easily taken, easily forgotten. The thought traced across his mind, vanished.

Because Cort had no intention of forgetting her. Or this.

He tore his mouth away, dragged in a ragged breath before moving his lips to trail a line of kisses down her neck. There was a pulse beating madly at the base and he lingered there, laving the spot with his tongue. The realization that she was as affected as he was small solace. Because their timing was just about as bad as it could get.

He lifted his head to look at her. "Listen," he started to say, then stopped, the word balling in his throat and nearly strangling him. Her eyes opened, lids heavy and the dazed look of desire in them nearly had him throwing caution to the winds.

He wanted to lay Emma back on the couch and slide his hand up under her tee shirt, feel the satiny skin there. He longed to strip her down, his mouth discovering each newly bared inch of skin until he learned every intimate secret. And even the thought of her seeing his amputated stump did little to cool the fever in his blood. And that notched her right up from desirable to dangerous.

Because he needed to be able to think, he looked away for a moment, tried to order his thoughts. They threatened to riot in the next moment when he felt her slightly roughened palm cup his jaw. "Cort."

Just one word. But spoken as it was in that rumpled silk voice, the word laden with meaning, it was enough to have him wanting to throw his head back and howl. It took every ounce of will he possessed to focus on the reason he was here.

"If you want to continue this when this is over . . . " He cleared his throat, wished he could clear his mind as easily. " . . . you better believe I'm interested." *Interested. Yeah, right. He was so primed he was ready to disgrace himself.* "But you might change your mind after hearing what I have to say."

He waited for the desire to fade from her expression. Mourned the loss. "Those phone calls I made before dinner? I touched base with a few of the townies that seem to make it their business to know everything about everyone in the area." He paused for an instant as she nodded in bemusement, before adding deliberately, "And I told all of them where you're staying."

Chapter Ten

Emma blinked, certain she couldn't have heard him correctly. "You wouldn't . . . " The look in his eyes said just the opposite. She sagged against the back of the couch, disbelief warring with panic. "Why would you? I trusted you, Cort!"

"I had some time to think this afternoon." His face was as grim as she'd ever seen it. "And I believe you may be wrong about your mother-in-law's intentions."

His words sent her temper from simmer to full boil. "You think I'm making too much of this?"

"No, you might be underestimating the danger. I'm not sure she's planning on kidnapping the kids at all. I think she may have hired someone to target you."

His words acted like a bucket of ice water on her anger. "Michelle Cunningham is ruthless when it comes to getting her own way, but she's not a murderer."

"Doesn't have to be. Money buys just about anything. Think about it." Cort shifted position, stretching his leg out. "If she steals the kids she's on the run for the rest of her life, looking over her shoulder for the police. For you. Why would she give up her friends, her lifestyle if there were another way to get what she wants? Who gets the children if something happens to you?"

"I . . . " She swallowed hard, her mind swirling. "I named my mother as their guardian." But his words were taking on an awful sort of sense. Helen Watkins was battling health problems that would make caring for two active youngsters a challenge. And if Michelle Cunningham took Emma's mother to court, her former mother-in-law's vast wealth might mean the custody outcome could turn out far differently than it had with Emma. She shook her head, but couldn't dislodge the horrible logic of his words.

"Bridgit Lewis—you remember her, she's worked at Al's Diner since we were in grade school—she said there was someone in just yesterday asking about your family. Mid-forties, thinning blond hair, about five ten or eleven, hazel eyes?" It was a moment before she realized what he was asking.

"No. I haven't seen anyone like that."

"He'll lurk around the area as long as he needs to, trying to gather information. We could wait for him to make his move. But by making sure he learns your location sooner, rather than later, we flip the advantage to our side. He'll come sniffing around here soon. He won't be able to help himself." That lethal air she'd noted before seemed to radiate from him now. If she didn't know better, Emma would think Cort was looking forward to the man's arrival.

"And when he does show up . . . I'll be waiting."

Chapter Eleven

The wait was excruciating. Which was ridiculous, Emma thought as she tossed the ball underhand to Matt and ducked when he hit it squarely with the bat. She'd been bracing for this moment since she left Palm Beach. Had recognized its inevitability.

But knowing the stranger was in town and knew where to find them made the situation even more nerve wracking.

She cheered her son around the makeshift bases while Molly scrambled after the ball. She glanced at the back window and saw Cort moving about the living room. Her throat dried. All day yesterday and again today he'd been working on the perimeter trip wires and the rest of the transmitter alarms. Each time a cloud of dust on the road indicated a vehicle coming this way, he'd headed back inside and watched the action on the monitors.

There wouldn't be much for a passerby to see. Cort had stowed his truck in the barn after making a swift trip back to his dad's to get some things two nights ago. There'd be no activity or possessions out front that would peg this as her residence.

A person would have to come closer than the road to be certain of that.

"Now my turn, my turn!" Molly demanded.

"Can I pitch, Mom?"

Emma gladly gave her son the plastic ball and turned again to check on Cort. Found him standing on the back porch, watching them with an enigmatic expression. Her legs feeling leaden, she joined him.

"Same silver Tahoe has gone by three times today," he murmured, his bright blue gaze steady. "The guy is wearing a ball cap. No way to tell if he's the one Bridgit described. But his vehicle has rental plates and he slows way down as he passes."

She nodded, unable to speak. There'd been binoculars on his shopping list a few days ago, and night vision goggles she'd had to find at her one and only trip to an army surplus store. Although he said nothing else, she knew what he was thinking.

Because she was thinking the same thing.

"Do you think he'll try to get a closer look tonight?"

"I'd be surprised if he didn't."

Ice pierced her veins and she stared blindly at her laughing children. "I'm still a fair shot. If he shows up here he'll have to go through me to get to the kids."

His arm slipped around her waist and he pulled her against his hard side. And for a moment—just one—she let herself lean into his strength.

"Serve him right if I set you loose on him." His words drew a smile, as they were meant to. It disappeared in the next moment. "But I have plans for him."

A chill skated over her skin at the promise in his voice. She knew she hadn't been mistaken in thinking he was looking forward to the fight. Her stomach clenched. For the first time Emma considered that by accepting Cort's help, she'd placed him in danger, too.

Chapter Twelve

Vince Baccino squinted through the shadows and considered his options. He wasn't a man to rush into things, despite demanding clients. He'd already determined that the best way to take the woman would be to wait for her to come out to her mailbox some afternoon and pick up her mail.

Hell of it was, the only way he was going to catch Emma Cunningham at her mailbox was if he set up camp somewhere nearby and waited. He'd been a sniper in Desert Storm before hiring out his skills for a different sort of work back in the States. He could wait for days for the perfect shot.

But the only cover for miles was the barn on her property and its shelter wouldn't offer a clear shot of the woman. Which left a home invasion as the next best option.

He considered the idea carefully. Kids made the plan slightly messier. There was to be no collateral damage, the client had been clear about that. But he was enough of a realist to know that the unexpected had to be planned for. The woman was going to die and anyone who got in his way was expendable.

He still had the picture of Cunningham in his pocket. It was a shame to kill a fine looking piece like that. Maybe he'd take a little time with her before slitting her throat. Give her a proper send off.

The thought had him hardening and provided the impetus he needed to move. Silently, he picked up his bag of tools and slipped from behind the barn toward the house.

There was little cloud cover but the moon was only a sliver. He wasn't worried, regardless. There would be no one up at three AM to notice his progress toward the old ranch house.

Baccino had already determined there was no way inside the fence so he continued to the front of the place. His steps up the porch steps were noiseless. He tried the front door because it was dumb not to look for the obvious entry. Wasn't surprised to find it locked. He turned immediately to the window to its right.

He set his bag down, opened it and retrieved the glasscutter. A few minutes later he'd scored a circle in the glass just above where the lock should be. He took his time. Haste led to mistakes. The cutter was put away and a piece of contact paper affixed to the scored circle. Then he tapped it lightly with the butt of his knife until the circular piece of glass sagged inward. Slowly peeling aside a corner of the paper, he removed the circular piece. It was easy enough then to reach inside and unlock the window. Raise the sash and slip inside.

Adrenaline started pumping. He'd already spent the advance for the job and looked forward to the final payment. Almost as much as he was looking forward to doing the woman. He waited a moment, allowing his eyes to adjust to the dark interior. He caught the slight movement to his right at the same time a voice spoke.

"I've been waiting for you."

Chapter Thirteen

The shadowy figure reacted quicker than Cort had expected, wheeling around with a kick that would have caught him in the chest if he hadn't moved back. The movement caused him to stumble and the intruder leapt at him, the glitter of a blade discernible in the darkness.

This time he was ready. He brought the crowbar he held crashing down on the wrist of the hand holding the knife, heard a sickening crunch. The weapon clattered to the floor. He kept moving, behind the guy's elbow now and used his momentum to push the intruder, intent on driving his head into the wall.

But the stranger wasn't cooperating. He spun away to dive at Cort, toppling him to the floor. The crowbar rolled out of his grasp.

The two men grappled and it quickly became apparent to Cort that his opponent had had some training of his own. The man grabbed Cort's throat with his uninjured hand, squeezed. Gray dots danced before his eyes as he struggled to breathe. Bringing both hands up, he jabbed his thumbs hard in the intruder's eyes until his grip loosened. Then, doubling his fist, he swung it with all his might at the man's temple. Once. Twice. Again.

When the man's body had gone limp he shoved him off him, bracing his good knee on the man's back. At the same moment, the lights flipped on in the room. Cort risked a quick glance at Emma, who'd moved into his peripheral vision. The Glock was gripped firmly in her hand, pointed at the stranger.

"I thought I told you to stay downstairs with the kids." His voice was mild.

"I'm not much good at doing what I'm told."

Her words had a crazy grin spreading across his face. She wouldn't be Emma if she took orders worth a damn. He bent the man's arms behind his back before he could start to stir. "Maybe you can make an exception this once and hand me those zip cords." When she cooperated he quickly secured the intruder's hands and feet before turning the guy over again.

"We make a pretty good team," she said lightly. There was a slight unevenness in her voice that had Cort giving her a quick look. What he saw in her eyes had warmth stealing through his system.

"Yeah. Somehow I'm not surprised."

It was nearly eight a.m. The sheriff had left a couple hours ago, escorting Emma's would be assailant off the property. The kids had just fallen back to sleep, but Emma knew sleep would be out of the question for her anytime soon. Cort had mentioned adrenaline crash, but she was still revved up, senses humming.

And the man sitting on the couch beside her was partially responsible for that.

She wrapped both hands more tightly around her coffee mug and sipped from it. "I can't believe Michelle Cunningham would have even known a man like that." Baccino hadn't been carrying ID, nor had any been found in the silver Tahoe parked just down the road. But Sheriff Lasher had called them with the man's identity when his fingerprints had shown up in the system. Vince Baccino was wanted for questioning in three unsolved murders.

"When you have enough money it just takes knowing someone with connections." Cort reached for her mug. When she handed it to him, he drank, his gaze meeting hers over the rim. "He doesn't have a record. It's possible he'll take my advice. Giving up the name of his client, and the job she hired him for will make things go easier for him in court."

"Do you think he will?"

"If there's a chance he can cut a deal, yeah. I think he'll take every opportunity offered."

She wanted, needed to believe that. Emma had seen the knife Cort had taken from the man. Had observed other items in the bag he'd brought in with him that still made her heart pound at her narrow escape. "I need to speak to the county attorney and urge him to offer that deal." Otherwise Michelle Cunningham would be free to send someone else, and then someone else until she finally found a hired gun who succeeded where Baccino had failed.

Cort leaned forward, placed the mug on the table. Reached over to clasp one of her hands in his. "We'll tie this attempt to her and I'll make damn sure she knows it." She shot him a startled look, but was momentarily distracted by the heat transferring from his touch. "I'm guessing dual threats of a police investigation and selling the story to a tabloid would bear some weight with her."

"I think the threat of media attention would scare her more than the police," she said ruefully. Michelle considered law enforcement as tools to be used to her own end. Having her name tied to a scandal however . . . for the first time in the last several days Emma felt the heaviness in her chest dissipate.

And it didn't escape her attention that Cort's hand was still on hers. Or that it had turned caressing. "So." She tried to collect her thoughts, which had abruptly scattered as soon as he touched her. "You're not too bad at this body guarding thing. You could start a business."

"Turns out I'm especially adept at it when I've a fondness for the body in question. More than a fondness, actually."

Her breath catching in her chest she turned toward him. Was caught by the light in his wicked blue eyes. "I have absolutely no idea what I want to do with the rest of my life," she began.

"Me either."

"Or where I want to live." They were closer somehow. Had he moved? Or had she? She was near enough to feel the heat he radiated. Like a moth to a flame she was drawn to it. To him.

"We'll figure it out." The words were murmured against her lips. "Together." The first kiss was whisper light. The second one firmer. She laid a hand against his chest as she leaned into him. Opened her lips beneath his and enjoyed the way his taste sent her senses rioting.

Together. The word was imbued with promise. A promise she reciprocated.

And one she had every intention of collecting on.

GOING DARK

Helen Brenna

Chapter One

"Four minutes twenty-five seconds, Griggs. The rest of the team is en route to the Humvee, objectives safe in hand."

Crouched behind an abandoned shell of a car, Chief Petty Officer Nate Griggs kept his assault rifle trained on the Somali rebel guards as Senior Chief Kyle Turnham's calm voice came over the wire.

"Any sign of Mohammed Ahmed?"

"Negative," Nate whispered. Too bad, too. He would've liked nothing better than to have nailed the Somali warlord with ties to al-Shabaab. Not only was the bastard one of the top three on the most wanted list, but he was also responsible for the deaths of tens of thousands of Somali refugees.

"Alright then," Turnham said, sighing. "Target is not at this site."

Basically, that meant their primary mission had failed. Intel had been wrong for the second time in less than ten minutes. The first screw-up had been in indicating that the hostages, the rescue of which was their secondary mission, were being held in one building. Instead, the kidnapped American citizens had been scattered throughout the abandoned village, forcing the SEAL team to split.

"Let's wrap this up, Griggs. We can't be here when the sun hits that horizon, and the only hostage we're missing is Pritchard."

"Figures," Nate said softly. The rest of the team had encountered no snafus, but then, by all accounts, their objectives had been lightly guarded. "I got four men between me and our kingpin." Two in front of what was most likely Pritchard's location, a small retail shop that had long since been abandoned. A third near an alleyway a couple buildings away. The fourth was apparently on rounds and had stopped for a smoke. "One of 'em will be leaving any second."

Mr. Cigarette, there was no doubt about it, rubbed Nate wrong. Maybe it was the cocky way he blew smoke into the air, or the way he puffed out his chest when he walked, like a peacock flirting with a peahen on a sunny Sunday afternoon. Didn't really matter. Nate shouldn't be trusting his gut these days, anyway. Not after what had happened with a certain redhead last month in Virginia Beach. From now on, he was a by-the-numbers, follow-orders-to-the-letter man.

Sure enough, the smoker flicked his butt to the ground, issued an order to the other men, and then went on his way. Obviously, Mr. Cigarette outranked the others. Could he be Mohammed Ahmed? Nate focused in on the man's face. Nope. Although there was only one known photograph of Ahmed, that picture clearly indicated a scar, resembling a sliver moon, on the man's right cheek. Mr. Cigarette's cheek was somewhat pockmarked and shiny with sweat, but scarless.

"Back down to three, Senior Chief. I got this." By the light of a fading moon, Nate moved in, passing a couple more abandoned vehicles.

One of Pritchard's guards, Mr. Smartass, started joking loudly with Corner Guard near the alley. Sounded like they were talking about someone. Pritchard? Another prisoner? Nate translated a word here or there, but couldn't make sense of the conversation. Whatever was going down was clearly bothering Pritchard's other guard, Mr. Serious.

A gust of dry, hot wind blew dirt into Nate's eyes and up his nostrils. He stopped behind a partially demolished concrete wall and waited for his eyes to clear. God, how he hated this place. For that matter, every man he knew hated this country with a passion. Unrelenting sun and heat, one drought and civil war after another, dirt upon dirt upon more dirt. Not to mention a culture that bred some of the most violent extremists on earth.

"Remind me again why we're doing this?" he whispered to Turnham.

"A little PR goes a long way as far as the Brass is concerned. Maybe next time Pritchard will think twice about bashing the military in his news reports."

Nate had never paid much attention to Donald Pritchard's muckraking TV news journal, *On Record,* until the man made things personal by sending a cold-hearted, red-headed bombshell Nate's way.

Kaley Andrews. She might have smelled as sweet as the cherry blossoms in the backyard of Nate's childhood home near Richmond, but, in truth, she was more like a man-eating Venus flytrap.

Had he known up front that the only reason she'd been at that Virginia Beach bar was to dig up information about a classified mission here in Somalia that had gone completely FUBAR, that night they'd met would've ended differently. Instead, the curious mixture of vulnerability and intensity in her eyes had lured him into a slow, moonlit walk on the beach. One night had led to three weeks of spending every moment of his off-duty hours together. Twenty-one days of heaven he wouldn't soon forget.

Well, almost heaven. The best of the heavenly part was supposed to have happened on a long weekend they'd planned to spend at his cabin in the Blue Ridge Mountains. Then, the morning they were to leave, he'd gone to her hotel and discovered she'd checked out not fifteen minutes before he'd arrived. No messages. Cell phone disconnected.

He'd been dazed and confused until Pritchard's *On Record* had aired on primetime a couple days later and for several long, agonizing minutes the camera had focused on a photojournalist named Carly Danson. Funny, but Ms. Danson had borne a striking resemblance to one Kaley Andrews. A body as curvy as Virginia's back roads topped by show-stopping red hair as bold as a sailor's favorite sunset.

Nate hadn't given the two-faced, lying piece of work any information about the medical team that had been slaughtered by Mohammed Ahmed's rebels, but Pritchard had made up what he'd needed, singling out Nate and his SEAL team as total losers.

Wham-bam-thank-you-ma'am, had Nate ever been screwed. Good thing Kaley, or Carly, or whatever the hell her name of the week was, hadn't been on the list of Pritchard's staff they were here to retrieve, or Nate might not have been accountable for his actions.

A scuffle suddenly broke out between the two guards in front of Pritchard's location. Mr. Smartass pushed Mr. Serious to the ground and then, taking the only lantern, sauntered toward Corner Guard. Those two then turned down the alley, disappearing out of sight. Didn't make sense, but it wasn't going to get any better than this for Nate. While the one remaining guard glanced angrily toward the entrance to the alleyway, Nate nailed him from behind, knocking him on the head with the butt of his rifle. He caught the instantly unconscious man and slipped into the building, dragging the body inside.

Sitting tied to a chair in the middle of the dark room was a man with a hood over his head. Nate had to verify he had Pritchard before heading back to the Humvee. He cut the ropes cinching the hood around the man's neck and lifted the hood. *Yep. Pritchard.* Gagged, too.

The man's bleary eyes widened at the sight of Nate. He mumbled wildly and bounced in his chair, making far too much noise. Nate cut Prichard's hands free, but held him still, gag intact. "There are two guards down the way," he whispered in Pritchard's ear. "Quiet down, or I'll leave you here. Understand?"

Pritchard nodded vigorously.

Nate removed the gag. "Got Pritchard, Senior Chief," he whispered. "We're on our way."

"One minute forty-five before we have to skedaddle to rendezvous with that Chinook."

Pritchard cringed. "I need water." He looked sweaty and dirty, but no worse for wear.

What a pansy-ass. "In a minute. Let's go." Signaling for Pritchard to follow, Nate headed toward the door. All was quiet.

They made it to the corner when Nate heard another scuffle. Faint lantern light emanated from the open door to another dilapidated building down the alleyway. More laughter. His gut told him not everyone in that hellhole was having fun, but he wasn't listening. *Not your concern, sailor.* He had to get Pritchard out of here before Mr. Cigarette came back around.

A muffled scream.

Nate stopped in his tracks. "They're holding a woman nearby, SC, and she doesn't sound happy. I'm going to take a look-see."

"Hold on, cowboy. Our number one objective was to take out Ahmed. Number two, to retrieve Pritchard's staff. Don't get sidetracked."

"You know—"

"I thought you were following orders these days. To the letter."

Turnham was right, as usual. Nate took several more steps in the direction of the Humvee when another round of laughter sounded from down the alleyway. Gut or no gut, Nate *could*, so he *had to* fix this. "This'll take thirty seconds."

"Griggs, listen to me . . . . "

Once upon a time, Nate might've claimed he was losing his SC's signal and then disconnected communications. But these days he was trying to be a good boy, so he simply ignored Turnham's intermittent stream of dialogue and turned to Pritchard. "Wait here."

"Oh, no!" Pritchard grabbed Nate's arm. "You're supposed to get *me* out of here!"

Nate shoved Pritchard through the front door of what had once been some form of a retail shop. "If you're not right here when I get back, I won't come looking for you. Understand?"

Pritchard nodded, and Nate glanced down at his stopwatch. One minute, thirty seconds. The woman's muted cry sounded again. Moving down the alley, Nate slid through the shadows. He glanced through a dirty, busted-up window to find Mr. Smartass and Corner Guard passing a woman, whose clothing looked American, back and forth between them. Like Pritchard, her hands were tied behind her back and a sack had been cinched around her head. Unlike Pritchard, they'd ripped open her shirt, exposing her bra and bare belly. Nate didn't have time for this crap.

Slipping through the doorway, he flicked off the lantern, startling the guards. Then he grabbed the first slime bucket, twisting his neck and killing him instantly. The other man released the woman and reached for his weapon. In the blink of an eye, Nate was behind him, silently slitting his throat.

Grabbing the woman's arm, Nate drew her with him toward the door. "It's okay," he whispered. "You're all right."

Mumbling something unintelligible, she struggled against him. She was likely gagged, too.

"Be quiet." He sliced the ropes off her wrists. "There are other guards. I'll get the bag off your head in a second."

The moment her hands were free, she fumbled ineffectively with the rope securing the burlap around her neck.

A sound in the alleyway. Footsteps?

He backed up out of sight, pulling the woman with him. "Someone's coming," he whispered into her ear.

She fell completely still. The only sound in the dark was the soft puff of her breath. Knowing they might have to move and move fast, Nate very carefully slipped his razor-sharp blade between the rope and woman's neck and gently tugged. "Quietly," he whispered. "Slowly."

She reached for the sack and gradually drew it off her—

Damn. It was Kaley or Carly, or whatever she was calling herself these days. The face might be smudged and dirty, but there was no mistaking that head of red hair. Or that cleavage. For a split second, his gaze was drawn down the open front of her blouse to the pale blue silk of her bra. Unbelievable. He would've sworn he caught the barest hint of cherry on her skin.

Even now, even after what she'd done, Nate's groin tightened at the memory of their last walk on the beach. Their last night together. By the time they'd made it back to her hotel, he would've bet another run through Hell Week she'd been ready to invite him up to her room. Instead, she'd wrapped her arms around his waist and kissed him, long and slow, for what seemed like forever. As if she'd been branding the memory of his mouth on her lips.

"I want to come up to your room," he'd whispered, as her scent, a mixture of cherry blossoms and the salty sea air, had been seared into his brain.

"This weekend," she'd whispered back. "In the mountains. I promise."

One thing was for sure. This woman knew how to torture a man. Maybe he should've left her to the mercy of the guards.

She glanced at Nate for the first time and seemed confused. Her eyes slowly widened as she silently dragged the gag down and off her mouth. Then her gaze shifted toward the dead bodies at her feet, and a soft, involuntary sound escaped her throat.

At that, the footsteps stopped in front of their building. Her terrified gaze flew to his face. He put his index finger to his lips and got ready to silence any intruder.

Mr. Cigarette kicked the door open. The watery light of the quickly vanishing moon illuminated the dead bodies on the ground. Just as Nate was about to take him out, the man pulled out his radio and sped down the alley.

"Let's go." Nate ran out of the building, stopping only to grab Pritchard. That's when the shit hit the fan. Loud shouts sounded from the village center. Shots were fired into the sky.

"You shouldn't have gone after her," Pritchard said, shaking his head.

"Shut up and follow me." Nate zigzagged through the empty alleyways, bypassing more abandoned vehicles, scrub brush and garbage.

"We're on our way," Nate said into his radio. "And I picked up a hitchhiker."

"Of course you have," muttered Turnham.

A siren sounded. Shouts sounded near the edge of the deserted village not far from where the rest of his team was waiting for them behind a thick stand of acacia and scrub brush. From this distance, Nate could only make out one fender of the Humvee. He glanced around the courtyard. The rebel guards were completely disorganized, but it was still going to be tricky getting past the clearing.

"What's your ETA?" Turnham asked. "We don't have much time before they locate out position."

"Ten seconds—"

"Are those your men?" Pritchard pointed toward the trees.

"Yes, but—"

Pritchard took off at a dead run. The lucky bastard made it to the Humvee just as several guards noticed him. Thanks to Pritchard, Ahmed's men had zeroed in on the extraction point.

"Lay down some cover," Nate shouted above the sound of rapid weapons fire. "We'll come around—"

"Too hot," Turnham said. "You know what to do."

"Roger that."

The Humvee sped away toward its rendezvous with the Chinook helicopter several clicks east. Nate clicked off his radio and glanced around, looking for the safest way out of this mess. There had to be fifty armed guards converging on where the Humvee had been parked.

"Let's move." He turned and headed back the way they had come.

"But wasn't the truck—"

"*Was* being the operative word." They had to get back to those abandoned cars. One of them looked like it might get them out of this dusty hellhole. "Your boss just ruined any chance we had of getting out of here today."

"No surprise there. Pritchard looks out for number one. Always has. Always will. So now what?"

"We have to get out of here. Fast. And we're going dark."

"What does that mean?"

"*Incommunicado.*" He smiled grimly. "Until we can make the alternate extraction point, it's just you and me, Red."

Chapter Two

Nate Griggs. *Of all the gin joints in the all the . . .*

Carly ran to keep up with him as he zigzagged through the deserted streets, her heart hammering from much more than the prospect of getting caught by Ahmed's men again. "Where is this alternate extraction point?"

"Outside Mogadishu. Along the coast. This time the chopper will come straight for us, but not until after sunset."

"Is there another option?"

"Sure. You could hang around for one of Ahmed's yahoos to find you and finish what the others started."

No way that was going to happen, but the alternative was not good. She couldn't leave this village, not yet, and especially not with Nate. In Virginia Beach, this man had almost thrown her off course. She was so close, so close to uncovering the truth. She couldn't let anything get in her way at this point, not even this hunk of a Navy SEAL.

Wait a minute. Maybe he'd help. If she explained, he'd understand. "Listen, Nate, Virginia Beach? I can—"

"No time for confessions, Red. Gotta put some distance between us and Ahmed's men."

"Do they know we got left behind?"

"Not yet." He glanced behind her. "But they're heading this way."

"What?"

"Relax. We'll get out of this."

"Relax. Sure. Why not? I get kidnapped and nearly raped every day."

Abruptly, he turned a corner, pushed her into an abandoned house and drew her into the shadows, leaving the door wide open. "Quiet," he whispered, shielding her behind him.

Carly held her breath as she brushed up against Nate's camouflage-covered back of steel. The sounds of men running came closer. Closer. Suddenly, the men stopped a mere six feet from their hiding place. One of the men was on his radio, speaking rapidly, and then listening. Then, suddenly, all of them turned and headed back the way they came.

Nate waited a moment and then stepped aside.

"Why did they leave?"

"We got lucky. They don't know we're here."

For now, it appeared, they were safe.

Nate's gaze flashed to her torn shirt and exposed bra. For a moment, raw desire flickered hot in his eyes, reminding her of every kiss they'd shared, every touch of his hand, both gentle and urgent. He'd wanted her in Virginia Beach. Worst of all, she'd wanted him back. But as quickly as desire had flared to life in his eyes, it had been doused, leaving only unfiltered menace.

Carly sucked in a quick breath. This soldier, this man, wasn't her Nate. The Nate she'd met and fell for in Virginia Beach would've pulled her into his arms and chased away every fear, every bad thought. This man was cold, hard, and very, very angry. At her. And he had every right to be.

Self-consciously, she tried pulling the torn blouse together, but the buttons had been ripped off.

He unzipped his pack and held out a black T-shirt. "Here. Put this on."

She grabbed the shirt and then hesitated as she caught the faint, but very familiar scent of a fresh sea breeze mixed with spicy aftershave.

"It's all I've got," he said. "Pink isn't in the Navy's repertoire."

The problem wasn't the color. The problem was wearing anything that smelled like Nate, but it's not as if there was a shopping mall nearby. "Thanks." She yanked the shirt over her head, squirmed out of her torn blouse and tossed it in the corner.

"So what are you doing here, anyway?" He glared at her. "You weren't on our list of Pritchard's staff."

"Just lucky, I guess."

His stare intensified.

"I quit Pritchard's group last week. I was in the hotel suite collecting a few things I'd forgotten when they . . . when they ambushed us. Forced us into a truck. And brought us to this . . . place."

For a moment, he eyed her, as if trying to decide whether or not she was telling the truth. Then without comment, he pulled out a GPS unit and studied their position.

"Don't you want to know why I quit?"

He didn't respond. Only studied the digital map.

Too bad. He was going to get an explanation whether he wanted it or not. "I quit because of you and what Pritchard did to your team's reputation with that show."

Without glancing at her, he shook his head. "And that's supposed to make it all better?"

She clenched her mouth shut. No way was she going to apologize, not with what was at stake, but she could explain.

"I guess all's fair in love and war," he muttered.

"Look. I thought Pritchard was running a legitimate investigation into how that medical team was killed. If I'd known he was going to distort things and lie . . . If I'd known he cared more about ratings that the truth, I never would've agreed to . . . . "

"Use me."

"If I remember correctly, you didn't seem to mind at the time."

At that, he glared up at her as if he might snap her in two with one hand, and at six foot two and two-hundred-twenty pounds of muscle, there was no doubt he could. "What I mind is being lied to and ditched without explanation. What I mind is being led on for weeks over dinners, long walks, moonlit nights."

The intimate conversations, the intense eye contact. The kisses they'd shared. She understood. That's why she'd left before going to the Blue Ridge Mountains with him. In truth, she'd been protecting herself as much as him. "What if I had a reason for doing what I did?"

"A lot of good people, a couple of them friends of mine, died that day in route to that refugee camp."

She understood far better than he realized.

"There is no reason good enough for putting any of them in a bad light."

Tears pricked at the corners of her eyes. Hadn't he gotten to know her at all in those three weeks they'd spent practically every waking moment together? A part of her wanted to explain everything, and another part of her wanted to slap him silly for not giving her the benefit of the doubt. Now was clearly not the time for either as the sound of footsteps crunched in the gravel outside.

"Back up," Nate said, snatching up his gear and heading back into the dark corner.

Carly glanced outside and froze. Suddenly, she couldn't breathe, couldn't move. She was a studio photographer, for God's sake. She took senior high school pictures and family photos. She had no business being in Somalia, of all places. Jason was the risk-taker. Not her.

Strong hands wrapped around her upper arms and she felt herself being pulled into the corner. Instantly memories of being held captive by the Somali radicals popped into her thoughts. Hunger, thirst, having to pee so badly she thought her bladder would burst inside her body. Then the guards man-handling her. *Oh, God.* She'd always thought she was strong. She'd thought she could handle coming here. For her parents' sake. She'd found out she wasn't strong at all.

The hands around her arms slowly loosened. "Hey," a soft masculine voice whispered. "They're gone. It's all right."

She glanced up.

Nate's gaze softened and a glimmer of the man she'd known slipped through a crack in his desert camouflage. Memories of other rescues, other kidnap victims—women—who hadn't been as lucky as Carly, seemed to pass through his thoughts. There he was, her Nate. "Did they hurt you?"

She swallowed. "No. Not really."

"You sure?"

She'd been punched and pawed, but there was no real damage, at least not on the outside. Inside, Carly felt as raw as hamburger and, obviously, it showed. "I'm okay," she whispered, absently rubbing her wrists.

"Good." And just like that, the focused soldier was back, intent on his objective. "We have to find some transportation. Cover some distance before it gets any lighter."

He glanced out the window and beaded in on an old, beat up beige Fiat parked near a half-dead acacia. Other than the fact that it had only three tires and one of the doors had been battered in, it looked serviceable. "Wait here for a minute." He left the house and returned moments later with a wheel and an old gas can.

"Where'd you get that stuff?" she asked, heading outside.

"Off another car down the street." In a matter of minutes, he'd jacked up the vehicle and was replacing the flat tire.

"How long before we have to meet that chopper?"

He glanced at his watch. "Twelve hours, sixteen minutes and forty-five seconds."

A half a day to go fifty miles. That was enough time.

Before she knew it, he'd replaced the tire, had hotwired the Fiat, and had tossed his gear into the back seat. "Get in."

Everything in her screamed to follow his order and get as far away from these Somali rebels as possible, but she forced herself to stay put. She was here. She had to do this.

"I said get in, Red. Now."

"No." She calmed her racing heart as he glared over at her, clenched her sweating palms together and held his stern gaze. "I can't leave. Not yet."

Chapter Three

"What the hell is that supposed to mean?" Dumbfounded, Nate stared at Carly. The woman had balls. He'd give her that.

"I can't—I won't—leave this village. Not voluntarily."

Well, then, that only left *involuntarily*. "Listen," he said, heading round the car toward the five foot two, one-hundred-twenty pound piece of cake.

"Oh, no you don't." She backed up, keeping what she apparently considered a safe distance between them.

He almost smiled. Almost. There she stood, swimming like a little kid in his oversized T-shirt with dried blood in the corner of her mouth and a nasty scrape across her cheek and still she acted as if she was calling the shots. Then he looked again. Beneath the bravado was heart-wrenching vulnerability, and an odd sense of protectiveness— maybe even possessiveness—passed through him, throwing him off his game.

Oh, no, you don't, Griggs. Do not let her fool you again.

"Hear me out first before you overpower me and shove me in that car," she went on. "Once you hear what I have to say, you might even offer to help."

Wouldn't count on it. He stopped, but stayed on the ready. Any minute the sun was going to rise above the horizon, and they'd be sitting ducks. "Okay. I'm listening."

"No, you're not." She backed up even farther. "You're just waiting for your opportunity. I can see it in your eyes."

For having known him only a few weeks she sure as hell could read him well. "All right, fine." He crossed his arms and leaned against the wall. "You going to tell me what's going on or should we play twenty questions?"

She took a deep, shaky breath. "My brother's name is Dr. Jason Danson."

The name sounded familiar.

"About a year ago, he came to Somalia to provide humanitarian aid to the refugees."

Nate had a feeling he knew where this was leading, and it wasn't pretty.

"Yeah. You got it." She held his gaze. "Jason was with that medical team that was ambushed last month."

Ah, hell.

"Military personnel came to my parents' house and told them what had happened. Or should I say they gave Mom and Dad the pat explanation that had been given to the press. The medical team was being escorted from one refugee camp to another when they were ambushed by Mohammed Ahmed's men. No survivors. No remains."

That was about it in a nutshell. There was only one piece of info she was missing.

Tearing up, she turned away. He could've grabbed her at that point and they could've been on their way, but he'd seen what had been left of that medical team after Ahmed's band of militants had been through with them.

"Something about the explanation didn't feel right to me," she went on. "So I did some digging. Every file on Jason's death was sealed. Classified. I was desperate to find the whole truth for my parents. For myself. No matter what the cost."

"So you came to Virginia Beach. Were you targeting any SEAL from my team or was I the only lucky son of a bitch?"

She hesitated. "Anyone."

Unbelievable. He had the worst instincts in the world. "Why didn't you just tell me this from the beginning?"

"Would it have made a difference?" She blinked away her tears. "Would you have told me about what happened?"

Classified, meant classified. His gaze wavered.

"Orders are orders, right?"

"Is the truth worth your parents losing two children?"

"No, but I won't be able to face them again after what I've discovered." She paused, swallowed. "While Ahmed's men held us here, I saw some things. Heard some things. I think part of that medical team might still be alive."

"No way. I was there. No one survived that massacre."

"But you weren't there when they attacked, were you, Nate?"

She knew.

"I saw some of Ahmed's injured men carried off to the other side of his compound. I heard them talking about a doctor. I think Ahmed's men needed medical people. I think there's a possibility they kept Jason alive and brought him back here."

"A possibility. That's all you got, Red?"

"For a brother, that's all I need. And my name isn't Red."

"Oh, right. *Kaley.*"

"My name is Carly." She held his gaze. "We have twelve hours before we need to be at that extraction point. Help me find out if Jason is still alive."

As she stood her ground, dawn threatened to expose them to the light of day, and a spark of respect for her flickered to life inside him. But that didn't change what he had to do, not really. Already, he'd waited too long. He'd have to knock her out. There was no way she'd get in that car still conscious.

Just then the sounds of loud shouts and vehicle engines revving came from the direction of the village square.

"What's going on?"

"I don't know, but I need to find out." With Carly behind him, Nate carefully made his way back to the village square. Like ants moving anthills, men were coming every which way out of buildings carrying crates of weapons and supplies into a caravan of waiting cars and trucks.

"They're packing up and moving," she whispered.

"Their location has been compromised, so they're heading to greener pastures."

"After Pritchard and his staff were rescued why didn't our military come and blow the shit out of this place while they had the chance?"

"Because we aren't supposed to be here. If a village, even a deserted one like this, was suddenly reduced to rubble, the Somali powers that be might just kick all of the humanitarian aid workers out of their country." And then the U.S. would lose its cover for its covert hunt for Mohammed Ahmed.

"So Ahmed's men move and get to continue to terrorize the poor people of this country."

"It's not our country. Not our rules."

As the last of the supplies were loaded, Ahmed's men climbed into the waiting vehicles and the caravan rolled out of town, leaving nothing but a trail of dust in its wake. After the last vehicle had left, Carly shot out of their hiding place and headed straight into the nearest building Ahmed's men had occupied.

"What are you doing?"

"Maybe they left Jason here." Frantically, she raced from one building to the next.

From what Nate could see, all Ahmed's men had left behind was garbage. Realizing there was little he could do except wait for her to run out of steam, he stood in the shade and waited. Each time she came out of a building, her features had grown more and more worry worn. When she came out of one of the last buildings holding something in her hand and with a distinctly different look on her face, he snapped to attention.

"We need to follow that caravan, Nate."

"What? Why?"

"That building was used as a makeshift hospital," she said, holding out a handful of empty syringes, discarded rolls of bloodied gauze. "What if they kept Jason alive—kept a couple of nurses alive—to treat their wounded?"

"My orders are to make my way to that alternate extraction point ASAP."

"Do you have siblings?" she asked.

He didn't answer, but the images of his two older sisters flashed through his mind.

"What if it was your brother or sister?" she whispered. "What then?"

Chances were this was a wild goose chase, but his gut—his damned gut again—told him she could be right. And what had his gut done for him lately other than to get him into trouble? Still, the *facts* were that amidst those charred remains, there'd been no way to tell one body from the next.

Nate glanced toward the quickly dwindling trail of dust left my Ahmed's caravan and knew he didn't have a choice. He may have been following orders when he and the other SEALs had left that medical team minimally guarded to go hunt down Ahmed's second in command, but he still felt responsible for what had happened in his absence. Besides, there was only one road from here to Mogadishu, so he'd still be, in effect, following orders by following Ahmed's men.

"I'll make a deal with you," he said. "We'll follow them. For now. If we run out of time or Ahmed's men veer too far from the extraction point and we've seen neither hide nor hair of your brother or any other Americans—"

"Then I'll go with you. No questions asked."

No questions asked. Sure. But at least he'd be doing what he could to help and wouldn't feel the slightest bit of remorse when he eventually threw her over his shoulder and hauled her away. "Okay, Red. Let's get on that trail of dust before it drifts out of sight."

Chapter Four

"Have you seen anything?" Carly asked hopefully.

"You mean in the five minutes since the last time you asked?" Nate didn't even glance up from his binoculars. In fact, he'd barely moved in the almost four hours since they'd followed Ahmed's men from that deserted village into this rundown section of suburban Mogadishu.

She had no clue how he could be so patient. "I hate this place. This country. This city." She dragged her booted toe over the dusty floorboard. "Everywhere I turn, there's this fine layer of dirt."

"Why don't you sit down and relax? You're making me antsy."

Him antsy? As if that was possible. Since agreeing to help find Jason, Nate had moved quickly and quite calmly. He'd not only followed Ahmed's men all the way to the gates of their walled compound without being noticed, he'd also located this building on his GPS and found an unoccupied apartment on the top floor with a relatively unobstructed view of the compound. Regardless of how this all turned out, she wasn't sure how she'd be able to thank him.

She could start, she supposed, by burying the hatchet. Plopping down, she sighed deeply. "Thank you for doing this."

"I haven't *done* anything. Yet. And I'm still not convinced I won't be dragging you off to our extraction point when the time comes."

His surly tone cut to the bone, but what bothered her most was that he had every right to be angry at her. If not for her, he would've never missed that Humvee. "Thank you for saving my life. Back at that village. If you hadn't . . . killed those guards, I don't even want to think about what would've happened to me."

"Just doing my job."

"But I wasn't part of your job, remember? I wasn't on your list."

He didn't turn. Didn't say a word.

But there was something more personal for which she had to atone. Walking out on him in Virginia Beach. "I'm sorry," she whispered, the words coming from deep inside. "No goodbye. No explanations. What I did to you wasn't right."

Silent. Again.

"I never meant to hurt you, Nate. I didn't think three weeks with me . . . would . . . . "

"Mean anything to me?" He turned then, but his gaze had softened. "You telling me that it didn't mean anything to you?"

"That's not what I said." The time she'd spent with Nate had been nothing short of magical for her. He'd distracted her so much that she'd almost forgotten her ultimate goal had been to find out what had happened to Jason's medical team.

"Yeah, well," he said, turning back to his binoculars. "I might've done the same thing if I'd been in your situation. He's your brother. You were desperate."

She'd been desperate for answers, all right. She still felt desperate. What if Jason was really dead? What then? She glanced at the back of Nate's head, down his tanned neck, his broad shoulders, remembering what it had felt like to be held by him, wanting to be held by him now. Holding back an unexpected rush of tears, Carly looked away.

"Hey." Nate's warm hand settled on her shoulder. "Just because I haven't seen anything out this window, doesn't mean they don't still have hostages. It just means that if they are holding anyone, they're smart enough to keep them out of sight."

"But if you don't see anything—"

"We'll cross that bridge when—if—we come to it. Okay?" He went back to looking through his binoculars. Suddenly, he went very still and whispered, "Hold everything. We got action."

"What?" She jumped up and glanced over his shoulders, but the compound was too far away to make heads or tails out of any of the movement with the naked eye. "What's happening?"

"Two trucks just raced through the gate." He shook his head. "They pulled up into the courtyard."

"And?"

"Mr. Cigarette is back. One of the guards I recognize from where you were being held. They're carrying something—someone—out of the back of one of the trucks. He looks hurt. There are two more coming out of the other truck bed." Nate adjusted the focus. "I'll be damned. That's it."

"What? What's it?"

"You could be right, Red. They just might have set up a makeshift hospital."

"What about Jason? Did you see him?"

"No. But I can't see the entire area. Looks like they might be taking the wounded to that small building near the main house. If Jason's in that compound, that's where they'd be holding—wait a minute. There. That man's not a Somali. Look. Quick." He thrust the binoculars into her hands. "Just this side of the main building. See the two vehicles? Is that man Jason?"

"He looks American," she whispered, her hope dwindling. "But he's not Jason."

"You sure?"

"Positive. Jason's hair is as red as mine." She handed him back his binoculars and started packing things up. "But we have to get that man out of there. Whoever he is. Maybe he knows something about my brother."

"Whoa, whoa, whoa. Slow down, Red. We can't head in there in broad daylight. Too many guards."

"So there's nothing we can do but wait?"

"After dark we make our move." He went through his plan. "You're going to wait by the car. If anything goes wrong." He pulled out a handgun and prepped her on using it. "Don't worry about where you hit your target. Just hit him. Anywhere."

She nodded. "When do we leave?"

He glanced at his watch and then into the sky. Already the sun was dipping toward the horizon. "Two, maybe three more hours."

"And in the meantime? What if they hurt that man?"

"They won't. They need him."

She rubbed her arms at a sudden chill in the air.

He dug into his pack and held out some supplies, a canteen and some foil packages. "Drink some water. Eat. You need to keep up your strength."

The fact that he opened the package before handing it to her might've seemed ridiculous in other circumstances, but not now. At this moment, she was supremely grateful for Nate Griggs. "What about you? Aren't you hungry?"

"I'm fine." He went back to staring through his binoculars.

"Do you think they're feeding him?"

"Yeah. Like I said, they need him alive."

Carly broke off a chunk and tossed it in her mouth. Either the bar was grainy and tasteless, or she simply didn't have an appetite. She swallowed as a tear slipped down her cheek. "The last time I talked to Jason, we fought. I told him he was being selfish for coming here. For risking his life in joining that humanitarian medical team."

"This country needs help."

Everywhere she'd looked since coming here, there'd been starving men, women and children. People beaten and harassed by Mohammed Ahmed's men. Injured people needing medical care. "I just want the chance to tell Jason I'm sorry."

Nate smiled gently. "If he's there, Carly, I'll get him out."

She could fall for this man. Hard. It was too bad she'd screwed things up between them. Regret hung over her like a heavy, damp cloud. Suddenly, she was cold, oh so cold. As if the events of the last couple of days had finally caught up with her, she shivered, thought she could even hear her teeth chatter.

Before she comprehended he was moving, Nate was at her side, rubbing her bare arms. "You're as cold as the trout stream by my cabin."

"Bet you say that to all the girls." She tried to smile, but her mouth felt frozen.

"Come here." As if she were no heavier than his pack, he lifted her between his spread legs and wrapped his arms around her.

She was too tired to fight. In truth, she didn't want to fight. The warmth of his body was so inviting, she found herself curling into him. "Just for a few minutes," she whispered.

For several long, quiet moments she held completely still in his arms. A few minutes turned into ten. Fifteen. Suddenly, his embraced tightened, as if he was preparing her for something. "I think you should know," he said softly. "There's no big secret about your brother's medical team getting ambushed and killed. What happened is classified, but there's no big conspiracy."

She held her breath, hoping he'd continue.

"Our SEAL team was assisting in transporting the doctors, nurses and a truckload of supplies from one refugee camp to another when we got news that Mohammed Ahmed's second in command was nearby. At the time, it seemed like too good an opportunity to pass up. We left behind what we thought was adequate protection for the civilians, but we were wrong. Ahmed's men wanted those medical supplies. The four marines and two SEALs we'd left behind didn't stand a chance."

"Did you get Ahmed's man?"

"Yeah," he said, regret filling the tone of his voice. "But if I had to do it over again, I would've stayed behind."

She ran her hand over his chest, hoping to comfort him some small amount. "Thank you for telling me."

"So you were wasting your time in Virginia Beach."

"No, I wasn't, and there's one thing I'll never be sorry for."

"What's that?"

"Kissing you." There'd been nothing fake or pretend about how much she'd wanted him then, how much she wanted him now. "For your sake, for both of us, I had to leave before either of us had gotten in too deep."

"Well, you were about two weeks and six days too late for that, Red. I was in too deep the first night I met you." His eyes darkened as he reached out to cup her cheek and run the pad of his thumb over her upper lip.

"That makes two of us." She closed her eyes and kissed the palm of his hand.

He groaned. "Virginia Beach was almost perfect."

"Almost?"

He tilted her head back and looked into her eyes. "I wish I'd made love to you."

What if neither of them made out of Mogadishu alive? Could she leave this world without regrets? No. Not yet. There was one thing she still needed to do. Wrapping her arms around Nate's neck, she pulled him toward her and kissed him, whispering, "Better late than never."

Chapter Five

He was in too deep, all right.

Nate studied every line, every pore, of Carly's sleeping face. Making love with her just now had been as perfect as perfect got, better than he'd dreamt it would be. Damned if his heart was ever going to recover from the likes of Carly Danson.

As soon as they were done here, as soon as her brother was safe, she'd have no more use for him. No doubt she'd walk off into the sunset with his heart in her hand. Whoever the hell had said better to have loved and lost than never to have loved at all was full of shit. Might as well get the pain over with sooner rather than later.

Gently, he nudged her. "Carly." While she'd been sleeping, he'd left to secure a more reliable vehicle with a full tank of gas. The rest of the time, he'd been watching the rebel compound. Everyone but five night watch guards were buttoned down for the night. "Wake up. It's time to move."

Slowly, she opened her eyes, gazed at him, and a lazy smile spread across her face. She'd clearly forgotten where they were and why they were here.

For a moment—one blissfully contented moment—he allowed himself to do the same. He imagined they were at his cabin, nestled amidst the thick spruce and firs. The trout stream in back trickling softly and the chestnut trees rustling in a cool night breeze. He'd never taken a woman there, never wanted to before Carly.

He bent his head and kissed her slowly, luxuriously, as if they had all the time in the world. She sighed and yielded to him as he dipped his tongue inside her warm, sweet mouth. When she wrapped her leg around him, pulling him close, he let himself sink into her softness. One heartbeat, two. Ten. A lifetime would never be enough. Damn. His gut had been right all along. She was the one. Reluctantly, he pulled away.

She blinked and suddenly jolted upright as reality seemed to hit.

"How long was I out?"

"Coupla hours." He looked away, giving himself a minute, and then held out his canteen.

She took a swig of water and wiped her mouth. "Listen. About what just happened between us—"

"Now isn't the time." He stood and grabbed his pack. "Later."

"What if there isn't a later?"

He extended his hand. "Then explanations, apologies, promises. None of it'll matter."

She put her hand in his and pulled herself upright, all the while holding his gaze. "Nate—"

"Focus on the objective," he stated with as little emotion as possible. "I get that man out of there. I look for your brother. And then we get the hell out of Mogadishu. One thing at a time."

"Okay." She nodded. "I'm ready."

He went through the plan one more time. They would park the vehicle beside the compound wall. She was to stay there for ten minutes. If he didn't come back, she was to, without hesitation, head directly to the coordinates on his GPS. "If all goes according to plan, we'll be out of here in no time."

Again, she nodded.

They exited the apartment building and, while Carly steered, he pushed the old Mercedes to a spot near the wall of the compound. "This is it," he whispered, signaling for her to get out of the car. "This is closest to their makeshift medical clinic." He took the supplies and weapons he needed out of his pack and set it in the back seat. Then he handed her his 9mm and suppressor, climbed onto the roof of the car and surveyed the compound through his binoculars. One guard at the main building. One at the gate. And three making rounds. His window of opportunity was right . . . now.

He glanced down at Carly. For the first time ever, there was a woman he wanted to come back to, safe and sound. "You ready for this?"

"Yes."

She looked about as ready as any civilian could be for the possible fight of her life. "You'll do fine."

"Be careful," she whispered. "I—"

Before she had the chance to say another word, he climbed over the wall. Within minutes, he'd made it inside the building the rebels seemed to be using as a medical clinic by climbing through a rear window. The main room of the house was, indeed, outfitted like a small rustic hospital. Two Somalis, Ahmed's rebels, both heavily bandaged in various parts of their bodies, lay sleeping on cots. A guard sat conked out in a chair, semi-automatic weapon across his lap. Nate made quick work of all three. No point in taking the chance any of them would awaken.

Now to find that male prisoner. A search of the other four rooms, a kitchen, bathroom and two bedrooms yielded no results. That left only the closet off the main room. It was locked. Bingo.

A key from the now dead guard's shirt pocket opened the door. The man—and a woman—their clothes stained with dirt, blood and sweat, were huddled close to each other in the dark. No Jason. Without enough time to address the obvious fear in the hostages' eyes, Nate held out his hand. "Can you speak English?"

"Oh, thank God, you're American," the woman cried softly as a tear spilled down her cheek.

"You *are* here to rescue us," the man said, pulling himself up and turning to help the woman. "Aren't you?"

"Yes, sir. I'm getting you out of here right now."

"I'm Ed. This is Amy. We were on a medical—" The two came into the room and, clearly terrified, stared at the rebels.

"Don't worry. They won't ever hurt anyone again," Nate whispered. "Is there anyone else from your team who survived?"

"Yes." Amy's eyes went wide with worry. "Jason."

"At least he was alive this morning," Ed added with bitterness. "But when he wouldn't treat one of their men they beat him. Badly. We haven't seen him since they dragged him out of here."

"Do you know where they took him?"

"It looked like they went into the main building," Amy said, nodding toward the windows. "Through that side door you can see from here."

"After the beating he took, he's bound to have internal bleeding," Ed added. "If he's alive, he'll be in bad shape."

The only reason Ahmed's men would've taken Jason away from the medical team was if they wanted him to die. How was Nate going to tell Carly? First things first, and they had to hurry. There were running out of time to get to the extraction location. "Let's get you two out of here."

They left the building and made it back to the car with three minutes to spare. Carly helped Ed and Amy into the back seat of the car and then turned expectantly toward him. Nate relayed everything the two hostages had told him about Jason.

"So we don't know whether or not he's alive," Carly said, clearly struggling to hold herself together.

"I'm going back to look for him." He didn't want to tell her that this time was going to be riskier. Even if he managed to find Jason, he wasn't sure what kind of shape Carly's brother would be in. Nate would have a tough time carrying a man's dead weight over that eight-foot wall. "We need a new plan."

As he gathered more supplies, he gave her new instructions. "With any luck, the guard will leave the front gate unattended. If he holds his post, you may have to use that weapon, Carly."

She looked scared, but would that fear immobilize her?

"You can do this. I know you can." He climbed back up onto the roof of the car and studied the grounds. Same three men on rounds. Same guard at the gate. Same man at the main build—

Hold everything. Mr. Cigarette. What do you know? The man stepped outside, lit up and blew a lungful of smoke into the air as he arrogantly puffed out his chest. Then he turned to talk to the other guard. That's when Nate saw it. *Dammit.* On Mr. Cigarette's left cheek was a half moon scar just like Mohammed Ahmed's. "How can that . . . "

"Nate, what is it?" Carly asked.

Every other time Nate had seen Mr. Cigarette it'd been from his right side. But how could—? Then it dawned on him. The photo identifying the man had been a reflection. "It's him," Nate murmured. Mr. Cigarette *was* Mohammed Ahmed.

"Nate?"

He glanced at Carly. They were running out of time to get to the extraction point. He was going to have to choose. Take out Ahmed, his primary mission objective, or save Jason? The answer was obvious.

"Do not, and I mean this Carly, do not wait for me." He took one last look at her face, and then hopped over the wall.

Chapter Six

Something was wrong. Carly had seen in on Nate's face. Strong emotion. Conflict. He'd looked as if he was being torn in two. Over what? Or . . . *who?* She'd heard him whisper something. It's him? Yes, that's what he said. *It's him.* Could he have been talking about Mohammed Ahmed? Could Nate's primary mission be here? If Ahmed was here, Nate would do his job. No matter what. *Oh, God. Jason.* What if Nate had to leave him here?

She climbed into the car and turned toward Ed and Amy. "How bad was Jason?" she asked. "Do you think he could make it another day?" If he was still alive, could he make it until Nate's team came back for him?

"He was bad." Ed shook his head. "I'm not sure he'll see the sunrise without medical attention."

She spun back around and stared in shock out the dusty windshield. She might never see her brother again.

Just then an explosion boomed through the silence, shaking the ground. She jolted with surprise as the black sky lit with bright lights and plumes of smoke. That was her signal. Signal for what, though? Her mind went black as panic threatened.

You have to remember. You need to—

Time. She had to keep track of the time.

Quickly, she clicked the stopwatch Nate had given her earlier. In exactly two minutes, she was supposed to drive the car to the front gate. If Nate didn't show within thirty seconds, she was to leave, with or without him. These were going to be the longest two minutes of her life.

Gunfire erupted inside the compound. One minute and thirty seconds of rapid fire back and forth as one frantic thought after another raced through her mind. Damn Nate and his commitment to duty. But was it fair to fault him for doing his job?

"We need to go," Amy said, nearly hysterical with fear. "We need to get out of here."

"Sorry, Amy, we have to wait just a little bit more. To give Nate time to get back to the gate." Carly stared at the watch, counting down those last thirty seconds. "Now we can go."

She started the engine and eased toward the gate. Too late, she realized the guard hadn't been distracted, as expected, by the explosion Nate had set. The guard pointed his gun at her, some kind of heavy-duty automatic thing, and yelled for her to get out of the car. She opened the door and slid out, keeping the gun Nate had given her behind her back and praying for a chance to shoot.

A second explosion crackled through the air. This was it. Her chance. She aimed the gun. The guard turned back to her and she froze. She couldn't do it.

Then past the guard, inside the compound, motion drew her gaze. It was Nate running toward them. And he was carrying a body over his shoulders. Jason! She'd have known that head of red hair anywhere. He'd rescued Jason. Carly squeezed the trigger, hitting the guard in his gut. She hit him again, forcing him to the ground, as she raced to open the gate.

"I'm driving!" Nate called out as he ran toward her.

She flew to the passenger's side and helped Nate get her unconscious brother into the back seat. She climbed into the front passenger seat, Nate slid behind the wheel, and they took off before the doors where even closed.

"Is Jason alive?" she asked, turning to see if there was anything she could do.

"I don't know," Nate said as he sped through the deserted city streets.

"He's alive," Ed said, his hand on Jason's limp wrist.

The car's motion jostled her back and forth as Nate drove as fast as he could through the deserted streets, but she couldn't take her eyes off her brother. He was laid out on the seat, his head in the doctor's lap. The nurse held his feet. His face was a mass of blood and bruises. His clothes were torn, dirty.

Slowly, Jason cracked open one puffy and bruised eye. When he saw her, he smiled faintly. "You came to Somalia, Carls," he murmured, his words slurred. "I'm impressed."

"Stay alive and I'll tell you a few stories that'll impress you even more."

"Oh, I'll be all right." His words were little more than exhaled breath and then his eye drifted closed and his mouth went slack.

"Jason?" When he didn't respond, she turned to Ed. "Is he going to be okay?"

"His blood pressure is dropping. I need an operating table and lots of medical supplies. Fast."

"Everything you need will be on the carrier," Nate said. "But we gotta get there first."

"Did you take out Mohammed Ahmed?" she asked.

"No. Had to follow my gut. It's usually right."

Just then headlights popped up through the haze of dirt being kicked up behind them. Someone was tailing them. "We've got company," Carly said.

"I see that," Nate muttered, glancing in the rearview mirror. He flicked on his radio and contacted the chopper. "I'm coming in hot."

"Looks like your tail is gaining," said Master Chief Turnham.

"I've got four passengers, so I'm going to need some help."

"Roger that."

Suddenly, the rear window was shattered by gunfire. "Get down!" Nate called.

"I've got a better idea!" Carly shouted as Ed and Amy ducked. Fueled by adrenaline rushing through her veins and anger over what Ahmed and his men had done to Jason, she aimed out the rear window and fired. Over and over. The truck, a gunman in the rear bed, swerved, but kept coming.

"That's Mohammed Ahmed in the front passenger seat," Nate said. "Take him out."

"Me?"

"You're the one with the gun."

She fired several more times. The truck slowed slightly, but it wasn't enough.

"The chopper's landing just ahead of us," Nate said. "You gotta do better than that."

The truck closed in again. Carly fired several times, missing her mark. Another few shots and this time she managed to hit the front windshield. The truck swerved and the gunman lost his balance.

"Get ready. As soon as I stop this vehicle, everybody out. Chopper side. Get Jason to safety as fast as you can. Do not stop to look back. And keep your heads down. They'll be throwing down some cover fire. Understand?"

"Yes!"

"Showtime." Nate swerved the car sharply just in front of the chopper and jerked to a stop, throwing up a veil of dirt and dust. "Run!"

"What about you—"

"Go!"

She flew out the door and helped Ed with Jason as Amy ran to the chopper. Amidst the storm of dust kicked up by the rotating helicopter blades, four SEALs hopped to the ground and ran past Carly. Someone helped her up into the chopper and she turned to watch.

Nate had climbed out behind her and was using the car as a shield as he fired at Ahmed's truck. Ahmed's men had almost overtaken Nate when the other SEALs joined Nate's side. That's when Ahmed's truck made an abrupt about-face and sped off back toward Mogadishu. Nate grabbed what looked like a couple grenades and launched them toward Ahmed and his men. A split second later, the truck blew to pieces.

Nate and the others ran full out back to the chopper. The moment they were inside, the pilot took off. Nate put on a radio headset. "So long to Mohammed Ahmed," he said into the radio, holding Carly's gaze.

A round of cheers erupted amongst the SEALs. In a matter of minutes, the chopper was over water. They'd no sooner landed on the carrier deck than a medical team flew toward them with a stretcher. Everything happened in a flash. As they transferred Jason, Ed relayed Jason's vital signs.

"Prep him for surgery. I'm right behind you." Ed glanced at her. "I think we got him just in time, Carly. He's going to be okay."

Carly hopped out of the chopper and ran behind them, wanting—needing—to be with Jason. But something—someone—tugged at her heartstrings. She turned and found Nate watching her as the chopper blades rotated over his head. This man had risked his life for her, for her brother. She could risk her heart.

"The Blue Ridge Mountains," she called. After everything they'd been through, would he still want to see her? "Your cabin."

"What about it?" he said, his gaze intense.

"I owe you a weekend." She held her breath. "Still interested?"

"Yes, ma'am." He smiled softly. "But my gut's telling me a long weekend won't be nearly long enough."

FINDING HOME

HelenKay Dimon

Chapter One

Megan White balanced her palms on her desk, kicked off her three-inch black pumps, and nearly groaned in relief. Her arches ached and her cramped toes tingled to painful life after an hour of numbness. The carpet under her was little more than a mat. A co-op of local women wove it together from the thick leaves of a huge pink flowering plant, the name of which Megan kept forgetting. The flooring wasn't soft or cushy, but she wanted to hug each of the women for creating something that felt like a fluffy pillow compared to the stiff shoes.

She'd been on the tiny island of Erites for exactly eleven days and felt as if she hadn't sat down for more than ten minutes. She didn't have time to rest now either. The first-ever U.S. Ambassador and the diplomatic envoy charged with getting the new embassy up and running stood together in the doorway between the Ambassador's temporary private home office and the open area outside his door that eventually would house his security team and an assistant once those people arrived. The two men poured over military reports as Ambassador Templeton, a lifetime State Department employee and former Assistant Secretary, shook his head and grumbled.

Ambassador Templeton wasn't even supposed to be here yet. His top-secret early arrival meant a limited security detail, few office workers and virtually no assistance except her. He had a series of meetings scheduled with the Erites Prime Minister and his top advisors to ease the transition from no U.S. presence to an active embassy.

Despite its strategic location in the middle of the ocean, thousands of miles north of Hawaii, no one had bothered with Erites for decades. Powerful countries dismissed the people of Erites as uncivilized and saw little benefit to offset the expense of making an ally out of a strip of land approximately the size of California. Then the photograph of a secret meeting between Erites Prime Minister Hakandu and the U.S. President surfaced and Erites became an area of great interest.

Conflicting rumors swirled for months about a U.S. military base being built there and Korea's hold over Erites' military leadership who long fought with elected Prime Minister Hakandu over the country's need for a mobilized fighting force. In the middle of it all, Megan and a small crew had been dispatched from Washington, D.C. to set up and charge ahead.

Thanks to the secret nature of the visit they hadn't expected a welcoming committee, but death squads were a horrible surprise.

"How many are dead?" The Ambassador looked at Megan as he asked the question.

The answer stuck in her throat, but she pushed it out. "Fourteen unarmed men slaughtered while they slept, several more missing, and every thatched shack burned to the ground as the women and children scattered."

When news broke of the United States' interest in Erites, rebel military forces had moved from threats to action and the once peaceful nation erupted in chaos. Last night brought the second attack on established settlements along the southern shoreline in two days, a place long quiet except for the steady thump of work as fishermen dragged nets off the Pacific Ocean.

The Ambassador swore under his breath. "A planned bloodbath."

"Even way out here, this far away, it will be difficult to keep this news from hitting the mainstream media back home." Skip Ellison already had his cell out as he spoke.

For a diplomatic liaison Megan found Skip only had a passing acquaintance with the definition of diplomacy. Yes, she was a management officer and not a political appointee with Erites expertise like Skip, but she was also career government. She'd been stationed in Germany and Turkey in her seven years since graduating from college and joining the Foreign Service. She deserved respect and he deserved a good kick. She vowed to figure out a way to give him one without getting her butt fired before this assignment ended.

"Shouldn't everyone know what's happening on the ground here?" she asked.

Skip frowned. "How do you figure?"

"People need to know there's unrest. That the military is out of control."

Skip stared at her as if she'd started speaking Farsi. "For God's sake, why?"

Fourteen unarmed men dead. By Megan's way of thinking that should be more than enough.

The man's lack of compassion would derail his career . . . at least she hoped that was true. There was a difference between being strong and being a jackass and Skip had no idea where that line fell.

The Ambassador's voice broke through the beat of silence before she could unleash or otherwise do something to put her own career in jeopardy. "What did you find out about local custom?"

Megan called up her briefing notes from memory. "Tradition dictates the dead be laid out in front of their homes on a special table called a *kaku* for two days while friends and family visit and bring offerings. The bodies are then cremated and the ashes buried in a cavern-like structure constructed of lava rock on the property by the grieving families."

But there was so much more and all of it heartbreaking. During those days, the women would sit, rocking back and forth as they sang songs of mourning in their native language. Megan had heard the voices that morning, deep drawling tones in a mix of wailing and pain. She did not understand most of the words but the blinding despair crashed over her. Even now, she closed her eyes and tried to block out the memory of the haunting sound.

"Megan?" Ambassador Templeton's voice pushed out the haunting sounds of crying women that would not leave her head.

"Yes, sir?"

He finally looked up from his report, his eyebrows still drawn in concern. "We need to get the Secretary on the phone. Tell his office we have an emergency that needs containment and potential intervention. I need immediate access."

She knew that meant Secretary of State and a lot of relaying and waiting. She agreed but the U.S. reaction wasn't their only concern. "The Prime Minister's representative will be here in—"

"That was an order." Skip delivered his verbal slap then put a hand on the Ambassador's back and guided the older man into the office.

As soon as Skip slammed the door she exhaled, letting the

unspent scream of frustration die in her throat. She bent her knees and felt around under her desk with her foot until she found them. Pink fluffy slippers and the only thing that got her through a late work evening in the office after a day of coordinating meetings and preparing personnel files for the staff yet to arrive.

"Pure heaven," she whispered with relief as her feet slid inside.

A crash of glass made her jump. Her palm slammed against the telephone keypad when she flinched. Air hiccupped in her lungs then jumpstarted again when the tat-tat-tat of gunfire sent her falling to her knees. Her fingers dug into the mat as her heartbeat thundered in her ears.

"What's happening?" Her harsh whisper echoed through her body, rattling her bones as she forced her mind to focus.

"Down, now!"

She didn't recognize the sharp male voice but heard the panicked edge and heavy accent through the closed door as loud as if he were standing right over her. The pounding and shaking started a second later, as if someone repeatedly threw something heavy against the wall. All the noise rumbled from inside the Ambassador's office. Wood cracked and crackled as if being ripped to shreds in a grinder.

She curled into a ball with her hands over her head, certain at any moment the house would crumble down around her. She peeked up and saw a switch at the very edge of the underside of the desk. Reaching up, she clicked the emergency button and kept hitting it, unable to stop her finger from tapping against it. Voices called out all around her. She tried to make out the words through the shouting in Eritesan, but the constant slams against the wall blended with barking rapid-fire commands until all she heard was a loud roar.

The Ambassador's voice rose above the din. "Calm down. Everyone stop so we can work this out."

The words that followed were muffled. She put her hand behind her ear, straining to make out the conversation but couldn't. From her position on the floor, she glanced around trying to guess the distance to the door and her chance of getting there without getting caught or killed. The heavy drapes at the far end of the room were drawn, but through the slit she saw gray move across the bright blue sky. She blinked a few times. When the sky seemingly morphed into daytime darkness, she realized smoke filled the air. She couldn't smell it through the bulletproof glass, but she could see it.

Her mind raced as she tried to piece together how someone could break into the Ambassador's office through the security, why no one was answering her emergency call, as the male voices rose again to screaming insanity. The attackers spoke fast and loud in Eritesan and the Ambassador answered in English, insisting the other people in the room lower their weapons.

"No! There is no one else here," he said in a voice creeping ever louder.

She knew he yelled that information to tip her off. She had to move because sitting there guaranteed getting captured. Gulping in air, she tried to calm her breathing so she could think. She needed to get somewhere and find help.

"Call the Prime Minister." Strings of Eritesan drowned out the Ambassador's ragged request. "Call his office. Call—" The Ambassador's voice cut off in the middle of his pleading. A sudden deathly silence filled the room.

Megan knew it was too late.

Chapter Two

Hal Robertson lowered his weapon and stared at his partner on the two-man recon team. There had been grumblings of trouble for weeks. His SEAL group, a five-man fire team, left Coronado and hit Erites two days before. They divided up and this shift belonged to Clark Beamer and him. Their job was to gather intel for a possible move on the rebel leader.

A mole deep inside the rebel camp had warned of impending concentrated attacks on civilians and a war on the capital city of Maka. The rebels' long-term plan involved destabilizing the country and destroying the Prime Minister's existing government—the U.S.-friendly government. Watching now as commandos easily breached what should have been the Ambassador's secure private residence, Hal mentally shifted the operation from recon to tactical.

He guessed the rebels weren't the only ones with a leak. The bad guys were getting help from someone and the fires rising in the distance and the sudden presence of armed militia walking the streets suggested the coup had started.

Hal needed the entire team moving and the few Marines who arrived with the Ambassador to step up. Americans likely had to be evacuated. Erites sat too far away from any U.S. military base to mobilize quickly. That meant the majority of the work fell to Hal and his men.

Clark slumped down with his back against the stacked stones and glanced up at Hal. They were fifty feet away with limited visibility but out of site from the rebels. "Thought we had until next week to develop a strategy."

"Someone moved up the time table. I'm guessing word got out about the Ambassador's arrival and this is a message. Likely a deadly one." Hal broke radio silence with the pre-arranged signal. Four clicks, silence then four more clicks. "We've gotta get those people out the house and hide them."

A voice barely above a whisper crackled over the radio. "Hotel secure."

Hal blew out a long breath. "Lock it down. You've got guns in the street. You'll need the personnel there."

"The hotel gets the Marines and the rest of our team?" Clark smiled as if he relished the odds of two SEALs against a rebel platoon.

"We get the three targets in the house. The rest of our team and a bunch of Marines will handle the rest." Hal sighted his weapon and saw the woman duck then drop to the floor. "Tell me about her."

"Foreign service with limited arms training."

"I was hoping for undercover CIA."

"Not sure if that would be good or bad."

Three targets and, at last count, sixteen gunmen. Not the best odds but Hal had experienced worse. "I'm going to get in there. You circle around try to get eyes on that room."

"And if I have a shot?"

Clark's sniper skills were legendary. The three people inside that house needed those skills now. "Take it to save the targets. Otherwise, wait for my signal. We can handle the guns here but we've got to march these folks out safely."

"We'll have rebels crawling all over us." Clark shrugged. "But I don't see that as a problem."

"Right." Hal smiled then because he knew Clark actually meant it.

Ever since BUD/S training, the twenty-eight week Basic Underwater Demolition/SEAL school when almost ninety percent of their class dropped out before completion, Clark insisted those who stayed and survived the nearly four months of training could withstand anything. So far he'd been correct except for one.

Hal adjusted his weapon. "Let's go."

Megan slipped her shoulder out of her hiding place and peered around the desk. The door to the office remained closed but the shouting had stopped. She couldn't even hear a low rumble of voices, which touched off a free-fall in her stomach.

She cleared the throat, trying to fight off the cough tickling her. Smoke choked the room now. A steady stream of gray haze moved through the one-story building. That meant there was an open window somewhere and either a huge lapse in protocol or a situation too horrible to contemplate.

She shifted to her knees, ignoring the hard shaking that moved her body from side to side. She'd keep low, crawl then run. She repeated the plan until it was the only thought running through her mind.

"Don't stop." She mouthed the words, surprised when they escaped her lips as a soft groan.

She tried to get a foot under her when something moved in front of her. A face peeked around the doorway connecting the area to the hallway running to the back door and kitchen. A scream raced up her throat but she stopped it in time when the figure put a finger to his lips. Black pants, black long-sleeved tee, black hair. The man almost blended into the dark wall, which she guessed was the point.

Even from across the room, a good fifteen feet away, she could make out his shocking blue eyes. The black watch and razor short haircut shouted military but she'd met every Marine protecting the Ambassador on this mission and he wasn't one of them. She'd remember that face, lean with a strong chin and a serious frown that comforted rather than scared her.

Ducking low, he ran in a line straight for her. Crouched and soundless. Focused and determined. He reached her before she could lift her hands to fend him off.

Then he balanced in front of her, right at the small opening under the desk. "Lieutenant Commander Hal Robertson, U.S. Navy."

Relief raced through her, zapping every ounce of strength as it went. "You're a SEAL."

It wasn't a question because she knew. The steely determination, the absolute lack of fear. He walked into a disaster, his gaze constantly surveying as if he were analyzing and dissecting every move and every exit.

"Yes, ma'am." He lowered his weapon as he stared straight into her eyes. "You are?"

"Megan White." She held out her hand.

He folded her cold fingers in his palms, heating them with a gentle rub. "Are you hurt, Megan White?"

"Scared witless."

A small smile tugged at the corner of his mouth. "Understood."

Right behind the relief came a rush of guilt. She'd hid under a desk while her boss fought off who knew how many men. "The Ambassador?"

"Wait here." Hal stood up and stalked, not stopping or landing even one loud footstep, on his way to the office door.

She guessed then he'd had the building under surveillance. He knew where to look and the layout, which she hoped meant there were others out there ready to move in for a rescue. Scrambling out of the tiny hole and using the desk as a shield, she watched him. Long and lean, he moved with the grace of a jungle cat with the air crackling around him. His body in perfect control. His mind centered on the door.

She heard a knock and a faint voice. "Clear."

The tension across Hal's shoulders eased as the barrel of his gun slowly shifted toward the floor. As she stood up, the office door opened. Panic crashed into her, nailing her to the floor. She couldn't move, couldn't breathe. She doubted her heart pumped one ounce of blood.

Hal nodded in the direction of the blond-haired man with the matching haircut who stepped into the doorway. "This is Chief Petty Officer Clark Beamer."

A violent shaking overtook her body. The cold seeped through every pore until her back teeth tapped together. Somehow she forced out two words. "The Ambassador?"

In a move so quick she almost missed it, Hal glanced at Clark then back to her. He shifted his position until he stood next to Clark, blocking her access and view into the office. "I'm sorry."

Her mouth dropped open. She could feel it and couldn't stop it. "He's dead?"

Clark nodded.

When she tried to push through and see for herself, Hal grabbed her arms. His firm grip didn't bite into her but didn't let her move either. "It's better you don't look."

Through the wall of their joint broad shoulders she could see pieces of broken furniture, splashes of blood and a huge ragged hole on the far side where the wall once stood. Papers and glass covered the floor and she could make out the tip of a man's shoe lying sideways in the corner.

Hal walked her backwards, his gaze scanning the room behind her as he took her out of viewing distance. "Others are coming. We need to leave."

She shook her head, trying to pull her mind back to the present and away from the grinding loss that threatened to envelop her. "Skip?"

Hal frowned. "Excuse me?"

"Skip Ellison, the diplomatic envoy."

Hal looked over his shoulder but Clark didn't say anything until Hal gave him a curt nod. "There's only one body but a blood trail. They likely took Ellison with him."

"We have to help him." She reached up and grabbed Hal's arms. "Skip is a weasel, but no one deserves—"

"Agreed." Hal shifted until she stood at his side with her hands still clenching at one of his arms and focused on Clark. "Follow the trail and check in. I'll take Ms. White—"

"Megan." Hal smiled this time. The grin left as soon as it came, but the impression stuck with her. Under all the gruff no-nonsense beat the heart of a man with dimples and a mouth to die for. "Please. And where are we going?"

"Somewhere safe." Hal turned and talked with Clark in a voice too low for her to hear. Whatever it was Hal said had Clark threading through the demolished office and disappearing into the street beyond. Hal turned back to her. "Ready?"

Dizziness slammed into her. She tightened her grip to keep from sliding to the floor. "I don't know if there's anywhere safe in Erites anymore."

"There is." He loosened her death grip in his arm and held her hand.

"You sure?"

"With me."

The boast stopped the room from spinning. "You won't hear an argument from me."

"Hold on here." He put her hand on his waistband and positioned her slightly behind him. "It lets me have full range of movement in case I need to get off a shot."

The thought of more killing made her stomach heave. "Okay." Her fingers curled into the material and she felt nothing but firm muscles and skin radiating warmth through his shirt.

"One question before we go." He glanced down. "What's with the pink shoes?"

"It's either these or impossibly high heels."

He nodded, his mouth stretched into a grim line but his voice filled with amusement. "Bunnies it is."

Chapter Three

Hal guided her through the room to the far hallway. Gun up and ready to pounce, he intended to get them out through the kitchen and through a planned zigzag of small homes and dirt alleys. He had to take care of a few problems first.

He stopped. Since Megan had a death drip on his pants and her body plastered against his back, the move slammed her into him. "Megan?"

"Yes?" Her whisper blew across the back of his neck, causing a blip in his concentration. But the real problem was the way she tugged on his pants. She'd hiked them into danger territory.

He propped his shoulder against the wall and tucked her in behind him. "Few things. First, you're shuffling."

"What does that mean?"

He slid her flat against the wall and shifted until he loomed over her. The only thing holding their bodies apart was her hands, which she had balanced between them.

His gaze traveled around the enclosed space just in case the owners of the voices he heard on the street decided to step inside. "You need to pick up your feet. The goal is quiet."

"Sorry." A pink stain raced up her neck and colored her cheeks.

When she started rubbing her hands together, her fingers brushed against his stomach and both of them froze. This close, he could see the green flecks in her eyes and the round angel face with full lips that begged for him to run a finger across them. She was a beautiful woman, curvy behind her conservative black suit and tall enough for her mouth to reach his chin. The lacy white shirt under her blazer hinted at her feminine side.

And her ability to stay calm and on her feet while the world crumbled around her . . . well, that was sexier than any of her other obvious female attributes.

He put his hand over hers and held them against his stomach.

Something sparked in her eyes and her body went still. He sensed the second she remembered where they were.

"You are safe with me." He waited until she nodded to go on. "Hold my pants or my shirt. Do not let go."

"Got it."

"Also might be a good idea for you not to yank the pants up so high."

He gaze shifted to his lower half and her mouth dropped open. "I didn't—"

"Any higher and my belt will be at my neck. I can fight through most things, but having my pants at my ears will slow down my running speed."

She let out a half-laugh that sounded more like a squeak then put her hand over her mouth. "I'm so sorry."

"I've got swim trunks on, so we're fine." When her shoulders stopped shaking, he skipped to the tougher stuff. "The sun is at full power. You need to lose the jacket."

At this time of year, the temperature bounced from cool fifties at night to boiling high-nineties with no wind in the afternoon. A dark blazer might hide her identity but heat stroke could kill her. Wearing nothing but a blinding white shirt would put a target on her back.

She slipped the blazer off her shoulders and let it fall to the floor. He tried not to notice her bare shoulders or the way the shirt stretched across her breasts. The slight definition of muscles down her tanned arms suggested she worked out. His brain processed the fact and stored it for later use in their escape. The not-so-smart part of him wanted to reach out and test her skin to see if it was as smooth as it looked.

She rubbed her hands over her exposed arms. "Better?"

"Yeah." He untucked his shirt and slipped it over his head, leaving the top of his wet suit on. "Slip this over your shirt. It will give you a bit of camouflage"

When she just stood there staring at him, he tried again. "Megan?"

She visibly snapped back to attention. "Right."

The shirt fell to her upper thighs. The baggy clothes took her from business and in charge to vulnerable. The bunny slippers probably had something to do with the change.

"We're going to get to the edge of this neighborhood then wait for the signal. Once we're clear, we'll get to the water and get you out."

She swallowed hard enough to make her throat move. "You do

mean by boat and not by swimming."

"Are you afraid of the water?" He could knock her out if he had to, but he sure as hell hoped it didn't come to that.

"Terrified of sharks."

A phobia he could handle. "Won't let them near you. Promise."

She pushed away from the wall and put a hand on the back of his shirt. "Ready."

"I like your style, Megan White."

They crept along the hall until they hit the kitchen. The place was abandoned and looked as if no one had moved in. No groceries or signs of life other than the coffee maker and a few dirty mugs in the sink.

"No one eat around here?" Hal asked.

"I can barely boil water." And that wasn't an exaggeration. She'd lived in a series of small apartments overseas with limited cooking facilities and a host of restaurants right outside her door. One didn't even have a stove. A mix of embassy receptions and late night take-out substituted for a healthy diet. Good thing she liked to run or she'd weigh twice as much as she did now.

He stopped at the refrigerator long enough to grab two bottles of water. He slid one into each of the lower pockets on his cargo pants. "I have some energy bars if you need them."

"In your pants?"

He shot her one of those deadly sexy smiles. "You'd be amazed what I have in there."

"You can show me later." Once the words were out there she couldn't call them back.

"I might just do that." He motioned for her to stay still as he cracked open the back door and peered out.

With his gun up and his body pulled tight as he prowled, he stepped outside. She couldn't hear him walking around, but she knew he was out there. She repeated that fact several times to keep her heartbeat from racing straight to a heart attack.

The door creaked open and he held out a hand to her. "Remember. Do what I say when I say."

"I can guarantee it." Her fingers brushed against his on the way to his waistband.

They took two steps down into the sandy yard. She tugged on his shirt to get him to stop. "Wait."

The flat line of his mouth and the way a nerve in his cheek ticked, she knew he didn't like the delay. Without stopping to explain, she bent down and scooped up a handful of the dark brown sand that made up the terrain of the island. With a few pats, she turned her clean fuzzy slippers to a dirty mess. The important thing is they no longer stood out as much.

Hal flashed rows of shiny white teeth. "Nicely done, Ms. White."

"Since I intend to hug the crap out of you once you get me out of here alive, you should probably stick to calling me Megan."

Something in those blue eyes sparkled. "Fair enough."

He kept an arm pressed against her side as they jogged through the small yard behind the house to the shack just over the property line at the back of the property. Gunfire echoed in the distance. Men chanted and the sky to the north lit up with orange.

"A fire." She pointed.

"We're not going that way." He veered to the right, taking them past a row of worker houses, which resembled oversized storage sheds.

Pebbles and grit crunched beneath her feet as they pressed against the grimy wall of an alley, following the wall until it turned to the right at the end. Hal didn't stop or knock at the door in front of them. He pushed it open, ignoring the squeak, and pulled her inside behind him.

It took a second for her eyes to adjust to the near-black space. Without windows or light, the walls closed in on her and the stale air clogged her throat. Despite Hal's need to be able to move, she pressed up against him and wrapped her fingers around his arm. "Where are we?"

"Safety."

She inhaled and coughed on the cloying smell of old incense. People on Erites burned it during many of their traditional ceremonies. The smell lingered over the island. In the tiny five-by-five square, it was concentrated to the point of sucking all the fresh air out of the space.

"Does someone live here?" she asked.

"It's used for storage. I staked it out. We'll be safe here for a few hours."

"Hours?" The idea of hanging around for more than another five minutes made the bit of breakfast she had earlier churn in her stomach.

She felt him shift then heard the scrape of metal on metal and dug her fingernails into his forearm. A slim band of light sliced across the floor and far wall. With the sun she could see dried herbs hanging on the wall and jars lining the shelves on the wall next to her head. Not everything shifted into focus, but she could see a bit and it was enough to keep her from jumping at every little sound.

"Sit."

She didn't see the slim bench until he pointed to it. With her head balanced against the wall and her feet stretched out in front of her, she let her body relax for the first time since the Ambassador started reviewing his reports that morning. When she moved her head, she crushed the herbs beneath her hair and strong puff of lavender fell over them.

The wood groaned when Hal sat down next to her. "You okay?"

"Believe it or not, this is not my usual workday."

"Really? It's what mine tend to look like."

She laughed until he smiled, then she realized she could spend the whole day staring at him. Even this awful day. She'd initially noticed the broad shoulders and obvious strength. Now she saw a man, handsome with high cheekbones and slightly crooked nose. A white scar stretched diagonal from the bottom of his cheek and ran down his chin. He didn't have the perfect look of an untried boy. He wore the marks of a warrior.

"Is Hal your real name?"

His head fell to the side as his gaze wandered over her face. "You think I made up a name?"

"I'm wondering if it's short for something."

"Just Hal." He must have picked up on her skepticism because he smiled. "Only child of Harry and Alice."

"Where are they now?" She chatted about nonsense because it stopped her nerves from jumping around in her belly. And the soothing sound of his deep voice let her believe she might just survive this day.

"My parents live in the small once-thriving but now barely functioning mining town in Pennsylvania." He shifted his leg until his thigh rested against hers. "And you?"

"Parents are college professors in D.C. Older sister is, as of a few months ago, a college professor in D.C."

He snorted. "I'm sensing a pattern."

"They are plan people." When he frowned she guessed he didn't get it. "They plan out everything. Schools, careers, life events. There's no room for surprise or adventure. The fact I'm not working my way toward tenure at a prestigious university is a constant source of anxiety for them."

"You're not exactly living a wild life. From what I understand, the foreign service is pretty regimented."

"It's an embarrassment for them." She rubbed the space right under her breasts to ease the growing tension there. "The older I get the more I wonder if my need for travel and excitement is really just a way to prove my independence. If I'm trying to find something or run from something."

The words long unspoken rushed out of her. Amazing how the darkness and not knowing someone made it easier for her to dissect her life. Thoughts she pushed out of her head every day came flooding in but accepting that her life may have veered in the wrong direction was another.

But today wasn't the day for big decisions. The shock of the attack still hadn't left her system and danger still lingered. She had to push it all out and concentrate on surviving.

"Since we're sharing . . . " Hal let the sentence drop.

"No husband." She bit her bottom lip to keep from saying anything else stupid. She wanted to know if he had a wife or anyone waiting for him, but she knew her thoughts were silly and misguided.

She might not teach like everyone else in her family, but she had her master's degree. She'd worked in this field for years. She knew how this worked. No matter how handsome he was, how safe she felt by his side, this moment was about adrenalin and fear. He thrived on it. She stumbled through it.

When this was over, he'd sneak back under the protective tent of privacy the SEALs provided. She'd be debriefed and shipped somewhere else, probably to a desk job for a rotation. Once he got them out of there she would never see him again. That was the right answer but it still left her feeling hollow.

"That wasn't my question but it's good to know." He lowered his head until his mouth hovered right over her ear. "I thought we'd talk about that hug you want to give me."

"I was kidding."

He exhaled, blowing a warm breath across her cheek. "I'm sorry to hear that."

Chapter Four

Megan turned her head right as he leaned in. Another inch and his mouth would cover hers.

A huge red warning light flashed in Hal's brain.

He eased back, ignoring the desire flaring in her eyes and the need boiling in his gut. He'd never messed up a job. He'd never lost his concentration. If anything, after ten years with the SEALs, he'd learned to block out the world except for the assignments in front of him. He'd lost two semi-serious girlfriends who needed more than he could give, or so their notes said. He regretted not having someone to come home to but never saw a future with either, so the break-ups left him more confused than upset.

But over the last year his priorities had shifted without him knowing it. For years the job had been enough. Now he wanted more. Finding a woman who understood and accepted the danger and could handle the secrecy proved impossible. Not that he tried. He'd always insisted he lacked the energy to handle more than a few nights, but as he got older he wondered if a guy could change.

She brushed her hand over his cheek. "I know it's inappropriate, but I think you should kiss me."

He didn't realize he was staring at her mouth until she spoke. He shook his head to break the spell sitting so close to her wove around him.

"We have to stay focused," he said, trying to ignore the soft caress of her skin against his.

"Do I threaten that?"

He flipped over her hand and kissed the center of her palm. "Hell, yes."

The steady thrum of conversation from the street grew louder. The roll of truck tires stopped close to their position. Hal pressed his hand against her mouth. When she nodded, he let his hand slide down to rest below her chin.

Heavy footsteps sounded all around them. Walking and talking, Hal guessed the voices came from rebels checking the area. The marching sounded synchronized and every now and then one of them would fire a weapon. Since he didn't hear the sounds of victims' screams or a house-to-house search, he assumed the gunfire was nothing more than warning shots.

But a search was a huge concern. If the rebels started looking, Hal's limited options decreased even further.

As he sat with Megan, stiff and unmoving, the talking passed right outside their door, increasing in volume then receding again. Hal didn't breathe until all evidence of soldiers and potential attacks died out.

He exhaled, letting his shoulders fall as he slowly removed his hand from Megan's face to rest on her collarbone. "We're okay."

"That was close." Her wide eyes didn't blink.

"The kiss or the attackers?" He regretted the words as soon as he said them. He needed to let this topic drop before—

She kissed him. Her soft mouth danced over his, light and unsure. She pulled back as quickly as she'd started. He nearly followed her back and dragged her down on the wobbly bench beneath them.

If possible, her eyes grew wide enough to take over her whole face. As if in a trance, she rubbed the tip of her finger over his lips. "I don't usually do stuff like this. I mean, I date but I don't throw myself . . . "

He tried to swallow but something was blocking his airway. "It's a reaction to the danger."

She sighed. "Yes."

He waved his hand, hoping to take the memory of her mouth with it. "The proximity."

"Exactly."

He nodded. Sat there. Balled his hands into fists. None of it worked.

"Screw it." He slipped his hand around the back of her neck and pulled her in close. "One time."

Then he kissed her. Not a light touch of thank you. This was a hot mouth, blow-your-mind kiss. His lips slanted over hers. His tongue swept into her mouth. Every cell in his body sparked to heated life. When her hand fell against his chest and her tongue touched his, the last of his control snapped. All that mattered was holding her, touching her.

The click of his radio bounced off of every surface of the small room and right into his brain. He stopped kissing her and focused on reining his breathing to a normal level. Megan pulled back, taking her body right out of his arms as she glanced around the room. Her movements were jerky as she shoved against him.

He rushed to calm her building panic. "It's okay." He reached up for his earpiece and removed it, bringing it between them so they could both lean in and listen. "Beamer? I need a status."

Clark's voice came through a clear as if he was standing in the room with them. "Our ride is here and the hotel is empty."

Hal considered ignoring Megan's presence for the rest of the call, but she sat there, staring and listening to every word. He gave up trying to hide any of the harsh truths from her and pressed in closer. "Ellison?"

"Still looking."

Hal shoved the piece back in his ear. He stood up and took Megan's hand to drag her with him. "We're on the move."

He adjusted his belt and checked his gun for the tenth time in a half hour. He was about to fill her in on their next move when she started talking.

"Why are you here?" she asked.

He shrugged. "I was doing some recon. Saw the men break into the house and—"

"I mean on Erites."

There was no need to pretty this part up either. "Intel on a military coup. The U.S. position on the military leadership keeps changing. We're here to gather some information."

She rolled her eyes. "Wish someone had warned me there was a potential problem. All I got was the peaceful beach nation speech."

"In the State Department's defense, word was we had another week." He put his hand on her lower back and brought her to his side at the door. "We're headed for the water."

"I'm ready."

He glanced down at her. The small shake to her voice was the only indication of her worry. She stood still, ready and waiting for directions. No panic or screaming. She was ready to follow orders and do what she had to do to get out of there alive. He was tempted to kiss her again but refrained.

With her at his back, they slipped down the alley, her footsteps heavier than his but not loud. She followed his lead and kept her head down. Her breath pounded against the back of his neck, but she never got winded.

Houses passed in a blur as they ran from cover to cover. The closer they got to the open square where the neighborhood park stood, the more people he saw. None were facing his way. They laughed and pointed at something in front of them. When they reached the far side of the park and faced the last dash to safety, he took one final look through the buildings and stopped. There, in the distance, was a man in a suit. The same man Hal had seen with the ambassador.

Megan must have noticed the gathering because her steps slammed to a stop. There, out in the open, she stood in scuffed slippers and a skirt that had inched up her thighs as she ran. Her chest rose and fell on harsh breaths.

No one had noticed them and Hal didn't wait to be discovered. He tugged her along after him until their backs flattened against the wall of a small home. Hal motioned for her to stay quiet and still as he peeked around the corner for a better look.

"That's Ellison. You have to save him." Her comment came from right behind him.

As Hal watched, Ellison rolled out a long piece of paper and pointed to areas while he spoke in Eritesan. A quick visual tour of the crowd and Ellison told Hal what he needed to know. He was meeting with the power cell of the rebels and Ellison didn't have an injury and wasn't calling out for help. The man was exactly where he was supposed to be.

"Wait. He's in on it?" Shock threaded through Megan's voice as she said the thought that played in Hal's mind.

Hal knew what they were seeing didn't necessarily mean what Megan thought it did. "Looks that way. It's either a CIA operation or he's dirty."

She shot Hal a you've-lost-your-mind look that women did so well. "Skip isn't CIA."

"I'm betting you're wrong about that, but it doesn't guarantee this is an approved op. More likely a power grab using Ellison's intel. But we'll figure that out later."

"And before then?"

They had to get out of there alive first and now was the best chance. With a significant number of soldiers gathered in one place that meant fewer on the streets. They had to move. "We run like hell for the water."

He'd no sooner said the plan than two armed men turned the

corner and headed right for them. The men were talking and didn't notice a problem until one of them tripped over Megan. Hal pushed her out of the way and stepped into the line of fire. Before the men could yell for help, Hal nailed the guy under the chin with an elbow, sending his head flying back. Bones snapped as the man let out a keening wail. Wanting to keep their position quiet, Hal kicked out at the other attacker, catching him behind the knee and sending him crashing to the sandy ground and his gun spinning in the sand.

Hal didn't waste time. He stepped on one man's wrist to keep him from lunging for the gun. When the one with the leg injury tried to get up, Megan kicked out the elbow he was using for balance and sent the man sprawling. While he was down, Hal landed a second kick to his forehead, knocking him out on contact.

The one with the head injury wasn't going down as easily. He opened his mouth to yell and Hal reached an arm around his neck. Legs flailed and shoes scraped against the ground. The guy's hands slapped and punched against Hal's arm, but Hal never eased up on his hold. He pressed against the man's throat until he gagged and wheezed. Then his body went slack and slipped to the ground. Two down but alive.

When Hal looked up again, Megan held one of the attacker's guns on the fallen men. With her legs braced as far apart as her slim skirt would allow, she switched her aim from one unconscious man to the other. The barrel bounced all over the place as her hands shook.

Hal respect for her grew even bigger. "You okay?"

"Yeah." Her clipped speech reeked of panicked aftermath.

He decided to take the weapon before she accidentally shot him. He slid his hand over hers and lowered the barrel to the ground. "You can be my partner any time."

Her eyes finally focused on his face. "Get me out of here and we'll talk about it."

Flirting had to be a good sign. "Deal."

Chapter Five

Megan stood in the family room of her short-term business rental in southwest D.C. and looked out her window at the Potomac River. Not having a home and not being able to stay with her parents after two dinners which consisted of lectures on "a proper career," she was stuck in a temporary apartment filled with furniture and belongings that weren't hers. What little she owned sat in a storage locker in Erites, so she doubted she'd see any of that soon.

She'd been there for ten days. The raft ride over the rough Pacific led her to an aircraft carrier. Hal had gotten her up on deck then disappeared. She hadn't seen him on the ship, at the airport in Honolulu, or in any of the offices she sat in while being briefed over the last week in D.C.

She was on something called mandatory temporary leave. Apparently that was protocol after an attack situation. Foreign service officers got pulled out of the field. Most took off for a few weeks of vacation, but she didn't have anywhere to go. She didn't even have a permanent address. When she sent a message through the proper channels to Hal she could only provide this hotel address.

And she doubted he ever got her note. The Navy didn't breach the privacy of the SEALs. No one would even admit his existence. But she knew he was out there and prayed he was fine.

She was so lost in thought that she barely heard the knock. When the pounding grew louder, she went to the door, careful to check the peephole first. The sight that greeted her had her blinking and questioning her sanity even as the blood raced through her veins, heating as it went.

Jeans and a polo. Hair he kept combing with his fingers. The broadest shoulders and the sexiest mouth she'd ever tasted. She pulled open the door and drank him in.

"Hal."

He smiled until it lit up his face. "Megan White."

"I can't believe you're here."

"These are for you." He held up a half-crumpled bag.

She would have been wary but that sparkle in his eyes suggested the surprise, whatever it was, likely was the good kind. She unrolled the top and peeked inside. A fluffy mound of pink and four black-button eyes greeted her. She burst into laughter a second later.

"I thought you could use a new pair. I doubt the last pair survived the sand and water."

She lifted her foot to show off her white socks, a huge grin tugging on her lips the whole time. "I couldn't save the bunnies, so thank you."

"How have you been?" His voice swept over her with the softness of a sweet caress.

"I left a message for you."

"And here I am." He stared at the space behind her. "May I come in?"

Her thoughts splintered and her hands shook, but somehow she stepped aside and let him come in. "You're okay."

"I had to go back to Erites." He walked into the room and kept going until she motioned for him to take a seat on the couch.

She sat next to him with her legs curled underneath her. "Can you tell me what happened?"

"Need to know, but the news reports about U.S. policy toward Erites being in flux are correct." Hal's arm slipped across the back of her couch cushions and his hand slipped into her hair. "Ellison is alive, on the ground and doing the job he was sent to do."

That was the information she got from her interviewers. If Ellison was a spy, he was theirs not the rebels'.

With the tough part out of the way, she focused on Hal. She beat back the urge to jump in his arms. "I've been interrogated to the point where I can't remember anything but my name."

His thumb caressed her cheek. "Gotta love protocol."

"I'm grounded. I have a thirty-day hold before my next assignment." She leaned in, letting the warmth of his palm wash through her. "Of course, since I've been through what they term 'an ordeal,' I have the pick of my next assignment."

His eyebrow lifted. "Where do you want to go?"

"I'm not sure I want to go anywhere."

"Finally stop running?"

His soothing touch made her realize what was missing. The

comfort of closeness with someone else. Of being able to discuss fears without being judged and verbally berated about her life decisions. "I'm still trying to find something."

He glanced around, his eyes narrowing as he went. "You think you're going to find it in here?"

She laughed and her head fell sideways until it rested on his shoulder. Being this close to him, wrapped in the safety of his strong arms, her messed up world shifted right again. "No."

"Can I make a suggestion?"

She felt his lips move against her hair and closed her eyes to enjoy the sensation. "Sure."

"San Diego."

Afraid to move to fast or read between the lines, she lifted her head and chose her words carefully. "What are you saying?"

"You have thirty days. I have a condo." He placed a kiss on her nose then another high on her cheekbone. "Thought we could see if this attraction still sparked without the danger and gunfire pushing it. With your career background, you understand mine. And I sure as hell know I've thought about you non-stop since I put you on that ship."

Her gaze met his and she couldn't look away. "So, I become your houseguest."

This time his mouth lingered over hers before he spoke again. "You sleep in my bed. We go out, though I would prefer to stay in as much as possible, and we see if whatever you're looking for is in California with me."

Her heart jumped. It actually bounced hard enough to knock her breathless for a second. The terror and aftermath were behind them. He was a man of few words but she understood what he didn't say. This was about moving forward. About a possible future.

"On one condition."

His head snapped back as his eyes grew wide with what sure looked like excitement. "Name it."

"We don't wait on that bedroom thing." She pointed at the closed door in front of them. "We start that part right now."

The downright decadent grin spread over his mouth. He looked ready to pounce as his arms tightened around her. "I like the way you think."

She remembered the first time she asked and tried it again. "Then shut up and kiss me."

He did and neither of them said anything for a very long time.

SEALed WITH A KISS
(A Black Ops, Inc. story)

Cindy Gerard

Chapter 1

Luke Coulter was no poet. But as he lay on the private Palau beach, smelling of cocoa butter and sun, sipping something rum and fruity, and enjoying the *hell* out of watching his beautiful bride emerge from a gently rolling surf, it was all he could do to keep from bursting out in iambic pentameter.

> *Lord, thank you*
> *Life is good*
> *It's turned out just*
> *The way it should*

Hokey. That's it. No more rum for him.

"You going to lay there and be lazy all day, Doctorman?"

Val stood over him wearing a soft smile and an electric-blue string bikini. Water rivulets trickled down her magnificent, golden curves; salt water dripped from her long black hair and beaded on her thick lashes. With her ebony eyes and melting-pot heritage of Latino, Irish, African American and Cherokee, she looked like an exotic sea nymph, risen from the depths of Atlantis to entice him—like one of the handmaidens the goddess Persephone had sent to lure the Argonauts to their deaths with their bewitching siren songs.

Bewitching. Yeah. That was Val. Only she'd lured him back to life, not death. She still didn't realize how close he'd been to the abyss when they'd met on that chance encounter in the Andes on a midnight train to nowhere. She thought *he'd* saved *her* life when he'd rescued her from assassins sent to kill her. On that level, yeah, he had saved her. But she still didn't get that she'd saved more than his soul from sinking into the deep, into the dark and . . . Whoa. He wasn't going back there again. Not today. Not here. Not with his woman.

He tipped up his sunglasses. "With a view like this every day, yep. I think I might get good and lazy." He gave her a long, leisurely once-over. "And the scenery isn't bad either," he added with a grin that had her rolling her eyes.

And to think, he'd balked at the idea of making this trip when she'd brought it up two weeks ago . . .

"Palm trees, tropical beaches, sun and surf." His new bride had spread an array of brochures featuring Palau over their dining room table. "What about paradise doesn't appeal to you, darling?"

"Paradise, with you? Very appealing. Paradise with a full camera, production, and technical crew ogling you in a bikini? Not so much."

Valentina—known to the world by one name like Cher or Beyonce—had been a hot ticket in the fashion industry for over a decade. And like fine wine, she had only improved with age. That's why she was still a highly sought after model— and the number-one pick for the cover of the Sports Illustrated swimsuit edition.

"So join me when the photo shoot is over," she'd coaxed. "We'll rent a house on a private island and stay on for a few days after they finish shooting. We can be Emmeline and Richard and swim naked in our very own Blue Lagoon."

She'd settled onto his lap—a tactic that never failed to arrest him—and looped her arms around his neck. "Come on, Luke. I really want you to go with me. We'll make it our honeymoon—the one we've never found time to schedule."

She'd been right, of course. They'd been married two months, and if a mission for his boss, Nate Black, with his Black Ops., Inc. team hadn't tromped all over their honeymoon plans, then one of her photo gigs had.

"We can go snorkeling," she'd persisted with a temptress grin. "And you can scuba dive to your heart's content."

The woman knew how to cut straight to his Navy SEAL heart.

He'd pressed his forehead to hers. "Well, since you mentioned my favorite word—"

"Scuba?"

Smiling, he'd brushed a fall of hair behind her ear. "Yeah. Um, no. Nekked."

So, now, here they were.

He breathed deep as the tropical breeze washed over him. Val had been right on all counts. Palau *was* paradise. It was also a diver's dream. As a former SEAL, he'd scuba-dived and snorkeled as many reefs as his time had allowed. But the Republic of Palau had never made it to his 'been there, done that' list.

Five-hundred miles east of the Philippines in Micronesia, the Pacific island nation had long been his dream destination. He'd drooled over online photos of the psychedelic reefs, blue holes, dramatic drop-offs, World War II wrecks and over 1,200 species of fish. Yesterday, he'd joined the mantas when they'd congregated at the German Channel's cleaning station; the day before, he'd gone swimming with the reef sharks as they surfed the currents at Blue Corner. And the day before that, he'd explored the Big Drop-off, the world's best dive wall, according to *National Geographic*.

The only thing that would have made it perfect was if Val could have made the dives with him. He gave her a big A for effort but her issues with claustrophobia had proven to be too much for her. A sudden anger swept over him. The bastard who had kidnapped her when she was a little girl, then held her captive in a root cellar, could be damn glad the judge had ordered a life sentence because if he *ever* set foot outside that prison and Luke ran into him . . . well... he wasn't going to think about that now, either. Or about the bleak look on Val's face when she'd finally thrown in the towel after three valiant dive efforts.

What he was going to think about was *now*. And the way she looked all sun-kissed and wet. He really liked her wet.

"This was a great idea, babe," he said as the swish of the turquoise blue waves on the outer reef, the rustle of a soothing breeze swayed through the coconut palms, and the melodic cry of the gulls played in the background. "I could happily get used to being a beach bum."

She spread a towel onto the golden sand beside him. Then she stretched out on her stomach, rested her cheek on her folded hands, and got comfy. "The job does have its perks."

He rolled to his side, propped his head on his palm. "Yeah, plus I distinctly remember something about the word *naked* in conjunction with beach." He toyed with the string on her bikini top.

She smiled, never opening her eyes. "And *I* distinctly remember that we fed that fantasy several times since we've been here. Time to start weaning you back to life in the real world. It's our last day here, then—"

"Shh." He leaned over her, pressed a kiss to the small of her back and tugged the string until it gave. "No more talk about the real world."

With a gentle nudge, he rolled her to her back and moved over her, sliding his thigh over sun warmed, sweetly oiled skin then untied a couple more strings. "You are so beautiful."

He leaned in and kissed her mouth, her throat, and felt a swell of longing when her body hummed to life with a simmering sexual heat. Moving slowly downward, he strafed her bare breast with the tip of his tongue then made the most of the sun and the sea and her sultry sighs.

Damn. He was a lucky SOB.

Chapter 2

Val was deliriously spent and dozing in the shade of the palm when a coconut plopped heavily on the sand between them, missing Luke's head by inches.

"Incoming," Luke growled, jerked to a sitting position and swiveled his head around until he spotted the culprit. "If I ever catch that damn monkey, I swear, I'm going to cold-cock him," he muttered darkly.

She laughed as she sat up and reached for her bikini. The little macaque monkey had shown up their very first day on the island. Tango—a fitting name given his terrorist tactics—had become both a source of amusement and a pest. "He just wants to play."

"Then why can't he dance for his bananas like any other monkey?" he grumbled while, overhead, Tango screeched with glee. "Get down here you little creep. It's past time you had an attitude adjustment."

Val tied up her loose bikini strings and reached into her beach bag for the banana she'd brought just in case the monkey showed up. "Okay, you do realize you're trying to reason with a monkey, right?" She'd learned early on that she'd better have a treat for Tango or he'd continue to lob his coconuts like hand grenades.

"Here you go, Tango." She made coaxing noises and held out her hand.

Seeing the banana, the monkey scrambled down the tree, then sat a safe three yards away, eyes on the prize.

"He's going to bite you," Luke warned.

"Only if I don't give him what he wants." She tossed the banana.

Tango skuttled over on all fours, snatched it on the fly then scampered back to the palm tree, scaling it like a cockroach scaling a wall.

"Just like a man," she said with a teasing smile. "Gets what he wants then hits the road."

"Not *this* man." Luke leaned in and touched his mouth to hers. "I know a good thing when I see it. You're stuck with me, Princess.

Better get used to it."

Oh, she planned to. And, oh, how she loved this man.

He kissed her hard then rose to his feet. All six, glorious, naked feet of him.

"I'm going to go get wet. Save my spot. And you," he shook a finger at Tango, who was happily munching away. "Stay away from my woman."

Val leaned back on her elbows and watched him walk toward the gentle surf. She felt a renewed stirring of arousal as the sunlight played over his tanned back and lean hips then danced over the flex of muscle as his powerful legs propelled him into a shallow dive.

He was like a fish in the water. Fluid and fast and in his element. Only the scar slashing from high on his ribs to low on his abdomen reminded her how vulnerable he really was. And how afraid she sometimes was for him.

She'd married a warrior. A former Navy SEAL. A medic. Now a key member of Black Ops, Inc., a covert paramilitary team that 'unofficially' worked for the U.S. government, taking on missions that were too hot for the sanctioned government agencies to handle.

Danger came with the territory. She was still reconciling herself to that fact, counting on his strength and his skills and his team to keep him coming home to her. And she was working on being a woman worthy of his devotion.

She wrapped her arms around her up-drawn knees and watched as he swam steadily back toward her with sure, commanding strokes. And she wished she hadn't let him down. Snorkeling was a stretch for her but, she'd swallowed back her claustrophobia and, for him, she'd done it. Had even started to enjoy it.

But scuba—she expelled a sigh of defeat and lowered her head onto her crossed forearms. Scuba had been her downfall. She'd tried. She'd really tried . . . but the mask, the mouthpiece, the bubbles blowing past her face, keeping track of her air, the weight of the belts and the tanks, and the fathomless depths and darkness of the water all joined forces against her.

Three times she'd tried. Three times she'd felt the pressure start to build in her chest, the nausea rise to her throat, and the memories of her abduction surged back like it was yesterday. *She was a terrified ten year old again. Back in that root cellar. Alone with the rats. And the bugs. And the endless, horrifying darkness.*

And the fear that she'd worked for years to combat, would grab her by the throat, seize her lungs, and the next thing she knew she was in a full blown panic.

Thank God Luke had been right by her side. Guiding her to the surface. Praising her for her bravery. Lulling her into believing she wasn't the biggest coward known to mankind.

"Hey."

She snapped her head up, startled to see him standing in front of her, dripping with salt water.

"Hey," he repeated with gentle concern and dropped to his knees. "Where were you, Princess? What's with the tears?" He reached out, tenderly brushed his thumb over her cheek.

"Happy tears," she lied and put on her game face. "I'm just so happy to be here with you." That much was the truth.

He searched her face. She looked away when she saw that he knew she was fudging. Nothing got past this man.

"You're beating yourself up again over the scuba diving, aren't you?"

Apparently her silence was answer enough.

"Val." He cupped her face between his big hands and made her look at him. "It's okay. Hell, our boy, Reed, self-professed toughest, kick-ass warrior of the universe, is scared to death of spiders. We all have fears. Scuba is not everyone's cuppa. And you, of all people, have more reason to have trouble with it than most. Yet you tried. I've never been more proud of anyone in my life. You should be proud, too."

He was the most amazing man. Only Luke could turn her failure into a victory.

She covered his hands with hers, leaned forward and kissed him.

"So . . . Johnny Duane Reed." She smiled, thinking of the blond Adonis bad boy. "Arachnophobia? Seriously?" There was something deliciously comforting thinking about the former Recon Marine and Luke's team mate at BOI squealing like a girl at the sight of a spider.

"Yeah, I thought you'd like that picture," he said, grinning. "But you didn't hear it from me, okay? He'd kick my ass from here to next year if he knew I'd been telling stories out of school."

"My lips are sealed."

He sat back on his heels, apparently satisfied that he'd dragged her out of her funk. "So . . . our last day, huh? What do you want to do with the rest of it?"

She'd be perfectly content to while away the hours right here on the sand. But she knew what he wanted to do.

"Let's snorkel that little cove . . . the one that's intrigued you ever since we arrived."

His eyes lit up. "Seriously?"

"You've got my curiosity piqued."

He'd been looking through the binoculars and checking it out ever since they'd first walked down from the house and viewed their temporary new home from the beach.

Their island was small and mostly jungle that gave way to this beautiful beach that curved in a graceful horseshoe on the question mark shaped island. The cove that so interested him was at the tail of the question mark, about a hundred yards away.

"Why don't you go get our gear," she suggested, encouraging him. She knew he was worried that she really didn't want to go. "We need to get going before high tide starts moving in.

"And put some swim trunks on, would you?" she added when he still hesitated. "I don't want any curious fishies mistaking my favorite dangly parts for dinner."

He laughed and pushed to his feet. "Since they're my favorite dangly parts, too, I'm happy to oblige. Be right back."

Chapter 3

The water temp was a sweet eighty-plus degrees, the visibility at least one-hundred feet as Luke and Val snorkeled their way toward the cove. Color exploded around them as schools of clown and zebra fish darted among the seagrass and rocks scattered along the sandy floor of the cozy bay. A lumbering, fat-lipped grouper nosed lazily along the bottom.

Beside him, Val was doing great. He'd made certain they stopped often and just floated, heads up, to give her a break from the confinement of the mask. The last thing he wanted to do was push her too hard . . . especially now that she was doing so well.

God, he was proud of her as she resettled her mask again, adjusted her mouth piece and bravely went face down for another look. Even though he could tell she was enjoying herself to a degree, she was still tense but pushing through her claustrophobia. He quickly caught up with her and touched her arm directing her attention to a school of rainbow trigger fish that flitted in and out of the sea grass then swam out of sight.

It took them a little over thirty minutes to reach the part of the cove that had captured his interest. As they neared the end of the land mass, the water grew so shallow they could both touch bottom, so they stood for a moment, and tugged their masks below their chins.

This tip of the island wasn't as sheltered from the wind as their little bay so they had to brace against the waves washing in from the bigger water and rocking against them with more force.

"Beautiful," Val said, sounding a little breathless from the exertion of their swim and the stunning view.

The water kissing the shore was an amazing aqua blue but shifted and gradually deepened to a saturated marine where it headed out to open ocean. The wind was also stronger out here and had whipped up a little foam where water met a shore made mostly of black, lava-like rocks interspersed with sand.

"So . . . worth the trip?" Val asked, latching on to his arm for balance when a wave slapped up against her.

"Any trip with you is worth it," he said, pulling her into his arms and kissing her. Damn, he never got tired of kissing her. "Why don't you go perch on that big, flat rock and feed my mermaid fantasy while I nose around . . . see if I can find any evidence that there really was a ship loaded with gold doubloons that sank off this point."

She smirked. "Seriously? What *guide for suckers* have you been reading?"

"Hey." He took a stab at looking offended but knew his grin minimized the impact. "You wound me. I don't fall for that tourist crap. I got this intel straight from a guy with an eye patch, a peg leg and a parrot."

"Oh. Well. In that case, it *must* be legit. So go find me some treasure."

"Greedy wench."

"Damn betcha."

He took her hand, helping her maneuver the rocky bottom and get settled on the rock. Since he'd be wading as much as anything else, he slipped out of his flippers and handed them to her. "Be right back."

Val watched her hunky husband—she was still getting used to that term—alternately snorkel then wade through the shallow water and thought, *I am the luckiest woman on earth.* This man loved her. This man protected her. This man accepted her for what she could bring to the relationship and for what she couldn't. She was already stronger because of him. Not strong enough, but she was getting there.

Baby steps, Val, she reminded herself. If he could be patient with her, then she could be patient with herself.

She drew her knees to her chest and hugged her arms around them, squinting against the brilliant sun. Luke had wandered a good twenty yards away. She watched him, spellbound as he rose like an Adonis in the chest-deep surf, water cascading off his golden shoulders, sunlight glinting through his hair.

"Are we rich yet?" she called out.

When he didn't hear her, she realized that the wind had picked up enough that the surf sounds had risen and drowned her out.

She cupped her hands around her mouth and tried again.

This time he turned, gave her a crooked grin and a thumbs down.

"Maybe we'd better head back." She felt a sudden uneasiness with the increasing chop. And their little beach suddenly seemed like a long swim away.

"Couple more minutes, okay?" Then he disappeared again, only the tip of his snorkel visible above the surface of the increasingly undulating water.

He was like a kid in the proverbial candy store around water. She wished she felt as comfortable in it. Determined to stay relaxed, she lowered her head to her knees and focused on the soothing sound of the gulls, the slap of the surf against the rocks, the rustle of the wind through the palms further up on the shore and let time drift lazily away. Her head came up abruptly though, when a wave washed up and doused her toes.

The tide was coming in fast, she realized, looking around and realizing her once dry perch would soon be covered in water.

She looked for Luke. Told herself not to panic when she didn't immediately spot him, then breathed a huge sigh of relief when his head broke the surface about ten yards away.

"Okay, fish boy. Play time's over. The tide's coming in."

"That's fish *man* to you, lady." His manufactured scowl made her laugh. "There's one more spot I want to check out. I saw a really nice golden cowrie wedged between a couple of rocks. You're going to love it."

And he was gone again. After a shell. She sighed then went to work getting back into her flippers.

Good to his word, a few seconds later, his hand emerged triumphantly from the water, his fingers wrapped around the shell. His head followed. And his grin out shown the sun.

"Is this a treasure or what?" He looked very pleased with himself.

Yeah, she thought. This moment was, for a fact, a treasure.

"You ready to go now?" She grabbed her mask, dipped it into the water to rinse the salt residue off the lens and settled it on top of her head.

He was already wading toward her as she eased into the choppy water that had once been chest deep but now came up to her chin. "Yes, ma'am. But I expect you to thank me real nice for—whoa!"

She'd been concentrating on her footing and her balance against a fairly strong undercurrent when his sudden yelp brought her head up.

"What's wrong?"

"Um . . . not sure yet. I slipped. My foot's caught. Hold on."

A little ripple of alarm skittered through her body. Fighting the current, she half waded, half paddled over to him.

"Did you get it?"

He handed her the shell. "Not yet. Don't suppose you've got any butter on you? Oh wait, we used it all up last night."

"This is not funny," she said as the ripple of alarm turned into a tidal wave.

"No," he agreed, all trace of humor gone. "It's not. What it is, is stupid. I can't believe I let this happen."

He drew in a deep breath then ducked under the surface. Val watched through the crystal clear water as he latched on to the rock that trapped his foot about four inches above his ankle, wedging his foot tight against another rock. And as strong as he was, the rock wasn't budging.

Finally he surfaced, gasping for air, a grim, angry look on his face.

"Maybe we can move it together." She tossed the shell aside. It sank slowly to the bottom. "Tell me when you're ready."

Her gaze locked on his, she waited for his nod, then drew in a breath and dove. The both tugged and shoved and pulled and pushed. And got nothing. No movement. Not even an inkling that the heavy black stone might move. If anything his ankle seemed to be wedged in tighter.

Luke latched on to her arm and dragged her to the surface with him.

She sucked in air and tried to catch her breath.

She was scared now. Good and scared. The wind was still picking up. The waves were getting stronger. The water getting deeper. It was lapping over her mouth. Up to Luke's armpits. And it was rising fast.

"We need something to pry the rock free. Something to give us a little leverage," Luke said, his voice calm as he scanned the shoreline.

Beside him, Val willed herself to follow his lead. To keep her composure. But her mind was racing and she fought a terrifying image of the water rising above his head. Of him drowning before they could get him free.

"Do you see anything?" she asked abruptly, tearing her thoughts away from that picture.

He shook his head. "'Fraid not. Let's give it another try. On three, okay?"

She nodded, then dove down with him one more time.

And one more time they accomplished nothing . . . except to make him bleed. He'd pulled so hard, the rock had gouged his skin.

And now a new threat lurked in the shadows of her mind,

haunting her.

Sharks.

Oh, God. Sharks could smell blood from miles away.

"Keep it together," Luke said, gripping her shoulders gently when they surfaced. "I need you to keep it together for me now, Princess. You with me?"

She nodded. Yeah, she was with him. And more terrified than ever because she could see in his eyes that he knew his life was in grave danger.

Chapter 4

Holy Mary and all the vestal virgins, Luke thought. He'd screwed up royally.

All because he'd wanted to show off for Val. Bring her back something special. A remembrance of their special time in this special place.

Well, dumbass, it doesn't get more special than this.

He mentally calculated how long they'd been out here. Best estimate, based on the sun, about forty-five minutes plus the half-hour or so it had taken them to swim this far. The tide had risen six inches since then. It was up to his armpits now. That meant another twelve inches and his nose would be under water. That gave him an hour and a half . . . give or take . . . to get himself unstuck.

Only, he already knew that wasn't going to happen. Not without a pry bar. Or an act of God. He wasn't banking on either showing up any time soon.

"Let's try again," Val said, looking and sounding determined to keep desperation at bay.

"On three," he said, because, damn, there weren't a lot of options.

They both went under. Both tugged and shoved and grunted and failed.

"It's no good," he said on a gasp as they surfaced. "That sucker's not budging."

She floated up against him, breathless, wrapped her arms around his neck and held him so tight his heart broke. "What are we going to do?"

"Well," he said, gripping her around the waist and setting her back away from him. "I'm going to hang around here and work on my tan."

"Stop it!"

"Sorry," he said, reacting to her frustration. "Here's what has to happen." He brushed the wet hair out of her eyes, determined to show her calm, steady confidence when the truth was, he knew they were running out of time. "You're going to swim back to the beach."

"No," she blurted out, tears filling her eyes. "I can't leave you here. The tide's coming in."

"Baby . . . that's exactly why you have to go. Listen to me. You swim back to the beach, okay? First thing you do when you get there is call the emergency number. Tell them what's going on and to get someone out here yesterday. Then get my scuba tank and regulator out of the closet and bring it back here. That'll buy some time. Then we sit back and we wait for the Calvary to arrive. We're golden, okay?"

Only they were more like tin than gold. She didn't need to know that. He'd purposefully left the tank low after his last dive, knowing he was done diving for this trip and wanting to lessen the weight for their flight home. If he remembered right, he'd left the tank with 500 psi—one-fourth full. Theoretically, the average diver could get an hour out of a tank. So, that left fifteen minutes of air for a recreational diver. With his SEAL training, he might be able to stretch that out to twenty to twenty-five minutes as long as he kept his cool and didn't exert himself too much.

Speaking of exertion—that tank was going to be all Val could handle. Even only one quarter full the sucker would weigh her down.

"You need to go, babe," he said with an encouraging nod even though his mental calculations of time vs. distance left him helplessly on the short end. Thirty minutes for her to get back to the cabana, five to make the call and gather his gear. Then weighted down by the gear—even the nearly empty the tank would weigh around forty pounds—it would take another forty-five minutes for her to get back to him. An hour and twenty minutes total.

It was cutting it close that she'd make it back with the air tank before he met Davy Jones. And even if she did make it, he only had fifteen minutes of air—twenty-five max—between now and the afterlife. Factor in that after her thirty-minute swim and a call to the mainland, a chopper or a boat needed a minimum of sixty minutes to get out here and then *find* him . . . well, he was a betting man but this hand was coming up deuces and treys. It was a loser. And so, he figured, was he.

"Pace yourself, okay?" he said thickly, knowing that this might be the last time he ever looked upon her face. "You can do this."

"Oh, God."

"It'll be fine. *I'll* be fine. "

Her eyes told him he wasn't fooling her. She knew that every second counted and they were on the short end of a race against the clock. And she wasn't stupid. As fast as the tide was rising, the odds of help arriving to free him before he ran out of air were sinking by the second.

"Just go, babe. And while you're there, check out that little shed behind the cabana. I figure it's a gardener's shed or something. It's bound to be full of tools." He swallowed thickly. This was going to be even harder to say than it had been to think. "You'd better look for a hand saw. Bring it back with the tanks."

It took a moment before the significance of the saw registered. She started crying then.

"You can do this, babe."

She cupped his face in her hands, searched his eyes then kissed him. Hard. "You are not going to die. I'm not going to let you."

Then she was gone.

He watched her swim steadily toward the beach. Thought of how much he loved her. Thought of how romantic it had sounded being alone on this private island . . . civilization a good hour away by boat or chopper. And that was figuring she could even *reach* civilization on a phone system that was sporadic and unreliable at best.

Damning his stupidity, he watched until her head was only a speck on the surface of undulating aqua blue. Until the water started lapping over his shoulders. Then he sucked in a deep breath, dove down and tried to move the rock again.

He surfaced spitting sea water, swearing and hoping to God that she wouldn't have to watch him die.

Thirty minutes later, Val half swam, half crawled to shore. She stumbled and fell down on all fours when she finally hit the beach. Winded, muscles burning from the hard swim and shaking with fear for Luke, she ran to the house, flew inside and dialed the emergency number.

"Please, please, please," she begged, gripping the receiver with both hands as the sound of broken rings beat faintly across the line.

"Oh, thank God," she breathed when someone finally answered. She quickly told them what had happened.

"We're on our way," a disembodied voice answered. "ETA—sixty minutes."

"Please . . . you have to get here faster. I don't know if he can last that long. The tide's coming in fast."

"Sixty is the best we can do, ma'am. I'm dispatching a chopper now."

The line went dead.

She had a moment of stunned numbness. She stood, dripping on the floor, hands trembling and she could not move.

Luke was counting on her. Luke's life depended on her.

"You can do this, babe."

She heard his voice as clearly as if he'd whispered in her ear. And in that moment, she knew exactly what she had to do. She had to save him. Help was not going to get here in time.

She tore through the kitchen, remembered seeing a hammer and screwdriver and a flashlight in one of the cabinet drawers. She found the drawer on the second try, grabbed all three items and raced back outside. The stone walk way was warm under her feet as she ran to the shed. The door was padlocked shut. She didn't hesitate. She slammed the lock with the hammer. Over and over until she was screaming in anger and frustration. Finally, the lock's hinge broke away from the wooden doorframe.

The door swung open with a creak. It was dark inside. Like a cave. Like a cellar. She pushed past the familiar rise of claustrophobia and shined the flashlight around. The first thing she saw made her heart stop. A hacksaw. She grabbed it from its hook on the wall and tossed it outside. She breathed a huge sigh of relief when she found a long, heavy metal bar with a flattened edge. The bar was almost five feet long . . . must have weighed thirty pounds but adrenaline had a hold on her and she lifted it away from the corner where it leaned against the wall and heaved it outside with the saw.

With that and the scuba gear, she could help him. The question was how to get it all out there in one trip—no way in hell was she heading back there without the pry bar. There had to be more she could use. She shined the light toward the little shed's roof and almost wept with joy when she spotted four big white bumpers—the kind used to hang over the side of a boat to protect it from bumping the dock—tucked in the rafters.

They were too high up for her to reach. She found a wooden crate and quickly moved it to the center of the shed, stepped up on it and dragged all four bumpers down. After finding several lengths of rope, she was ready to head for the beach.

First she dragged the pry bar, bumpers, rope and the horrifying saw to the water's edge. Then she ran back for the scuba gear, hauling the heavy tank through the sand with the help of adrenaline and single-minded determination. Her muscles burned with fatigue by the time she'd fashioned a sling between the bumpers—two on each side—then secured the scuba gear, pry bar and saw between them with the ropes.

One final, muscle-wrenching drag and she had her 'raft' in the water.

It actually floated! Too overcome by her sense of urgency to celebrate her small victory, she tied a rope attached to the raft around her waist. Before heading out, and figuring it would be much easier to get his tanks ready on land than in the water, she quickly connected the octopus to the tank and opened the valve, checked the pressure and tested the regulator—thanking God that Luke had taught her how to prepare for a dive.

Satisfied that she'd set everything up correctly, she headed back to Luke.

She didn't think about the fact that forty-five minutes had passed since she'd left him. That another forty-five would pass before help would arrive. That with the weight of the scuba gear and the pry bar and the current going against her, it might possibly take her another forty-five minutes to get to him.

Forty-five minutes. His life had come down to that.

Her life had come down to that because without him, she didn't think she could go on living.

So she swam. Didn't think about sharks. Didn't think about high tide. Didn't think about failing. She thought about him. About the life he'd breathed into hers. About his smile that made her feel fifteen and carefree and renewed. About how he'd once risked all to save her and she could not fail him.

Her lungs screamed for air as she slogged on, towing her heavy weight. Her muscles burned with fatigue as she stroked steadily onward. To Luke. To life. To everything that mattered in her world.

Chapter 5

In the field, as the team medic, the guys depended on Luke to have a cool head, steady hands and nerves of steel. They did not expect him to screw up. If he did, someone would most likely die.

Well, he'd screwed up. Big time. And it was starting to look like he'd dodged his last bullet. A Mara Salvatrucha hit squad had almost gotten his number in San Salvador last year. He'd almost bought the farm. That hadn't been his fault.

This was.

And he'd miscalculated. The tide had risen faster than he'd thought. Val hadn't been gone an hour when the seawater had risen to his chin. Fifteen minutes ago, it started lapping over his nose. Only his mask and snorkel were keeping him breathing air and hanging on.

He'd tried—many times—to pull his foot free after she'd left. All he'd gotten for his efforts was blood and pain . . . and yeah, a constant three-sixty head swivel to watch out for the sharks that so loved blood and warm, tropical water. So far, his luck was holding on that count.

But luck was a relative term, wasn't it? And training was only as good as the circumstances permitted. Hell, to pass drown-proofing in BUD/S training he'd had to jump into a nine-foot-deep pool with his hands and feet tied, bob for five minutes, float for five minutes, swim 100 meters, bob for 2 more minutes, do a forward flip, a backward flip, survive a mask grab and bob some more until he was finally called out. He'd aced the challenge. Of course, there hadn't been a frickin' rock involved.

And there'd been an instructor on standby to pull him out if it looked like he was going to drown. He hadn't panicked then.

Alone, out here with nothing but miles of endless ocean, he'd passed panic fifteen minutes ago. And then he'd settled, somewhat reluctantly, into acceptance. He was going to die here. It royally pissed him off. He'd wanted so much more time with her. Wanted to make beautiful brown-eyed babies and watch them suckle at her breast. Wanted to teach his son to toss a baseball, ride a bike. Wanted to teach his daughter how to protect herself. Wanted . . . hell. He'd wanted to

make Val happy. She'd had so little happiness in her life and now . . .
God. Now she was going to come back and find him dead.

It so wasn't fair to her.

A huge wave pounded overhead, filled his snorkel, and he sucked
in a draft of salt water. He coughed around the mouth piece . . .
managed to choke himself before he finally cleared the snorkel and
dragged in a breath of dry air.

Close. When the next big wave rolled in it was going to be all
over.

His ears were already plugged with water. Thin wisps of blood
drifted up from his captured ankle around his face. He felt very tired
suddenly. And very sad. He'd failed her.

He didn't consciously close his eyes. They just drifted shut as he,
too, drifted back and forth in the water, tethered to his ocean grave by
an anchor of rock.

She'd made it. She was sure she'd made it. This was where she'd
left Luke. Val treaded water and searched frantically for signs of him.
Nothing. Maybe she'd miscalculated. Maybe she'd overshot his
position. The waves had grown more volatile. The chop was a good
two feet, churning up the water and sand and cutting surface and dive
visibility to almost nothing.

She fought panic as she whipped her head back and forth,
searching, searching . . . and finally spotted the very tip of a snorkel
sticking out of the water not ten feet away.

Oh, God.

She swam frantically toward him, dragging her raft behind her.
And cried out in anger and denial when she ducked beneath the
surface and saw that his eyes were closed. His arms floated listlessly
out to his side.

Refusing to believe he was gone, she grabbed the regulator and
opened the valve. Then she reached for Luke, jerked the snorkel out of
his mouth and shoved the mouthpiece between his lips.

"Breathe, baby. Breathe!" she demanded, sobbing and fighting
and praying all in one breath. For an eternity it seemed, he didn't
respond. She scrambled to remember what he'd taught her.

"Scuba regulators are demand valves. You only get air when you inhale."

She had to do something to make him inhale.

So she punched him hard in the chest. Once. Again. Finally, thank

God, he coughed and clutched at her hand.

"Breathe!" she pleaded again, until she could see the life returning to his eyes and the strength returning to his limbs.

And her life became worth living again.

Relieved and hopeful but knowing they weren't out of the woods, she sank beneath the surface so he could see her face.

"Hold on," she mouthed then squeezed him hard when he nodded.

Bobbing up above the water again, she pulled and pushed and finally maneuvered the pry bar to the edge of the raft. This was going to be tricky. Once she slid it completely off, it would sink like lead and take her with it into around seven feet of water.

Making certain Luke had a good grip on the raft holding the air tank, she untied the rope from around her waist, breathed deep several times, sucked in a huge breath and pulled the pry bar free.

They sank to the floor together. Still it was easier to handle it in the water than on dry land. She struggled and worked and finally maneuvered the tip of the bar between the two rocks trapping his foot. By then, she was out of breath.

Luke's hand reached down and steadied the bar while she shot to the surface. She clung to the raft, refilling her lungs and, when she felt strong enough, dove down again. This time, she was able to get under the bar and pull down.

The rock moved a fraction of an inch.

Revved on adrenaline, she tugged again, putting all of her weight into it. It shifted a little more.

For several minutes, she repeated the process. Surfacing, replenishing, diving, tugging. On her last trip down, she got a look at the gauge on the octopus connected to Luke's air tank. The digital read out said the tank was empty.

This was it. She had to get it this time.

She dove again and this time Luke had regained enough strength that he was able to drop down with her. He pressed his free foot on top of the bar and bounced while she swam under it again and tugged. Finally, just when it looked like nothing was going to happen, the rock tipped then rolled to the side and Luke's foot slipped free.

She shot to the surface with him, laughing and crying and hugging him so hard she dragged them both under again. Luke's strength pushed them back up. He grabbed the raft, hooked an arm over the top of a bumper, and hugged her to his side.

"I thought I'd lost you." She wrapped her arms around his neck and her legs around his waist and hung on like Tango hanging on to a banana leaf.

"I thought you had too, Princess," he whispered tiredly into her hair and clung while overhead, a chopper flew into sight. "I thought you had, too."

Chapter 6

"So," Luke said, setting his crutches aside and propping his bandaged foot up on the conference room table at BOI headquarters in Buenos Aires a week later. "I've got another poem."

The entire situation room lapsed into suspended silence.

Johnny Reed was the first of the assembled BOI team to break it. "I thought you hurt your ankle in Palau. Didn't know there was a brain injury involved."

"Har, har," Luke grumbled. "Just shut up and listen."

"Listen to what?"

Luke whipped his head around when he heard Val's voice. God, he loved knowing that she was a part of his world now. *This* world. Black Ops, Inc. No, she hadn't joined the team like Rafe's wife, B.J., or like Johnny's Crystal had, but she was still a regular around BOI headquarters, stopping by to check in on him and the guys, or to bring them those amazing éclairs she'd discovered at the Hotel Sofitel, just off Cinco de Julio in downtown B.A.

"Hey, babe." He held out a hand to her. "I have another poem for you."

Her smile was filled with the kind of indulgence one reserves for the village idiot. "Another one?"

"What?" Luke glance around the room where the rest of the team was making kissy faces his way. "A guy can't express himself around here unless it involves an action plan, C-4 or an M-16?"

"Nothing wrong with self-expression." His boss, Nate Black, tossed a stack of files on the table. "But please don't call the drivel you've been spouting poetry."

"The sea is green, the sky is blue," Reed said in a mocking, singsong. "Colter once was a SEAL, now he's a tool."

"That doesn't even rhyme," Luke muttered. "And I don't write like that."

"Yes, darling," Val said gently as she pressed a kiss to his forehead, "you do. But I love your poems anyway. They come from the heart."

"Maybe you should consider writing for one of those greeting card companies," Rafe Mendoza suggested with a crooked grin. "You know . . . make up rhymes to help people feel good when their life turns to crap."

Okay. Maybe he deserved this grief they were dishing out. Since he and Val had returned from Palau, he *had* gone a little off the deep end in the 'expressing his love' department.

But she'd saved his life. Overcome her own fears, charged in like the heroine she was, and literally saved him in the nick of time. He'd been gone. For real. Sounded hokey but he'd actually felt his—hell, he didn't know what to call it. His spirit? His essence? His soul? Whatever, he'd felt it leave his body. Known it was all over. And then she was there. Offering him precious air. Willing him back to life. Using her ingenuity and clear thinking to bring the tools she'd needed to free him from that cursed rock.

He wouldn't have made it until the chopper crew arrived. They'd shown up in time for the mop up. Airlifted them back to the mainland. Stabilized him because damn, he'd lost a helluva lot of blood.

So yeah, thanks to his amazing, beautiful, intelligent, brave wife, he was back at BOI—still on the DL for a couple more weeks—but he would soon be back in fighting form, instead of six feet under.

"I want to hear Luke's poem," Crystal said, and earned a chorus of groans. "Knock it off, you guys." She gave Luke an encouraging smile. "Go ahead, Doc. Read it for us."

"Thank you, Crystal." Vindicated, he cleared his throat and unfolded his paper. "This is for you, babe," he said and winked at Val.

"O my Luve's like the melodie
That's sweetly play'd in tune!
As fair thou art, my bonnie lass,
So deep in love am I:
And I will love thee still, my dear,
Till a' the seas gang dry:
Till a' the seas gang dry, my dear,
And the rocks melt with the sun;
I will luve thee still, my dear
When the sands of life shall run.
And fare thee weel, my only Luve,
And fare thee weel a while!
And I will come again, my Luve,

Tho' it were ten thousand mile."

The room had grown reverently silent by the time he'd finished. When he looked up, the guys were all watching him with narrow-eyed interest. Reed was staring at him like he wanted to say something but couldn't quite find the words. Crystal was dabbing at her eyes. Nate was smiling into his chest.

And Val . . . Val was giving him an arched look.

Alrighty then.

"Well." He reached for his crutches and stood abruptly. "If you'll excuse us, ladies and gents, I think I'm going to call it a day."

No one said a word as he and Val walked out of the situation room.

"What?" he asked, attempting to look innocent as they reached their car in the underground garage.

"That poem was beautiful." She helped him into the passenger seat.

"I meant every word." He took her hand after she'd settled in behind the wheel.

"I'm sure you did. But you didn't write it, darling. Robert Burns did."

"Oh. So . . . we're going to split hairs?"

She grinned. "You really thought you'd get that past us?"

"You? No. Them? Just long enough to see those looks on their faces. And they were priceless. God, I love to gloat."

He leaned over in the seat and kissed her. "Let's go home. I just thought of another way to thank you for saving my life. You're going to like it. It involves whipped cream."

She laughed, shifted into gear and drove out of the underground parking garage into the daylight.

More content than he'd ever thought he could possibly be, Luke turned his face to the sun.

Lord, thank you
Life is good
It's turned out just
The way it should.

PANAMA JACK

Tara Janzen

Chapter One

Darien Gap, Panama

"You've got that low-crawl down real good, ma'am, very fine action on the move. Very fine, indeed." Panama Jack Corday had a reputation for calling 'em like he saw 'em, and the girl wiggling up next to him in this godforsaken jungle had a backside worthy of worship.

"Watch yourself, Flipper," she said, handing him an MRE—Meal Ready to Eat—and settling back into her rifle. "I've got enough trouble without you getting all worked up staring at my derriere."

She also had a mouth on her. Flipper. Hell. Nobody had ever had the guts to call him Flipper, but she did it regularly. Her little way of trying to keep him in line, he guessed.

Fat chance.

He grinned. "I love it when you talk dirty."

"Derriere?" She slanted him a quick glance over the top of her rifle. "That's not dirty, it's French."

"Dirty French." His grin broadened.

"*In your dreams,*" she said under her breath, resting her cheek back on the rifle's stock and peering through the scope.

She had that right—*in his dreams*. Hell, if he'd had a night in the last two months when she hadn't been in his dreams, he didn't remember it. Oh, hell, no. Little Miss Blondie with the O.G.A., Other Government Agency, a.k.a. the C.I.A., had been popping in and out of Panama City on a damn near weekly basis, and every week she requested one operator to take her deep into the overgrown danger zone between Panama and Colombia known as the Darien Gap. Every week she requested him, Jack Corday, U.S. Navy SEAL on special assignment.

Special assignment to cover Little Miss Blondie's very fine derriere. *Yeah*, he'd finally figured it out.

But he hadn't figured her out.

He opened up the package of cookies in the MRE and handed her a couple, then put his eye back to the spotting scope and scanned the area in front of them.

Nothing about the Ice Queen made sense. She was half spook, half sniper, and all gorgeous. Agents like her usually ended up in European embassies, carrying a pocket pistol and collecting intelligence from tuxedoed diplomats.

This girl was in the middle of the big, bad nowhere, sweating her guts out and toting a M40, a fully accurized .308 with a scope that cost more than his first car.

"So, do you ever take a day off?" Yep, that was him, all right, a real smooth guy.

"Not in this lifetime," she said dryly.

"Maybe you should try it, with me."

"Maybe not." Without an instant's hesitation, she turned him down, but he was a U.S. Navy SEAL and SEALs never gave up. Never.

"I could take you fishing." He was good at fishing.

Her little snort of derision implied that fishing might be a long shot.

Grinning, he popped the last cookie into his mouth and glanced over at her. "If you'd tell me what you're looking for, maybe I could help you find it." After eight times of getting dropped into this hellhole and bushwhacking their way to the same damn hillside to stare down at the same damn abandoned farmhouse, and getting nowhere doing it, he figured she might be ready for a little professional guidance.

He'd figured wrong.

"That's real sweet of you, Squidbreath," she said, keeping her gaze focused through the scope and for damn sure looking like she knew what she was doing. "But if I told you what I'm looking for, I'd have to kill you."

He grinned again, and checked his watch. *Squidbreath?*

"We're running out of time," he told her. "We need to get to the

LZ." If all had gone according to plan, the helo designated to pick them up was on its way.

"Five more minutes," she said. "Then we'll pack it in, which means we'll be right back here doing this again next week."

That was all right by him. He'd had worse missions, far worse than being teamed up with Little Miss Blondie.

"So when are you going to tell me your name?" he asked.

"You know my name."

"Oh, yeah, Smith, Jane Smith," he recalled. "Or was it Johnson? Jane Johnson?"

"I always heard SEALs were real smart," she said. "You got it right the first time. Smith Jane Smith."

"So should I be calling you Smith or Jane?"

"You can keep calling me what you've been calling me—'Yes, ma'am.'"

She had that right. He'd been "Yes, ma'aming," Little Miss Blondie from the moment they'd met.

"Two o'clock," she whispered, going very still next to him on the jungle floor.

Yeah, he heard it, too, the soft cough of an engine coming off the mountain pass north of the abandoned farm. He angled the spotting scope in that direction, following the winding path of the dirt road up through the trees until he saw an old deuce-and-a-half lumbering toward the valley below.

"Delivery time?" he asked.

"I sure as hell hope so," she said, and for the first time, he detected an honest, unguarded emotion in her voice—naked anticipation. She wanted this, whatever "this" was. It could be anything, weapons, drugs, a squad of narco-guerillas. For sure, it would be trouble.

"You've got a plan for whatever comes out of that truck, right?"

"Right." She nestled in closer to her rifle.

"Want to tell me what it is, in case I need to step in and save the day?"

"You just keep doing what you're doing, Corday, and everything will be just fine."

Oh, man, he could hardly believe the size of her *cojones*. But when he'd been given this assignment, his commanding officer had made it crystal clear that he was going to be working for "Jane Smith," not the other way around. She called the shots. She gave the orders, and he got her where she wanted to go and got her back out.

The minutes ticked by in silence, both of them watching the truck slowly rumble its way down the gullies and over the rocks in the road. Sweat ran down his face. Doubt edged into his mind. Wasn't it just like a damn C.I.A. agent to drag him into something without telling him what in the hell was going on? PSD, he'd been told, a Personal Security Detail. But who in the world ever did a PSD for a fricking sniper?

No one, that's who.

The truck started across the valley, heading for the farmhouse. When it reached the path leading to the adjoining, ramshackle barn, it stopped. A man wearing jungle boots and camouflage got out of the cab and headed around to the back of the deuce-and-a-half, no doubt getting ready to unload whatever it was Smith was hoping to score.

Jack did a quick mental check of all his gear, which most definitely included an M4 carbine and a .45 caliber pistol with plenty of extra magazines for both. He was ready. He was always ready.

But nothing came out of the back of the truck—no drugs, no weapons, no narco-guerillas. The driver kicked the tires, checked a load strap, looked at the farm and empty pastures for a few seconds, then came back around to the front of the truck, got into the cab, and started up the deuce. The engine sputtered and coughed, and finally turned over a couple of times, and then it died.

Jack didn't move, not so much as a muscle twitch. Beside him, Smith had gone pure mannequin, her gaze glued to the scope, her breathing so soft as to be damn near imperceptible.

Down below, the driver gave another long go of cranking the engine, and just when Jack was thinking it was time for the guy to give up, the old truck roared to life. Mission accomplished—or maybe not. Next to him, he caught the slight movement of Smith's finger sliding onto the trigger.

The driver sure as hell had screwed up something, and it was going to cost him his life. At four hundred meters with no wind, the girl wasn't going to miss. She'd been dialed in on the guy's location for the last five hours. But the truck didn't move, and she didn't shoot. Everybody was waiting for something, but he'd be damned if he knew what, until the driver reached out the window with a red rag in his hand and cleaned off the side mirror. Next to him, Smith eased her finger off the trigger. When the driver followed up the red rag with a bright yellow one, giving the outside mirror a real thorough polishing, she whispered one, succinct word.

"Bingo."

She'd gotten what she wanted, and he knew it was more than just a clean mirror on some damn paramilitary deuce-and-a-half. A message had been passed, and Smith liked the news.

Down below, the driver finished with the mirror and started grinding the gears, looking for first. When he got it right, the truck took off with a lurch and a roll and continued down the valley.

Jack glanced over and caught Smith looking at him with a big, sweet grin on her face, a wide curve of soft lips, perfect white teeth, and so-help-him-God dimples that for a second turned him just a little bit inside out, but just for a second. Then he recovered.

Just in time for her to jerk his chain again.

"Are you ready to kick this game up a notch and have some fun?" she asked, her pale green eyes lit with excitement. Her grin broadened, deepening those so-help-him-God dimples, and all of a sudden he was just a little bit inside out again.

Oh, yeah, he silently answered. He was ready for just about anything with Little Miss Blondie, had been for weeks, and *oh, yeah,* he was in trouble here—real trouble.

"Born ready," he said with a curt nod, ignoring whatever emotion was getting all churned up in his chest. Or maybe whatever was getting churned up was a little farther down his anatomy. "But I'm damned curious about what just happened, and about what didn't happen. If the guy hadn't cleaned his mirror . . . " He let the question trail off.

"I had him in my crosshairs with a half pound of pressure on a two-and-a-half pound trigger," she said, confirming exactly what he'd thought. "If he wasn't my messenger boy, then we'd been compromised, and he was a bad guy in the wrong place at the wrong time."

Good enough for Jack—and he was impressed as hell. He liked working with people who knew what it took to get the job done and get out in one piece.

"So what have you got in mind?" He was up for damn near anything.

"Drinks," she said. "At Las Palmas in Casco Viejo."

For a moment, all he could do was look at her, completely caught off guard. Weeks of ignoring him, and now she was asking him out for a drink? Highly trained operative that he was, he recovered quickly and gave her another nod.

"What time would you like to be picked up?" Having a drink

together wasn't his *numero uno* hot, green-eyed blonde fantasy. In his *numero uno* fantasy, he and secret agent Jane Smith spent the night tearing up the sheets in the downtown bungalow where he always stayed, compliments of a buddy of his, J.T. Chronopolous. But she had definitely nailed the far distant number two or three spot on his current personal hit parade—Las Palmas, an elegant waterfront hotel in Panama City's historic district, Casco Viejo, drinks to start, maybe moving onto wine and dinner, and her, Little Miss Blondie, illuminated by candlelight without any visible firearms at the table.

But she was shaking her head.

"I'll meet you there, at midnight. I'll be bringing you a small gift, but don't feel obliged to return the favor. Just take a seat at the bar and order a drink. I'll come up and set my cigarette case down next to your glass. When I leave, pick up the case, and deliver it to Benjamin Neville's office at the U.S. Embassy, where we met. He'll be expecting you."

From bodyguard to delivery boy—she'd done it again, caught him off guard and put him in his place.

"Yes, ma'am." Apparently, they'd gotten everything they'd come for, and he was ready to blow this pop stand, but she wasn't finished.

"How long have you been with the SEALs?" she asked, sizing him up, cool and steady with her green-eyed gaze. It didn't make him uncomfortable in the least. He knew who he was, and he could take all comers, including beautiful C.I.A. agents.

"Five years, ma'am."

"Seen a lot of action?"

"Some." A whole lot of "some." Iraq, Afghanistan, all over Central America, and a dozen other places, but somehow ending up in Panama enough that it felt like home. The surfing was great, the beer was cold, and every now and then something damned interesting landed in his lap—like Smith Jane Smith, a.k.a. Little Miss Blondie. Not that he'd be calling her that to her face anytime soon.

"I need you watching my back tonight in Casco Viejo," she said, her gaze still so cool and steady. "Get to the bar an hour before me and keep your eyes open."

"Yes, ma'am." Amazingly, not one lewd, smart-ass thought even went through his mind about watching her back or her backside. She was damned serious, and rightly so. Las Palmas was a classy place, but beyond its elegant walls, the neighborhood of Casco Viejo was dangerously sketchy after dark.

"Powell," she said, obviously coming to a decision about him. "Alanna Powell, but you can call me Lani." She stuck out her hand.

"Lani." He took her hand in his and gave it a firm shake, grinning. "Corday. Squidbreath Corday, but you can call me Flipper."

Her smile and her dimples returned, and there the two of them were, sweat-stained and mud-streaked, holding hands in the jungle and grinning like a couple of hormone-addled teenagers instead of two of Uncle Sam's finest and brightest.

Right in the nick of time to keep him from doing or saying anything too stupid, the sound of the helo coming in over the mountains broke the silence, and the two of them got to work. In less than a minute, they'd stowed their gear and were heading down the trail.

Chapter Two

Casco Viejo, Panama City

She was late.

Lani stepped out of the smoke-filled Club Firenze and moved quickly across the cobblestone street, tucking a small silver case into the bodice of her mini-dress. Zebra-striped and strapless, the dress had a built-in underwire bra with a secret pocket for the case and enough spandex to fit her like a second skin. With her short blond hair spiked up, black leather cuffs on each wrist, big white hoop earrings, and a small black clutch purse slung over her shoulder she was perfectly camouflaged for the Panama City dance-club scene, equal parts urban-punk lion tamer and Sheba, Queen of the Jungle.

Behind her, hard rock music blared out of the packed club. Ahead of her, two blocks away, she could see Las Palmas, the pale stucco of its Spanish Colonial façade rising above the shops and restaurants clustered around the upper-end condominium buildings on the waterfront.

Casco Viejo was part slum, part construction site, part trendy tourist attraction, and no place for a *gringa* walking alone at midnight. But it wasn't the sullen-faced group of young men eyeing her from the corner that set her on edge. Oh, no. Her contact had done that quite nicely at their meeting.

A quick glance behind her proved Vasily Nikolayevich was still on the second-floor balcony of the club where she'd left him, watching her. Their meeting had gone longer than planned, with him stepping out twice to take a phone call, and Lani's unease had increased with every delay. She'd come to Panama to close a deal with Nikolayevich, a former KGB agent turned illegal arms dealer, a deal she'd been working on for over a year. In exchange for a substantial cash payment, and to put himself in the good graces of the U.S. government, should he ever need them, he had offered her a cigarette case electro-magnetically encrypted with the port designation, arrival date, and the BIC-Code of a shipping container transporting a load of shoulder-fired surface to air missiles, SAMs, destined for the Taliban from their comrades in arms, the Colombian guerillas known as the National Revolutionary Forces, the NRF—a deal guaranteed to fan the flames of the global war on terror.

Mission accomplished.

Except Nikolayevich had been two months late getting to Panama—two months he'd spent holed up in Colombian jungle with the damned NRF. Two months when her superiors had started to doubt the veracity of her information and her ability to get Nikolayevich to the table. Today, the tide had turned in her direction. The red flag at the farmhouse had told her Nikolayevich had finally crossed the border into Panama. The yellow flag had been the code for a meeting in Panama City.

And the sudden rising of the hair on the back of her neck told her she was being followed. It wasn't Nikolayevich. Grossly overweight and out of shape, he couldn't have fought his way through the crowd gyrating on the Club Firenze dance floor without giving himself a heart attack.

But there was a chance he had sold her out. He might not have come to Panama City alone. But neither had she. Lieutenant Jack Corday, U.S. Navy SEAL, nearly six feet of rock-hard brawn and Mensa caliber brains nicknamed Panama Jack, all of him honed and trained to a razor's edge of operational skill, was on her side.

And on her mind way too much since the first day he'd walked into Benjamin Neville's office at the U.S. Embassy and been introduced as her assigned escort. In his dress whites, he'd been impossible to ignore, dark-haired and blue-eyed, and so supremely self-assured that he'd just about broken her heart without doing a damn thing but stand there. When he'd flashed her a cocksure grin during their briefing, the deed had been done—*Yes, ma'am, I can take care of you, one hundred percent guaranteed.* Sure, she'd kept her cool, but a week later she'd made mistake number one: She'd requested him by name when she'd found herself back in Panama. He was irreverent and intelligent, and gorgeous, and hot, and interested, and so help her God, she knew better. Eight separate times, she'd known better, and eight separate times, when Benjamin Neville had asked who she wanted, she'd said Lieutenant Corday. She called him Squidbreath to keep herself in line, not him.

In five more steps, she reached the well-lit entryway of Las Palmas and passed under the pale pink arch into the luxurious hotel. Inside, crystal chandeliers cast a soft golden glow over marble floors and paneled teak walls. Without breaking her stride or looking anywhere except dead-ahead through the French doors leading to the bar, she pulled a cigarette case out of her purse and opened it. The case had a built-in lighter, and after selecting a cigarette and putting it between her lips, she stopped, seemingly by happenstance, next to a super-sized bouquet of tropical flowers and lit up. Cupping the flame, she inhaled, then blew out a long breath of smoke and with a slight flick of her wrist, dropped the case into the elaborate flower arrangement.

Whoever was following her was practically required by secret agent law to pillage the bouquet, giving her time to make the real drop in the bar, and that would be that. *Sayonara,* Navy SEAL. *Adios,* Corday. Goodbye, Flipper, and hello promotion. The lieutenant would head for the embassy, and she'd be on the next flight to Virginia.

Passing through the open glass doors, she picked him out of the crowd jamming the long, mahogany curve of the Las Palmas bar, and damn but the boy cleaned up good. Crisp, black T-shirt under a white suit jacket with black slacks, and swear to God, Italian leather loafers all but shouted "GQ." Add his chiseled jaw, deep-set blue eyes, the scar cutting across his left eyebrow, and that damn crooked grin of his, and all she could see was "Heartbreaker."

She wasn't the only one. A leggy redhead in tight gold pants and a green halter top was sidled up close to him, bending in close for Jack to light her cigarette. It was the perfect cover for the drop—and perfectly annoying.

Repressing a sigh, she worked her way up to the bar and leaned in next to him.

"Mojito," she called out to the bartender, flashing a twenty dollar bill she'd pulled out of her purse and completely ignoring the broad back she was brushing up against.

Sure she was.

She stubbed out her cigarette in the ashtray next to his beer. She needed a life. Something more than just a job that kept her on the road and on the run twelve months out of twelve. Honestly, she did.

Hell, for all she knew, she might like fishing.

Glancing back, she took note of the man digging through the tropical bouquet in the lobby—gray-haired and pock-marked and unquestionably Slavic. It had occurred to her more than once that the Russians might be keeping track of Nikolayevich, the same way they kept track of so many of their former comrades, especially those in the arms trade.

But this old guy didn't have a chance against her. Even at five feet, five inches and a hundred and twenty pounds she was one of the agency's big bad girls—and most of the time she had enough sense to stay away from the big bad boys. Why Corday was different, she didn't even want to know.

Her mojito came, and in between paying for it and pocketing her change, she slipped the silver cigarette case out of her bodice and set it next to Jack's beer with her hand covering it.

Or maybe all she needed was a vacation, just a little time off to recharge.

"Thanks, sugar," the redhead drawled on Jack's other side. "Or should I be saying *muchas gracias, azúcar?*"

Despite her best efforts, Lani's damn annoyed sigh escaped her.

Squidbreath did not seem to notice.

"It's no problem, ma'am," he said. "I'm happy to help."

Lani didn't doubt it for a moment. Every guy she knew was happy to help redheads who were practically falling out of their halter tops.

"I like a helpful man," the redhead said, her voice a low, intimate purr. "Maybe we could get together later and party."

"Maybe we could, ma'am."

Oh, for crying out loud, Lani thought.

With the cigarette case on the bar between them, it was time for her to pick up her drink and wander off. Instead, in her estimation, and much to her irritation, Panama Jack was far too distracted by the redheaded woman to be left alone with the case. Damn Benjamin Neville for bringing a tradecraft rookie in on her mission, and why in the hell hadn't she noticed Lieutenant Corday's shortcomings earlier?

Because you spent too much time staring at his butt, Lani girl.

Well, hell. She couldn't deny it.

Stalling, she took a sip of the mojito and let her gaze drift across the mirror behind the bar—until it slammed into a black-eyed gaze locked onto her like a tractor beam, Alek Zhivkov, a.k.a. Zhivkov the Butcher. She swore one succinct word. She had eleven rounds in an XDM Compact .45 in her purse, and if this deal got salty, his name was going on the one she kept in the chamber. Zhivkov had a long, sordid list of international crimes as a Russian Mafia enforcer, mostly in human trafficking, and she hated to see him branching out into her neck of the woods, illegal arms sales. As for Nikolayevich, if Zhivkov was checking up on him, she gave him a month on the outside, before he was dead.

It was time to run, and the smart money said she should take the case with her, but she no sooner closed her hand around it, than Corday's hand came around hers, holding onto her like he was never going to let her go.

Twenty minutes, Jack thought. That's how late she'd been getting to Las Palmas, twenty minutes of hell, and now she thought she was going to skip out on him?

He didn't think so. A minute ago, she could have left as planned. Thirty seconds ago, he might still have let her go, but not now, not under the current circumstances.

"Later then, sugar," the flirty redhead said, turning and walking away, thankfully at an angle that didn't impede his line of sight to the lobby.

Jack turned back to his beer, shifting his gaze to the mirror to keep everyone in sight, including his hand-holding partner. The light in the bar was dim, but he still got an eyeful.

Zebra stripes. *Wow.* If he'd thought she looked good in muddy camos, Lani Powell flat-out owned him in a strapless, black and white-striped mini-dress, and here he was again, just a little bit upside down and inside out.

"You were followed," he said. Despite the redhead trying to distract him, he'd known the instant Lani had entered Las Palmas, and he'd known the instant she'd slipped in next to him at the bar, but he hadn't known that the bare curves of her shoulders and the upper curves of her breasts were so creamily, silkily beautiful, or that her skin had a golden glow. He hadn't known he had such a weakness for bad-girl make-up and leather cuff bracelets.

He had known he had a weakness for her, and the damned torturous twenty minutes he'd spent wondering where in the hell she was had proved it the hard way.

"Roger, that," she acknowledged.

"And the guy who followed you, the one lost in the flowers back in the lobby, has called in his reinforcements. The black-haired man coming in through the French doors and staring a hole in your back looks like rough trade, and the bald guy walking in from the rear of the bar is planning on cutting off your escape."

He saw her shift her gaze beyond the bar to the far corner of the room.

"Rough trade's name is Alek Zhivkov," she said, "also known as Zhivkov the Butcher. Baldy is Dmitri Yudin."

Somehow, her knowing all these guys didn't improve his mood.

"Anglo-Saxon jungle queen doing business with old-school Russians in the heart of Panama City, I guess that's what globalization is all about," he said, trying to keep the tightness out of his voice, and failing. "We can either fight our way out of here or give them what they want. How important is the silver case under your hand?"

"It's electro-magnetically encrypted with the BIC-code of a shipping container holding a load of stolen, third generation SAMs, French Mistral, Russian SA-18, and Stinger B missiles headed toward Afghanistan."

Fight to the death, then, dammit. Their deaths, not his, and sure as hell not hers, which meant run.

"There's a stairway on the balcony that leads to the rooftop restaurant, and—"

"A fire escape down the back of the hotel," she interrupted him.

Good, he thought. They'd both done their homework, and with enough speed, they should be able to get some distance on the Russians.

"You take the case, babe, and run like hell."

Smart girl, she didn't waste a second buying into his plan. Scooping up the case, she turned away from the bar and slipped into the crowd. He was right behind her—and right behind them were the Russians. He heard the commotion of them bulling their way through the people packing the room.

Quick on her feet, his girl made it to the balcony five yards ahead of him. In the few extra seconds it took him to get outside, she had already covered the open ground to the broad, stone staircase and was halfway to the first landing, darting her way through people heading upstairs to dine. At midnight, the restaurant would still be busy, and there was a good chance they could slip onto the fire escape before the Russians spotted them.

He caught her on the second landing, and as unobtrusively as possible, the two of them breezed past the hostess and crossed through the maze of tables and diners, heading to the north wall of the building. When they reached the fire escape, Lani quickly stepped over the side, onto the top rung, and started down. He followed, damned impressed that they'd shaken the bad guys.

But then someone swore and she stopped.

"Oh, excuse me," she said between a rapid-fire stream of angry Spanish. "I'm sorry, oh . . . excuse me."

What in the hell was going on, he wondered, trying to look below him. He couldn't see much, staring down into darkness, but she at least started moving again, even though she was still murmuring apologies and someone else was still swearing. A few more rungs down, when he reached the first landing, the situation became crystal clear. Anywhere else in the world, a metal ladder bolted to the side of a building and occasionally interspersed with small metal landings was called a fire escape. In Casco Viejo on a Friday night fueled by *seco con leche* and rum, it was called Lover's Lane.

Clothing was coming off here and there, a jacket, a scarf, a shoe, and buttons were coming undone on every landing all the way to the street.

So much for the afternoon he'd spent planning escape routes. He shrugged out of his too-damn-easy-to-spot white suit jacket and left it hanging on the railing with the other folks' clothes.

When they reached the second landing, someone from above shouted down in thick, Russian-accented Spanish, "*Alto!*" Stop!

Not very damn likely, Jack thought. Some of these folks were past the "stopping" part of the evening. Except he stopped, and Lani stopped, and in the instant of silence between the shouted command and the torrent of verbal abuse directed back up from the people crowding the fire escape, he had a brilliantly tactical idea—camouflage.

Pulling her close, he wrapped her zebra-striped curves in his arms and pressed her up against the building. Instinct more than brains brought his mouth down on hers, and pure, unadulterated pleasure, sweet and intense, kept it there, moment after lush, sensual moment as her lips parted, welcoming him inside, and so it would have gone, an endless kiss into something more, with her hot body pressed up against his, if the Russians had left.

They did not.

Over the side they came, pushing and shouting for the lovers to get out of their way.

He obliged, pushing Lani ahead of him down the last rungs of the fire escape. Back on the ground, he took her hand in his, and they ran down the nearest alley. In less than a block, they'd left the elegant and brightly lit world of Las Palmas behind and entered the maze of cobblestone streets and narrow walkways that made up the barrio section of the historic old town. He held to a northwest course, making for one of the main streets where they could catch a taxi to the embassy.

The music coming from the hotel's bar grew fainter with every step they took, giving him ample opportunity to silently wonder what in the ever-loving world had he be thinking? He'd manhandled a C.I.A. agent, kissed a spy, ran his hands up the side of her amazing curves and loved every second of it. And in the middle of a rocky escape, way too much of his brain was wondering how to do it again.

The sound of a gunshot zipping down the alley cleared all that nonsense out of his mind in a nano-second. He shoved his shoulder hard against the first wooden door he saw, wrenching the door handle at the same time, and the two of them burst into the overgrown courtyard of an abandoned house.

One thing he really liked about working with her, besides the rare opportunity to kiss the stuffing out of her, was that the two of them thought a lot alike. If this was going to turn into a shoot-out, they needed cover, which she spotted the same time he did, a set of large iron doors hanging half open on the ground floor that must have served as the home's service entrance. She all but dove inside, with him right behind her, almost on top of her, with another shot whacking into the door behind them.

"Cripes!" she swore, breathing hard, her face dirt-streaked, her dress ruined. She was low to the ground, crouched behind the door, looking out the door with a semi-auto pistol in her hands that looked to be .45 caliber—his favorite.

"We've got two problems," he said, his gaze quartering the part of the courtyard he could see without exposing himself. He could tell she was doing the same over on her side

"The Russians and the cops," she said.

"Exactly." Neither of them wanted to explain their situation to the Panamanian government, local or otherwise. "There's got to be a door that opens onto the street, and we're less than a block off the sea wall. If we can get to the water, we can get to a boat."

"You're thinking like a SEAL."

He almost grinned. "Sweetheart, I *am* a SEAL."

Another shot hit the iron door, and he aimed for the muzzle flash, squeezing off a round that hit something that grunted and moaned.

"Down by one," she said, then fired. "Make that two."

Yeah, he'd heard something else collapse out there with a groan, but there was still a lot of rustling and stumbling going on in the courtyard.

"I think there are more than just the three guys we saw in the Las Palmas," he said.

"I agree. We need to move out, if we're going to get out."

God, they were good together.

"I'll lay down some fire, try to hold their attention back here while you go out the front."

"I'll meet you at the sea wall." Once again, there was no debate. She took the plan and ran with it, literally, and after a moment's hesitation at the front door to check out the street, she disappeared into the darkness.

He fired a couple more rounds into the courtyard to give the Russians something to think about, and followed her out. They were going to make it.

Then he heard a shot.

Lani heard it, too.

Worse, she'd felt it burn a path across her shoulder. Halfway over the sea wall, she dropped like a stone onto the beach, shocked into losing her grip. She'd never been shot before, and the pain was disorientating. She tried to catch her breath and check herself out, and cursed herself for losing her gun. Before she'd even begun to think straight, let alone decide if she'd done more damage to herself by falling than by getting shot, Jack was there by her side, grim-faced and serious.

"Lani?"

"Flipper?" Okay, she wasn't dying, and a few tentative moves convinced her she hadn't broken anything. "Help me up."

"You're bleeding. Where are you hurt?" His voice was smooth and calm, and just hearing it helped sooth her jangled nerves. He was with her, and they were going to make it out of here—*Yes, ma'am, I can take care of you, one hundred percent guaranteed.*

"My right shoulder."

He looked at the wound and swore softly under his breath. "You're just skinned, babe, but I'm going to carry you."

"Good idea." It was going to take more time than they had for her to get steady on her feet, a fact proved by the shot fired from above. It hit the water, ten feet out, but was still way too damn close.

He turned and raised his pistol in one smooth move, aiming a precise shot toward the top of the wall, and a body came over the side, landing in the sand with a deathly thud.

"Change in plans," he said, kicking off his shoes and stripping off his slacks. "We're heading out to sea."

Another good idea, really, but Lani didn't see a boat anywhere close to where they were beached. Then she did see some boats, a lot of boats, moored at the *Muelle Fiscal* wharf, but the wharf was a long way away.

"How far can you swim?" She thought it was a question worth asking, especially as how he'd already picked her up and was carrying her out into the water.

"Miles," he assured her.

"Yes, but how far can you swim with me?" With the Pacific Ocean lapping at her butt, that was the sticking point.

He just grinned and kissed the tip of her nose as they sunk into the water and he turned her over onto her back. "Miles," he said. "Miles and miles and miles."

"The saltwater hurts like hell." And it did, burning like a brand where the bullet had sliced her skin open. For a moment, all she wanted was *out* of the water, and she started to panic.

But his voice came to her, steady as a rock. "I was born in Alabama, in the northern part of the state, and when I was five, my folks packed us all up, my two brothers, one sister, and me and we moved over to Louisiana. Now there's a great state."

Stroke after stroke, they headed into deeper water on a course that would take them to the wharf, where—in between telling her his life story—he informed her they would "borrow" a boat.

He never faltered, not once, not for an instant, but she did. By the time he got her into one of the motorized canoes the locals called *piraguas,* she felt half dead, feverish, and like she might not make it. But he knew better.

"You're doing great, Lani. Just hang in there. We're almost home. Everything is going to be okay."

Home was the U.S. Embassy. Across the bay, she could see the lights of central Panama City, and as they came up to the Balboa Monument, she knew he was right. Home wasn't very far away.

Slowly, with effort, she brought her hand up to the bodice of her dress and felt the silver cigarette case still secure in the secret pocket.

Yes, she thought. Everything was going to be okay.

Epilogue

Four months later, somewhere in Louisiana

"Hey, babe, you want to hand me that bait can?" she asked.

Fishing had been his idea. Jack would be the first to admit it, but who in the world would have guessed his secret agent girlfriend would take to it like a duck to water?

Not him, that was for damn sure, or he might have held off for a few years.

Whether she was after largemouth bass, crappie, or a mess of bream and shellcracker for supper, Little Miss Blondie left his bed way too damn early every morning to get down to the lake and start casting her line.

From where he was stretched out on the dock, he rolled over and looked in the white plastic bucket she'd brought down. The water was murky in the bucket.

"What have you got in here?"

"Ditch shrimp."

"You go, girl," he said around a yawn, pushing the bait bucket in her direction.

He was on leave, and she was still on hiatus, and hiatus looked good on her, almost as good as her Daisy Duke cut-offs and bikini top. Barefoot and suntanned, her hair had gotten long enough for a little ponytail in back, and he knew she liked sporting one around.

He liked sporting her around, taking her down to the nearest backwater roadhouse for crawfish and zydeco, and every night, bringing her back to their cabin in the swamp oak and tupelo forest, where he made love to her by the light of a southern moon.

Down on the end of the dock, she got a bite, her cane pole dipping toward the water, and with a dimpled smile and a short laugh, she pulled the fish in and got busy baiting another shrimp on her line. From this angle, he could see the scar across her shoulder from the night she'd been shot. She thought it made her look tough.

He thought she *was* tough.

"What did you get?" he asked, more to be polite than any actual interest. It was too early in the morning to be interested in fish.

"Bluegill." She looked up with the smile still on her face.

God, she was beautiful. No wonder he loved her. The truth had been staring him down for weeks. Smart, funny, gorgeous women were hard to find, but he'd done it, and he wasn't going to let her go.

He wasn't going to rush things, though. He wanted to give her plenty of time to figure out she was crazy about him, too. So he'd gotten her something special to let her know how he felt. This morning's phone call had cinched it for him.

"I heard from a friend of mine this morning, the guy whose house I was staying in while I was stationed in Panama."

"J.T. Chronopolous, right?" She threw her line back in, casting it into the weed beds lining the bank.

"Yep. Seems he and this group of guys he works with out of a place called Steele Street in Denver tracked down a shipping container full of stolen shoulder-launched surface to air missiles at a port in Yemen."

That got her attention.

She turned to face him so quickly, she almost dropped her pole.

"They found the Stingers?"

"And the Mistrals and the Russian SA-18s." There had been doubts. The encryption on the cigarette case hadn't been as definitive as Nikolayevich had promised. "It's all thanks to you, babe. You saved a lot of lives."

She was beaming, the sunlight caressing her skin and turning it that peachy golden color that made her look good enough to eat. "They found the SAMs."

Oh, yeah. He was in love.

Pushing himself upright, he rolled to his feet and padded down to her end of the dock just to drop down next to her and take her in his arms. She snuggled in close, and he kissed the top of her head. She was warm, and he was in love, and the time was right for the box in his pocket.

"J.T. has a sister-in-law who's an artist, and I had her design and make up something for you." He reached into the pocket of his shorts.

Lani leaned a little ways back, and he opened the box between them. Nestled inside was a necklace, a silver chain with three charms hanging from the middle, two in gold and one in silver.

"Oh, Jack," she whispered, reaching out to take the necklace and hold it in her hand. "It's beautiful, but what . . . "

She was a smart girl, she'd recognize the charms in a minute.

It took less than that.

"Missiles?" She looked up, her expression a fascinating mix of confusion and delight. "You had somebody design little missiles for me?"

He just grinned. Yes, he was the man who knew how to deliver.

"Ohmigosh." A rapturous smile spread across her face. "This is so awesome."

"One of a kind, sweetheart. Just like you. But a couple of the girls down at Steele Street—"

"The place in Denver," she clarified.

"Yes. They liked your necklace so much, they'd like to have a couple more made. I told them I would check with you. What do you think? Would you mind if Skeeter and Red Dog had necklaces like yours?"

Her eyes widened a little. "I think any woman with enough guts to wear missiles on a chain around her neck ought to have exactly what she wants. And Skeeter? Red Dog? Cripes, babe, do names even get cooler than that?"

"They're cool, all right. Cool like you." He reached over and took the necklace out of her hand and clasped it around her neck. "Maybe you'll get to meet them someday."

"I'd like that." She looked down and ran the tips of her fingers over the three charms.

"Yeah, I think you would." He leaned in closer and kissed her cheek, and her forehead, and the tip of her nose. "Can we go back to bed, now. Dawn is long gone, thank God, and the fish won't start biting again until noon."

"But, sweetie-pie, it's a gorgeous day out here. What in the world are we going to do in bed?"

His grin broadened. Right, he thought. Like that was a mystery.

In answer, he scooped her up into his arms and started back up the dock. "Oh, I'm guessing we'll figure something out."

She laughed and leaned in close to whisper in his ear. "You know I love you, Flipper."

Yeah, he knew, and my, oh, my, wasn't it really just a damn fine day.

WRAPPED AND SEALed

Leslie Kelly

Chapter One

Tanner Boudreau wasn't intimidated by much.

He'd endured the seven months of grueling torment that the U.S. Navy called BUD/S training, capped off by a hell week to rival Dante's. He'd swum waters frigid enough to stop a man's heart. He'd seen battle. He'd leapt out of planes and dangled from helicopters and crawled through caves as dark as a demon's soul. And while all of those experiences could—and had—caused a twinge of anxiety here or a moment of concern there, none had ever really scared him.

But this? This intimidated the hell out of him. "Gram, I just don't—"

"Oh, Tanner, it would mean so much to me," his elderly grandmother said, casting him one of those melting, *I'm-just-a-weak-old-lady* looks. "I'll be so disappointed if you say no."

And that was it. He was done for. Because she'd dragged out the "d" word.

Disappointing this kind, loving old woman, who, along with Gramps, had raised him and his sister after their parents had died, was the one thing Tanner truly couldn't handle. He could face physical danger, discomfort and even the threat of his own death, but he could not deal with causing his grandparents a moment of grief or sadness. He'd already put them through enough when he'd decided, on September 12, 2001, to enlist in the Navy, with the intention of becoming a SEAL. And God knows they'd had a lot of scary moments since. Fortunately, that would soon change. When he gave them the gift of his news on Christmas morning, and they realized he would soon be home for good, their worries and fears would be lifted.

"It would just be for an hour?" he asked, stalling. "I do have stuff to do."

Nearby, someone snickered. He shot a glare at his kid sister, Marie, who sat in a chair in the corner, busily sewing. She obviously saw right through him, knowing he'd never been able to refuse his grandmother any reasonable request. And while this one was stretching that word—reasonable—to its utter Webster limits, he knew he couldn't now.

"Yeah, Gram, you know how busy Tanner's been this week with his mysterious nights out," Marie said. "I bet some random bimbo is already kindling her Yule log for tomorrow night."

He could have retorted that his "mysterious" nights out hadn't had anything to do with a random women—just his search for a very specific one, whose last name he didn't even know. But he didn't want to go there, not with these two, already so in his business they might as well live in his back pocket. Besides, what could he say? That he was literally haunted by someone he'd met years ago, someone with whom he'd shared coffee and grief on a violent night filled with pain, blood and loss? That he had been scouring hospitals in the area, knowing she'd said she was from this area, too? That every time he closed his eyes, he could still see her beautiful smile, even though the last time he'd seen her she'd been wrists-deep in a wounded man's guts, looking so exhausted but also utterly determined to save his life?

That he'd never forgotten her—and he never would?

No. He wasn't about to share any of those things. Because sometimes he wondered if that woman—*Jessica, her name was Jessica*—was even real, or if he'd conjured her up on a night when he'd needed to feel warm and sane and normal.

"An hour will be fine, dear. So will you do it?" Gram said.

He stalled, not meeting her eye, looking around the room for inspiration. As his gaze skimmed over his sister, something drew his attention. It finally registered that the fabric Marie was torturing with the needle was red and fluffy.

The truth hit him. She was making his costume. She had been, since before he'd walked into his grandparents' house. "I never had any choice in this, did I."

"Well, of course you did. If you refuse, I will find another way." His grandmother shook her head sadly, then pulled out the first nail and hammered it into his coffin. "Of course, it might mean your grandfather has to do it, and with his heart—"

His grandfather's recent heart attack was one reason Ty had pulled every string he could to get this holiday leave.

"Or," she added, hammering nail number two, "I could spend *all* the entertainment budget on hiring the one professional not already busy, meaning I'd have to cancel the Glenn Miller tribute band from the New Year's Eve party. Of course, the seniors do so love to dance and the news would probably be enough to ruin Christmas."

That was so below the belt.

"Or maybe we should just cancel both events, it's getting so complicated."

Nail three. "I'll do it, I'll do it," he snapped.

Marie, laughing loudly now, pulled out a big bag of fluffy, white pillow stuffing.

He groaned. "Please tell me that's not for me."

"You have to have a big belly—Santa."

Santa. Freaking Santa Claus. He could not believe he was gonna dress up as the fat guy in red and play the part of the jolly old elf at an assisted living facility's Christmas party.

"Thank you so much dear," Gram said. "The residents of Rolling Hills would have been heartbroken if anything ruined their holiday party. For some, it's the only day of the year they get to see their families. Some people don't even make the effort to visit more often than that."

His heart twisting, he bit back any further commentary. Just the thought of his own grandparents ending up feeling so neglected made him queasy. It was enough that his seventy-eight year old grandmother devoted so much of her time volunteering in the place.

Besides, it wasn't that much to ask, one hour in a silly costume to make a lot of people happy. But this sure wasn't how he'd pictured his first Christmas at home in so many years. Honestly, he hadn't experienced a real Christmas in so long, he didn't know what he'd been picturing. Eggnog, carols, presents?

Well, it appeared *he* was the present, being wrapped with a bow and gifted by the bossy—lovable—women of his family. And, for the first time in a decade, Tanner was unable to think of one single thing he could do to save himself from his fate.

"So, little girl, what do *you* want for Christmas? Why don't you sit on Santa's lap and tell him all about it?"

The comment was accompanied by a leer, but Jessica D'Angelo wasn't exactly excited by the flirtation. Because the man doing the flirting was grey-haired, denture-wearing, and married. Considering the pathetic state of her love life, she might soon have to stop being so picky, and shorten her list of requirements in a man. But "married" would be a total non-starter no matter what. Dentures were pretty much a deal-breaker, too.

"Now, Mr. Shaughnessy, remember what happened the last time your wife got jealous of your flirting? She exchanged your denture cream for hemorrhoidal ointment."

The eighty-four year old frowned deeply, his bushy brows veeing over his eyes. "I wasn't talking about *my* lap," he said. "Santa Claus is right over there, and from what I hear, he's a young fella. You oughta go climb aboard, Doc. If anybody needs a little romance in her life, it's you."

She didn't need romance. Sure, it might be nice to have some, but needing and wanting were two different things. Besides, she was too busy to meet any eligible men. Her patients were elderly veterans and their spouses or widows, and since coming to work here, taking over as in-house physician at the assisted-living community, which also had an intensive nursing wing, she'd had no time for socializing. And she certainly wouldn't look for some by "climbing aboard" the lap of some random Santa.

That said, though, she had to concede, having caught a glimpse of him earlier, that the Santa in question did look extremely nice from behind. If his red coat had been checked with white, he might have been mistaken for a table in an Italian restaurant—his shoulders were *that* broad.

"Forget it," she said, as much to herself as to Mr. Shaughnessy.

"Scared, huh?"

"Of course not."

"I dare ya."

"Not even if you triple-dog it."

"Come on, it'll make everybody laugh." The elderly man gestured toward the few seniors sitting alone. Those whose families hadn't come. Those who quietly watched other residents share special moments with their grandchildren.

Those who looked so damned sad they made her heart ache in her chest.

"They all love you, and it would give them a smile," he added, all humor gone now. "I think a few folks could use some cheering up with all this partying going on."

He was right, as crazy as it sounded.

Jess wanted to make her lonely patients smile. Wanted to do so much for them, to brighten their days. And heck, considering they all had, at one time or another, commented on the fact that she was an all-work-and-no-play kind of "gal," she knew they'd get a kick out of seeing her being a little silly.

This is crazy, a voice whispered in her head. But she ignored it, edging closer to Santa and his throne. All the kids had had their turns, and a few nurses, too—obviously she wasn't the only one who'd noticed the build under the costume. Right now, he sat alone, posture straight, his hands griping the armrests of his chair, his lap totally empty.

Still, she couldn't make her feet go further.

"Chicken!" Mr. Shaughnessy whispered.

She shot him a glare. Then, looking around and seeing so many of those sad, lonely expressions on the faces of her patients, Jess went ahead and made a fool of herself.

She walked over and plopped right down on Santa's knee.

Chapter Two

Tanner let out a little oomph, surprised when an adult crash-landed on him without warning. He hadn't even spotted her coming, which said a lot about how ridiculous he felt. Because in his line of work, letting somebody sneak up on you was a big no-no.

"Ho, ho, ho," he remembered to say, casting another quick glance at the clock on the wall. It had been nearly two hours since he'd arrived, well over his agreed-upon sixty minutes. But every time he moved to stand up, another munchkin showed up with a wish list as long as his arm.

"Check out the doc!" someone called.

A voice whooped and another person whistled, which was enough to get him curious. He stared at his lap's new occupant. Looking at a cloud of thick, dark hair pulled back at the nape, as well as the pretty profile—high cheekbones, pert nose, lush lips—he felt a tingle of recognition. When she turned her face toward him, Tanner finally saw her springtime green eyes, flecked with gold. Wide, luminous eyes. Beautiful eyes.

Eyes he knew.

His breath left him. "You!"

"Sorry to ambush you," she whispered, "I'm just trying to give some of them a laugh."

She might have given the seniors a laugh, but all she'd given him was one hell of a shock. Because it was her, Jessica. His mystery woman. The one he hadn't even been sure existed.

"Tell 'im what you want, Doc!" someone called.

"She needs a man, that's what she needs!" a woman called.

She stiffened, and Tanner reflexively slid his arms around her waist, afraid she was going to regret her impulse and shoot to her feet. "Stay," he ordered, his voice low, for her ears only.

She looked down at him, those eyes widening, a hint of pink appearing in her cheeks. As their stares met and locked, her lovely lips parted and she sucked an audible breath through them. Finally she murmured, "Do I know you?"

He nodded once. "How ya doin' Doc?"

"How—who—"

He reached for his fluffy white beard, then, at the last second, remembered he couldn't just yank it off and give her a good look at his face. He'd probably scar for life some kid who still totally bought the whole Santa thing.

"We met a long time ago," he admitted, wondering if she heard the rawness in his voice.

She shifted a little more, which, considering the crowd of seniors and children all around them, shouldn't have elicited the hot, instantaneous reaction, but still did. He felt the heat of her ass against his thigh, the way her calves dangled between his. Hell, even the warmth of her breath on his brow as she leaned closer to look at him was a total turn-on.

She smelled like cinnamon. It wasn't because of the holiday cookies or the eggnog. That was one thing he'd always remembered about his mystery woman—the cinnamon-tinged perfume she'd been wearing that night. The way that scent had filled his head when he'd done the unthinkable and kissed her—a perfect stranger—before walking out of her life forever.

Well, not forever. Just until now.

Suddenly, she gasped. Against all odds—against time and space, considering they'd met in another world, far removed from this small California town—she had recognized him by nothing more than his voice and his eyes.

"Yemen. 2008," she whispered.

He nodded.

"You brought in that village boy; he'd broken his leg."

"Yeah. After you patched him up, I bought you a cup of coffee."

"The coffee was free, Lieutenant Boudreau," she said with a wry smile.

"It was the thought that counted—Jessica."

She hesitated, her lashes lowering over her eyes. "You kissed me."

"You kissed me back."

Oh, yeah, she had definitely kissed him back. It had been crazy, one of the most impulsive things he'd ever done—leaning over, sinking his hands into the thick, dark hair of a beautiful stranger, and tugging her against him. Their mouths had met and opened easily, hungrily. They'd been oblivious to time and place—at least until reality had come back with one hell of a bang.

They were silent for a moment, remembering. Wondering. Asking a million questions and answering them, without ever saying a word. *Where have you been? Why do you remember this? Did it mean as much to you as it did to me?*

Finally, she sighed. "And then the world blew up."

"It sure did."

That one cup of coffee, the brief conversation, the shared laughter, and oh, God, that kiss, had inspired memories and dreams in Tanner ever since. He'd wondered, many times, what might have happened had the Doctors Without Borders clinic not been overrun by wounded villagers fleeing the kind of massacre that would give a grown man nightmares. Whether they'd have had time to learn more about each other. To at least exchange their full names.

But the moment had passed. Blood and violence had landed on them both like a truck-load of cement. He'd raced to get back to his unit, she had begun saving lives. Their paths had firmly diverged.

Now they'd come back together again. As if they'd always been meant to. As if the search he'd been conducting since arriving home on leave—the needle of the name Jessica in the haystack called the southern California medical industry—had been rewarded.

She was here, the woman he'd never forgotten, sitting right on his lap, as if deposited there, the one gift he'd been waiting years to receive.

Torn between wanting to sink deeper onto this man's lap and wrap her arms around his neck, and wanting to leap up and hurry out of the social hall before she made even more of a fool of herself, Jess chose a third option: *Play it cool.*

Easier said than done, considering she'd already been decidedly uncool. How hard would it have been to pretend it had taken her longer than twenty-point-four seconds to recognize him? Maybe then he wouldn't suspect she'd spent a lot of hours over the past three-and-a-half years thinking about him. *Thinking. Wishing. Wondering.*

Only one thing kept her glued in place—it had taken even less time for him to recognize her. So maybe he'd been doing some thinking, wishing, wondering, too.

Which seemed ridiculous. This big, incredibly powerful,

intimidating-looking military man could probably have any woman he wanted. Not just because he was so damned gorgeous, with those chocolate brown eyes that crinkled at the corners, that dark brown hair, the flash of dimple in his cheek when he laughed—but because, at least from the little she knew of him, he was funny, generous, honorable, and, strange as it had seemed at the time, even gentle. Would any other bad-ass Navy SEAL have taken time out to pick up a village kid and bring him to the local clinic, carrying him in his arms and shouting for help because the boy had broken his leg?

Not many. But this one had.

Something compelled her to admit, "I've looked for you."

"Ditto."

That voice. So deep and smooth. It had filled her dreams for a long time.

She nibbled her bottom lip. "I actually Facebook stalked you, even though I only ever knew your last name."

"My first name's Tanner," he said.

Tanner. A nice name. Sexy and masculine. Like him.

"And I'm not on Facebook. I wish I'd thought to do that, though. I've been staking out VA hospitals all week, hoping to spot you."

Her brow shot up. "Seriously?"

"Yeah. This is the first time I've been home in a few years. Thought you might have come back to SoCal too—you said you probably would when your volunteer tour was up, and that you wanted to work with veterans." He looked around the crowded room. "I guess you still are."

"Just from earlier wars," she said, seeing her patients as he must see them—bent with age, arthritic, white-haired, but still so proud, still wearing that invisible badge of honor that said they'd served their country and would do it again in a heartbeat. Then, wondering what had brought him back, and whether he was here for good, she asked, "What about you? Have you been discharged? What do you do now?

He shook his head. "Still in the service. I'm just home on leave, visiting family. I leave again the morning after Christmas."

Disappointment stabbed her. Two more days, and then he'd be gone again. Out of her life almost as quickly as he'd entered and exited it the last time. Were they destined to cross paths, then move in different directions, never having a chance to see what these sparks, this instant connection between them, meant? Had she found the man of her dreams again, only to watch him march back into battle?

Man of your dreams? Who are you kidding?!

Considering all she'd seen during her years overseas—the wars, the violence, the blood—the man of her dreams *should* be a quiet college professor who spouted poetry and wouldn't lift a flyswatter against an insect. Not a guy like this. Not a guy who lived for the thrill, who put his neck out every single day. Jess had known enough about the military to have recognized that he was a SEAL. There weren't many jobs more dangerous than that one. He'd probably take fewer risks wrestling alligators for a living.

She was thirty-four years old, professionally established, with a great job and a home, and should be thinking only of finding someone stable—someone who didn't get shot at for a living—to share that life with.

But she had to admit it: He was the *only* man she'd wanted for a very long time.

"I wanna see Santa!" a child's voice screeched. A little boy with chocolate-smeared cheeks, whose diaper-lumpy pants looked suspiciously damp, was frowning at them.

"I should let you get back to work," she said, pulling away from him. Even though she'd spent the past minute telling herself why he was all wrong for her, she immediately found herself missing the warmth of his body, the strength of his arms around her waist.

He hesitated for a moment, then let her go. "What time do you get off?"

"I'm here all night tonight," she admitted. "Why?"

"Wanna meet me in the cafeteria after I'm finished?" Beneath the beard, she saw one corner of his mouth lift in a half-smile. "I'll buy you a cup of coffee."

She couldn't contain a laugh. "I'm on staff. The coffee's free."

"Then you buy *me* a cup of coffee."

She shouldn't. Heaven knew she shouldn't. But even as a refusal formed on her lips... she knew she would. "Okay, Lieutenant Boudreau. Coffee is on me."

Chapter Three

It started as just coffee. Small-talk. Light laughter.

Then it turned into dinner. Cafeteria-food dinner, but dinner nonetheless.

Then dessert. More coffee. More talking between her rounds and her check-ins with the staff. At one point they'd ended up in the lounge watching *It's A Wonderful Life* with one of the residents, an old man she'd called Mr. Preston, who apparently suffered from severe insomnia. Even the taciturn Mr. Preston liked playing matchmaker for his beloved "Doc," because he slipped a sprig of mistletoe in the buttonhole of Jess's pristine white coat.

Hadn't *that* led to some interesting thoughts. Not just about kissing her mouth, but about kissing her everywhere beneath that mistletoe.

He had it bad for her. Was attracted to her the way he had never been attracted to another woman. Maybe it was because of unsatisfied desire from their first meeting, but he didn't think so. He suspected he could make love to Jess every night for the rest of his life and still want her the next day.

Love at first sight? Who knew? He wasn't willing to label it. He just knew he wanted her, in his bed, and out of it. For as long as he could have her.

"I can't believe you've stayed here all evening," she said as the two of them sat in her office, waiting for Christmas Eve to become Christmas Day.

It was nearly midnight, and Tanner would need to get back to his grandparents' place soon. They'd be in bed, but he wanted to be sure he was there on Christmas morning.

"It's the excellent coffee," he said with a shrug.

She grimaced.

"Okay, scratch that."

"Well, I know it's not the food."

"I dunno, that gelatin surprise stuff was pretty unforgettable."

"Maybe as compared to MRE's."

He shuddered. Meals-ready-to-eat were one thing he would be very happy to leave behind when he left the military. There was only so much freeze-dried shit-on-a-shingle one person should have to eat in a lifetime. "Believe me, I've been getting as much home-cooking as I can stand. I think my grandmother wants to fatten me up to fit in that red suit."

She glanced at him, her stare sliding from his jaw, down his neck, over his T-shirt covered shoulders and chest. Her bottom lip disappeared between her teeth, and he knew, watching her nibble that pretty lip, what she was thinking.

The heat went up a few degrees. It had been going up from the minute she'd sat on his lip, until he'd shucked off the costume and joined her in the cafeteria earlier tonight, and every hour since. She was as physically aware of him as he was of her.

He didn't know what else was going to happen tonight, given how little of it was left. But he'd sooner lose his shooting hand than walk out of here without kissing her one more time.

"Besides, who says I was sticking around just for you? I finally got to see the end *of It's A Wonderful Life*. Mr. Preston was pretty shocked that I'd never seen the whole thing."

"He's a lovely man," she said. "Always a little sad. I'm glad you spent some time with him."

"Doesn't he have any family?"

"None that come to visit. Apparently he never married—he was badly affected by the war."

Tanner made an immediate assumption. "World War II?"

"Yes. He was in your line of work."

A sailor? No wonder he and the older man had shared an instant affinity. Perhaps deep down they'd just recognized a brother.

"Apparently he survived some awful battle, and it affected him. He was on a ship called, um, the Indianapolis."

Stunned, immediately understanding the ramifications—and thinking of the sad, lonely life Mr. Preston had lived after what had been one of the greatest Navy tragedies of all time, he could only swallow hard and murmur, "Wow."

"You've heard of it?"

"Of course. Every American should have," he replied. Because every person alive owed a debt to that generation. What they'd fought for, lived for, died for, had changed the world. And the men on the Indianapolis had paid an especially brutal price for their country.

"I've been meaning to research it," she admitted.

"Seen the movie Jaws?" he asked her, knowing that would be the quickest pop culture frame of reference.

She nodded slowly. "Yes, but not for a long time."

"Watch it again and you'll understand."

"I will," she promised. "You military men have a real bond, don't you?"

"An unbreakable one."

She didn't speak for a moment. Then, as if wanting to change the subject, to stop thinking of dark things on this night that had been only about talking and laughter and holiday cheer, she smiled brightly. "I still can't believe you're Miss Marge's grandson."

"And I still can't believe you're the pretty lady-doc she always talks about."

They'd talked earlier in the evening about his family. About how his parents had died and his mother's parents had raised him and his sister. He hadn't tried to hide his feelings for them—his gratitude, his love, his loyalty. There was no game-playing between them, no holding-back-the-cards. It was as if they both knew they had a very short time and didn't want to waste it.

She'd been just as open when talking about her less-than-happy childhood, her wealthy, neglectful parents, who'd been so critical when she'd "wasted" so much time helping the poor in other countries when she could be pulling down big bucks back home. That had sounded so ridiculous to him—as if she'd ever value money over helping other people.

How funny that they'd know her all her life, yet he already knew her better.

The clock continued to tick, growing loud as silence again descended between them. As if they both knew he'd be walking out the door in a few minutes, and didn't quite know what to say to each other now.

In the end, they said nothing. Instead, he rose from his chair, walked over to hers, took her hand and tugged her up. Her eyes widened in curiosity, but he didn't explain, didn't ask permission. He simply did what he'd been wanting to do for hours. For *years*.

He slid his fingers into her hair, cupped her head, tugged her to him and caught her mouth in a hot, open-mouthed kiss.

She fell against his body, wrapping her arms around his neck. Her soft curves surrendered to his hard angles; they just fit, from neck to knee. She tasted as sweet as he'd remembered, but there was no shock, no shyness this time. They both dove into the kiss, their tongues dancing, tangling in a hot exploration that acknowledged that this was the wrong time and the wrong place, but was absolutely the right thing to do.

Within moments, she was turning to lean against her desk, one of her legs twining around his. Their desire was a thick, tangible thing and for a few long, pleasurable minutes, Tanner let himself be carried away by it. By the feel of her soft curves, her spicy smell, the heat rising and swirling and filling the room.

Finally, though, a voice in the corridor reminded him where they were. He ended the kiss—regretfully—and stepped back. Drawing in a few deep, ragged breaths, he watched her do the same, straightening her clothes, smoothing her hair.

She shook her head hard, as if angry at herself. "That was a bad idea."

He merely smiled.

"I mean it. This isn't what I want."

He stared at her swollen, parted lips, then dropped his attention to her still-quivering body, the puckered nipples thrusting against her blouse, the way her legs had grown so weak she still had to lean against the desk.

"Yeah. Right."

"I mean, I don't *want* to want this."

Her serious tone began to dig through the lust-haze in his brain. "Care to explain?"

She paused, then, to his surprise, said, "I wish you weren't in the Navy."

His jaw dropped. "What?"

"I hate that you're going back to active duty so soon."

He opened his mouth to tell her wouldn't be gone long, to share with her the news he would be sharing with his grandparents in the morning—that he'd accepted an offer to teach new recruits at the Coronado training facility. That he was coming home for good.

Before he could say anything, she went on, her voice gaining a hint of bitterness. "I honestly don't know how you career guys do it. Stay sane while you're surrounded with all that. I worked in a war zone for a year and still have nightmares that wake me up screaming."

"Look, Jess—"

"I guess what I'm trying to say is, this has been a wonderful night. One I'm never going to forget. But I really don't want to go down this road with you."

"What road?"

"The bloody, always-in-danger, might-never-come-back road," she admitted with a frown. "I would rather never have this than get a tiny taste of it and then lose it forever."

This. Them. Him.

He took a step back. Thoughts whirled in his brain. He wanted to tell her the truth—that he'd be back soon, that the risk would be nearly nonexistent once he was an instructor. That he'd be serving the rest of his active duty here in California and would probably be out for good within five years.

But there were still those four months to go. Four months more of being on the front line, where, he knew from experience, life didn't have much value. The past few months had not been kind to SEALs in Afghanistan—which was where he was going.

So maybe it would be kinder to let it go. Let her have her way. And God willing, when he got back next spring, find her ready to pick up where they'd left off.

"Okay," he told her with a brief nod. "I understand. It was great seeing you again."

Her jaw fell open, as if she hadn't really expected to get what she'd asked for. Tanner hesitated, waiting for her to change her mind. But she remained silent.

Finally, with one shaky smile, he said, "Merry Christmas, Jess." Then he turned and left her office without another word.

But he didn't leave the building right away. He had a stop to make first—in the lounge area. After he'd made it, exchanging a few words with the person he'd been seeking, he left the building.

It was five after twelve when he got into his rental car. Christmas: the day he'd been looking forward to sharing with his family for a long time. But right now, all he could think about was how much he wanted to get back on duty and claw through these last four months.

So maybe the life he'd secretly been hoping for could really begin.

Jess stayed in her office after Tanner left, evaluating what had been one of the strangest days of her life. She couldn't remember another one when she'd ridden such a roller coast of emotions, from shock, to near euphoria, to utter desire, to despair. All caused by presence of the same man. The man she'd just, basically, kicked out of her life.

"You are an idiot," she told herself, having reached that conclusion in ten minutes. Because, really, what kind of fool gave up the chance at something wonderful because she was too afraid of something bad that might come afterward?

Jess had never been a coward, but she'd sure acted like one tonight.

Still angry with herself about it, she went back out to prowl the corridors. As she passed the recreation room, she saw Mr. Preston, still sitting quietly in his chair, a blanket over his knees.

"Are you okay?" she asked.

"Fine thanks. Just gonna sit here a little longer, then I'll head up."

She sat beside him, sharing the silence.

"That friend of yours is a good sort," he finally said. "Nice of him to stop in and say goodbye before going home to his folks."

"He did?"

"Ayuh."

"What did he say?"

The old man never turned his head to look at her, but the faintest of smiles touched his lips and he sat up a bit straighter in his chair. "He shook my hand and said, 'Thank you for your service.' Then he saluted me and left."

Jess felt tears prick her eyes, seeing how very much the gesture had touched this proud, quiet old man. Tanner hadn't been happy when he'd left here, she knew that, yet he'd taken the time to reach out a hand in friendship and brotherhood to this complete stranger.

What a good man. What an amazingly wonderful man.

She'd found him twice in her life. Once she'd lost him due to fate and war and bad timing. This time, she'd let him slip right through her fingers.

That was a mistake she could rectify. It wasn't too late. She wouldn't let it be.

Unfortunately, she couldn't go after him now—she was on duty until six a.m. So she had to spend the night thinking about what she'd said, how he'd taken it, and what to do next. The hours stretched out interminably. She felt like a kid who couldn't sleep Christmas Eve because of the nervous anticipation about the morning to come. She only hoped she hadn't messed things up so badly that she wouldn't have the happy Christmas morning she was hoping for.

As soon as her shift was over, Jess went home. She had looked up Tanner's grandparents' home address before leaving the center, Miss Margie was a very popular volunteer and the info hadn't been hard to track down. But Jess would never have barged in on their Christmas morning. She didn't have anywhere else go to, considering her parents were, as usual, spending the holidays in the Caribbean, so she spent most of Christmas morning sleeping.

By noon, she couldn't wait any longer. Hoping she wasn't making a big mistake, she drove to the house, went to the door and rang the bell.

Miss Margie answered. "Why, Doctor D'Angelo, what are you doing here?"

"Merry Christmas," she said, trying to smile though her heart threatened to beat out of her chest. "I'd like to talk to Tanner for a few minutes, and I know he's leaving tomorrow."

"Come in, come in!"

She entered the house, immediately smelling the delightful aromas of baking turkey, pine and gingery spices. Tanner must have heard her voice, because he walked out of the nearby living room, his eyes wide, his mouth hanging open. "Jess?"

"Hi. I was wondering if we could talk?"

"If you'll excuse me," his grandmother said, "I have to check on dinner. You will stay, won't you, Doc?"

Jess looked at Tanner, then at Margie. "Can I wait and answer that after Tanner and I talk?"

"Of course," the older woman said.

Once they were alone, Tanner grabbed her hand and tugged her outside, onto the front porch. As if suddenly realizing she might not be here with good news, he asked, "Is everything okay?"

"It's fine. I've been thinking about what I said to you before you left last night."

He held up a hand, waving off her apology. "Don't worry about it, I really do understand."

She grabbed that hand, twining her fingers through his. "I was being stupid. Believe me, Lieutenant Boudreau, I am not a coward."

"I never thought you were," he said, lifting his hand to her face and brushing his fingertips against her skin.

She curled her cheek into his palm, noting, of course, his strength, but also the innate tenderness she'd seen in him from their very first meeting all those years ago. "I couldn't let you leave again, not so soon, not without taking advantage of the little time you have here. And not without letting you know that I care—very much—about when you're coming back." Taking a deep breath for courage, hoping she hadn't misread his feelings, that hers weren't one-sided, she added, "I'll be here waiting for you, if you want me to. I don't care how long it takes."

He smiled, then actually started to laugh.

She moved her lips to his rough palm. "What's so funny?"

"Oh, Doc. I've been waiting for you for more than three years."

She edged closer to him, loving the way his hands fit so perfectly in the indentation of her hips. He drew her close, staring down at her, those gentle brown eyes gleaming with emotion.

"Now come inside and you can be there when I share the news with my family, because the wait isn't going to be nearly as long as you think."

He wouldn't say more. Intrigued by the cryptic tone and the sexy smile, she couldn't wait to hear the rest. But first, she just needed to taste him. Feel his heart beating against her chest, share his warm breath, taste his tender mouth.

They melted together in a kiss as natural and easy as if they'd been long-time lovers. As if they'd always been meant to be together.

And somehow, though the future was still uncertain and she didn't know how long her wait might be, she suspected that someday they would.

Epilogue

NOTICE:

To all residents of Rolling Acres—Remember, this year's Christmas party will double as a wedding shower for our own "Doc" Jessica D'Angelo. Help us celebrate Doc's upcoming marriage to Miss Margie's grandson Tanner "Santa" Boudreau by bringing shower/housewarming gifts in lieu of holiday goodies.

And don't forget: The wedding will take place on New Year's Eve, right here in the common room and all are invited!

WORTH THE RISK

Elle Kennedy

Chapter One

Skylark Springs hadn't changed one damn bit. Still the same quaint little place, with its quaint houses and quaint shops and—well, quaint was the magic word when it came to Jason Anders's hometown. Somehow he'd thought it might be different, that coming home after all this time would fill him with a sense of peace and belonging. But no such luck. The moment he drove past the bright red sign welcoming him home, the claustrophobia set in.

Drawing in a breath, he eased on the gas pedal and did his best not to focus on the scenery or the curious eyes that landed on his shiny, cobalt-blue pickup truck as it ventured through town. Folks around here didn't like flashy cars. Not that his pickup was flashy by any means, but it was clearly brand-new, an impulse buy he hadn't been able to resist. No point in letting his recent inheritance sit in the bank collecting dust and interest.

As he drove down Main Street, he almost expected tomatoes to be thrown at his windshield. Either that, or a parade to welcome him. He suspected the people of Skylark Springs were torn between being proud to have a real-life hometown hero, or furious that said hero hadn't bothered attending the funeral of their *other* hero. He supposed it depended on which Anders they deemed more heroic—Jason or his late father.

But alas, no tomatoes *or* parade. Apparently the townsfolk didn't care about him one way or the other, and that was fine by him. There was only one person whose opinion he was interested in—and if any produce was going to be hurled, he knew it would be by the hand of Callie Carraway.

Unless she'd purchased a gun in these last four years.

Which was kind of a frightening thought.

He was uncharacteristically nervous as he neared Odds N' Ends, the corner shop that Callie's aunt owned and where Callie had been working since she was a teenager. It was one of those cheesy tourist stores, its merchandise consisting of postcards and crafts and pointless knickknacks people ended up throwing out years later, when they realized Skylark Springs wasn't worth remembering. It didn't even occur to him that Callie wouldn't be working at the store anymore. She'd gotten nice and comfortable in her rut years ago, and couldn't be convinced to step out of her comfort zone.

God knows he'd tried.

And now here he was, hoping to try again. Hoping that maybe this time she could be persuaded.

Good news was—she wasn't married. Call him a loser, but he'd checked out her Facebook page. Yep, he'd resorted to social networking to stalk the love of his life. Her status had been listed as single, which was a good sign, and she also hadn't unfriended him— another good sign. Unless he was so inconsequential to her that it hadn't even crossed her mind to unfriend him. In that case, a bad omen.

Quit overanalyzing.

With a slow exhale, he parked the pickup in front of the shop and hopped out, suddenly wishing he'd worn something more presentable. Like his Navy dress whites or something. Faded blue jeans with a hole in the knee might not bode well for him. Neither would his threadbare Metallica shirt. But those were his only clean clothes. He hadn't exactly stopped at a laundromat after leaving the naval base.

Rubbing his suddenly damp palms against the front of his jeans, he said a silent prayer and strode into the store. The little bell over the door chimed, announcing his arrival, and a second later, he heard a familiar female voice.

"Hi there, can I help you with anything—*you.*"

He met Callie Carraway's gorgeous brown eyes. "Me," he said ruefully.

Silence.

Jason gulped as Callie slid off the stool behind the cash counter and made her way toward him, her strides slow and wary, as if she were approaching a rabid dog. His pulse took off in a mad sprint. She looked even better than he remembered, much sexier than the woman whose picture he still carried in his wallet. She was tall, with long, colt-like legs and a seriously spectacular chest, but her hair was longer now, sliding over one shoulder in chestnut waves. The Callie in his wallet wore cutoff denim shorts and a pink tank top, her features flawless and make-up-free. The Callie in front of him wore a yellow sundress that swirled around her bare knees, and shiny lip-gloss that made her mouth look lush and utterly kissable.

Of course, that mouth tightened in a thin line when she approached him. "You're back," she said.

"Thank you for stating the obvious." His lips twitched. "For a moment there, I thought I was still at the base."

Callie rolled her eyes. "Did the Navy finally kick you out? I figured they would sooner or later, once they got to know you."

"Funny. Did you write that one down so you could save it for this very moment?"

"I sure did." She slanted her head, and a lock of shiny hair fell onto her forehead. "Though I didn't think I'd ever get to use it." She frowned. "You didn't show up for the funeral."

His jaw tightened. "I was overseas."

Callie sighed. "You wouldn't have come even if you were in the country, and we both know it."

She was right. He and his dad hadn't even been on speaking terms when the old man died. The last contact they'd had was when his father sent that letter informing Jason he was updating his will. *I'm leaving it all to you, but only because I can't find a charity I like.* And he'd signed the letter *Lewis.* Not Dad, not even 'Your father, Lewis.' Which said a lot about their relationship.

"He wouldn't have wanted me to come," Jason finally said, his voice gruff. "I was a disappointment to him, remember?"

She waved a careless hand. "Well, he was an asshole, remember?"

He had to grin. "How dare you speak ill of the dead?"

"He was a tyrant, Jase. His being dead doesn't change that."

Jase. His heart warmed at the familiar nickname. Nobody but Callie had ever called him that. He was surprised to hear her say it, and equally surprised that she was siding with him on the issue of his dad. Everyone in town considered Lewis Anders to be some sort of saint. Only Jason and Callie had known the truth. And sure, maybe Jason should have made more of an effort to attend the damn funeral, but he hadn't been able to muster up the motivation. He had no desire to sit there listening to everyone sing his father's praises. Lewis Anders the town savior. The businessman who'd swooped in and brought jobs and money to Skylark Springs. The mayor who'd protected the town.

The man who'd beat the shit out of his son . . .

Choking down a lump of bitterness, Jason shoved his hands in his pockets. "Let's not talk about him."

There it was again, that shrewd tilt of her head. He'd seen the gesture so many times he knew exactly what was coming.

No-holds-barred sarcasm.

"Then should we talk about how you re-upped without telling me, left town without saying goodbye, and disappeared for four years?"

He felt his face go hot. "Callie . . . "

"Or I could tell you what I had for breakfast that day," she went on, an angry blush creeping into her cheeks. "You know, when I was waiting for you at the diner, when you didn't show up, and I had to find out from Eddie the barber that you left town?"

"Callie . . . "

"Oh, I know what I can tell you." She flashed him a stony smile. "Get lost."

He raised both eyebrows. "Are you serious?"

"Yep." Her smile widened. "Get lost, Jason. I don't know why you're back, and I don't particularly care."

"You won't even give me the chance to explain?" There was an edge to his voice. He valiantly tried to rein in his indignation, but as usual, Callie brought out his argumentative nature. It was the sarcasm. It always drove him nuts.

"You don't have to explain." She placed her hands on her hips. "I got the message loud and clear."

"And what message was that?" he said in a low voice.

"That being a SEAL meant more to you than being with me. That I meant so little to you that you couldn't even be bothered to say goodbye."

Jason shook his head. "That's bullshit, and you know it."

"All I know is that I've moved on with my life. And like I said, I don't know why you came home—"

"I came back for you," he blurted out.

She just stared at him. Then she laughed. "*Four* years later! Gee, that's so romantic."

He stared right back. "Can you just quit it with the sarcastic remarks and hear me out?"

"Sorry, can't. As you can see, I'm super busy. I don't have time to talk right now."

"The shop's empty," he grumbled.

She shrugged. "I have inventory to do in the back."

"Fine." He flashed her the little-boy grin that had always made her melt in the past. "Then we'll talk later."

"I'm busy later."

"Doing what?" he challenged.

"Having dinner. With my fiancé."

He faltered. For a second. "You're lying," he said with a laugh.

"Nope. I'm engaged."

"Where's the ring?"

"I don't believe in material displays of love and commitment."

"Fine. Who's the guy?"

"Oh, you don't know him."

Another laugh lodged in his chest. "What's his name?"

"Bob."

The laugh spilled out. "You're marrying a guy named Bob?"

"What, you've got something against that name?" Callie seemed to be fighting her own amusement, which told him he had her right where he wanted her. "Bob is a very distinguished name, you know. Think of all the Bobs who've done such great things. Bob Dylan, Bob Marley, Bob Barker, does Billy Bob Thorton count? He's got a Bob in there. Uh, Bobby Kennedy—"

"Okay, I get it," Jason cut in, doing his best not to show her just how entertained he was. "So now here's what's gonna happen, baby."

"Don't you dare call me ba—"

"I'm going to let you get back to this monstrous amount of work you claim to have," he continued as if she hadn't spoken. "And when you're done, you can decide if you want to have dinner with your fake Bob, or come to my motel like a mature adult so we can have a mature conversation. I'm staying at the Skylark Motel."

"Never heard of it."

He smothered a laugh. "You can Google it." His voice grew serious. "Look, I know you're pissed at me—I deserve it. But I'm only in town for one night, Callie. One night, and then you'll never have to see me again."

She didn't answer.

"At least give me the chance to explain before I go. You owe it to our history together to give me that chance."

Her delicate throat worked as she swallowed. "I'll have to talk it over with Bob."

An unwitting grin tugged at his mouth. "You know where to find me, Callie."

Without giving her the opportunity to get the last word in, he spun on his heel and dashed out of the shop. He didn't need to turn around to see the frown marring her mouth—he could feel it burning into his back.

But that was okay. He'd gotten what he'd wanted out of this visit. A chance to see Callie. A chance to make things right again.

And he knew she would show up tonight. There was no doubt in his mind.

Chapter Two

Why did men only get more attractive as they grew older? Jason was thirty years old—wasn't that the time when things started to go downhill? The beer gut and receding hairline and all that fun stuff? But no, not Jason the-hottest-body-ever Anders. He, of course, had to look even sexier than before.

Jerk.

Callie locked up the shop and set the alarm, then walked around the side of the building toward the small parking lot. She headed for her rust-covered Toyota hatchback and unlocked the driver's door. Sliding in, she started the engine, reached for the gearshift, and . . . hesitated.

One night.

Why was he only in town for one night? Why had he even come back? He'd said he was here for her, but she wasn't about to buy *that* one.

Her heart squeezed as she remembered that awful day. He'd *left*. Stood her up, hopped a bus to Little Creek. No kiss goodbye. No goodbye, period. He hadn't even called her once over the past four years. Oh, she'd gotten his packages—all jammed full of photographs he'd taken during his travels. Really good photographs, she grudgingly admitted to herself. But no surprise there. Jason had always been talented with a camera.

And now he was back. To explain apparently, but did she really want to hear what he had to say? They'd been dating since they were eighteen years old. She'd patiently waited while he'd served two tours in the Navy, while he'd joined the SEALs and risked his life every day for so long. Four years ago, he was supposed to be done. He was getting out, he'd told her. Ready to settle down and start a life with her.

But he left.

Just like that.

"Screw it," she mumbled to herself, putting the car in drive.

She wasn't going to fall under his spell again. Jason Anders was the most charming man she'd ever known. Smart, funny, incredibly attractive. He'd had it tough growing up—she'd witnessed that firsthand—but she'd thought he'd managed to come out of it even stronger. But then he'd bailed on her, and she'd spent the last four years picking up the pieces of her broken heart. Now that her heart was intact again, she refused to let Jason take another stab at it.

The sun had already set, and Main Street was bathed in the yellow glow from the lampposts lining the sidewalk. With the shops closed and the streets empty, the town was deserted. The sight normally brought her a sense of tranquility, but tonight it just annoyed her. Every day in Skylark Springs was the same as the one before. People woke up, went to work, went home, had dinner, went to bed, then did it all over again. A part of her had always envied Jason for managing to avoid the monotony of it all. God, she'd been tempted to leave this place too, so many times, but unlike Jason, she had responsibilities. A store to run, an aunt who depended on her, bills to pay.

Sighing, she halted at a stop sign, realizing she was nearing the turnoff that led to the Skylark Motel. Take a left, and she'd be at Jason's door. Take a right, and she'd be on the road to Aunt Susan's place, safe and sound in her little guesthouse on her aunt's property.

She kept driving, her foot hovering over the gas pedal as she neared the intersection. Left or right.

Did he even deserve the chance to explain?

Did she even want to hear what he had to say?

"Aw, shit!" she burst out.

At the very last second, she yanked on the wheel and turned left.

Jason answered the door in nothing but a towel.

Callie's mouth instantly turned into the Sahara Desert. Her eyes were assaulted by his sleek golden chest, the sculpted muscles and rippled abdomen, the dusting of dark hair arrowing down to his groin. There was a new scar on his upper arm, three-inches long, white and puckered. Her fingers tingled with the impulse to touch it. To touch him.

Swallowing hard, she tore her gaze from his spectacular chest and lifted it to his spectacular eyes. Ice blue, like a crisp, cool glacier moving languidly through the water. He was so damn gorgeous she wanted to hit him for it. Perfect classic features, a sensual mouth, dark stubble slashing across his defined jaw.

She'd never been attracted to anyone the way she was attracted to Jason. It was crazy and primal and confusing, and it irked that he still managed to evoke that same jolt of heat inside of her, even after all these years.

"Hey," he drawled, his eyes lighting up at the sight of her. "Bob gave you the okay to come, huh?"

At his slight smirk, her cheeks went hot. Okay, so maybe conjuring up a fake fiancé hadn't been her finest moment. But he'd caught her off guard, darn it. The last thing she'd expected when she'd gone to work today was a spontaneous reunion with Jason Anders.

"Bob doesn't exist," she said with a sigh.

"Shocker."

With a scowl, she brushed past him and entered the motel room. She glanced around, taking in the ugly patterned bedspread and splintered wood furniture, then the unzipped duffel bag sitting on the faded carpet.

"Why are you only in town for a night?" she asked, turning to face him.

He adjusted his towel, drawing her gaze to his trim hips. "I'm eager to get started."

She furrowed her brows. "Get started on what?"

"Life." With a shrug, he sank down on the edge of the bed. "I'm going to do some traveling. Start off here, driving across the country, and then I'll tackle the rest of the world."

"Sounds liberating," she said, an edge to her voice. "Aren't you going to put some clothes on?"

His lips twitched. "Nope." He cocked his head. "Why, is the sight of me in a towel getting you hot?"

Of course. He was trying to distract her with his potent masculinity.

Determined not to take the bait, she leaned against the tall cedar dresser next to the bed and crossed her arms. "So, let's hear it."

He faltered.

"Explain," she clarified. "Tell me why you left."

He was quiet for so long she didn't think he'd answer, but then he gulped a couple of times and met her gaze head-on. "I couldn't stay in this town a second longer."

Not even for me? she wanted to cry out, but swallowed the words.

"I tried, Cal," he went on, his voice husky. "After I came back from overseas, I tried to settle down here, and for a while, I thought I was actually happy. We were living in the guesthouse, I was taking pictures, trying to make a career of it, but this town . . . this town suffocates me."

She bit her lip. "You only gave it two months."

"That was enough. Enough to know I didn't want to be here. Faking smiles when people raved about how wonderful Lewis Anders was, those shitty dinners with my dad, where he pretended he hadn't hit me until I got big enough to defend myself. I couldn't do it anymore."

There was a raw, helpless chord in his voice. Callie steeled herself against it, trying not to sympathize, not to care. Lewis Anders had been a real piece of work. A nasty drunk with an even nastier tempter, a father who couldn't fathom why his son was more interested in photographs than business.

But Jason wasn't the only one who'd had a tough upbringing. Her own parents had died within days of each other—her mother from complications during childbirth, her dad in a car accident two days later. Her aunt was amazing, but after Susan had been diagnosed with multiple sclerosis, Callie had been forced to take on more and more responsibility. Susan had been wheelchair bound for the past five years, which meant Callie had to take on an even bigger burden in order to pay the mortgage and run the store.

"I know you think I ran away," Jason finished, his blue eyes flickering with regret. "But I didn't, Callie. I didn't run *from* something, I ran *to* something. I don't belong here. I never did."

A lump rose in her throat. "That doesn't explain why you didn't talk to me about it, why you didn't say goodbye."

"I tried to talk to you. I told you how much I wanted to get out of here. I even asked you to go with me." He sighed. "I loved you so damn much. Leaving you was the hardest thing I ever did, Cal. When you said you never wanted to leave Skylark, I panicked. I had to get out, so I reenlisted."

Callie's lips tightened. "I didn't say I never wanted to leave. I said I *couldn't* leave."

"Because of Susan."

"Yes, because of Susan. She needed me. She still does."

He shook his head. "No, she doesn't. And she was right there beside me, urging you to leave."

Callie battled a burst of aggravation. "Deep down she didn't want that, though."

"But she did. She feels so guilty that you're stuck here, taking care of her. She feels terrible that you're not pursuing your writing, that you're working at her store because she's too sick to do it."

She stubbornly shook her head. "I know you claim she told you that, but I don't believe it."

"Well, it's true."

Frustration rolled in her belly. God, she shouldn't have come here. What was the point in rehashing the past? Jason had made it clear how he felt about her when he'd skipped town four years ago. And now he was leaving again.

"I have to go," she murmured, edging toward the door.

He was on his feet before she could blink, and suddenly his hands were cupping her chin. "No," he said in a ragged voice. "Don't go, please."

She tried pushing his hands away, but he just tightened his grip, running his thumb over her cheek. "I just want you to understand that my leaving was never about you. I loved you, baby. I never stopped loving you. And I knew I couldn't call you, knew I couldn't stand listening to the pain in your voice if I did, so I sent you pictures. Every time I took a picture, I thought of you."

The lump in her throat thickened. "I got the pictures."

"You looked at them?"

"Yeah."

He stroked both of her cheeks. "Please. Just don't go. I'm here for one night. So stay. Just stay with me tonight, and let's pretend none of that shit in the past happened. Let's lose ourselves in each other."

It sounded tempting. So damn tempting. Her heart pounded like crazy from his mere proximity. Her thighs quivered, her breasts achy and sensitive. She'd loved this man since she was sixteen years old. He was her first love, her first lover. He'd been her everything.

She *wanted* to lose herself in him. She wanted to feel the naked emotion and raw desire that only Jason Anders could make her feel.

But she wanted to preserve her heart too.

"I can't," she whispered.

"Yes, you can."

Before she could protest, his mouth came down on hers. The kiss robbed her of breath and common sense, and just like that, the years and heartache melted away. His lips were warm, firm. His taste was spicy and familiar. And his tongue . . . his tongue slid into her mouth

SEAL of My Dreams

like it belonged there and teased her into oblivion.

Unable to stop herself, she twined her arms around his neck and got lost in the kiss. She'd never been much of a romantic, or a believer in soul mates, but as Jason's lips moved over hers, she couldn't deny that something powerful existed between them.

Breathing heavily, she wrenched her mouth away. "We shouldn't do this. There's no point. You're leaving again."

His eyes shone with passion and warmth. "You could come with me this time."

She gave a startled squeak, but he bent down again and swallowed the sound, kissing her so deeply she forgot all about the terrifying idea he'd just voiced. As her pulse drummed in her ears, Callie closed her eyes and kissed him back, knowing it was too late to stop the disastrous runaway train she'd just boarded.

Chapter Three

She was back in his arms again. A thrill shot up Jason's spine at the feel of Callie's curvy body pressed against his. Her lips were as warm and lush as he remembered, and just as addictive. He'd never stopped fantasizing about those lips. No matter where he was, no matter what he was doing, he'd thought about Callie. He'd brought her memory with him on every dangerous mission, every chopper ride, every trek through the jungle. And he'd been thinking of her when that bullet had ripped into his flesh, when he'd endured months of grueling physical therapy learning how to use his arm again.

It had always been Callie. And as her tongue eagerly swirled over his, he knew it would always *be* Callie.

"I'm still mad at you," she muttered against his mouth.

"I know," he muttered back, and then he kissed her again, while his hands drifted down her body to cup her firm ass.

Somehow they stumbled onto the bed. Somehow their clothes disappeared. Somehow a condom founds it way onto his thick, throbbing erection.

Callie gasped when he entered her, digging her nails into his back, hard enough to bring the sting of pain.

He didn't mind. Their lovemaking had always been frantic, out of control. A furious joining of bodies, a desperate joining of hearts. And then it would slow down, turn lazy and tender, as it did now. He thrust into her slowly, watching the haze of desire flood her big brown eyes. She wrapped her arms around him and yanked his head down for a kiss, slipping her tongue into his mouth as her hips lifted beneath him.

"I've missed you," he choked out, burying his head in the crook of her neck.

Her breath tickled his shoulder. "I've missed you too."

Those four words drove him wild, had him picking up the pace again, until they were both gasping and moaning in sheer abandon. When Callie cried out in pleasure and shuddered in release, Jason finally allowed himself to let go. His climax crashed into him, sending waves of pleasure to every inch of his body, making every nerve ending crackle. With a groan, he lost himself in the mind-blowing sensations.

He lost himself in Callie.

She got dressed in a hurry. She was rattled—he didn't need to be a genius to figure that one out. Sighing, Jason slid up into a sitting position, unconcerned with his nakedness. He watched as Callie slipped her feet into her sandals, as she smoothed out her tousled hair.

"Cal," he said softly.

She slowly met his eyes. "This was a mistake, Jase."

"It wasn't a mistake."

"You *left* me." Her voice cracked. "God, I'm the biggest loser on the planet, huh? You disappear, waltz back into town four years later, and what do I do? Hop into bed with you."

He let out a heavy breath. "You said you missed me."

"People say dumb things in the throes of passion."

"You meant it." He softened his tone. "And I meant what I said too. I want you to come with me."

Her agitation seemed to deepen, making her fidget with the hem of her sundress. "That's ridiculous."

"Why?" he shot back. "Why is it ridiculous?"

"Because I can't go with you," she sputtered. "Because I don't want to."

"Yes, you do." He shot her a knowing look. "You wanted it four years ago, too."

"But I couldn't then. And now, I don't want to, no matter what you think." She shook her head. "We're not together anymore, Jase. I might have slept with you right now, but that doesn't mean we're back together. It doesn't mean anything."

"It means everything," he corrected.

As determination hardened his jaw, he rose to his feet, striding naked toward her. He noticed her eyes rest on his crotch, on the erection that thickened the closer he got to her. She swallowed, then averted her gaze.

"This is it, baby. You and me." He captured her chin with two fingers and forced her to look at him. "We belong together. Always have, always will."

"Jase . . ."

"Remember how when we were teenagers, we'd talk about traveling the world together? You'd write, I'd take photographs. We'd roam the planet and go on adventures?"

She shot him a wry smile. "That's kid fantasy stuff."

"It's not a fantasy. It can be a reality." He took a breath. "If you leave Skylark with me tomorrow."

"I can't—"

"I paid off Susan's mortgage."

Callie gaped at him. "What?"

He dropped his hands from her face and rested them on his bare hips. "I paid your aunt's mortgage. The day my inheritance cleared at the bank. I bought Odds 'N Ends too. Well, the building it sits in."

Callie looked utterly stunned. "Are you serious? When the hell did you do this?"

"A couple of months ago."

"But Aunt Susan never said anything . . . "

"I asked her not to," he confessed. "I was planning on coming back to Skylark to tell you myself, but my physio took longer than I thought."

Her brown eyes rested on the scar marring his right arm. "Physio . . . you were hurt. Bad?"

"Pretty bad." Pain lined his throat. "I've got full use of the arm again, but I still get these spasms every now and then. Definitely can't hold a weapon without shaking. I was honorably discharged after I recovered."

She sounded genuinely regretful as she said, "Oh, Jase, I'm sorry."

"I'm not." He shrugged. "I told you, I reenlisted because I didn't think I had a better option. You didn't want to leave Skylark, and I didn't want to travel without you. I'm happy to be out, though. I think I'm getting too old to play hero."

She gave a faint smile. "You're never too old for that."

"Yes, I am. It's time for me to focus on other things. Photography. You." He hesitated. "If you'll let me."

"Will you . . . " Her voice cracked. "If I don't want to go, will you stay here?"

He knew she'd ask that. And as much as he wanted to tell her that he would, he couldn't bring himself to do it.

"I can't, Cal. And it's not just because of all the shitty memories I have of this place. I can't stay here with you because in my heart, I know that *you* don't belong here either." He locked his gaze with hers.

"You've been aching to leave this town since we were kids. You would've done it too, if Susan hadn't gotten sick after graduation. So no, I won't stay."

"But you want me to follow you." Bitterness tinged her voice.

"I want you to follow your dreams," he said gruffly. "I want you to write that book you've always talked about."

"I can write it here," she protested.

"Have you started it? Written a single word?"

Her silence was all the answer he needed.

"Come with me," Jason murmured. "Susan doesn't need you anymore. She's got her house, her store. When I spoke to her on the phone, she even admitted she's eager to go back to work. She's bored, sitting in that chair all day while you take care of everything."

"She said that?" Callie whispered.

"She did. So damn it, come with me."

Hesitation dug a crease into her forehead. "I . . . don't know if I can."

Jason stared at her in frustration.

"You can't just come back after four years and expect me to drop everything," she burst out. "Expect me to trust you again. You broke my heart, you insensitive ass."

Guilt prickled his skin. "I know. And I kick myself for it every day. I'll keep kicking myself until I finally earn your forgiveness."

She sighed. "Jase . . . "

"Go home, Cal," he said gruffly.

Her eyes widened. "What?"

"Go home. Talk to Susan. Sit on the porch swing and think about it." He suddenly realized he was still as naked as the day he was born, and quickly bent down to swipe his jeans off the floor. Slipping them on, he fixed her with a somber look. "I won't push you, okay? I won't pressure you to give up the life you have here and go on the road with me. But rain or shine, I'm leaving tomorrow, Cal. I'm going to live out the fantasy we always talked about. So go home, baby, and think about it. Really think about it."

She swallowed.

"Think about the life you wanted, the life you have." He reached out and tucked a strand of hair behind her ears. "Think about the life we can have together, if you just let yourself take that leap of faith. You never know, you might land somewhere you never thought you would."

Chapter Four

When Callie came to a stop at the end of the long driveway leading up to the main house, it didn't surprise her to see that all the lights were on. Aunt Susan was a night owl. She'd always claimed the disease took a break after the sun went down.

Rather than heading over to the guesthouse, Callie climbed the rickety porch steps of her aunt's house and let herself in. This was truly Susan's house now, she realized. Jason had bought it. And the store. She still couldn't believe he'd done that. Yes, Lewis Anders had been the wealthiest man in town, which meant Jason had money to spare now, but she hadn't expected him to make such a grand gesture.

It would definitely take the heat off Callie now, not struggling to pay the bills. Susan could even sell the store if she wanted, now that she didn't need to worry about a mortgage.

And you could leave town with Jason.

The thought hung in her mind, bringing both unease and a trickle of anticipation. Leave Skylark Springs. God, that had always been her biggest goal in life, to get out of this town. She'd dreamt of traveling, seeing new things, gathering up experiences and using what she learned to write her book.

She had the chance to do that now. With Jason.

Maybe that was reason for the unease. With *Jason*. The man who'd walked out on her. The love of her life.

Tonight had confirmed that she hadn't managed to get him out of her system, even after four years. When he'd touched her earlier, when he'd kissed her, her entire body had sung with joy. Her heart had felt weightless and full at the same time.

"Cal, is that you, honey?"

Callie poked her head into the living room to find Susan sitting by the window in her wheelchair, a blanket draped over her legs and a hardcover edition of *Great Expectations* in her hands.

"I saw the lights on and decided to come in and say hello," she told her aunt, walking over to kiss the top of Susan's head.

Susan glanced at the intricate grandfather clock across the room. "You're home late."

"Yeah . . . I was . . . " She took a breath. "Jason is back in town."

To her surprise, her aunt's face broke out in a big smile. "Finally. I expected him back sooner."

Shaking her head, Callie flopped down on the armchair by the window. "Why didn't you tell me he paid off the house?"

"He wanted to tell you himself."

"So you've just been chatting it up with my ex-boyfriend for the past couple of months behind my back?" Her voice was laced with weariness. She wasn't upset with Susan. Just the situation.

"He's not your ex-boyfriend," Susan replied, the smile never leaving her face. "He's the one."

"The one what?"

"The *one*." Her aunt rolled her eyes. "You know, the one you're meant to be with."

"I'd be more inclined to agree if he hadn't left town four years ago and never looked back."

"But he did look back. He *came* back. And now it's time for you to go with him."

She swallowed. "I can't leave you."

"Sure you can. How many times do I need to say it before you actually listen? You should have left me years ago, honey." Susan made a tsking sound. "And you've been using me as an excuse the entire time. I'll admit, I did need you, when I first wound up in this chair, but things are different now. I can take care of myself. And you, my darling, need to stop being so scared and take care of *you*."

"I'm not scared," Callie protested. But she had to wonder. Her aunt had been encouraging her for years to follow her dreams, but Callie had always brushed it off, convincing herself that Susan didn't really mean it. That her aunt wouldn't survive if she left.

Had that been an excuse, though? Was it truly fear holding her back?

"Hey, I'm not judging," Susan said, setting down her book on the table under the window. "It's a scary thought, leaving your familiar surroundings, stepping out of your comfort zone. Writing a book that the world may or may not read. It's a risk, Callie."

"But is it worth the risk?"

"That's something you'll find out. Either way, it's time for you to go. I refuse to hold you back a second longer."

Callie chewed on the inside of her cheek. Her aunt made it sound so damn easy. Just pack up, leave town, see where she ended up. And yes, it had been her dream for so long, but over the years, the dream had faded, dulled, seemingly so far out of reach that she could barely see it anymore.

But she was seeing it now. The shiny glimmer of promise, of new horizons and adventure. All she had to do was stick her hand out and grab it. But that meant opening her heart to Jason again.

"You're right," she murmured. "I'm scared. Most of all, I'm scared to love him again."

Susan laughed. "When did you ever stop?"

She wanted to frown, but ended up smiling instead. She still remembered the day Jason had slid into the seat beside hers in English class during their junior year. They'd immediately gotten into an argument over something—she couldn't even remember what they'd fought about anymore. But she did remember falling for him that day. Immediately. Any guy who could match her sarcastic remark for sarcastic remark was definitely a keeper.

They'd dated all throughout high school. Long-distance when he joined Navy. Lived together for those two months before he left again. And in these four years he'd been gone, she hadn't been on a single date, or felt even an inkling of interest toward another man.

"Come on, tell me," Susan said in a teasing voice. "When did you ever stop loving him?"

Callie shuddered out a breath. "I guess I never did."

Chapter Five

She wasn't coming.

Jason forced himself to swallow that devastating dose of reality as he tossed his duffel into the cab of his new pickup. He glanced around the deserted motel parking lot for the hundredth time, then at the empty road beyond it. It was past noon, and he'd spent the entire morning sitting in that drab motel room. Waiting. Hoping.

A part of him knew he was being unfair—storming back into Callie's life, asking her to drop everything and leave town—but he was tired of wasting time. He and Callie had been dreaming of leaving this place since they were sixteen. He was thirty now. He'd had a long military career, he'd kicked ass and taken names and tried to save the world. And now it was time for something new. It was time to put Skylark Springs behind him, time to put the past—and his father—away and take the next step of his life's journey.

But damn . . . he'd really wanted to take that step with Callie.

You broke her heart. She's not coming. End of story.

Letting out a ragged breath, he unlocked the truck and slid into the driver's seat.

And then he heard a car engine.

In the side mirror, he noticed a little red hatchback pulling into the parking lot. His pulse kicked up a notch. When he made out Callie's pretty face and chestnut hair through the windshield, a grin swept across his face.

He was out of the pickup and at her door in a nanosecond. Looking hesitant, Callie stepped out of the car. "Hey," she said.

Uneasiness tugged at his gut when she didn't continue. Oh crap. Had she come here to dump him in person? To spit on his truck as he drove out of town?

But no, she was reaching into the backseat, pulling out a . . . suitcase.

His heart soared.

"You're coming with me," he said in wonder.

A smile lifted her mouth. "I'm coming with you."

"And Susan?"

"She's staying here." Callie rolled her eyes. "Unless you want her to come with us."

"Lovely thought, but no." He grinned. "We need some alone time. Got four years to make up for, remember?"

"I remember."

She set the suitcase on the pavement and met his eyes. "You're not going to abandon me at a gas station or anything, right?"

He choked back a laugh. "Nope."

"Leave me in a motel room in some random state?"

"Not at all."

"Tell me you're meeting me at a diner and then never show up?"

Pain circled his heart. "Never again."

She moistened her lips nervously. "Don't make me regret this, Jase."

"I promise you, baby, you'll never experience a single regret for the rest of your life, not if I have anything to say about it."

He watched her face, the way color seeped into her cheeks, the apprehension melting out of her eyes, transforming into a sheen of clarity and excitement.

"Then let's do it," she said softly. "Let's live out the fantasy."

With a grin, he reached for her hand, tugged on it, and pulled her into his arms. "Best idea I've heard in a long time."

TWENTY-ONE HOURS

Alison Kent

10:00

Teri Stokes stopped the rented box truck in front of her parents'
house, fearing she'd arrived too late. Not two hours ago she and her
father decided she'd pick up the truck in Austin, he'd recruit local
manpower to load it, and the two of them, along with her mother,
would get the family's barn full of irreplaceable antiques out of Crow
Hill.

But the wildfire eating its way across the drought-ravaged
grasslands of their south central Texas county wasn't sticking to the
plan. And now, counting the men at the controls of bulldozers and
plows clearing brush and cutting firebreaks, and those on ladders
wetting the barn's tinderbox roof, she couldn't imagine any local
manpower remained to tap.

Meaning . . . she could get her parents to safety, and say goodbye
to the antique business that had been her mother's life, or she could
roll up her sleeves, take her turn swinging buckets with the rest of the
brigade, and pray. Not much of a choice, really. This was her family.
This was their home. This was where she belonged.

Jumping from the truck's cab was like jumping into an open
barbecue pit. Heat blasted her face, sucked the air from her lungs. She
blinked against the irritating haze, scrunched her nose at the acrid
scent—both strong enough to sting her throat from miles away.

Gale force gusts whipped her hair, plastered her white cotton top
to her torso. She dug an elastic tie from her bag and wound her hair
into a knot, shoved her sunglasses tight against her head, and pocketed
her keys. And that was when she saw him.

A laptop on the hood of a fancy pickup, a clipboard in his hand, a
pair of dark green fatigues hugging an ass she dropped her tinted
shades to see better. The black T-shirt stretched to accommodate his
shoulders and his biceps drew another appreciative and admittedly

lustful look, as did his strong jaw and cheekbones, the buzz cut of his dark blond hair.

He lifted his head in answer to another man's call, shouting and pointing toward the break of trees along the dry creek bed behind the barn. He knew what he was doing, the crew of volunteers following his orders without question.

His gadgetry put him as the man in charge, as did the respect given him by the others and his authoritarian air. But his eyes and a good part of his brow were hidden by a pair of wraparound shades, leaving her with a single question.

Who was he?

She'd grown up in Crow Hill. She returned often to see her folks. They kept her apprised of the locals' comings and goings. Neither her mother or father had said anything about a new man in town. Strange, since they were usually anxious to report on additions to the area's bachelor pool.

"Teri!" Nora Stokes yelled from the porch, waving. "There you are!"

Shaking off her musings, Teri hurried toward the house. She met her mother at the bottom of the stairs and pulled her into a hug. The past week of worry seemed to have taken at least five pounds from the older woman's already petite frame and added a new web of wrinkles at the corners of her eyes.

"Oh, Mom." Aching at her mother's distress, Teri stood with her arm around the other woman's waist, watching as in the distance, the blue sky disappeared behind the gray and white plumes rising from the fire. "I had no idea things were so bad."

Her mother shook her head, her gaze on the same frightening view. "They weren't until yesterday. Something about highs and lows and the jet stream. The wind shifted when no one was looking."

"Is it predicted to get worse?"

"The forecasters say no, but they didn't anticipate what happened yesterday either."

"Who's the hot shot down there with all the equipment?" *Because, of course, that was important. Sheesh, Teri. Priorities?*

It took her mother a long moment to answer, and the hair at Teri's nape began to tingle even before her mother spoke.

"That's Shane Gregor." She stroked a wisp of Teri's hair, her hand trembling. "You remember Shane, don't you?"

No. Uh-uh. Impossible.

He'd been Crow Hill High's star wide receiver, an eighteen year old built for speed. This man was ... more. Broad and defined and well-aged, his neck corded, his skin bronzed, his bearing large and impressive and nothing like that of the boy she'd tutored.

Her stomach tumbled, and she wondered what he was thinking, coming here. Where he got the nerve after the things that had passed between them. If he'd thought about her even once since leaving, or about the extent of her humiliation at his hands.

His hands. She remembered the feel of his fingers closing around hers. And then she made a fist. "He's back? In Crow Hill?"

"Teri, he's here to help." Her mother's voice held a warning note: let bygones be bygones.

But it wasn't her mother who carried the memory of those days. "Help? Seriously? Is that what he's calling it?"

"Enough," her mother said. "We don't have time for this. And there's something you need to know."

Not if it was about Shane Gregor. "What?"

"Shane's father and stepmother were killed in an automobile accident last month."

Oh, God. Teri whipped her gaze back to her mother's, her heart a jackhammer in her chest. "What?"

Her mother nodded. "They had an eight-year-old daughter. Shane's half-sister. Shannon. He's taken leave to see to her."

Wait a minute. Neither one of her parents had mentioned any of this before today. "Taken leave?"

"He's in the navy. I don't know how long he'll be here. I guess he's her only family now. Such a shame."

A shame. A tragedy. Absolutely heartbreaking. Teri didn't know what to say. "I'm sorry. What can I do?"

The older woman took a deep breath as if thankful to move on. "Your father's down at the barn. You go on and help him."

"What about you?" she asked, turning her back on her past.

"I'm fine here. I'm gathering up documents and photos and things we can't afford to lose in case we have to leave in a hurry."

"Okay," she said, kissing her mother's cheek. "I'll see what Dad needs."

She hurried to the barn, swearing she'd do anything to see her parents didn't lose their belongings. If she had to take orders from the man in charge, so be it.

But she would stay as far out of his way as possible, and not for a moment would she wonder what had compelled him to show up at her childhood home and run this operation.

Shane Gregor might be somebody's hero, but he meant nothing to her anymore.

10:20

Shane Gregor's focus was on the fire, the ground and air temps, the humidity, the barometric pressure, but especially on the wind.

He'd been a volunteer firefighter in high school, been schooled at Brayton Fire Training Field in College Station while attending A&M, been accepted as a wildland firefighter for the Texas Forest Service after graduation.

A short two years later, in those initial disbelieving days of fear and panic and patriotic duty that swept the country post 9/11, he'd enlisted in the navy, gone through the grueling months of BUD/S training, and been a SEAL ever since.

So he knew about focus. He knew about discipline. He knew the true strength of the mind and that of the body. He could be a team player as well as lead. And he hadn't forgotten the challenge of successfully fighting a fire with fire.

But none of those deeply instilled qualities kept him from noticing the arrival of the bright yellow truck or the woman behind the wheel.

Teri Stokes.

He pictured her looking like she had the night she'd changed his life. Her blonde hair in an intricate braid against the back of her head, tendrils loose around her face, her blue eyes wide as he lowered his head to kiss her.

He hadn't expected it to happen. He hadn't expected to carry so much guilt for his treatment of her after it had.

Most of all, he hadn't expected her to kiss him back—with more intensity, more involvement, more intimacy than his seventeen-year-old self had known what to do with.

He'd lived with the memory for sixteen years. He hadn't cherished it, or been obsessed with it, but it had been there inside of him, breathing of its own accord, keeping him going, keeping him alive.

He'd taken it out once in awhile and let it ground him. Let it, too, remind him of the amends he needed to make.

"Shane! Over here!"

He watched Teri disappear into the barn's dark interior, then trotted across the property to where he was needed. Before the end of the day, no matter what happened with the fire, he would get her alone.

It might be his last chance to tell her the things he'd been saving up all this time.

10:40

"Daddy?" As the darkness of the barn wrapped around her, Teri removed her sunglasses, hooked the earpiece in her blouse's neckline, and used the low angled slats of the sunlight to look around for her dad.

Ladders banged against the side of the structure. Footsteps pounded overhead. The water pouring from buckets and streaming from hoses brought to mind afternoon showers, short bursts, then silence, the cycle repeated again and again.

If the truth of things hadn't been so frightening, the sounds would've had her climbing into the hayloft and curling up with a flashlight and a good book the way she'd done so many times in the past.

But because she *was* frightened, she breathed deeply, drawing in the scents of hay and leather and horse that the years hadn't been able to erase, as well as those of linseed oil and aged wood, of dry dust—all of it underscored by the incoming smoke.

Insidious, it fingered its way through knotholes and loosely hinged doors and window casings and gaps in the weathered planks which had stood their ground against a half century of punishing elements. So much history. So easily wiped out by fire.

Shivering not with cold but with apprehension and awe, she rubbed her hands up and down her arms. "Daddy?"

"Back here, Teri," Gavin Stokes called.

She turned toward her father's voice, saw him waving from beside a row of framed paintings covered with blankets and leaning against the wall. Winding her way that direction, she ran her fingertips over a cast iron headboard, along the front of a highboy, across the smooth surface of a mahogany pedestal table.

A row of long bulbs lit the side of the barn where her father was working. He ducked out from beneath the low-hanging roof created by the floor of the hayloft above, his tall body lean and limber. He met her for a long wordless hug, his fears broadcast by the length of time it took him to set her away.

Both hands on her shoulders, he looked down, his blue eyes—her eyes—bleary from the pollution poisoning the air. "Were you able to get a truck?"

She nodded. "Are you still going to pack up? It looks like the whole population of Crow Hill is outside helping."

"We'll pack as much as we can. And by *we* I mean you and I. Your mother can load some of the smaller pieces. And I imagine Shane can grab a couple of men for the most valuable of the larger ones." He dropped his hands from her arms, his gaze to the floor, swallowing once before looking up again. "I guess you saw Shane."

"I did." It was all she said. It was enough.

"You going to be okay with him here?"

She thought of the past. She thought of the present. Her present. Shane's. "Of course. Mom told me what he's been through. What he's still going through."

"He turned out to be a hell of a man."

She wasn't sure what to say to that. She only knew the boy who had hurt her. "What do you want me to do?"

Her father pointed toward the far corner of the barn. "Start at the back. There's a stack of moving blankets and rolls of bubble wrap in the supply stall. You lived with your mom long enough to know what she'd want to take."

"Got it." She gave the contents of the barn a cursory glance, dazed by the scope of the job that lay ahead of them, wondering how much time they had, wondering if her first instinct to get the hell out of here hadn't been right after all. Then she shook off her doubts. They were doing nothing but getting in the way. "We'll be okay, right? We'll get through this?"

"We'll be fine. Even if we lose everything, we'll be fine." Her father dropped a kiss to her forehead as he'd done thousands of times in the past. "I'm going to go check on things with your mother. And Shane."

Teri nodded once, and then she got to work.

11:00

Once he finished advising Gavin Stokes, Shane turned toward the barn. The volunteers had things under control, and he had some overdue business. The long hours ahead would be interminable if he and Teri had to spend them walking on eggshells. They'd done enough of that their senior year, and he wasn't that boy anymore.

He entered the building, his steps silent, his breathing soundless and measured. Even had he been a bull and the barn a china shop, he doubted anyone inside would've heard his approach. Overhead, the water showered down like rubble, and in the near distance, diesel engines shook the ground with the roar of heavy artillery.

In contrast to the controlled chaos outside, the barn's interior was still as a holding pattern. He cocked his head, his eyes adjusting to the shadows. A soft grunt followed by banging drew him toward the structure's northeast corner, and as he passed a head-high stack of storage crates, she came into view. He slowed, stopped, stared.

Her back was to him, her hair—still blonde and crazy with waves—caught in a careless knot. She wore jeans and a white top that was already smudged with cobwebs and dirt, and as she bent to reach for a moving pad, the fabric rode up her back.

He stared harder, remembering the feel of her skin beneath her clothing, her warmth when the air outside had been so cold, the light in her eyes in a night so dark . . . just not dark enough to keep them from being seen.

She straightened then, turned, and noticed him there.

Her intake of breath shook him, but he didn't move, just gave her a moment to acclimate while their gazes held, while the past flashed like a stun grenade between them.

Then he nodded and simply said, "Teri."

"Shane." She stood still, her hands hidden in the folds of the pad, her pulse visible at the base of her neck. "How have you been?"

"Good." He shrugged, cleared his throat and added, "Relatively speaking."

She pulled one hand from the pad and tucked the hair that had escaped her band behind her ears. "I'm so sorry about your parents. Mom just told me. I didn't know or I would've . . . . "

She let the sentence trail, and he wondered what she would've said, what she would've done. If with all the things hanging between them, she wouldn't have stayed away and let the gulf of silence between them widen further.

He wouldn't have blamed her. She owed him nothing.

"Thanks. Dad and I were never close," he said, burying years of regrets with the confession. "And I'd only met Shannon's mother once, but it's still a tough one. It's been especially so for her."

She picked at the moving pad's loose threads, a smile softening her features. "It's hard to think of you having a little sister. Especially this you."

She didn't know the half of it, Shane mused, grinning in return and breathing better as the tension between them eased. "Shannon's a pistol. Cute as a button. Of course, she doesn't know me at all, so she's staying with a friend from school while we work things out."

"I can't imagine she won't love having a big brother. Once y'all are more comfortable together."

"I hope so. Mostly she's missing her folks." Balancing the world of weight he carried on wide-spread feet, he looked down and shoved his hands in his pockets, his shoulders hunched. "It's hard being the guy telling her they're not coming back."

"I'm so sorry, Shane," she said, her voice shaky, battered. "And again, thank you. For being here. For helping. Especially with all you have on your plate. Being suddenly responsible for an eight year old can't be easy."

"It's more intimidating than anything," he admitted with a coarse laugh. "I've been responsible for getting a lot of armed men in and out of some really tight spots, so this is a new one for me."

"That's right. Mom said you're in the navy." She spread out the moving pad on a giant spool empty of cable.

He let that go without comment because he wasn't here to talk about his military career or the upheaval in his personal life. He was here for only one thing. "Teri, I owe you an apology."

"For what?" she asked, her hands that had been smoothing the pad going still.

"For high school. For the way I treated you. For what I let happen."

She blinked once, then turned her attention to the three music boxes she was preparing for transport. "It was a long time ago. It doesn't matter. We're both older. We've both moved on."

He came closer, ducking beneath a beam, holding onto it with one hand as splinters pierced his palm. "It does matter. I shouldn't have let it go all this time without making it right."

"C'mon, Shane," she said, her voice sharper now, though she still refused him her gaze. "You kissed me and then you blew me off. I'm not the first teenage girl that's happened to. I won't be the last. It wasn't the end—"

"Teri." He stepped forward into her space, planting his hands on the spool and leaning close. "You were the best friend I had in school and I ruined it."

She shook her head as if not wanting to hear. "What are you talking about? You were friends with everyone."

"Friendly, not friends. Big difference." One that had been hammered home continually over the years. He gave a gruff snort. "I'm not even sure I was friends with Karen."

Finally, she looked up, her gaze searching his for the truth. "You two dated for three years. How could you date her and not be friends?"

"It was high school. Dating's not always about liking someone as much as being part of something, or the attention." And damn if that wasn't humiliating to stomach. "You gave me all the things she didn't."

"What did I give you?" she asked with a scoffing laugh. "Grief over your horrible handwriting? A hard time about checking your watch?"

A kiss I will never forget. "You gave me your full attention and didn't expect anything in return."

"That's not quite true. I expected you to listen," she said, and then grew silent as if realizing he was asking the same of her now. "Shane—"

"I know I hurt you. I've wanted to make it right for a long time, but I wasn't sure when or if I'd ever get back to Texas."

"You could've called. Or emailed. If it was that important to you."

"It was that important. It *is* that important." *Why wasn't this coming out right? Why couldn't he find the words?* "Important enough that it had to be said face to face."

"Fine. You've said it. Apology accepted." Her hands shook as she covered the music boxes with bubble wrap, storing one after the other in a crate. "Was there anything else?"

Crap. He rubbed at his forehead, then jammed his hands to his waist. "I meant it, you know. When I kissed you. I wasn't trying to score. I liked you. I liked you a lot."

She picked up the crate, shoved it at him, her gaze steely and lacking the vulnerability she'd let slip earlier. "Set this behind the truck, will you? Save me one trip out at least."

"Sure." He took it from her hands, ducked to avoid the beam as he stepped back. She said nothing more, done with him, and he turned to walk away, faltering only once when he swore he heard his name whispered on a sigh.

16:00

Standing near the copse of cottonwoods down the rise behind the house, Teri stared into the distance. Facing away from the fire, it was almost possible to believe the flames weren't licking their way toward Crow Hill. Almost, because the scent of burning earth scorched the air and scratched at her lungs when she breathed.

She was sweaty, dirty. Her muscles ached from the heavy lifting teaching kindergarten never required. After hours of digging, sorting, wrapping and packing, she'd taken a break to eat. Then she'd needed more. An escape, a moment of silence, something. Anything to help her get a grip on the things Shane had said.

That he'd liked her. Liked her a lot.

That she had been his best friend.

Their reunion hadn't been at all what she'd expected, and with each word he'd spoken, her childish animosity had fizzled another degree. And why wouldn't it? He'd been her first real grown-up kiss. The first boy she'd let beneath her clothes. But he'd made her no promises.

Neither had he been the one to raise a hand against her.

And his voice hadn't been the one to make threats.

Looking back, their contact had been innocent, nothing to raise the eyebrows it had, to start the gossip mill churning. Especially compared to the things she knew her friends were doing. Things Shane had been doing with Karen Best. The ones Karen explained in great detail when cornering Teri in the locker room and ordering her to lay off.

Their confrontation wouldn't have been so bad if Teri hadn't been alone, and Karen surrounded by her cheerleading posse, the girls moving in, shoving her, kicking her, each with her own pairs of scissors, and leaving ragged snips of Teri's hair on the floor.

Behind her, she heard the rustle of long grass, legs moving through the dry brush, whooshing, but she was back on the hard wet floor, her eyes crushed closed as she listened to the slice of the blades.

"You doing okay?" Shane asked, and she nodded, her eyes coming open to him handing her a bottle of water.

The icy plastic felt like heaven in her hands. She twisted off the top, brought it to her mouth, watched Shane do the same with his. And then she stopped drinking because looking at him reminded her of her where she was, that the past was the past, that this was the present and Shane had chosen to be here. With her.

His throat worked as he sucked the contents from the bottle, his Adam's apple bobbing, the tendons in his neck drawing her eyes to his shoulders, to his biceps, triceps, the stained pit of his arm, the tufts of hair peaking from his sleeve that strained around his muscles.

And then she realized the time she'd spent in the barn had left its mark—on her skin, her clothing, her hair. Lovely.

"I'm a mess." She set the bottle between her boots, turned into the wind and pulled the tie from her hair, capturing the tangled strands and twisting them into a knot that was probably as untidy as what she'd started with.

"We're all a mess today. I don't think anyone's going to care or notice."

He wasn't a mess. He was beautiful, in his element, man against nature. Yes, he was sweaty, dirt clinging to the golden hairs at his wrists, matted in the hollow of his throat, but he was perfect, and she was staring, and she felt like she was seventeen again, waiting in the library for him to finish football practice, to sit beside her and lean into her space while she pointed out the missing logic in his English essay.

"I always liked your hair long," he said out of the blue. "I'm glad you grew it back out."

"I never really wanted to cut it," she admitted, stopping because he didn't need to know the reason she had.

Except he did know. She saw it in the tic at his temple before he spoke.

"When we called it quits, Karen told me what she'd done. Threw it in my face, actually. I should've come to you then, but I couldn't think of anything to say. Or a way to make it up to you." He bit down hard on some choice words, keeping them under his breath. "How could anyone make up for something like that?"

She shrugged. "I'm just glad they didn't chop off my fingers or something."

"Someone got too close." He reached out, ran his thumb along the tiny scar on her jaw, lingering there, his own jaw tight as if wishing he could go back and stop the attack.

She took his hand, held it for a moment then let him go. "Shane, it's okay. It was high school. Like you said, teenagers aren't known for thinking straight."

She watched as he looked to the ground, and it struck her again how much time they'd both wasted, how much needless baggage they'd carried when all either of them needed to do was talk. "How're things going? With the firebreaks?"

"Pretty good. We've done just about all we can here. We'll keep the water going, and watch the wind." He turned, looked behind them, his profile strong, his jaw determined.

She imagined his gaze being equally so as he studied the very scene she'd come out here to escape. "How do you do it?"

"Do what?" he asked, coming back to her, the lines on his face softening as she became the object of his concentration.

She remembered what he'd said earlier in the day and used his words instead of wrangling her thoughts. "Get armed men in and out of tight spots."

He shrugged. "You train. You learn. You put it into practice."

"Where?"

"Wherever I'm needed."

"No. Where did you train? Coronado?"

He gave a single nod. "There. Some at Fort Benning."

"I thought so."

"It's not a big deal. It's just what I do."

Something she would expect a SEAL to say. She laid her palm on his wrist and wrapped her fingers as far around as she could. "It's a very big deal, Shane. A very big deal."

He looked down to her hand, turned his beneath hers to lace their fingers. "I took you with me. You were there in my head telling me to pay attention, to focus, to be smart. Funny that yours was the voice I heard when so many after you drilled home the same things. A little more forcefully, but yeah. I always came back to you."

When he lifted his head, she stepped closer, bringing their joined hands behind her. She felt the beat of his heart as she pressed against him, as her own blood rushed through her veins.

She rose on tiptoes, found his lips with hers, and closed her eyes, humbled, frightened, honored. The kiss was tentative, an exploration of new feelings, so soft and tender, a memory of their first. He tasted the same, but different. He felt the same, but nothing like he had. She knew who he was, but she didn't know him at all.

And then she stepped away.

He rested his forehead on hers. "Sometimes, when I'm on a mission, and it's quiet, and we can't do anything but wait, I think about you. I think about you a lot, actually. About making it out and seeing you again."

"But you've never come back. Until now."

His lashes swept down, swept up. "I told myself it was all in my head. That I didn't have anything to come for. There was no reason you would want to see me."

Her heart wanted to break but held on. "Why would you think that?"

"You were bullied and I didn't stop it."

"You didn't know it was happening."

"I knew later."

"By then it was over and done with."

"I still should've—"

"Shh." She used her fingertips to silence him. "Don't. We're here now. That's all that matters."

"I need to get back to things," he said after a long moment of mingled breath, regret thick, longing thicker still.

"I know."

"I'll be around later."

"I know."

"I won't leave you again."

"I know."

18:30

Hooking the earpiece of his sunglasses in his T-shirt's neckband, Shane leaned close to his laptop, adjusting it this way and that on the front seat of his truck to better see the screen. The satellite imagery and wind models had his hopes up. They verified what he'd thought he was seeing, watching the smoke change directions.

Teri initiating that kiss had his hopes up even more. Different hopes, yeah, but ones he'd been entertaining since returning to Crow Hill.

He hadn't intended to follow her again. Going after her into the barn had seemed like enough stalking for one day, but the unfinished business between them had only been stirred, not settled. He'd seen her walk off, watched her disappear behind the house. He'd fought with himself and lost the battle. He was so glad he had.

"Shane?"

He turned. Teri stood five feet away holding a paper bag from the Blackbird Diner. He breathed deeply and smelled what he was pretty sure were a burger and fries. But he also smelled soap and shampoo, and hunger of another sort gripped him deep.

"Daddy had burgers sent over from the diner. I thought you might be hungry."

His stomach rumbled loudly enough to be heard over the one tractor idling nearby. "I could eat."

"It's not much, especially after the day all of y'all have put in."

It was everything. The food and the fact that she'd brought it to him. He took her in, her boots, her faded jeans, her damp hair twisted on top of her head. Her face clean of makeup. Her sleeveless shirt closed with only three strategically placed snaps.

He thought about popping them, burying his face against her chest and breathing her in. "It's plenty. Anything more and I'd probably pass out from a food coma."

Their hands brushed when he reached for the bag, and he lingered, wanting to take her by the wrist and pull her to him. Wanting to feel her mouth beneath his, her breasts against his chest, her hips pressed to his and begging.

Clearing his throat, he turned and pushed the laptop into the passenger seat, boosted sideways into the driver's. Elbows on his knees, he opened the bag and dug in.

"What?" he asked moments later, his mouth full.

Her smile was shy, tentative, but not innocent. "There's something about watching a hungry man eat."

He could tell her about being hungry. The ways he'd wanted her. The things he'd said to her when she wasn't there to hear. "I went eight days once living on a single MRE a day. We got stuck on a mission and had to ration our rations while staying invisible. You should've seen us chowing down once we got back to base camp."

"Does it scare you?" she asked, her smile fading. "What you do?"

"I have a healthy respect for all the ways things can go wrong. I do what I can to make sure they don't," he said, then shoved a handful of fries in his mouth.

"I guess you've seen some bad things."

Bad people. Bad situations. "I've seen a lot of good, too."

"And done a lot of good."

"It puts life in perspective."

"Like your sister losing both of her parents."

He took another bite, chewed to gather his thoughts. "That shouldn't have happened. She'll be fine, but she should've had these years free of that sort of tragedy. It's going to change who she is, the choices she makes."

"Are you talking from experience?"

"Human experience as much as my own, I guess."

"Did you enlist after 9/11?"

He nodded. "I'd been fighting wildfires for the state a couple of years. Had an engineering degree. Thought I could put some of that to better use."

"And yet here you are, jumping in to save one single barn."

He caught her gaze, held it. "I jumped in because of you."

"Me?" She frowned, and after a long moment asked, "Are you saying if it had been the Campbell's house threatened you wouldn't be trying to keep it from burning down?"

"Sure I would, but for a less personal reason."

"Shane—"

"I wasn't quite telling the truth when I said you'd been my best friend. You were a whole lot more," he said because in for a penny, why not the whole pound?

"Shane—"

"It's crazy, isn't it, how I've never been able to let you go?" He ran a napkin over his mouth, tossed the garbage to the seat behind him. "I was pretty damn happy when I found out you were still single."

She scuffed the toe of one boot at the ground, hiding behind her sunglasses, hands in her back pockets.

"I got my degree, started teaching. Just never really dated much."

"Not to sound selfish, but I'm glad." Because the thought of another man's hands on her . . . .

Her gaze came back to his, her pulse throbbing in her throat. "I don't know what to say to that."

Oh, baby. Blinking hard, he grabbed his sunglasses and shoved them on. "Don't say anything. Just know."

02:30

Not to sound selfish, but I'm glad.

Eight hours now, and that was the only thing Teri could think about.

Shane being selfishly glad that she was single. So many responses had tumbled into her head, and what had she said?

I don't know what to say to that.

Yeah. She was some prize. She couldn't even tell him the truth.

That she'd given him her heart in high school. That she hadn't thought it fair to raise the hopes of another man when she knew Shane would always be there in the back of her mind.

She would wonder. She would wait. She would hope.

What she wouldn't do, it seemed, was sleep. She tossed off the bedding, and walked to the window, looking at the moon and the paper thin ribbons of smoke drifting beneath it. When she'd gone to bed, the fire had been eighty percent contained, and the volunteers working to save her family's belongings on their way home.

All but Shane.

He was standing at the back of his truck, staring at the same view. Knowing she was looking at the rest of her life, she slid her bare feet into her boots, used her sheet like a shawl to cover her pajamas, and made her way out of the house and across the yard to where he stood guard. To where he waited.

"It's the middle of the night," she said, moving to his side.

"I know," he said without looking at her.

"What are you doing out here?"

"Just watching. Making sure."

A kick of worry ached in her chest. "I thought you said—"

"Teri," he said, cutting her off and turning toward her. "Watching and making sure doesn't mean anything I said earlier has changed."

"Okay. If you're sure."

"I am. C'mere." He reached for her, lifted her to sit on the tailgate then hopped up beside her. Right beside her. Their thighs touching from hip to knee, his shoulders broad and like a wall behind hers as he braced his palms on the truck bed and leaned back.

She couldn't help it. She dropped her head to his shoulder, nuzzled her face against his T-shirt that smelled of sweat and smoke. The afternoon's kiss came back, swimming over her until she thought she might drown in the things she was feeling. Had he been so much a part of her life all this time that she'd kept herself for him?

Before she could find her voice, he turned into her, loomed above her, his eyes glittering in the darkness. He covered her, pressed her down. The liner in the bed of his truck was smooth and hard beneath her back. She didn't care. She dropped her sheet behind her and raised her arms, looping them around his neck and bringing him down.

He supported himself on one elbow, splayed his other hand on her belly, working his fingers beneath her thin cotton tank while holding her gaze. She said nothing. She only breathed and held on as he covered one of her breasts, thumbing her nipple before moving the same hand lower, to the drawstring waist of her low-riding knee shorts.

He freed the knot, slid his hand beneath the fabric, into her panties. She pulled her heels to her hips and spread her legs, her hands kneading the balls of his shoulders. As he slid a finger between her folds, she bit at her lower lip, and when he moved lower, entered her and pushed deep, she gasped and began tugging his T-shirt up his back.

He sat up, stripped it away, and went to work on his fly. She swallowed, watching the play of the moonlight on his body, his wide shoulders, the dusting of fine hair on his chest. The thicker hair trailing behind his dark briefs.

She scooted further into the truck bed, and he kneeled between her legs. When she lifted her hips, he tugged down her bottoms and her panties, then shoved his briefs to his knees. He was thick and full, and she stared as he rolled on a condom, then could see nothing but his face as he crawled above her, entered her, making everything in her world right for the very first time.

He held himself still, his forearms bearing the brunt of his weight, and she reached for him, her hands on his neck, her thumbs skimming along his jawline, his skin dirty, scruffy, sunburned and beautiful.

"It scares me to think of you in danger."

"Then don't. Think of me inside of you."

"It scares me to think of losing you."

"Then don't. Think of being with me."

"It scares me to think of never seeing you again."

"Then don't. Think of seeing me until you're sick of my face."

"I'll never get sick of your face."

"What about the rest of me?"

"I'll never get enough of the rest of you."

He loved her then, moving his body over hers, into hers, with hers until they were one. The beat of their hearts. The cadence as they rocked.

The rhythm of their shared breath. They finished together, and she arched into him, burying her cry of passion in the crook of his neck, soaring as he carried her places too high to bear.

She waited until his breathing had slowed and his shudders had stopped before asking, "What are you going to do now?"

"Besides put on my pants and hope your parents are still asleep?"

That made her grin. "About your sister. About where you're going to live."

"I'm moving back to Crow Hill. But my sister's only a part of it."

"Oh?"

"I've been in love with you for sixteen years, Teri Stokes." He stroked a finger down her cheek, her neck, circling it in the hollow of her throat and pulsing inside of her as he hardened again. "I think it's time I let you know exactly how much."

07:00

Standing on the Stokes's front porch, Shane buried a yawn in his fist. It had been a long twenty-one hours, physically, mentally. Emotionally. A totally different exhaustion than what followed his SEAL team's missions, those keeping him awake for days at a time. But tired or not, he had miles to cover before he could sleep.

His first order of business? Stopping to see Shannon. To let her know he was fine. That the fire was out and no longer a danger. That no matter how often he might be gone, or for how long, he'd fight heaven and hell to get back to her.

He would write. He would call. He'd get her a computer so they could video chat no matter where in the world his job might take him. They were family. And families stuck together, thick or thin. Shannon. Teri. They were his. To care for. To provide for. To keep safe. Now and forever.

Behind him, the Stokes's front door opened, and Gavin walked out with two steaming mugs of coffee. Nora, holding hers, shut the door. He handed one to Shane, who as dirty as he was, had declined to join the older couple inside.

The three of them drank their coffee in silence, watching the sun rise over the grass that was as dry and yellow-brown as yesterday, over the barn that was weathered to gray and wet, but was still standing proud and strong.

Before another yawn took him, Shane turned. "I guess I'll head out."

"You should get some sleep, Shane," Gavin said. "You have our undying gratitude, but you need to see to you and yours. Reports this morning have the blaze at ninety percent contained. I think we're out of the woods."

"Trust me. Sleep's on my schedule. Just a few things to take care of between here and there." He gestured toward the barn. "I thought you might need help moving things back inside."

"No rush on that. Teri rented the truck for a few days. She'll get it back to Austin in plenty of time."

"Sounds good." Handing his empty mug to Nora, Shane shook Gavin Stokes's hand, then made his way back to his pickup.

Teri was waiting in the driver's seat, the door open, her knee shorts and thin white tank making him hard as he remembered the body beneath. He stepped between her spread legs, set one hand at her waist, threaded the fingers of the other into her loose hair that he loved.

"Know what I realized as I was talking to your folks?"

"That they *were* asleep last night and didn't see a thing?"

He felt his face coloring. "Besides that?"

"What?"

"You don't live in Crow Hill anymore."

"Hmm." She twisted her lips to one side, nuzzled his wrist where it grazed her cheek. "Guess I'll have to do something about that."

"Or Shannon and I can get a place in Austin."

"That wouldn't be fair to her. Uprooting her after all she's lost? Besides, she'll need her friends close when you're deployed."

He liked that her first thought was of a little girl's needs. "I don't want to make things hard on you either. If you need to stay for your job, we can do something long distance."

"Long distance?" She arched a wicked brow. "After last night?"

He leaned his forehead against hers, closed his eyes and breathed. She was here. She was his. It was almost too much to believe. "After last night I'm having trouble loading up to leave."

"I'll be here a few more days. We'll talk. Make a plan. We've got time."

He shook his head. "I wasted sixteen years. I'm not wasting a minute more. You know that, right?"

"I do," she said.

It hit him, then, like a shot to the center of his chest, that he wanted to hear her say that while their friends and families, and hell, even his team, looked on, while she wore a long white dress, flowers in her hands and in her hair.

He brought her to him, kissed her hard, fierce and possessive. "I love you, Teri. All these years. I kept you with me."

"Oh, Shane. I love you, too. I never forgot you. Not for a minute."

"I'm going to make sure you never do."

NOT WAVING BUT DROWNING

Jo Leigh

He'd taken his time driving up the mountain. Nine thousand feet was pretty damn high, but most of the way the brilliant colors of September trees had given him some peace.

Dan Hogan was on leave, away from the burning sands of Afghanistan or the warm Pacific of Coronado Beach. He hadn't been in the mountains in a long time. Three years, he figured, although he didn't measure time in years but in missions.

Parking the rental Jeep next to Renee's old Outback, he figured she knew he was there, would have heard the car amongst all this silence. As he stepped out of the vehicle, he registered the speed of the wind on his face, the height of the sun by the length of the shadows, the underscore of quaking aspens and somewhere close, a creek. When he finally looked at the cabin he was there to fix up, Renee Crocker opened the door and stepped out on the front porch.

Seeing her again made his chest tight and his cock pay attention. They weren't even lovers, but try telling his johnson that when she was so damn beautiful. He'd thought about it, so had she. Talked about it. But the timing had never worked out in college, then he was in training, and once he made it as a SEAL he'd decided it would be better not go there. Ever.

"You waiting for applause or something?" she asked, folding her arms across her chest. Her dark hair was windblown and wavy, cut blunt above her shoulders. Last time he'd seen her it had been red, a deep red that matched her temper, but this looked good, too. Not as dramatic, but then she was stuck way the hell up on a mountaintop in Utah for a year, so who did she need to be dramatic for? He was pretty sure he recognized her worn-in jeans, but he hadn't seen her in a flannel shirt before. He preferred her in softer clothes, dresses that showed off her legs, although he'd never tell her that.

"Getting my bearings," he said. "It smells like Christmas."

"Pine trees will do that," she said. Then she smiled at him and the pressure in his chest relaxed. "I was about to have some lunch. Get your gear. You can scope out the cabin after."

His duffel bag was in the back of the car, along with a present for Renee. He'd bought a painting from a street artist in Soviet Georgia that he'd meant to give her. Instead, he had a bottle of Jameson 18 Year Old Limited Reserve. They both liked whiskey, and this was the best he'd ever tried. She'd like it. She would.

It was weird not to be in load out, although damn straight he had his Sig Sauer and his Recon rifle with him. He took another look around, checked the dirt road to the highway, then back at the cabin. The wind had picked up some. The sound of his boots on gravel carried differently this high up. Sixteen-percent oxygen. There were two windows on this side of the cabin, big enough for a man to crawl through, easy.

She'd left the door open for him and there she was in the dimmer light, her smile taking him straight back to the smell of coffee in the common room, the sound of her laughing so loud in the library they were kicked out seven different times. She was a year younger, thirty-three now, and she looked better than she had at seventeen.

"You're leaner than the last time I saw you," she said. "You look good."

"You do, too."

Her head tilted to the left. "Something wrong with your hugging muscles?"

He ignored the loud thunk on the floor as he dropped his kit. Two steps later he scooped her up in his arms and let himself have this. He closed his eyes, even though he didn't know what was behind any of the doors, even though it was pure indulgence, and Christ, she smelled incredible. He buried his nose behind her ear, right where hair met scalp, and he breathed her in as if he could store it up for a rainy day.

But then she was sniffing him back, loudly, and he laughed, which he hadn't done in too long. He still didn't open his eyes, though. Just kept on hugging her, the feel of her pressed against him reminding him of everything good. When the lump came to his throat, he backed off, picked up his duffel bag and handed her the whiskey. "Where am I sleeping?"

"Out back. I dug a ditch just for you. Figured you'd like to feel at home."

"You're hilarious, Renee. And you better not be putting me in some futon crap. I'll steal your bed from right under you, I swear to God."

"You and what army?"

He gave her his most evil squint-eye. "Say what?"

"Wow, you are such a cry baby. Thought you'd grow out of that by now." Her lips twitched in a faint smile, and she turned as if she expected him to follow.

He did, toward the back of the cabin where there were three doors off a tiny hallway. One had to be her bedroom, one the bathroom, and one her office, so he had every reason to be concerned about a fold out crap thing. She'd done it to him before.

She turned left at the first door, and he stopped. "This is your office."

"What was your first clue?"

His gaze was already on the back wall, on the huge map of tacked up pictures, note cards, business cards, torn out pages, all kinds of crazy things, some with brightly colored yarn connecting them via push pins. "That's some fancy mural you have going there."

"That's three years' worth of research on that wall, so watch your step in here."

Dan turned to face her. "If there's any chance I could screw this up, even by accident—"

She touched his upper arm, gave it a squeeze. "You're the world's most stealthy fighter, Danny. I trust you not to walk into the wall, even if you do drink all the whiskey."

After stepping closer to the queen-sized bed, he put his shit down, checked out the lock on the window.

"I've done everything I'm supposed to," she said. "Window guards everywhere, that dead bolt you told me to get. And my rifle is clean and ready for bear."

He smiled. "When's the last time you shot it?"

"Uh . . . ."

"Add that to the to-do list. You said something about lunch?"

Renee nodded. "Unpack, freshen up. After, I'll show you the tools and materials and we can go over the work schedule. I'm not gonna let you relax for a minute."

"You're not, huh?"

She wanted to go hug him again, and she wasn't sure why. "You can have nights off. There's a fine bottle of whiskey in the house, and I want to hear all about your top secret missions."

He chuffed a laugh, and she left the bedroom, her smile dropping the moment she walked into the hall. Something was off. She couldn't pinpoint what it was. It was a feeling, and when it came to Dan she trusted her instincts.

They'd known each other since freshman year at Northwestern. They'd both lived in the same dorm, and for awhile, they'd both been pursuing pre-law. That's not how they met, though. She'd been dating Mark Hunter. Mark Hunter had been in ROTC with Dan. While things had fizzled with Mark, Renee's friendship with Dan had not just continued but grown deep and strong. She loved Dan. Not quite like a brother, but not like a lover, either. Although she'd dallied with the idea, she doubted they'd have lasted this long if they had hooked up, so she was happy.

She saw him as often as anyone outside of his team and his parents. In fact, she wondered if he was going to visit them in San Diego after he finished helping her fix up the cabin.

As she pulled out a platter of cold cuts from the fridge, she thought about how little she knew about Dan's life, and yet how well she knew him. Since day one in SEAL training, he hadn't spoken a word he shouldn't have. She never knew where he was, what he was doing, how he was doing. If he were alive or dead.

That was the hard part, naturally, but she'd signed up for it. He'd wanted the SEALs from the age of fifteen, swore he'd been born for it, and he'd been right. He was not just the smartest guy she'd ever met, but he was also the single most focused individual. Nothing could keep Dan Hogan from getting what he was after, and he'd proved that too many times to count.

He was also aware of the fact that he was the smartest guy in the room, and that he could outmaneuver, outfox, outrun and out gun pretty much every person on the planet. Modesty was not a prized characteristic in his circle.

She'd never cared about that part, because Dan was also the best guy she knew. He walked the walk, and he'd move heaven and earth to make sure the people he loved were taken care of. Not to mention the fact that he put his life on the line day in and day out to serve a purpose so much greater than himself it humbled her more than the all the forests and the oceans and the stars.

That something was *off* bothered her one hell of a lot. She got out the bread, the mustard and mayo, pickles, of course, and beer. Then she pulled out one of the treats she had stocked up on just for him. Salt and vinegar potato chips. He was gonna be working with her for four days, so she had four bags.

He was normally a disgustingly healthy eater. He liked his beer, good hard liquor, sometimes even a soda, but he never indulged himself. Except when he was with her. Probably had something to do with him being there for so many of her breakups. She'd show up on his doorstep with chips, salsa and ice cream, and she'd eat herself into a coma. She was convinced he ate the junk food with her as a humanitarian effort. Sometimes he made it hard to be his friend.

"That looks more than decent," he said. "You spoil me, I swear. It would be even better if you did the extra five miles I'll have to sweat through after eating all this evil food."

"I would like to see the day you'd let me run five feet for you. You're a glutton for punishment."

He pulled out a seat at the table and plopped himself down. "Must be why I keep coming back to you."

She whacked him upside the head before she put his beer in front of him. She thought about asking him what was wrong, but that would be about as useful as asking him what his last mission had been. He'd learned the fine art of keeping himself bottled up, and he'd done as well at that as he'd done in sharp shooting. That was his specialty. Amazingly, she was allowed to know that bit. Just not what weapons he used, or any other detail.

He started building his sandwich straight off, and she sat across from him. Taking a sip of beer, she looked at him while he was occupied. It wasn't the least bit fair, but the man was so good looking it hurt. Just under six feet, he'd never gone after muscles as much as he'd wanted strength and speed. He'd been a swimmer in college, won a lot of races. He also fenced, which she'd made fun of since the day they'd met, played tennis, baseball, ran track and was an expert archer. That was aside from his love affair with guns. That had been his father's doing.

"Most of the work's gonna be on the roof, I assume?"

She watched him pile ham on his turkey. "Thanks for asking, Dan. I'm doing well. The book is gonna be a challenge, especially given the deadline I've got, but I'm looking forward to being away from L.A. and all that mess. And, no, I'm not seeing anyone. I was, but he turned out to be a real jerk, so I sent him packing. The only thing I'm wondering is if I should break down and get myself a dog. Course I won't be able to get too large a breed, because he'll have to fit into my life back home. You?"

Dan took a big bite out of his sandwich, then chewed, his jaw muscle flexing like crazy. He stared at her as if their conversation was every bit as normal as his wholewheat bread. Finally, he swallowed, took a hit off his beer, then nodded. "I've missed you," he said. "You drive me crazy, but it turns out I like that from time to time."

"I'm so delighted to serve."

He put down the food, rested his hands on his thighs. She knew from experience how hard those thighs were. Like rocks. His whole body was like that. Well, all the parts she'd felt. There were a few she couldn't comment on, but his chest? His legs? His back? Not an inch of anything but muscle and sinew. Enough fat to keep him from freezing on a bitter night, not that it showed. He'd gotten her into shape way back when, and it had always seemed easier to maintain it than to have to start from scratch, so she ran, did yoga, stretched, lifted weights. She wasn't insane, though, and if she wanted some damn macaroni and cheese, she ate macaroni and cheese.

"It's been a tough year," he said. "Full of challenges. I'm not acclimated to the real world yet, you'll have to forgive me."

She sighed and moved over to the chair next to his. "It's good to have you here," she said. "Especially considering I'm making you work your ass off when you should be out cattin' around with hot and cold running women all over you."

He looked out the front window. "It's quiet up here. Nice. But you're gonna have snow up to your eyeballs come winter."

"I know. It'll be a whole new experience. I've got enough cut wood to last at least two months and more will be delivered when necessary. I have a satellite phone and internet, and also a nice couple with a really big truck who'll come and save me come the apocalypse. So I'm all set."

"It sounds great."

She slapped him on that iron thigh. "If I hate it, I'll leave. Go back home."

"There you go." He picked up his sandwich again, but the moan she heard wasn't about meat and cheese. "You got my chips."

She'd understood him, even though he'd had a mouthful. "Yes. I did."

He had that bag open so fast the salt and vinegar smell hit her like a slap. "You are the best."

"I know. It's the least I could do."

He swallowed this time, before he said, "I think you're right. It is the least."

"I also got you Rocky Road ice cream."

He closed his eyes and rolled his head all the way back. "Oh, my God. You're trying to kill me." He straightened and stared at her. "How much?"

"Four pints."

"Damn, you are the perfect woman, you know that?"

She got up, went to get more napkins. Put them down on the napkins that were already on the table. "How are your folks?"

"Good. Fine. Busy. Dad's got some big conference next month up in Paris, and he's taking Mom along so she can shop."

"You going to see them after here?"

He grunted something as he chewed, which she thought might be a yes.

"I hope you know something about plumbing," she said. "Although I did pick up a how-to book that's for people who aren't Rhodes Scholars, so even if you don't, together we can tackle it, yes?"

"What's wrong with the plumbing?" His voice was low, guarded.

She went to the sink and turned on the hot water. Noises, mostly unholy loud bangs, started way before any water showed up. The entire sink vibrated like it was trying to get away from the banging as quickly as possible. Finally, a trickle came out, not quite as rust colored as it had been when she'd first arrived.

"I don't think there's gonna be enough time to replace all the pipes in this cabin before I leave," he said.

"I didn't say we had to replace all of them. According to William, a few will do. He wrote down their names. I bought them. The man at the store marked them in the book. I bought an internal nipple wrench. And other tools with less interesting names. I have no doubt whatsoever that you'll be able to figure it all out with one glance."

Dan looked at her with his deep blue eyes and an attitude that fit him better than his stone washed jeans. "First, you are the least helpless female that I know, so knock it off. I'm going to help, whether you bat your eyelashes or not."

"I did not—"

"Second," he said, cutting her right off, "why the hell didn't you rent a cabin that was functional? There must be plenty of places like that on this mountain."

"I'll address the second issue. Because William needs this cabin to be in working order next spring so he can rent it out for decent money. He's getting up there in years, and he doesn't have the wherewithal to keep this place up. I need solitude with minimal opportunities for distractions until I finish this damn book."

"You still have William?"

"Of course I do. He's my Dad."

"He was one of your many stepfathers. But he was the nice one, so good for you. You don't bring him up much, though."

"You're one to talk."

"True." He took a couple of chips and slipped them into his sandwich. Before he took another bite, he started on sandwich number three. She was glad she'd stocked up on everything before he'd arrived.

"Oh, and as for the first issue," she said, "kiss my ass."

He smiled. It made her feel marginally better, but there was still something going on. If every bit of his life wasn't top secret, she'd have asked him straight out about his work. It had to be work, because he didn't have anything outside the SEALs, except his folks and her. Maybe his parents weren't so peachy?

Dan came over to the sink, grabbed her hand, then put the third sandwich in it. "Eat," he said. "We're both working on this place. You need your strength. And quit trying to figure me out. It's not gonna happen. There's nothing wrong."

"Did I say anything?"

He rolled his eyes. "You would be the worst poker player ever, have I mentioned that?"

"Once or twice."

"Eat. Then lets break down the jobs and figure out how we're going to handle the next few days."

She took a big bite out of her sandwich, pleased he'd remembered she didn't combine mustard and mayo, ever. He was a cocky bastard, but he was also a sweet pea. He hated it when she called him that.

"I need coffee first."

"No one needs coffee before a run, Crocker."

"This is my house. If I say I need coffee, I goddamn well mean I need coffee. So sit down and shut up."

"I could run on my own."

Renee had her mug in one hand, the coffee pot in the other. "You know where the door is."

Dan sighed as if all hope of a decent world had vanished. "Fine. Drink your coffee. I don't mind completely wasting my time."

She ignored him while she sniffed the strong Columbian, letting the scent wake her and please her at the same time.

Dan was in jeans, a Navy T-shirt and a hoodie. His running shoes looked so high tech she wouldn't be surprised if they launched grenades.

She wore her running gear as well, nothing fancy about any of it. Just Lycra, a girl's best friend, and old fashioned Nikes. It would be chilly out there, but the run up the mountain would get her warm fast.

She'd be coming back alone, as always. She ran a couple miles a day. Dan? He ran the circumference of the earth or something close to it, in the time it would take her to get home, shower, dress, and dry her hair. She'd given up keeping up after their first run. She'd never known a person to be so disciplined. If he'd been a writer, he wouldn't have had to resort to hiding on mountaintops to meet his deadlines. His deadlines would crawl on their bellies and give him fifty.

On the other hand, the whole reason he was here bitching instead of leaving without her was because if he did go, he'd feel badly about it all day. Guilty. Not because she was a woman, but because she was his friend, the unfailingly polite bastard. She doubted he was that courteous when he was engaging the enemy, but she wouldn't discount the notion completely.

"You're staring. You're not drinking."

"Excuse me if I don't want to scald my palate."

He grunted as he abandoned the kitchen for the living room. He ran his hand over the brick of the fireplace, then the mantel. "The construction of the cabin isn't bad. The bones are still good."

"Except the kitchen plumbing."

"Yeah, except that. But we'll get into it when I come back. It's good that the pipes aren't buried. That's in our favor."

"It got down to minus twenty-seven last winter."

"Chilly."

"Yeah, even you might need a parka."

He looked at her with an almost smile, then away, quick. Weird. "Drink," he said, checking out the sink.

He was playing her all wrong if he didn't want her to worry.

Which actually told her more than the darting glances. He was smart and he knew her as well as any person ever had. It's not that he minded manipulating her. She'd once driven from Los Angeles to San Diego at four in the morning because his friend needed a lift. Dan hadn't even driven back with them.

It finally struck her. He wanted her to know. He would never volunteer the information. Not even obliquely. But every time he didn't meet her gaze, he was sending up a flare. All she had to do was figure out what he expected her to do. Then do the opposite.

The night wasn't quiet at all. There were animals on the prowl, night birds, trees meeting wind, creaks from the old cabin. Dan had his eyes open, one arm behind his head, the other on his chest. It was a dark he was used to, not pitch black because of the three-quarter moon, which was good for some operations, bad for others. The stars would be gorgeous at this altitude, with no major cities for hundreds of miles

He guessed the time at just past two a.m. and he wished like hell he'd worked harder before the sun had gone down. He counted on exhaustion to put him to sleep these days, which wasn't good. To do what he did, as well as he was able, he needed to totally own sleep. He was trained to do whatever was required no matter how long he'd been awake, but a smart man used the opportunities he was handed to rest, to regroup, recharge.

Since the mission in Sangin when his C.O.—

Dan turned over, punched his pillow. Made himself inhale for ten, hold for six, exhale for ten until he felt lightheaded. After, he ran through the pinpoint exercise, focusing on a single spot in his body for twenty seconds, starting at his toes and moving up. Every time his mind started to move outside the lines, he pulled it back.

The center of his left calf. The scar on his right knee. The bruise on his right thigh.

He kept on task, concentrating until the part of him that wanted to relive the worst night of his life gave it up.

Dan had to use Renee's satellite phone because his personal unit didn't have a signal. He hadn't wanted to make the call at all, but it had to be done.

"Hello."

Just hearing his mother's voice made him realize how big the problem was. "Hi, Mom."

"Danny! Oh, my goodness. You and your secret phones, I had no idea you were going to call. Your dad and I were on our way out. To think five minutes later we would have missed you."

"I can call another time. I don't want to mess up your plans."

"Don't be silly, honey. What could be more important than you?"

He walked over to the wood pile and kicked the shit out of a log. "How are you?"

"We're fine. Have you been getting our letters? I know Dad's been sending email and it's hard not to worry a bit when you can't answer right away . . . . "

"This was a long stretch. I'm sorry."

"It's okay. I'm just so glad to hear from you. Can we expect a visit, too?"

Dan closed his eyes. "Not yet, Mom. I'm sorry. We're not gonna be stateside for awhile. But don't worry. I'm fine. I'm really good. Feeling great. Doing fine. I just miss you. Both of you."

His mother didn't answer straight away. When she did, her voice sounded tight. "We miss you terribly, honey. But we love you and support you completely. Remember that, okay?"

Renee hadn't intended to eavesdrop until the opportunity presented itself. She'd had to get hammers. It wasn't her fault that Dan had taken her phone outside, right around the corner from where she was now pressed against the wall. Besides, her definition of friendship had always been fluid, but this was a no-brainer. The man was in trouble and now she had proof.

Dan was many things, but he wasn't a liar. Whatever was going on with him had to be bad. He'd never hurt his mother willingly, so in his head, he was reasonably certain that visiting his parents while he was on leave was worse than lying outright.

"Renee's fine," he said. "I'll see her when I come, but she's doing well. Writing another true crime book. She keeps herself busy."

That, at least, was true. She heard Dan's boots crunch then his voice grew softer as he walked away from the cabin toward the road. She waited until she couldn't hear him, then dashed back to the equipment shed where she pulled out two hammers. One huge mother, and one she could use.

The plumbing problem had turned out to be almost as simple as promised, and she now had actual running water on demand, without all the sound effects.

Dan and she had worked until the sun went down, then stayed up kind of late reminiscing. The whole time, for all the laughing they'd done, she'd seen the sadness in him. He'd always fit inside his skin better than anyone she'd ever known. This trip? He was a skinwalker, a man who didn't belong. Completely unnerving, especially the way he was playing at being fine. Perhaps the act would have worked on someone who didn't know him, but she did. She was an expert on Dan Hogan.

She was still trying to figure out why he'd spent so much time talking about her ex-boyfriends. He had the whole list in his head, and all their faults down to the guy who'd dared to lose her apartment key twice.

She'd wanted to ask if they'd made a mistake not getting together back then. If they were making a mistake now. But if they ever did choose to cross that gap between friend and lover, she wanted him sober and happy. Last night he hadn't been either.

"So, did you get enough information out there, because I can replay the whole conversation verbatim if you need me to."

She'd jumped about a foot at Dan's voice directly behind her. She spun around, her heart slamming in her chest. "You scared me half to death."

"Well?" His arms were crossed, and his eyes had narrowed, but that didn't mean much. The little vein at his temple was throbbing like a sonofabitch, and that did.

"Want to tell me why you lied to your mother?"

"No."

"What kind of an answer is that?"

"Better than it's none of your goddamn business."

That stopped her. A chill ran down to her toes, and it was all she could do not to tear up. Not because she was a delicate flower, but because her friend, a man she loved more than anyone on the planet, was in deep, deep trouble.

Same bed, different night, wide awake. Dan was getting sick of this shit. Sick of his traitorous mind, his memories. Of his goddamn feelings.

He'd thought it might be better, being with Renee, but it wasn't. She was his favorite person. To be near her had always meant relaxation and fun and closeness. Just because they'd decided not to get naked together didn't mean he didn't love her, which he did. He had for a long time. But that only made the situation worse.

Disgusted with himself, he broke down and looked at the bedside alarm. 1:50 a.m. Shit. The breathing thing was taking longer every night, and each night it became harder to concentrate on anything that wasn't that mission. But he didn't have a lot of options, so he inhaled for ten, held it—

Two taps on the door then it opened. He exhaled quietly, his body as tense as a bow even though he knew it was Renee. She didn't turn on the light as she shut the door behind her.

God, she was wearing nothing. Almost. Just panties and a tank T. It wasn't the first time he'd seen her in her preferred sleepwear, but it was cold up here and he'd assumed . . . .

She was at his bed, and he raised himself on his elbow. "What—"

"Shhh. Lay back down," she whispered.

He did as she'd asked, but why whisper? It was only the two of them. She wasn't scared, there was no sign that someone or something was outside trying to get it. But the next thing he knew, she was standing on his bed, her bare feet on either side of his chest.

One more step put her on the side by the wall where she crouched, lifted up his covers, and started to slide in next to him.

"What are you doing?" Shit, he was whispering, too. And thinking this was something they should have talked about.

"Scoot over," she said, wiggling her way down, rubbing up against his bare chest, his boxers, and her foot was freezing as it brushed his thigh.

He let out a huff, but he moved, letting his infuriating friend take over his space, unnerved that it wouldn't take much for him to get completely hard. She had the gall to pull out the pillow from underneath his head and adjust it behind her back.

This time his huff had a growl to it, but she didn't even pause. She was too busy arranging him. She yanked, tugged and poked him when he wasn't moving fast enough, but finally he was lying on his side, his head nestled against her shoulder, her arm bracing his back. One of her legs had curled around his so the two of them were twined together.

It was anything but comfortable. He wasn't used to being the one who got held. If it had been anyone else, he'd have broken out of her grasp so damn fast her head would have spun. But this was Renee, and she got special dispensation. Besides, he owed her for being such a prick this afternoon.

"I can hear you thinking," she said. "Stop it. You're not suddenly losing all your machismo because I'm holding you. And I know it's not going to be easy, but I need you to relax."

"Why?"

Her hand, the one that had been cradling his shoulder, moved to his head. Her fingertips brushed from his temples through his hair. Short, gentle strokes. "Because we need to talk. And because you love me, you're going to listen."

He wanted to argue. His body was still fighting him, though. He didn't like the position, the vulnerability. It didn't help that he'd been so wound up before she'd even tapped on his door.

"Hush," she said, lowering her voice so he barely heard her. "Let it go. No one can see you. It's just the two of us. You're safe. You're fine."

The only thing he could think of was to do the breathing thing. In for ten, hold for six, out for ten. She kept petting him and he kept inhaling, exhaling, listening to her murmur soft words, some he couldn't make out, some he figured weren't words at all.

"That's right," she said. "That's it."

He noticed his shoulders had relaxed, that he'd stopped fighting. He let himself be cocooned in her soft embrace, let himself fall into her sweet, womanly scent. Every stroke of her fingertips made his heart calm a little bit more.

"Now comes the talking part," she said. "I know you can't tell me much. I don't expect or want you to give away your secrets. But there are things you can say. Something's eating at you, sweetie. Something big. And as strong as you are, my love, you can't carry everything by yourself. Talk to me. Tell me what's tying you in knots. Because it is my business. Whether you like it or not. But you don't have to worry. I'll listen, I'll hear you, and when you've said it all, I'll still love you. I'll still be the same Renee. And you'll be my Dan."

He tensed again but didn't move. He could be out of the bed in a heartbeat, and she'd understand, she would because she knew him better than anyone. So why didn't she understand that he couldn't tell her? Not this.

She kissed the top of his head. "I promise. You're safe here."

He pulled the edge of the sheet off the mattress as the pain in his chest tried to bust its way out. The ache in his bones seared him like a burn until his whole goddamn body was shaking.

She kissed his cheek, then his lips so gently it tore the resistance right out of him.

Closing his eyes, he exhaled slowly, praying, struggling for that last shred of self-control to stop him. Maybe if she hadn't been holding him, he'd have more fight left, but this was Renee . . . .

Something broke inside. The damn that had been choking the life out of him. It was probably the worst idea ever to start talking now, but he couldn't keep it inside. Everything he'd tried had failed. This might be his only shot.

He took the deepest breath he could, then forged ahead. "I had a friend," he said, and Jesus, his voice sounded wrecked. "His name was John, and he was my C.O. He was the best man I ever knew. Stronger and smarter than any SEAL I'd ever heard of. He was everything I wanted to be. I trained with him, and he didn't let up, not once. But he believed in me. He was fearless, and he made me fearless. Our whole team, we could do anything. Anything. No task was too tough for us, because we all knew John could take it, and if he could, we could.

"He must have gotten mixed up, somehow. He was fine, everything had been fine, the mission, the plan, there was no confusion, it was all copasetic. But he walked out the wrong way. He walked out, turned left instead of right, and they killed him. They just blew his head off, because he wasn't even ducking.

"We were all over them before the smoke cleared, but it was too late for John. The mission was successful, except he was dead. For no reason. He turned the wrong way."

"God, I'm sorry," she whispered, holding him as tight as she could. "So sorry."

"I went to see his family. His wife. His mother. They were . . . God, they were devastated, and I couldn't help them."

He sniffed, looked up, even though he couldn't make out her eyes in the dark. "I got scared, Renee. I can't have that. There's no room for that shit. I have to know who I am with every step. I can't go out there with a chink in my armor. I have to get over it. Let it go. I can't be worrying about someone going to see my parents. Coming to see you. I can't."

She squeezed him tight for a minute, then she went back to stroking his hair, breathing deep and easy, her body all around him.

"Okay then," she said. "Here's what we're gonna do. You're going to give me that doubt. You're gonna just hand it to me, and I'm going to hold it for you. I'm gonna keep it for as long as you need me to. For the rest of our lives. I will be your safe place. The place you get to be soft. Right here, just like this. When you leave my arms, you leave whole. Because you already are.

"You're not broken, sweetie, you're human. You're incredibly strong. You're a wonder. You'll return to your team as the warrior you've always been. And you'll know that at any time, you can come to me, and you'll know that my arms are strong enough."

For a long time, Dan couldn't move. He breathed and he felt the warmth of her body, the softness of her touch, the strength of her offer. He felt tears on his cheeks, but he didn't bother to wipe them away.

He missed his friend, and he despaired that he would never know what had happened. For the first time since that mission, he let himself grieve.

When he looked up at her again, the night wasn't as dark. "What about you?" he asked.

"What about me?"

"Things could change. I don't know how long I'll be out there."

"I signed up for the duration, Danny. So don't you worry about me. There's really no chance of you getting rid of me at all."

Gently, he moved. It was a slow shift, but he knew where he wanted to end up. When she was finally in his arms, and he could look into her eyes and see that she had meant every word, he smiled. "I do love you, you know."

"Yeah."

"After . . . . "

She put two fingers on his lips. "I'm good," she said. "I can wait."

He nodded as he moved her fingers. Then he kissed her, and he was the man he was supposed to be, and he thought, *thank you, thank you, thank God for you.*

HER SECRET PIRATE
(A *Crossfire SEAL* Story)

Gennita Low

"The captain has determined that the Ambassador is in imminent danger of being discovered and that we must act now before dawn. The President has given the go-ahead orders. The four of you are tasked to take down the pirates. Zone, you've been cleared to go."

Zodenko "Zone" Zonovich swallowed his relief, retaining his calm demeanor as much as possible. "Thank you, sir!"

He'd downplayed his relationship with the Ambassador's daughter although he didn't think his commander believed him. Just a few dates, he'd assured, which was technically true. Rebecca Powers wasn't someone he could take out on a regular date, not when she was the personal aid to the Honorable Paul Powers, the U.S. ambassador to India, as well as his daughter. No, their secret meetings couldn't be called dates. And they'd agreed to . . . cool it . . . he guessed that would be the term because . . . damn, he didn't know why he'd agreed to it now. It was over an argument about, of all stupid things, war. He was a SEAL. Participating in warfare was his job.

He had better push all that out of his mind right now. The first order of the day was to follow instructions, go with his team to get the pirates before they turned on the news and found out Rebecca Powers was the Ambassador's daughter. That was what initiated the "imminent danger" decision; the media was naming names and in this day and age, it seemed that even pirates checked their Twitter accounts while terrorizing the seas.

His squad of four, including him, consisted of three of his closest friends, Cucumber, Mink, and Joker. Joker and he were snipers and their specialty would be needed once they'd snuck on board the taken vessel. The element of surprise had to be quick and deadly. Their target—the men guarding the captured crew. Four shots for four men. Cucumber and Mink's job was to take down the rest as quickly as possible while he located those who were still in hiding in the ship, Rebecca being one of them.

While they silently prepared for the mission, his commander, Hawk McMillan, finished his conversation on the satellite phone and turned to them, his expression revealing bad news ahead. Hawk and the rest of Zone's SEAL team were heading for another target, the "mother" ship coming this way.

"Listen up," he said. "These are well-prepared hostiles, armed with grenades, launchers, you name it, they probably have it. Their goal, presumably, had been the food aid on board. Everything was still fine at that point until the pirates found out the Ambassador was on board. The fucking media has broadcasted the news all over the channels. So now they're making threats and looking for the Ambassador.

"We know the Ambassador and his aid have hidden themselves in the safe rooms but they were somehow separated. The Ambassador has radioed in that he's okay but he's more concerned about his daughter. He said that if they find his daughter, he'll give himself up. Needless to say, your job is to make sure you find both of them when you get on board."

"How many on board, sir?" Cucumber asked.

"We see four securing the crew and we think eight searching the ship. The firefight took out two of the hostiles. The ambassador's men and the crew's shots has sunk their skiff, so they're angry and getting angrier, and they're starting to feel anxious waiting for their main ship to pick them up. Now, whether my crew and I succeed in delaying the other ship, you four have your orders. Unless they surrender, shoot to kill."

"Yes, sir!"

"It's dark. They've purposely killed the lights because they know about the possibility of snipers and they're using human shields. Study the map and photos, locate the safe rooms, and search them. Be aware that they're searching too so the ones in danger won't know you aren't the bad guys. Only the ambassador knows because he has the means to communicate. As far as we can tell, the rest in hiding know nothing so you have to exercise caution who you're taking out."

"Yes, sir!"

Zone looked down at the map, studying all the areas outlined in red. Swimming to the ship and slipping on board were the easy part, even though their usual eight-man team had been divided in half.

Taking out four hostiles? Hell, he could do that with one arm tied around his back. His finger touched Rebecca's photo, tracing the outline of her face. But making sure his woman wasn't harmed? That part made his chest area ached like never before. Where the hell was Rebecca hiding?

Rebecca had never been so afraid in her life. This morning, she'd been so excited about taking part in the international food aid treaty, knowing she was doing something about which she was passionate instead of just working the red tape. She was finally about see, with her own eyes, that the food and aid sent out reached the people that needed them most instead of being "lost" or confiscated once they reached port. Their entourage had boarded from the Seychelles Islands and started their goodwill voyage after signing the treaty, partly political publicity stunt and partly a sincere wish to see a good start to the food program. They were going to meet up with a navy ship, flying off to sign the treaty, and then later in the month, fly to India to meet the ship as it arrived at port there. Everything had been planned to a T, from meeting the VIPs to publicity shots to map routes to handing out the food to the villagers.

But that was this morning. All the planning hadn't covered *this*. Never in her life had she imagined that by dark, she would be hiding in the bowels of the ship being chased by pirates. She was afraid. For herself. And for her father, who had been separated from her when the lights went off. Someone had roughly grabbed her and she'd kicked out at him, just the way Zone had taught her when he was instructing her class, and she'd escaped.

Zone. Rebecca closed her eyes. She'd called him a pirate once. They'd snuck away on his motorcycle and once they were out in the country, they'd ridden around without their helmets. With the carelessly tied bandanna over his dark curly hair and his equally dark gypsy eyes, all he needed was an earring and longer braided hair. Pirate, she'd teased him. And he'd laughed and hauled her over his shoulder, threatening her with all sorts of delicious things pirates were supposed to do to their captives.

Rebecca opened her eyes. Dammit. This wasn't the time to think of Zone and her playing pirate. This was the real thing. With big evil men shooting up there and looking for her and Dad. She'd been in enough political maneuverings to understand now that without their getaway boat, the pirates were going to need hostages and they were looking for the most obvious. Her father, the ambassador would be the prime candidate. Of course, with them all separated, she had no idea whether they'd captured him. She prayed that he was safe.

Zone. She mouthed his name as she peered out into the darkness. They had an argument. It'd escalated from a simple discussion into their work; she was all about peace and he was all about war, or some such stupidly childish accusation. She'd been horrible, saying he was a killer. She was wrong. She knew it then but wouldn't take back her words. Now the universe was punishing her by showing her how wrong she was, because right now, real killers were looking for her. She almost screamed when somewhere above, a volley of gunfire interrupted the suffocating silence, almost in unison, like gunshots at a soldier's funeral. What was happening on the deck?

She drew back at a sound from around the corner, becoming louder. Flashlight zigzagged its way down the passageway towards her. Hurried footsteps. A loud thud. A curse in some language she didn't know.

Behind a stack of boxes, Rebecca flattened herself against the wall, trying not to breathe, trying to listen above her thudding heart. Her hand curled around the dinner knife she'd picked up. Training. She must remember all the moves she'd learned from Zone's self-defense class.

The flashlight came closer. She hoped her pursuer wouldn't see her till he actually came close enough to inspect. Then maybe she had a chance of surprising him. The light became brighter as the man came closer and she could hear the first of the boxes being shoved aside. She'd moved a few of them aside to get to her hiding spot and knew they weren't that heavy.

She braced one foot against the box in front of her, the cardboard cool and dry against her skin. She'd taken off her heels after running away from her pursuers; they were making too much noise. She could feel the beads of perspiration slowly traveling down her forehead as she waited. Two more. One. Then, with as much strength as she could muster, she kicked out, toppling the stack.

But her timing wasn't quite right. Too late Rebecca realized her mistake. The stack of boxes didn't fall over immediately, swaying for one precious second, giving her attacker time to leap out of the way. She saw the light swinging a wide arc to her left and made the quick decision to run for it from the right side. Something tripped her and she let out a small shriek as she fell on her knees. That something was a hand and it encircled her bare foot.

She tried to stand up anyway, knowing that she was done for if she let herself fall flat, blindly kicking out with her free foot. Her attacker let go. She turned to run. He was quick, somehow managing to grab hold of her skirt. Suddenly remembering the knife in her hand, she turned and swung out. It wasn't the sharp kind but it still went through flesh and the man yelled out in pain. Sickened, she turned again to escape but he still held on to her tightly. A big hand grabbed her neck. This time, she screamed in panic as she tried to wrench free.

The sudden flare of the emergency lights startled them both, freezing their struggle as their eyes tried to adjust. A figure, clad in black, appeared in the tight passageway. He walked toward them, weapon in hand.

"Let her go. It's over."

If it weren't connected to her skull, Rebecca's jaw would have fallen on the floor. Zone. She would recognize that husky voice with the slight accent anywhere, even coming from a stranger with black and green camouflage streaks painted on his face. He was the answer she'd been unconsciously praying for—powerful, dangerous, one hundred percent warrior. He glanced at her once, very briefly, his gaze cool, taking in the situation. Then his gaze returned to some point above her head.

"Come nearer and she dies," her captor warned, his accent thick. The hand around her neck pulled back threateningly, choking off her air. "She's coming with me and you're going to let me take the lifeboat to wait for my ship to pick me up. You'll do as I say or I kill her."

"You hurt one hair on her and you get a bullet right in the middle of your forehead. I don't miss. Let her go. Surrender and live."

Zone's toneless voice sent shivers down her spine. He'd never sounded so scary, even when he played the bad guy during class.

"No. You tell the captain I want to negotiate for a lifeboat. She's coming with me. You go tell whoever is in charge. Or I'll start using this knife on her."

How did he get hold of her knife? Zone kept advancing as her captor, pulling her along, kept backing away. She kept her gaze trained on Zone, trying to read his thoughts.

In class, Zone had emphasized three things in the act of self-defense. Scream a lot. The element of surprise. And if all failed, attack when the enemy least expected it. The thought of going with the pirate onto a lifeboat made her sick with fear. The knowledge that she might actually end up being a hostage away from the ship scared her into another split-second decision.

"Stay back! I say I'll cut—"

The women in her self-defense class had practiced the move many times because many attacks came from behind. Rebecca pivoted sharply to her right, at the same time throwing her right hand high in the air. Her elbow angled perfectly to break the pirate's hold. Then, using all her strength, she swept her other elbow up and backwards, powering all her momentum into his solar plexus.

He let out a gasp and toppled backwards.

The next part of her lesson was easy. Run.

Rebecca turned to hurry off in Zone's direction but he was already there, pulling her behind him as he trained his weapon on the fallen pirate. He kicked the fallen knife out of the way. She grabbed on to his back for a long moment. He felt so solid and safe. And familiar. She wanted to hang on to him. She wanted him to turn around and hold her tight. A hundred questions flooded her brain—why he was here, how, her father—but she understood that it wasn't over. Taking a deep breath, she took a few steps back to let Zone do his job.

She watched as he pulled a cord from a side pouch and went down on one knee. He worked unbelievably fast, gagging and tying up the downed man as if he were cattle. Then he turned, his gaze darting left and right, checking the surroundings.

His camouflaged face had a fierce expression as he reached for her. He cupped her face and gave her a hard kiss.

"Are you hurt?"

She shook her head. She opened her mouth to ask him all the questions swirling in her mind but he bent his head and kissed her again, this time more lingeringly. The taste of him, male and something indefinable, always made her go a little crazy. This time was no different. With adrenalin added to the mix, she responded with a passion that surprised him into allowing her to push him against the passage wall. She ran her hands all over his hair and his hard muscled body as her tongue tangled with his wildly, insistently. She'd missed him so much. Did he miss her?

Damn, he didn't want to stop. He'd kissed her to reassure himself. The sight of her in danger had given him a jolt of fear that he'd never felt before. And then she'd gone and taken care of her attacker with an efficiency that would make his SEAL brothers proud.

Just a quick kiss, he'd told himself. But her tongue and her hands tempted him to continue. She was kissing him with that sexy passion that made him want to take her then and there. How many times in the past months had he fantasized having her in his arms again? Naked. Sweaty. With hours . . . heat gathered where it shouldn't. Man. The timing sucked.

With great reluctance, Zone curled his hands around the sweet curve of her hips and put her away from him. "We've got to get back on deck to make sure the others have been taken down," he told her. He gave her a fleeting caress on the side of her face. "Later. You're mine later."

He grinned when she made a face at him. Her eyes were bright with unshed tears and he'd wanted to distract her from her fear. "Come on," he told her. "Follow close and keep quiet, just in case there's another lurking close by."

She nodded.

He activated the receiver in his belt. "Zone reporting in. Miss Powers is with me. Two hostiles are down on my end. Over."

"Bad news. The enemy has the ambassador," his commander told him through his ear mic. "He communicated with the satellite phone again."

That explained the emergency lights coming on. The head pirate must have activated it after capturing the ambassador. He didn't need to grope around in the dark now. "How many?" Zone asked.

"One, as far as we know. He's heading to the deck. He has asked for a lifeboat for him and his men. He doesn't know all his men on deck are down."

"He'll want to contact his ship to pick him up," Zone said. He shook his head at Rebecca's questioning gaze. "Are we negotiating?"

"We're almost to their main ship. We'll be delaying any contact from our end. Can you take out the lone pirate?"

"I've to go on deck and find a suitable location."

"Do it if you can. But the ambassador's safety comes first. Joker's listening in. You coordinate with him. Copy that? Over."

"Yes, sir, copy. Over."

The look on Zone's face had changed from teasing to serious as he

talked to the person on the other end. The conversation made her fear
for the worst.

"Zone?" she whispered when he finished. "Is it Dad ... the
Ambassador?"

He nodded. "He's been taken. Let's go up."

Rebecca shook her head. "Wait. We were down two levels when
the lights went off. Someone tried to grab me but I got away and ran
up here. I heard Dad calling me but we got separated. No one has
come up here. I've moved around but not far from the stairs."

Zone frowned. "The lights went off and you were attacked
immediately?"

"Yes."

"When did your security detail order you to come down?"

"When the pirates started firing at us and managed to come close
enough to board." It was her turn to frown. "They shouldn't be on us
so quickly, right? And the lights shouldn't have gone off that fast
either."

"Right." Zone clicked on his belt again. "Joker, count the security
personnel. Ask for who's missing. Any chance you can kill the
emergency lights from up there? ASAP. Suspicion of breach in the
ambassador's security detail. Over." He pointed to the boxes behind
which she had been hiding. "Rebecca, get back there now and stay out
of sight."

"Be careful," she mouthed.

She followed his order, squeezing behind a few disarrayed boxes.
Peering between them, she watched Zone kneel down in front of her
attacker. His hand struck downwards, fast like a snake coming at its
prey, and the tied man's head dropped sideways. She'd barely
processed what Zone had done when the lights gave a strange hum,
dimmed, and went out, and she was back in darkness once again.

This time, she wasn't as afraid. Zone was here, even though she
couldn't see or hear him. She pinched herself. Ow. Okay, she hadn't
fallen asleep and dreamed him up. He was really, really here. Her eyes
tried to pierce the veil of darkness.

"Copy." His voice floated to her.

It was just the merest whisper but it was reassuring to know he
was close by. He must still be communicating with members of his
team. What was his plan? She was worried about her father. Was he
injured? Zone hadn't said he was, just that he was coming up with the
pirate. No, not pirate. Zone's questions had planted the suspicion that

whoever had her father was one of their own. The idea that someone close had betrayed them explained the coincidence of the pirates' appearance just after most of the media had left and before the Navy ship's arrival to pick them up. She tried to remember who had been with them as they rushed down. Johnson? No, he was still on deck, instructing the other men. Sandow? No.

Panfilo. Rebecca bit her lip. Panfilo had been her personal guard for a few months now, accompanying her as she traveled back and forth from the States. He was a big man and was hired for his fighting skills. She needed to warn Zone.

The stairs doorway creaked. She froze, holding her breath, her eyes straining, trying to see. The footsteps sounded hesitant, as if the owner was unsure. A thud.

"Keep moving," a voice commanded. Then she heard her father's gasp.

Rebecca put a fist over her mouth. Panfilo. And the first set of footsteps, the one she heard stumbling, must be her father's.

The other stairway was through another door just around the corner. She hadn't dared climb them when she was alone, afraid that the noise of treading the metal steps would attract the other pirates. Zone would know they were heading that way.

Everything happened at once.

She heard Zone's crisply worded "Now." The lights came back on. She saw her father and Panfilo, both looking up, eyes squinting in surprise. Then Zone was there, reaching in, snapping Panfilo's arm back, and everything became a blur. She bit down on her knuckles as she watched the men struggle. Panfilo still had his weapon but his hold on her father had loosened as he fended off Zone's hits. Someone pushed her father out of the way.

Panfilo kicked out. To her relief, Zone averted it while still managing to hold on to Panfilo's hand. Then Zone swung the arm sideways and she heard a crack. The weapon dropped to the ground. But Panfilo didn't make a sound as he fought back with a vicious side punch that connected. He bent down to retrieve the gun but was slammed hard into the wall by Zone.

She had only seen beautifully choreographed exhibition fights, never like this, with life-or-death consequences. Zone had placed himself between her father and Panfilo, giving her father a chance to escape. Panfilo took the moment to dive for the gun on the floor. Zone fell on top of him and they rolled around, each trying to gain the upper hand.

When Panfilo's hand covered Zone's face, trying to push his fingers into his eyes, Rebecca couldn't take it anymore. She pushed the boxes aside, forgetting about everything except the urgency to help her man. She ignored her father's calling her name, her gaze riveted on the deadly struggle. Zone had somehow pried the man's hand away from his face. He head-butted Panfilo and, with a grunt, rolled on top of him. Move countered move. Another roll. Another. Her heart stopped as a gunshot rang out. Zone's body slumped and stopped moving for a long moment.

No! No, no, no, please God, no!

Rebecca choked out the strangled sobs that were stuck in her throat. Her feet felt like lead. Then she saw Zone sit up. His hand moved to his belt.

"Hostile down. Ambassador and Miss Powers safe. Is all clear to go up on deck? Over."

"Zone," she breathed out, relief making her knees weak. She fell into her father's arms. All she could say was, "Dad. Zone."

"With your permission, sir."

"Of course."

Suddenly it was Zone carrying her. She looked up, his face smeared with red, green and black, and never had he looked so good. She said his name again and felt like an idiot for having broken off with him because of a stupid argument. He wasn't a killer; he'd put her and her father's lives before his.

"It's all right," he reassured her. "Your father's safe and you're going to be okay."

"I didn't faint. I can walk," she said.

"I much prefer this."

He held her against his chest and it felt so good to hear his heartbeat. She reached up and touched his face. "I'm sorry about our argument. I was wrong."

He smiled that sinfully sexy smile, making her forget the rest of the planned apology. He shook his head, mouthing "okay" before setting her on her feet at the stairwell.

"Thank you," her father said, "for coming here in time. I never realized anything was wrong and let Panfilo into the safe room when he said it was him. It's Zone, isn't it? I barely recognize you without that bandanna."

"Yes, it's me, sir."

"All clear." Someone said from above. "We're escorting the Ambassador to our ship ASAP. His security detail will have to be verified."

It made sense that the SEALs weren't going to trust anyone right now. They went out on deck and Rebecca watched as the ambassador shook hands with the men dressed exactly like Zone. Only four of them against all the pirates? She knew about the SEALs' training, of course, but reading about their skills and watching them in action—okay, just one, but at close quarters—were two different things.

Contrast to the suffocating silence while she was hiding, there was now a frenzy of activity on deck. Those who had accompanied her father. The crew. The rest of the security detail. The only group not moving were the four SEALs, who stood and kept their attention on the Ambassador. She listened to their quiet exchange while her father went over to talk to Johnson, his security chief.

"All hostiles accounted for. All the security detail," one of them said. "The media's flying in. Let's hope we get off before they arrive."

"Yeah. At least we have our best make up on for their cameras."

"Damn, Cumber, we should've brought our Hollywood shades, man."

"Unlike you guys, I look great with or without them. Nice first shots there, three for three." The tallest of them thumbed toward the far end of the deck. "What happened to your face, Zone? Pirate got you?"

"Small resistance," Zone replied. "Nothing I couldn't handle."

"He was busy talking, I bet."

"Busy something-something, I bet."

"Can't blame him. I heard he and the Ambassador's daughter were . . . acquainted."

"Dude, he practically begged Hawk to let him come with us. Bet you they're more than—"

She tugged at Zone's belt. He took a step back and lowered his head so her words were for him alone.

"You'd better text me your next shore leave. We need to talk," she murmured. "After today, I definitely prefer you as the pirate."

His smile was slow and hot, the kind that promised more than talking. Instead of being in shock or hugging her father, she was standing in her bare feet, grinning foolishly like some infatuated teenager. But his smile . . . and that mouth . . . she went on tiptoe and kissed his chin. If there weren't three other SEALs looking at them with interested smirks, she'd have jumped back into his arms and kissed him silly. His head turned. His lips brushed against her ear.

"Arrrrr," he said.

Epilogue

Despite their best efforts, the media never got close to the SEALs. Rebecca saw a newspaper article detailing the incident at sea. There was a picture of the Ambassador and her. There were pictures of uniformed personnel escorting them to the boat that took them to the Navy ship. The four SEALs with the camouflaged faces weren't there. One moment, when she'd turned after joining her father, she saw them still standing watch in the shadows. Next, they were gone.

It was like a dream.

The man climbing off the motorcycle to meet her was more of a fantasy, though. Her heart fluttered at the sight of his familiar figure in leather jacket and jeans. He took the jacket off, hooked it over his shoulder, and headed her way. He didn't look as scary without that camouflage, but now she understood why she had been drawn to him when they first met. It wasn't just the undercurrent of danger and the hint of darkness behind that devastating smile. It was the way he walked—was walking now—that sure confident stride that never hesitated when he first saw her. She smiled. The way those legs filled out the worn jeans wasn't half bad either.

He stopped in front of her. She wrapped her arms around his waist, lifting her head for his kiss. Warm. Tender. A lover's embrace.

"Hey," Zone said, when he finally broke the kiss. His voice was husky.

"Hey. Miss you." And she didn't just mean since the hijack at sea.

"I love your emails. Sorry I'm not good at writing back."

"I didn't expect you to reply all of them." She figured a SEAL was busy all the time doing dangerous stuff. They started walking towards her apartment building . "I've been reading a lot about what you guys do."

"Is that right." It was more a statement than a question.

"Yes. And Dad has been telling me all kinds of stories too. I think he's afraid I'd get serious with you, and now that he knows you're not just a self-defense instructor . . . . " She trailed off, shrugging. She didn't have to explain political life.

"He approve now, huh?" Zone sounded amused. "Elite soldier much better sounding than part-time immigrant, right?"

She made a face. "You're not going to argue with him about politics again, are you?"

"I'd rather do other stuff, actually." He leaned closer. "Like play pirate. You gonna invite me in?"

She flushed at the heated look he gave her. She wanted him too. It had been too long. But things needed to be said and that was why she had met him down here and not up at her place, where it would be too easy to succumb to temptation.

She cocked her head and looked up at him. "Why do I get the feeling we aren't going to talk when we go up? You agreed to dinner, remember?"

He growled mockingly. "Me hungry," he said, emphasizing his accent. "Very. Sweets, you look good enough to eat." He held up a hand and added, "But if you want to talk, we will. I already emailed how I feel."

She laughed as she pulled out the card to unlock the building front doors. "Oh. You mean, 'everything is cool. I want to be with you' is how you feel?"

"I'm not great with words, I know." He shrugged. "The last time we discussed my job, when you found out what I do, we ended up arguing."

And she still felt ashamed of her thoughtlessness. "I know and I'm . . . "

"Quit apologizing, Rebecca. I'd rather we argue than not talk at all. Just don't give me the cold shoulder again. That's the part I didn't like."

They went inside and were silent as they waited for the elevator. She studied him and he looked back solemnly, as if that was all that was on his mind. She wasn't fooled at all.

When they were inside the elevator, she said, "It's the political brat in me. I promise to curb her tongue from now on. Like I said, I've been reading up about the SEALs. I wanted to know what you are, what you do, and not be ignorant anymore."

He sighed. "But you know me. I'm Zone. I'm crazy about you. I enjoy apple pie and ice cream. I love watching soccer. And right now, all I want to do is spend the night with you, showing you what an absolutely normal male I am."

His words warmed her insides. Sure, the man didn't say much but he'd always been good at showing her what he meant. They reached her floor and the door opened.

"Zone, we're talking about a long-distance relationship. With my dad's new appointment, I'll be traveling a lot the next year or so. It's going to be tough for us."

They paused outside her door. He turned. Tipped her chin up with his forefinger. "It's tough to be in any relationship. Ours will be challenging. All along, I've been willing to give it all I got, even with your dad's disapproval. The most important thing I want to know now is, are you tough enough to be with me?"

She met his eyes squarely. "Hey, you saw me knock down a bad guy twice my size. You think I'm not tough enough?"

His smile was slow. "Remembering you moving like that made all those hours on the floor mat with you worth it. Let's try it in bed. Are we through talking yet? 'Cause I'm hungry."

She opened the door. "Welcome home, sailor."

"Arrrrr." In one smooth move, he threw her over one shoulder and strode in, one foot kicking the door shut behind him.

Rebecca had her very own secret pirate. Not many women could boast that.

SEALed by Fate

Marliss Melton

Operation "Dumb Broad" was underway. The instant the Mark V-1 Special Operations Craft slid onto a deserted strip of shore along the Rio Grande River, Lt. Sam Sasseville stripped off his night ops jacket, stuffed it inside the gunwale locker, and leapt ashore with a lightweight pack.

Dressed to resemble a civilian, he wore black jeans, his pockets filled with extra ammo, and a baggy black T-shirt concealing the SIG Sauer P226 holstered to the small of his back. A Gerber blade was tucked inside his right sock, and his pack contained a helmet, radio, NVGs, MRE's, baby wipes, and a clean T-shirt.

Sam's jungle-green eyes appeared black under the drizzling night sky. His thick head of dark hair and the swarthy skin he'd inherited from his Cuban grandmother simplified his infiltration into the Mexican province of Tamaulipas.

Two of his teammates, Harley and Teddy, had a harder time disguising themselves as locals. Harley, who was fair and bald, had slathered himself in bronzing lotion and covered his shaved head with a bandana. Teddy, who was African American, wore a floppy hat to disguise his onyx skin. Only Vinny, a full-blooded Italian, merged into his present surroundings as easily as Sam—provided he kept his mouth shut. That would be the hardest part of the op for Vinny.

The lapping of water muffled the SEALs' trek across the mud to the predetermined location, deep in the scrub brush. As the K50S water jets on the Mark V carried the craft silently back to the Gulf, the squad rallied up, squatting to keep their heads low. They wouldn't need the Mark V again. If everything went as planned, they would exfiltrate the country via helo.

Sam checked his watch. He pulled his sat phone from his back pocket and called up headquarters.

"Homeplate," said the ops officer, who sat before a computer monitor at the Spec Ops Headquarters back in Virginia.

"This is Striker Team Lead, checking in, sir. We're at the infil site now, waiting for the OGA vehicle, over."

"Roger that, Team Lead. Keep me posted, over."

"Here it comes now," Harley said. He'd been sweeping their perimeter through the high powered scope on his sniper rifle. "Right on time."

Over the patter of rain, Sam detected the rumble of a car engine as it drew closer. Twin beams sheared the tops of the scrub brush around them. The other government agent, or OGA, was a DEA officer who'd volunteered to help out. He would escort them into Matamoros, the lawless town situated across the U.S. border from Brownsville, Texas. There, they would initiate a twenty-four hour reconnaissance, monitoring the movements in and around the site, before sweeping in to recover their target.

Then the OGA would drive like hell to a distant exfil point, where a Navy Seahawk would be waiting to swoop them all safely.

Piece. Of. Cake.

Sam slipped his sat phone back into his pocket, maintaining a tight leash on his temper. This whole goddamn op shouldn't be happening at all if Senator Paul Scott's idiot daughter had left Matamoros when the Embassy issued a mandatory evacuation for Americans. If not for her, he'd be headed for Malaysia now as part of the team tasked to take out an infamous Malaysian arms smuggler. Instead, he was playing nursemaid to a humanitarian aid worker who didn't have any sense of self-preservation. This mission had "Complete Waste of Time" stamped all over it, damn it. Sam hadn't fought to become a SEAL so he could waste his time. He'd done it to be part of something meaningful. And this was so not it.

What annoyed him most was if Miss Scott were anyone other than the daughter of the President's golfing buddy, Sam and his squad would be well on their way to Malaysia right now. He'd renamed this mission "Operation Dumb Broad" in honor of her idiocy.

"That's our guy," Harley confirmed, lowering his weapon. The OGA vehicle came to a stop and dimmed its lights.

"Go," Sam growled. As the officer in charge, it was up to him to call the shots.

Vinnie darted out of hide first, providing cover for Teddy and then Harley, who leapfrogged his position. Sam brought up the rear and was the first into the rust-colored taxi, taking shotgun. His three companions squeezed into the back seat, grunting at the tight fit. Cigarette smoke filled the car's interior. They slid on seats covered in plastic. The car even had a working meter.

"Welcome to hell," drawled the DEA officer, tossing his Marlboro out the window. Engaging the meter like he intended them to charge them for every kilometer, he hammered the accelerator. The crucifix hanging from the rear view mirror swung wildly.

Beyond the slapping windshield wipers, the glow of Matamoros beckoned them into danger.

Madison Scott jerked to her elbows and plumbed the dark dormitory for a threat. Something had wakened her. Her heart was trotting with terror, but the room looked exactly as it should beyond the mosquito netting.

It must have been a dream that disturbed her, brought on no doubt by the overpowering heat and the sounds of the city beyond the closed shutters. If only it were safe to open them. The fan secured to the crossbeam did nothing but stir the humid air.

Coated in sweat and desperate for relief, Maddy kicked off the sheet that felt shrink-wrapped to her body. It wasn't enough. She hauled the confining length of her cotton nightdress to her hips. The suggestion of cooler air had her pulling her arms out of the elbow-length sleeves, as well, and pushing the damp fabric to her waist.

Better. This was how she usually slept—stark naked—but as a teacher of an all-girls' school it was up to her to set a modest example. With a long-suffering sigh, Maddy flopped back down onto the bed and wondered if she'd ever get a good night's sleep again.

Hah. The real question was would she live to see her next birthday?

A startled scream erupting out of the alley behind the school, made her gasp. It curtailed abruptly with the shattering of glass. *Dear God.*

Fisting the damp bedding, Maddy swallowed fear that had leapt up her throat. How long could she keep the drug lords out of the school now that her colleagues had departed? The rest of the staff at *El Santuario* had abandoned the building weeks ago, all except for Maddy, who'd pleaded with her colleagues to stay.

What would happen to the girls without their protection? The perverse images that crept into her head left her feeling sick. Pimps controlled the streets of Matamoros, forcing girls as young as thirteen into prostitution. She couldn't just abandon them and hope they managed to fend for themselves. But she was starting to fear that she was going to end up dead. Or worse.

The compound was enclosed by cinderblock walls, all topped with broken bits of glass, but the security guard had fled with the rising violence. The only things keeping the predators out and the girls safely inside were the locks on the doors and shutters. And how long before those were compromised?

With a whimper of helplessness, she closed her eyes and clasped her hands together, raising them in prayer. "God, I need your protection here," she whispered. "Someone has to keep the girls safe—"

The faintest suggestion of a chuckle cut her petition short. She whipped her head toward the ghostly sound, every muscle in her body jerking with the realization that she was not alone.

Striker Team's orders were to nab the recovery target as quietly as possible. Her father had warned them that she might resist. They had entered Miss Scott's chamber with painstaking stealth, hoping to grab her while she slept.

Only, no sooner had they eased into the shadows of her darkened bedroom than she'd lurched awake. Sam, who was using NVGs to make a positive ID, had almost swallowed his tongue.

Viewed through the neon green of his lenses, with her auburn hair in disarray about her shoulders, Miss Scott struck him as the antithesis of a humanitarian aid worker. To him, she looked like an exotic flower, endangered and delicate.

As she stared fearfully into the dark, her breath rasping in the quiet, he ordered his brain to engage and his mouth to announce their presence.

Only the words never made it to his lips. In a flurry of movement, she kicked off the sheet, wriggled her gown over her hips and yanked it off her shoulders, exposing the prettiest thighs and tits this side of the Rio Grande.

Too stunned to speak, Sam watched her lie back down, clasp her hands together, and whisper a fervent prayer.

He was still reeling when Harley, who stood in the shadows behind him, loosed the chuckle he was holding in.

With a shriek of terror, Maddy scrambled to her knees. The shadow she'd mistaken for her wardrobe detached itself from the wall, taking the shape of a very large man. She could hear him speak as he moved in her direction, putting away what looked like ... binoculars? But blood roared past her eardrums muffling his softly-spoken words.

As he sprang toward her bed to haul aside the mosquito netting, Maddy bolted. She leapt off the far side of the mattress, just avoiding his outstretched hand. With a squeal of terror, she sprinted toward the door, only to draw up short as a second man intercepted her path. Spinning about, she loosed the scream building in her chest as they boxed her in.

A large hand clamped down over her nose and mouth, cutting her scream short. A thick arm encircled her waist and plucked her off her feet. Caught up against a hard, male body, Maddy fought desperately to free herself.

"Quiet," commanded a gruff voice as he squeezed the air from her diaphragm.

No problem. She couldn't draw enough breath to make a sound.

How can this be happening to me? She had fought so long and hard to eradicate human trafficking from the earth. Yet here it was, happening to her. These men were abducting her! She would disappear into the underworld, another victim caught up in the sex trade.

Denial surged into her bloodstream. *Not if I can help it.*

Determined, Maddy bared her teeth and sank them into her captor's palm, biting down with all defiance she could muster. He yelped, releasing her so suddenly that she crashed to the tiled floor. Pain radiated up her spine. Ignoring it, Maddy scrambled desperately toward the door. Freedom was only a few feet away; she could make it.

"Umph." A tremendous force hit her from behind, tackling her to the floor. Her right cheek struck the tiles. The coppery taste of blood filled her mouth. She tried to struggle free, but her attacker's weight kept her prisoner. With the air driven from her lungs, she grew lightheaded.

"Hold her still," hissed a voice she associated with the laughter earlier.

"I'm trying," panted a deeper voice in her ear. "She's a maniac."

"We can't hurt her."

"Well, tranquilize her, then, before she kills us both!"

Maddy thrashed and managed to draw a painful breath, at last. "No," she cried. But the man on top of her was triple her size. The

only part of her she could move was her head, so she threw it back
without warning, slamming her skull against his face.

Crunch.

"Ow. Damn it, woman! Hold still. We're not gonna hurt you."

The prick of a needle piercing the muscle of her upper arm made
a liar out of him. She wailed, dreading the immediate lethargy that
swamped her limbs and turned them into limp appendages.

Oh, God. They've drugged me. That was what they did to their victims,
creating addicts too high and too numb to protest the misuse of their
bodies.

"Ease up, LT," said the first voice, and the man crushing her to
the floor lifted his weight cautiously.

Maddy drew a second painful breath, but she couldn't move her
tongue at all to speak, let alone a muscle in her body. *Oh, God. So, this
was how it felt.*

"Roll her over. Crap, I hope we didn't bruise her."

"She broke my fuckin' nose," growled the other shadow.

For a pair of barbarians, their hands were surprisingly gentle. But
then they wouldn't want to mar the merchandise, would they? The
realization that they spoke English sawed at her outrage like a serrated
blade. How dare Americans participate in such savagery?

Please, she tried to cry, but the word came out as a puff of air.

The man who'd stabbed her with the needle looked up at his
companion, his blue eyes visible even in the darkness. "Aren't you
going to tell her?"

Maddy's gaze swiveled to the brute who nursed his nose while
eying her mulishly. *Tell me what?*

"Later," he said, on a terse note.

"Suit yourself."

They spoke with articulate efficiency, like they'd done this many
times before, the bastards.

Just then, the room brightened. A neighbor by the east wall had
flipped a light switch. Its radiance sliced through the cracks in the
shutters, illumining the bully's face. He struck Maddy as only partly
Hispanic. Blood was sliding from his swelling nose, and a frown was
carved between his eyebrows. In spite of either disfigurement, he was
the most ruthlessly handsome man she'd ever seen. His dark green
gaze looked her over with similar interest.

Oh, my God, I'm naked! The realization doused Maddy in horror.
She was lying on the floor with her nightgown in a twisted hoop

around her hips, no underwear.

"We need to cover her," said the brute on a regretful note.

What? Confusion addled Maddy's already-sluggish thoughts.

His companion openly grinned. "I have to say, sir, this is a first," he chortled.

Together they worked to make sense of her bunched and twisted gown. Inept and cursing under their breaths, they dressed her with surprising care. Maddy scurried to a safe, dark corner in her mind, fighting her awareness, while at the same time grateful that her brain was still functioning at all. If she could just keep her wits about her . . . Fingers brushed her taut belly. She ground her teeth in denial. *That's not pleasure I'm feeling.* It had to be the drugs they'd shot into her system, confusing her senses.

She felt the dark thug thread her arms through her sleeves. As the knuckles of his hand rode the outer curve of her breast, her breath congealed and her nipple stiffened. *I did not enjoy that!* she berated herself.

It was mortifying, degrading to feel pleasure at his touch. She refused to imagine what the rest of her ill-fated life would be like if she let them take her. *You've got to help me, God!*

Blue Eyes gave a final tug, and she was blessedly covered. "Okay let's move."

The first man's watch flared in the darkness. "We're three minutes behind," he clipped, sounding annoyed.

His companion squeezed a button on a cord she hadn't seen till now, hanging across his chest. "Target recovered," he murmured. "We're coming out now."

Target recovered. Target recovered.

The words both disturbed and comforted Maddy, but the tide of oblivion that had rendered her body useless was now seeping into her brain, keeping her thoughts from processing. *Target recovered* . . . What did it mean?

Her eyelids sank shut and would not open again, despite her efforts to keep awake. She felt the men hoist her off the floor, felt them carry her to the window on the far side of the room, beyond the wardrobe.

"Hand her down to me," said the bigger thug, lowering her feet to the floor. She heard the shutter creak, heard him clamber onto the ledge and jump. A light splash sounded in the courtyard below. His companion scooped her up and swung her feet-first out the window.

A wet mist sharpened Maddy's senses as she felt herself being lowered. Sure hands caught her knees. Powerful, protective arms encircled her thighs securely. The man above relinquished her, and she slid with little fear down the length of the bigger brute's body. *Good lord.* Even with her senses dulled, Maddy recognized what a ride that was.

Stay awake! Don't sleep! she commanded herself.

But a black-velvet current pulled her relentlessly toward oblivion. Her head, too heavy to hold up, lolled against a broad shoulder. Her nose slumped toward a warm neck that smelled like baby wipes and dryer sheets.

As the darkness encapsulated her, that last sensory detail left her bewildered. Weren't miscreants supposed to reek of body odor and villainy? Just what was that stuff they'd injected into her, anyway?

From their ongoing communications, Sam knew that Teddy and Vinny had cleared the compound, trussing and cuffing two stragglers who'd wandered drunk up the alleyway. He couldn't see any witnesses as he squeezed out of the gated schoolyard with the recovery target in his arms and waited in the shadows. Harley locked the gate from within to protect its sleeping inhabitants and climbed over the wall via the knotted rope they'd used for their insertion.

Then, with Vinny and Teddy covering them, Sam and Harley dashed across a trash-littered street and slipped into the waiting taxi. The other two dove in after them, wedging Harley into the back like a pair of oversized book ends, and the car took off. Operation Dumb Broad was nearing completion.

As they sped through a maze of streets, headed several miles out of town for the exfil site, the DEA officer cast a curious glance at the woman sprawled across Sam's lap and nearly plowed into an oncoming vehicle.

"Keep your eyes on the goddamn road," Sam growled, though he was having difficulty leading by example.

Miss Scott's nightgown had gone practically transparent in the rain. There wasn't any question she could win any wet T-shirt contest she entered, hands down. With every lurch of the taxi, her tits swayed enticingly under his nose.

From Sam's vantage, he could even see the shadow of her naval, the curve of her right hip and a suggestion of amber pubic hair at the apex of her thighs. The crazy woman slept without underwear.

Feeling his body respond, he jerked his attention back to maze of streets down which they raced, spraying water left and right, careening around corners. *Focus on the op, damn it.*

But her small, soft body remained such a distraction that he was forced to gather up her long auburn hair and draw it over her chest like a sash. There. Out of sight, out of mind.

Only, now the scent of her shampoo, utterly feminine and flowery, filled his head, ratcheting his awareness even higher. He could feel the curve of her ass, nestled right between his thighs, brushing his balls with every jolt of the shocks. The recollection of her satin-soft skin, how good it had felt when she'd slid down the front of his body, seduced him into a state of full-blown arousal.

Chagrined and praying she wouldn't wake up, he adjusted his hold on her. This was goddamn unprofessional of him.

But, hell, why was he upset with himself? She was the one who'd lacked the sense to leave Matamoros while the leaving was good. She was damn lucky she hadn't been raped or worse by now. Waking up to a boner jabbing at her sweet ass was nothing compared to what might have happened to her.

He had to give Miss Scott some credit, though. She'd resisted capture with the ferocity of a tigress. The woman had guts. And when she woke up and realized what had happened to her, she was going to be livid.

Remorse pinched Sam's conscience, followed by a shaft of real concern as the sweeping light of a passing truck illumed the swelling on her left cheek. *Oh, shit.* Maybe they had been a little rough with her. Sam's gulped against a suddenly dry mouth.

She was the daughter of a senator after all. She could ruin his career if she was really pissed off.

Maddy awoke to a throbbing in her cheek and the thunder of a helicopter chopping the air with a deafening *whuppa, whuppa, whuppa.* She lay flat on her back, strapped to some kind of a gurney. Too lethargic to open her eyes, she felt herself being lifted, jostled, then lowered into a gale-force wind that whipped her hair into her face. Light flickered beyond her weighty eyelids as she clawed her way to consciousness.

The wind and thunder faded abruptly, replaced by the cadence of heavy footsteps resonating with a metallic clang. They air felt still and close, now. The walls she sensed on either side emitted a low, throbbing hum.

What's going on? Where am I?

The gurney made a sharp, right turn, delivering her into a chilly space redolent with the scent of rubbing alcohol. Several pairs of hands went to work unstrapping her, then lifting and lowering her onto a mattress. Someone tossed a blanket over her shivering frame and stuffed a pillow under her head.

"Why is she comatose?" clipped a female in accents of authority. "And why is your nose bleeding, lieutenant?"

"She, uh, resisted us, ma'am."

The deep male voice sounded vaguely familiar, only Maddy couldn't identify the speaker any more than she could recall what had happened to bring her here. The last thing she remembered was falling asleep her in her bed at *El Santuario* . . .

"Just how much lorazepam did you administer?"

"Just two milligrams," said another male voice.

"Good," said the woman. "Then she ought to wake soon, only I expect she'll have trouble remembering."

Maddy's nerves tingled. Her urgency rose as her senses grew shaper. Remembering what? What had happened to her? How had she come to be like this?

"You bruised her face," stated the woman on a note of disapproval.

A tense silence filled the humming space.

"Her father's helicopter is still twenty minutes out," continued the woman. "If you're lucky, the swelling will go down before he sees her." Cool, deft fingers lifted Maddy's eyelids. Blinding light pierced either pupil. "She's coming out of it now. Stay with her while I fetch two icepacks." The tramp of her footsteps receded.

Maddy tried to swallow. Her throat felt raw, her mouth like it had been swabbed with cotton. She ran her tongue over her lips, finding them dry and cracked.

"She's waking up," said the familiar voice.

"Give her water," said the second man.

The sound of running water preceded the feel of a hand cradling the back of Maddy's head, lifting it off the pillow. "Here, take a sip, ma'am. It'll help."

Ma'am? The respectful term made her think of the military. As she swallowed a soothing draught, Maddy slitted her eyes and studied her Good Samaritan over the rim of the paper cup.

Definitely military, she confirmed. He was swarthy and gorgeous, still in his twenties. Blood ran in a sluggish line from his aquiline nose to his firmly held mouth. Dark green eyes regarded her with unnerving intensity.

"Who are you?" she croaked, as he lowered her head to the pillow, untangled his fingers from her hair.

"Lieutenant Sam Sasseville," he introduced himself. "This is my chief, Sean Harlan," he added, gesturing, and the second man stepped into her line of sight. This one wore a black bandana over his shaved head. Bright blue eyes shone out of an unnaturally tan face.

"Pleasure," said Chief Harlan, with a hint of a smile on his lips.

The blue eyes. The bandana. Something stirred in Maddy's memory. "Where am I? How did I get here?"

"You're aboard the *Harry S. Truman*, currently in the Gulf of Mexico," said the lieutenant dispassionately. "We're SEALs," he added. "We were tasked to recover you from Matamoros, at your father's request."

Maddy's heart began to palpitate. A pulse tapped at her eardrums. She tried sitting up, but the lieutenant laid a heavy hand on her shoulder, pushing her back down.

Another memory stirred. Something violent and frightening.

"You shouldn't move," he cautioned her.

"Take your hand off of me!" Her sudden panic startled them both. As she sorted through the rush of emotion, the lieutenant stepped back, his expression wary.

Under the SEALs' watchful regard, Maggie sat up slowly. The room went into a slow spin and then subsided. "You said, 'my father's request,'" she recollected, trying to piece it all together. "Then he's the reason I'm here."

"Yes," both men said simultaneously.

Damn it, Daddy. "And you—you what?—you slipped into the school while I slept and you grabbed me?" Of all the sneaky-underhanded maneuvers! They'd had no right to make that decision for her. No one did!

"Affirmative," said the lieutenant, his expression so inscrutable that she felt like he was hiding something.

The blue-eyed chief shifted uncomfortably on his feet.

A chuckle floated through Maddy's memory, like an untethered balloon.

The faces of her pupils rose up just as suddenly—Imelda, Graciela, Mercedes, and the other dozen girls at *El Santuario*. If they hadn't realized she was gone yet, they soon would. Maddy's heart clenched with alarm as she envisioned their confusion, followed by their fear when they realized what the loss of their teacher meant for them.

"What have you done?" she cried, directing her anger at her father first, and then at the two men hovering near the bed. "What have you done? They won't survive without me!"

Lieutenant Sassville's handsome face hardened. His companion clapped him on the shoulder. "She's all yours, sir," he stated with confidence. "Feel better soon, ma'am," he added, backing swiftly out of the hatch behind him.

Maggie wished the lieutenant would leave with him. The realization that she had failed her students lodged in her throat like a bitter pill, too awful to swallow.

In a matter of days—weeks if they were lucky—every girl in the school would be preyed upon by a man, her innocence forcibly taken from her.

A sob of denial escaped Maddy's strangled voice box. Dropping her face in her hands, she hid her crushing dismay from the commando studying her so apathetically. She had fooled herself into thinking she could make a critical difference in her students' lives. But who was she to hold back the tide of degradation overtaking Mexico?

"Go away," she choked, ashamed to be caught crying in front of a stranger. The pain in her chest made her double-over, but she was too unsettled by the lieutenant's presence to grieve openly. "Why are you still here?" she raged a moment later, pulling her wet hands from her face.

His eyes narrowed as if deliberating how much to say. "You realize you would've ended up raped or murdered if you'd stayed any longer," he bit out.

The harsh words sobered Maddy instantly. Dashing the moisture from her face, she sniffed and glared at him. "What's it to you?" she demanded, appalled by her childishness, but there'd been no cause for his remark.

"What's it to me? Nothing," he retorted unkindly. "I don't give a good damn what might have happened to you. Personally I think you deserved whatever you had coming."

Stung by his antagonism, all Maddy could do was to gape at him.

"You know what else?" he added, planting a hand on either side of her knees. He bent over her, his face mere inches from her own. Maddy's pulse leapt with alarm, only to subside as his scent stole into her nostrils. Baby wipes and dryer sheets. How dangerous could the man be?

"If not for you," he continued when she kept quiet, "I would be halfway around the world right now, putting an end to an arms smuggler who's been selling weapons to Al Qaeda." He bit out every word succinctly, quietly, his dark green eyes sparkling with resentment. "Instead, I had to rescue you from your own idiocy."

Memories bombarded Maddy, flickering through her mind so quickly she could scarcely get a read on them. She saw shadows in the darkness, heard a stifled chuckle. "You attacked me," she accused, recollecting how he'd approached her bed.

He straightened like she'd slapped him in the face. "No way. I told you who we were, and you resisted us, remember?"

All she could remember was him groping through the mosquito netting, trying to grab her. No, wait, he'd been saying something at the time, only she hadn't been able to hear him over her thundering heart.

"You dropped me on the floor and then you jumped on me," she added, reliving the pain of her face striking the tiles. She lifted a hand to her cheek where the warm, puffy flesh provided evidence that she was right. She sent him an accusing glare.

"You were a crazed lunatic," he corrected. "All we did was subdue you before you could hurt yourself worse."

"Hurt myself?" She glanced pointedly at his bloody nose. "Admit it. You were worried I would hurt you."

"Like I said. You were a lunatic."

"You scared me half to death while I was sleeping!" The details had returned with perfect clarity. "I thought you were locals coming to drag me off to a brothel."

"That's exactly my point, woman," he affirmed, his volume rising abruptly. "What the hell were you thinking staying in Matamoros after our government ordered you to leave?"

"Protecting the innocent!" Maddy shouted, undaunted by his thunder. "I was doing exactly what you do every day, you hypocrite!"

The epithet made him choke with laughter. He threw his head back and laughed out loud. After a moment's astonishment, Maggie joined in, albeit a bit hysterically.

Crinkled eyes and a flash of white teeth made him irresistible. His infectious laughter had her forgiving him begrudgingly.

"You couldn't begin to do what I do, Miss Scott," Sam Sasseville finally said, without conceit or rancor. His previous outrage seemed to have vanished. He now eyed her with something like compassion.

"I never said I do exactly what you do, lieutenant. You think I'd jump out of an airplane? No way. But am willing to put my life on line for a cause I believe in."

Maybe if she took the time to explain herself, she could convince him that her work was worthwhile. "For the last year and a half my colleagues and I have kept the girls at the school from turning to prostitution because they had no other choice." The recent events washed over her anew, and her heart sank. "Do you have any idea what's going to happen to my students without my protection?" she lamented as her grief returned. "Do you know what kind of life you've condemned them to?"

"Oh, no." He held both hands up as if warding her off. "You are not going to put that on me, lady."

She desperately wanted to blame somebody—anybody. But the problem was bigger than he was. "Fine. You're right," she conceded. "What's happening in Matamoros isn't your fault."

"Damn right it's not."

"I thought I could do more," she said, swallowing the lump that swelled in her throat. "I suppose . . . I suppose I should thank you for getting me out before something happened to me," she conceded. There, she'd extended him an olive branch. Surely he'd be gracious enough to take it.

He shifted on his feet, jammed his fingers into his pockets, and had the grace to look uncomfortable. "You can thank your father when you see him," he retorted, glancing at his watch. "In about ten minutes."

"Mmmm." Maddy tugged at a loose thread unraveling from the blanket that covered her legs. She wasn't looking forward to *that* reunion.

"What the hell is taking the commander so long?" The lieutenant swiveled abruptly, prowling toward the wall of cabinets. Opening a canister of gauze, he helped himself to several squares and wiped off the blood still oozing from his nose.

"Did I break it?" Maddy asked, with only the slightest twinge of remorse.

"Probably," he said, dropping the gauze into a receptacle marked HAZARDOUS WASTE.

"Sorry." She actually felt somewhat mollified at having ruined his obscene good looks.

"Sure you are. You know what I think?" he said, turning to face her again.

"What?"

"I think you're crazy," he averred.

The man didn't mince his words. "*I'm* crazy?" Maddy ran a dry gaze over his powerful physique, every inch of which suggested that he pushed himself to the limits of human endurance, daily. "I'm not the one who jumps out of airplanes into hostile territory," she quipped.

"No. You drive in with your band of humanitarian aid workers, headed like pigs into a slaughterhouse."

She blinked, her goodwill draining away with the blood that abruptly left her cheeks.

"I read your file, Miss Scott," he continued, taking a brave step closer. "You've participated in every disaster relief effort since 9/11. You've been in Bosnia, Uganda, Haiti—" He ticked the locations off his fingers, "—and Mexico. Enough already," he added on a note of exasperated concern. "Listen. I think you're an intelligent and beautiful woman. I don't want to hear one day that you got yourself killed in some shithole country where there's been infighting for four hundred years and nothing you did changed anything."

I think you're an intelligent and beautiful woman. He'd tried tempering his view with a compliment, but it did nothing to ease the blow of his low opinion of her work. Tears she refused to shed stung the backs of Maddy's eyes. Sam Sasseville had spouted off the same argument that her father always used. That she was too smart and beautiful to sacrifice herself for those less worthy.

Well, Maddy didn't see the suffering as less worthy than she. And she wasn't going to placate Sam Sasseville any more than she placated her father.

Lifting her chin into the air, she checked the emotion pressuring her chest and held his gaze unwaveringly. "Do you believe in what you do, lieutenant?" she inquired sharply.

He sent her a suspicious look and shrugged his massive shoulders. "Of course. I'm a SEAL."

"You feel like you make a positive difference in the world," she surmised.

"Yeah. When I'm not rescuing Americans from their own idiocy."

Ignore that, she ordered herself. "Then I take it you like your work to be meaningful, like putting an end to arms smuggling."

"Exactly."

"Well, so do I. The work I do is meaningful to me. We're exactly the same, Sam," she insisted, addressing him intentionally by his first name. "Whether you want to admit it or not, we're the same."

Madison Scott's assertion gave Sam pause. Hearing the slightest quaver in her voice, he realized that despite her willingness to engage him verbally, he'd dealt a little too harshly with her. She'd been through a lot in the past several hours—weeks, really, if he thought about it.

But she was every bit as crazy as he'd asserted earlier if she thought they were alike in any way. "No offense, Madison," Sam replied, using her first name the way she'd used his, "but there's a big difference between you and me." He propped his hands on his hips. "I've been trained to fight aggression. I know how to resist torture, how to survive in the wilderness, how to operate thirty-one different weapons with lethal precision. You don't know any of that." He raised his eyebrows at her.

"True." She conceded with surprising grace and a delicate shrug of her shoulders. "But I offer the world something other than physical protection." Her liquid amber gaze seemed to see deep down inside him.

"What else is there?" He was afraid to ask.

"Spiritual protection," she informed him solemnly. "Hope. Companionship. Compassion."

Her words had a strange effect on him. He felt his chest tighten, his throat constrict. At the same time, he realized that arguing with her was clearly a lesson in frustration. "Now I see how you drive your father crazy."

Her coral-colored lips quirked into a sad smile. She looked away from him, subdued but not defeated.

He stood there a moment longer, considering her fearlessness, her insanity. "Something tells me you're not going to stay away out of hotspots from now on," he guessed, his anger returning, simmering low deep down in his gut.

She looked up slowly. "Would you quit?" she asked him. "Just because someone worried about you?"

"It's not the same."

"Yes it is."

Fueled by frustration, Sam stalked toward the bed. Madison stiffened but she didn't shrink away from him when he caught her face lightly between his thumb and fingers. "You better hope I'm never taken off an assignment to rescue your sweet ass again," he warned her, altogether distracted by the way her lips parted and the tongue darted out to wet them. "Stay the hell out of the hot spots from now on," he added.

"Can't," she replied with an apologetic shrug.

That single syllable scarcely qualified as a smart-assed reply but, for some reason, it incensed Sam. Oh, what the hell. He'd been dying to kiss her since she'd lain across his lap like a damp angel. An angel with a temptress's body.

In the next instant, he was crushing his mouth to hers, punishing her for her obstinacy.

The defiant glide of her tongue hit his central nervous system like a jolt of electricity. He was about to gentle the kiss into something neither one of them would forget when the *tramp, tramp, tramp* of Commander Brady's boots intruded on the moment.

Sam straightened regretfully, his senses reeling; his faculties registering that he'd just given Miss Scott one more complaint to carry to her father: sexual harassment.

"Lieutenant, you're needed in the Tactical Ops Center, stat," the Navy doctor bit out, stepping through the hatch. "Here's an icepack," she added, slapping it into his hand as her sharp eyes slid suspiciously from his flushed face to the patient's.

"Yes, ma'am." Sam followed the commander's gaze and intercepted Maddy's dazed regard. She was looking at him with unguarded longing. The look made his gut clench in frustration. "Your, uh, your father should be here any minute," he said, his voice thick. "You're not gonna . . . " He touched his cheek to signify the bruise on her own face. "You're not going to blame us for that, are you?"

The look she sent him made him feel stupid for asking.

"Of course not," she replied. "Take care, Sam." She sent him a smile, her eyes so bright they looked like jewels.

"Stay out of the hot spots," he reiterated, pointing a warning finger at him.

Her lips pulled into a familiar, sad smile. "I'll see you around,

Lieutenant," she answered simply.

Damn it.

Ducking out of the hatch, Sam sent one last scowl over his shoulder and intercepted Maddy's shining gaze a final time. As he hurried down the long corridor to the TOC, he suffered the gut-churning certainty that he would, indeed, see her around.

SIGNED, SEALed, DELIVERED . . . I'M YOURS

Christie Ridgway

Thanksgiving is turning into a real turkey, Mandy Warner thought, as another explosion in her uncle's neighborhood rattled the tiny basement window and sent down a shower of plaster dust. She huddled deeper in her corner of the house's foundation, tucking into a smaller ball as she considered her other options.

Oh, yeah, there weren't any other options.

The door to the basement stairs was blocked by fallen debris. The sound of gunfire outside the walls told her that if she could have made it through, she would only face a dubious welcome from the trigger-happy rebels roaming the streets of the American district. Not for the first time in the last four hours did she curse her decision to spend Thanksgiving with her only living relative—her step-uncle, a top official in the U.S. foreign service, based in a stable region of Central America.

What *had* been a stable region.

A sharp ping against an outside wall goosed a shriek out of her, which she quickly stifled. Bullet ricochet was her best guess, though she had about as much experience with ammunition as she did with foreign travel. Why, oh why hadn't she stayed in her month-to-month leased apartment in L.A.? Sure, she didn't know anyone there, as her culinary school courses didn't start until January, but she could have made herself a nice little solo meal from a Cornish game hen and Brussels sprouts.

She despised Brussels sprouts, not that as a would-be chef she supposed she should admit despising any food. But right now, self-delusion didn't seem worth the effort.

Another barrage of gunfire began, more too-close-for-comfort pings. Drawing her knees nearer her chest, Mandy bit down on the denim of her jeans instead of screaming. Under the circumstances, her one idea for survival was not to give away that she was hidden here. Then, no rebels could capture her for ransom . . . or worse.

The basement of her uncle's house offered decent concealment. It was nearing noon now, but the electricity had gone out long before, and there was only the one, postage-stamp window to alleviate the deep gloom. Earlier explosions had tossed around the contents, so the small space was a warren of tumbled boxes and fallen shelving. The floor was littered with canned goods, water bottles, cleaning supplies, and other household overflow. Mandy was nestled in the space created by a tall, freestanding bookcase that had tipped against the rear wall.

The first skitter of sound didn't immediately register. There was so much going on outside the house: shouts, weapons discharging, loud explosive blasts. When she heard the quiet scratch and shuffle again, she tilted her head toward the noise. Then she thought—rats!

She moaned around the denim still clenched between her teeth. She didn't like rats. Or mice. Or spiders. Hell, she didn't even like pill bugs, when it came to that. It was just too bad she didn't have a fear of flying. She'd have stayed in L.A. and wouldn't be sitting here, waiting to be gnawed alive.

"Ma'am?" The voice was hushed, a colorless sound. "Miss Warner?"

Panic flushed through her veins. The rats knew her name! *No*, she thought, common sense prevailing. Of course it wasn't a rat calling to her. Still, she wasn't ready to trust that ghostly voice. Was this a terror-sourced auditory hallucination? Or one of the bad guys who wanted to flush her out?

The whisper came closer, even as she pressed harder against the concrete at her back. "Are you in here, ma'am? I've come to help, Miss Warner. I'm from the government. Your uncle—"

BOOM!

Throwing her arms over her head, she released a full-throated scream as the whole house was rocked on its foundation by a blast more powerful than any before. More chunks of plaster fell, more boxes toppled. She bit her tongue and tasted blood. From the murky shadows, a dark shape leaped forward. Before she could scream again, Mandy's balled figure was caged by a hard, lean, male body.

BOOM!

The stranger's large hand pushed her head low; he pressed his cheek against the side of her hair. The building shifted again, a box toppled from a shelf above, and the man surrounding her made an almost inaudible grunt as it glanced off his shoulder.

The world stopped moving. Silence descended. Even the gunfire seemed farther off.

Or maybe that was because Mandy could barely hear over her own harsh breaths, a counterpoint to the more measured ones of the man shielding her. Trying to calm herself, she inhaled deeper, taking in a combination of plaster dust and clean man-scent. The quiet voice spoke in her ear. "Are you hurt?"

She shook her head, trying to assess her new circumstances. The man's accent was American, his actions protective. After four frightened hours, was she finally rescued? "Who—" she had to break off to work some saliva over her dry tongue, "—are you?"

He sat back on his haunches, his arms still curled around her shoulders. It allowed Mandy room to lift her head. "I'm Josh," he said. "Your uncle sent me to find you."

She blinked, peering at him through the gloom. His hair was clipped close to his head and was darker than her honey-blonde. The hard-edged angles of his face told her he was closer to thirty than her own twenty-five. He was studying her in turn, and she couldn't guess what the anxious morning had wrought on her appearance. It seemed like a year ago that she'd put on jeans and a light cotton camisole top. Her straight hair wasn't tempted to wave even in this climate's humidity, so she'd left it loose to her shoulders. She did recall putting on a coat of mascara and a swipe of lip gloss, but who knew where the make-up had wandered to now?

His gaze followed the self-conscious journey her tongue took across her lower lip. She thought he might have made a sound, somewhere deep in his throat, but her hearing was off again, disrupted by a sudden stumble of her heart followed by its odd and unprovoked thundering. The man glanced down as if tracking the sound, and she saw that he had heavy, spiky lashes. They weren't feminine in the least, but as declaratively male as the rest of him.

At the thought, she remembered her earlier worry, and had to suppress a near-hysterical giggle. She felt as if she was sixteen again and drunk on wine coolers in the parking lot after the school dance. "I thought you were a rat."

A flash of white betrayed his quick, boyish smile. Mandy felt it, a visceral blow as real as those blasts that had rocked her world all morning. Her head made a drunken spin as warmth spread across her skin. She hoped the basement's shadows concealed her blushing face.

"Not quite a rat," he said. "I'm a SEAL."

Mandy blinked again. "A seal—" She thought of the animal. Then she bumped the heel of her hand against her forehead as logic took charge of her addled brain. Josh wore a T-shirt and a pair of camouflage pants tucked into workman-style boots. No, military boots. He'd said he was from the government. "You mean a SEAL, capital S, E, A, L."

He smiled again. "Capital Y, E, S." Then his long-fingered hands squeezed her shoulders. "Sit tight, okay? I'm going on a quick recon to see how those latest explosions left us."

When he made to rise, Mandy found herself clutching his wrists, cold alarm washing over her. "Don't." She didn't mean to say it any more than she meant to be squeezing him like a lifeline, but she had the sudden anxious thought that she couldn't lose him now. Not when she'd just found him! "Don't go."

He stilled and his gaze roamed over her face in a way that was almost . . . almost tender. His voice softened. "It's all right." He slid from her grasp only to take her hands in both of his. "You're not alone anymore, Miss Warner."

"Mandy." She felt the sting of stupid tears in her eyes. *You're not alone anymore.* It seemed like she'd been alone forever. Longer than the four hours in the basement, that was sure.

"Mandy," he repeated, chaffing her chilly hands between his. She felt the calluses on his palms and fingers. The small abrasion only made the touch feel more personal. Intimate.

Then he brushed his mouth against her knuckles. She told herself it was merely a kind and reassuring gesture. Something one human would offer to another. "It'll take me three minutes tops, Mandy. Then I'll be back with you."

God, how much she wanted him with her! Unnerved by the truth of that, Mandy forced herself to draw her fingers from his. "I'm fine now." *Get a hold of yourself, girl.* "Take your time."

"Sit tight," he said again.

"I'll be right here." *Where I will pull myself together.* When he returned he wouldn't guess she was, though now rescued, a shivery mess of confusion. Likely it was just a reaction to the morning's strain, but there was something about him that . . . that called to her. It was crazy, she knew it, so she would put from her mind the almost primitive attraction she was feeling for the hard-bodied man with the unexpectedly sweet smile.

Mandy wasn't surprised that Josh kept his word. When he returned to her corner he spent a few moments inspecting the stability of the fallen bookcase that was serving as the roof of her niche. As he removed the last of the boxes that remained on the shelving, she remembered now that one had fallen on him earlier.

"Are you okay?" she asked. When he bent over to meet her gaze, she pointed to his shoulder. "Something fell on you before."

"Didn't make a dent." He squatted again. "You chose a good spot to hunker down."

Uh-oh. "Does that mean we're not leaving anytime soon?" She winced as more gunfire sounded in the distance. "Or maybe that's for the best."

"We're here for a bit," he confirmed. "For one, the way I got in is now blocked. For two, I think it's still too hot out there for a secure extraction."

"I understand." Though she thought it was a little hot in here, too.

"My team will come for us when it's safer."

Mandy shifted to make room for him in her nook. "C'mon in, then. The water's fine."

That brought another of his quick grins. Then he crawled nearer and she shifted to the angle end of the isosceles triangle created by the tilted bookcase, leaving him the larger space. She couldn't risk any skin-to-skin contact, since clearly his short absence wasn't long enough to eradicate his appeal. His radiating body heat was enough to make her nerves jangle and her hands jitter. She couldn't imagine actual touching would help matters.

She slid him a sidelong glance. "My uncle's all right?" He'd gone to work at the embassy that morning, though he'd promised to be home early for the Thanksgiving dinner she'd been planning to cook.

"Just fine, beyond a bit frantic over you. When the trouble started, they closed the embassy. My team was in the area and we received an unofficial request to secure the U.S. civilians in jeopardy."

Mandy nodded. "I'm grateful. Thank you."

After a hesitation, Josh craned his neck to get a better look at her face. "Are you sure you weren't hurt? You didn't fall earlier or hit your head or . . ."

"No. Nothing happened. I came down here to collect some

canned chicken broth when I heard—and felt—the first explosions."

"Grenades and mortar rounds."

"Ah." She drew up her knees again and rested her chin on them, allowing her hair to fall forward and screen her face.

But Josh wasn't having that. One of his fingers slipped beneath the curtain it made. He drew a line across her cheek as he tucked the hair behind her ear. She felt the rim of her ear go hot. "Are you sure you're okay? I can tell you're trembling."

And here she thought she was holding it together fairly well. "Today has been a little . . . trying."

"I bet it was stressful." He touched her cheek again. "But you're going to be fine. I promise."

Countering the urge to lean closer, she edged away from him. "Thanks." *Was* this stress? Was her reaction to the morning's events this clamoring inclination to press herself against him? She slid a second look in his direction. He had his knees up too, his forearms propped on them, his hands dangling. Fascinated by them, she studied the wide palms and the long, limber digits. His nails were clipped close enough to show only a thin line of white.

Her gaze focused in on the forefinger of his right hand. *That's the one that touched me.* Drawing in a shaky breath, she tried dispelling the desire for it to touch her again. But the longer she stared, the more she wanted—and the more the atmosphere around them seemed to thicken. Yet he didn't appear to notice the heavy air and crackling tension sharing their small space. He remained still, his pose relaxed.

I'm nuts, Mandy thought. This . . . this . . . *whatever* . . . was clearly one-sided.

BOOM!

Mandy jumped—straight for Josh.

He yanked her between his knees and against his chest. Her face was pressed to his throat, her arms circled his neck, and she could feel the powerful thudding of his heart as their world rocked and rolled once more. When it was calm again, they both let out long breaths. His mouth moved against the top of her head. "Okay?"

She nodded.

Neither one of them made to break apart.

Beneath her, his chest rose in another long, careful inhale. The exhale stirred her hair, but she remained still, soaking in the intense rightness of being held by this man . . . this stranger. She was shivering, not as an aftershock to the explosion, but as a reaction to the sexual headiness of breathing in his scent and of being so close to his bare skin. His hand stroked down her back and she squeezed shut her eyes and turned her head just the tiniest fraction so that her lips touched the beating pulse at his throat.

His heartbeat accelerated—hers was pounding like crazy—and neither of them changed position for long, long moments. Then Josh stirred. "I should take another look around. See if that last one changed our circumstances."

"I think it definitely did," Mandy heard herself whisper.

He gave a soft laugh, then put her away from him. She didn't dare try reading his expression as he extricated himself from their shelter, because she wasn't sure what he was thinking about their impromptu embrace. But then he was back, and she thought she had her answer. Once he was seated again, without comment he reached for her and lifted her to sit between his knees, her back to his chest. Mandy rested against him, once more experiencing the intoxicating combination of desire and safety.

"We're going to be here a while more." Josh drew up the fallen strap of her camisole and then his thumb smoothed a circle on her bare shoulder as gunfire sounded in the distance. "I suggest we pass the time by you telling me all about Mandy Warner."

"No fair," Mandy said, feeling her nipples contract in response to the small strokes. "I want to know all about Josh . . . " She turned her head to look at his face and was close enough now to see that he had pale gray eyes. They should have appeared cool, but there was something in them that made it hard to swallow. Her skin felt tight on her bones and almost feverish. "Josh, um, what?"

"Josh—Joshua—Frye. Chief Special Operator, at your service."

Oh, yeah, she had some ideas of services he could provide. She whipped her head back around before he could read them on her face. "I don't know anything about the military."

"I'm an enlisted man. Joined up when I was twenty. A recruiter found me on the triathlon circuit. He convinced me with the SEAL motto, 'The *Only Easy Day Was Yesterday*'. Sounded like a challenge, and I couldn't resist."

She slapped a light hand on his outstretched leg. "Mr. Macho."

"Hey." He captured her hand on the hard muscle of his thigh. "That's Chief Mr. Macho to you."

With her fingers sandwiched by his body, his heat, her heart took a woozy, wobbly spin. She struggled for some intelligent thing to say that wasn't *touch me more, take me now, oh God, I've never felt like this before.* "Are you . . ." Her voice sounded hoarse, and she swallowed to lubricate her throat. "Are you from a Navy family?"

"Nope. My dad, my older brother, and my older sister are all doctors."

"You didn't want to do that as well?"

She felt him shake his head. "Blood makes me squeamish."

Her skeptical glance confirmed he was smiling. "Okay, the fact is I don't have the patience to deal with patients. My mom said I emerged from the womb feet first, I was that eager to start doing things. I like to be moving."

Feeling all that lean muscle surrounding her, she could believe it. "You seem to be pretty patient right now though."

He was quiet a moment, then he ran his free hand slowly over her hair. "I can wait when I need to. When I should. Plenty of experience with discipline in the military too."

Subtext: *This is going too fast.* And she couldn't deny it. The attraction *was* too fast and too crazy and she'd be really worried about herself if she didn't know it was also mutual. It had to be mutual, right? She could tell that by the way his heart was thudding against her spine and by the way he kept playing with her long hair.

"Now you," Josh said, tugging on the ends.

"I'm an orphan. My mom and her second husband died in a car crash four years ago."

He made a sympathetic noise and gave her shoulder a gentle squeeze.

She shrugged. "We weren't close. My dad was gone before that, and so the only relative I have left in the world is Uncle Jim—he was my stepdad's brother."

"He said you were visiting for the holiday."

"Yeah. I recently relocated to Los Angeles, and I was at loose ends because I don't start culinary school until January."

"You've always wanted to be a chef?"

"Not really. But I like to cook and bake and I hope it will be more interesting than the bookkeeping I've been doing since college. I've never really known what I want to *be*, only what I want to *have*."

He followed up with the natural question. "Which is?"

The answer welled up inside her, stilling all her jittering nerves, cooling all her hot desires. Though her limbs had gone suddenly leaden, Mandy forced herself to move away from Josh. He didn't say a word as she shifted away from him and into her angled corner. Wrapping her arms around her upraised knees again, she forced herself to face him.

He shifted as well, putting his back to the wall, the toes of his military-issue boots almost touching those of her sky-blue espadrilles. His gaze met hers, the expression in his pale eyes calm and serious. Expectant.

Still, she hesitated, not wanting to burst the bubble that their little place-beneath-the-bookcase had become. The street battle sounds had receded, though she didn't know if the skirmish was physically more distant or if the connection to Josh was so strong that it took the near-full attention of her senses. She listened to his steady breathing, his wide chest moving up and down beneath his T-shirt. His arms were roped with muscle, and for the first time she noticed there was a gun strapped to his hip. The handle of a knife protruded from a sheath buckled around his calf.

He was a warrior. More, a special kind of warrior, prepared to leave on a moment's notice . . . leaving loved ones behind. She'd done her share of reading about SEAL heroism and knew that his job meant long absences, long silences, lots of danger.

"What I've always wanted to have," Mandy said slowly, "is a . . . a partner. I've felt alone so much of my life. I want to have someone who will always be there. A man to come home to every night."

Josh didn't comment. He only nodded and after a moment she nodded back. Neither needed to say out loud that he was not that man.

Though she and Josh made it out of her uncle's damaged house by nightfall, there wasn't any Thanksgiving feast that day. Mandy actually didn't feel like eating at all, even once she was checked into a highly secure, luxury high-rise hotel in the city center. Uncle Jim had reserved his own room, but she guessed he wasn't spending any time there. His presence at the embassy was needed.

Mandy wasn't needed by anyone. Late Friday afternoon, wrapped in a thick terry robe and her own glum mood, she lay stretched on the bed clicking through the few English language channels on the television. The sound of a knock was a welcome relief from her own solitary company.

Still, she peered through the peephole before opening the door. Her breath and her heart seemed to collide in her chest as she saw Josh standing in the hall. Her skin flushed hot from her hairline to her ankles but that didn't stop her hand from yanking on the knob. With nothing separating them, they stared at each other from either side of the threshold.

He wore a pair of jeans, newish running shoes, and a button-down shirt, the cuffs folded back to his elbows. His pale eyes picked up the slate blue color. "Hi," he said, a faint smile on his face. He held up a familiar-looking suitcase. "I retrieved your things from your uncle's house."

Mandy clutched the lapels of her robe at her throat. She'd never expected to see him again—and she was thrilled to have a second chance to look at his starkly handsome face. Glum fled as gladness roared through her, a feeling so intense that a hot sting of tears pricked her eyes.

Josh's smile fled. "Mandy." He dropped the suitcase and took a quick step back. "I'll leave."

"No!" She flung out her hand. "No. I was just surprised to see you."

He eyed her with concern. "You're sure?"

"Please. Please, come in."

Still, he hesitated. "I was hoping I could buy you dinner."

He'd come to her, she thought, putting the back of her hand to her nose to stifle a watery sob. "I can't think of anything I'd rather do."

They ended up ordering room service. Mandy took her suitcase into the bathroom and slipped into a slightly wrinkled but very pretty organza sundress that was halter-styled and sported flirty ruffles at the knee-length hem. Wearing it, she felt feminine and even more so when she found he'd included her make-up bag. She was able to darken her lashes and smooth on her favorite lipstick. Her small bottle of perfume was intact and she dabbed on drops of that, too.

The result was worth the effort. Josh's eyes widened as she slipped into the main room. "You look beautiful," he said. "And you smell great."

"Thank you. A step up from plaster dust and desperation, huh?"

He shook his head. "You weren't desperate. You were handling yourself very well."

They stared at each other again, that palpable pull between them running as strong as the day before. One summer, Mandy had been caught in an ocean undertow. This was like that—a current more powerful than her strength and her will was carrying her toward this man. "Josh," she whispered, her heart aching with bittersweet yearning.

His eyes closed for a moment. "I know—"

Knuckles rapped on the hotel room door. They both started, and then Josh moved to the entry to allow in the room service cart. The waiter set it on the balcony outside her 31st-floor room. Dusk was falling and the air was warm but not unbearably humid. They feasted on a beans and rice dish, fresh fish, and a delicious concoction of corn-based dough, meat, vegetables, and spices wrapped in plantain leaves. For dessert, there were slices of tropical fruit.

Realizing she hadn't eaten much since the morning before, Mandy ate heartily. She felt greedy, storing up the moments with Josh sitting across her table. Her leg accidentally bumped his, and he captured it between his knees, a gentle clasp that sent her pulse soaring and her skin flushing warm.

She'd never expected to feel this happy again. And she'd never felt as happy as she'd been the day before. His voice echoed in her head then, the SEAL motto. *The Only Easy Day Was Yesterday.* It was so easy, so right, when the two of them were together.

At full dark, he wheeled the cart through the doors to her room and then out into the hall. They returned to the balcony, sitting in side-by-side chairs as they watched the bright lights of the city twinkle like holiday glitter in the darkness. "We're officially in the Christmas season," she said. "Where will you be on the 25th?"

"I'm based in San Diego," he replied. "It's where my family lives too."

She shot him a quick glance. "That's not far from L.A."

"You're right." He reached over and took her hand. Bending his head, he studied it like a precious object, stroking the palm, curling each finger then straightening it again.

A shiver rolled up the inside of her arm, and a voice whispered in her ear. *You could have a long-distance romance. It's not even a "long" distance. If you drove south and he drove north, you'd meet within an hour.*

It wouldn't last, of course, because she wanted to have that home-every-night guy. All her life she'd wished for that, but she could have Josh for a little while. Maybe a not-so-little while.

"The thing is, Mandy," he said now, running the back of her hand against the clean-shaven surface of his warm cheek, "I don't know when I'll be returning to California. We go wheels up again tomorrow. No return date guaranteed."

She could only have him tonight.

It made what came next simple—as simple as surrendering to that ocean current. She was ready to drown in Josh. Mandy stood, and he did too, and then they were kissing, sweet and gentle at first, hard and demanding soon after. He lifted her into his arms and she curled hers around his neck, their mouths still discovering all the delicious ways they could fit as he carried her to the bed.

He placed her there, and she watched through half-closed eyes as he drew the drapes and left just one light burning in the room. Then he sat on the mattress and cupped her face between his warrior's hands. His forehead touched hers. "Are you sure?"

"Yes." She pulled him down so his weight was on top of her, so wonderful to wriggle against. Her smile bloomed when she heard him groan. "You're sure too?"

His mouth trailed a hot, shivery path down her neck. "I've rarely been as certain of anything in my life."

Her hands yanked the tail of his shirt from his pants and she caressed the hot skin of his back, delighted at his shuddering response. In efficient moves, he shucked his clothes and then took a long time with hers, all two pieces, dress and panties. He kissed every inch of skin beneath the fabric, pushing it up, rolling it down, sliding it aside, until she was trembling and panting and still completely clothed.

It made her squirm even more, until he threw a leg over her thighs and kissed her pliant again, her skin throbbing with sensitivity, her mind dazed by lust. Then, finally, he removed her dress, making a big show of sliding the tickling ruffles at the hem over her twitching belly and berry-tight nipples. He ran his tongue along all the bared flesh, until she caught his head and drew it to one breast. He sucked strongly, and she rose into the hand wandering toward the apex of her thighs.

She sighed in agitated relief as he drew her panties down her legs. But his exploring mouth was still set on torture and she was begging for a surer touch than his teasing tongue. His fingers found her where she wanted him most, and pleasure rose in tornado spirals inside her, until it took off like a top, skittering bliss through her body in dizzy, delicious revolutions. Then he was right where she needed him, his condom-covered erection opening her, taking her, coming inside, shifting out, coming back in. Retreating and then returning, retreating and then returning, until his mouth fastened on hers, and he surged one last time and she clasped him to her, wishing this night could go on forever.

He had to leave by midnight, his orders requiring him to have himself and his gear ready for departure by two a.m. Dressed once more, he again sat on the edge of the bed and fiddled with the covers, tucking them around her shoulders. His expression was set, his mouth tight as he smoothed her hair from her face. "I don't know what to say," he finally confessed. "I don't know what I can change."

"Nothing," Mandy said, cupping his now whisker-gritted cheek in her palm. "I'm so proud of what you do. I'm so honored to know you."

"It's what I am."

"So we have nothing to regret. I know I don't." She tried smiling. "Someday I'll tell my grandchildren I shagged a Navy SEAL."

His gaze flew to hers. "What we did . . . that's private."

"I was teasing." It had been the most intimate act ever. "I'll never forget you."

"Mandy . . . " He looked away from her again. "Will you give me your email address? I know you want something different for your life, so I won't use it. But I'd like to pass it to my mom, in case—"

"Don't say it. Don't say anything like that," she said, her chest tightening.

"Just give me your address. Please."

And so Mandy did.

She heard nothing for weeks. Back in L.A., she scoured the newspapers and trolled the internet, trying to imagine what hot spot he might be in. She read blogs written by military families, and once she happened upon a group of military wives having coffee at her local Starbucks. She sat nearby, long after her latté was gone, listening to them share their burdens. Listening to the yearning in the voices of the women whose husbands were deployed. She knew the taste, the sound, the physical presence of that longing, because it accompanied her everywhere she went.

In a fit of unrequited energy, she started baking Christmas goodies, imagining what kind Josh might like. They hadn't gotten around to discussing favorite foods, but she made peppermint brownies and peanut butter cookies topped with chocolate kisses, sugar cookies in the shape of the SEAL trident and gingerbread men covered with camouflage icing.

But her email inbox stayed empty. Finally she admitted to herself she might never know or hear more about him.

On the morning of Christmas Eve, she boxed up all the treats she'd baked and decorated, determined to take them to a homeless shelter. She didn't have a tree or anything else festive set up, because there didn't seem to be any sense in pretending to celebrate. Maybe in the new year she'd find some respite from the relentless ache.

With her purse under arm and her car keys in hand, she paused by her laptop to check her email. Her inbox had a new addition. Subject line: *From Josh's mom.* Finger poised to open it, Mandy froze. What had he said? *I'd like to give it to my mom, in case—*

Was this bad news? No, she wouldn't believe that. She couldn't. Her hands shaking, she managed to press the button and the text flashed onto the screen. Moaning, she dropped her purse and slid into the chair by the desk.

He was all right. Though Josh had told his mother to contact Mandy only if there was an emergency, she'd decided to take the maternal prerogative. In case Mandy was interested, he'd be arriving on a commercial flight at the San Diego airport just before midnight.

Josh Frye couldn't calculate how many hours he'd been in transit. His team had scattered once they'd hit the States, most everyone heading for a few days with family. As he walked up the jetway he rubbed his gritty eyes, then rubbed them again as he rode down the escalator to baggage claim and the exit to the taxi stand. As he stepped onto solid ground, he heard his name.

"Mom," he said turning toward her. "Hey. Hey, Dad. I told you guys I'd visit in the morning. You didn't need to come tonight." He checked his watch, which he'd already changed to local time. "It's almost midnight."

His mother wore a blinking, "I'M VERY MERRY," pin on her red sweater. He had to grin at that, and at just how like herself she looked in her dark jeans and red suede boots. Always the fashionista. He hugged both her and his father, admitting to himself he was glad they'd come. It was a needed distraction. The long flights home he'd only had a single thing on his mind . . . that once he landed he'd be so maddeningly close to Mandy.

"There's someone else who came to greet you," his father said, his voice strangely gruff.

Josh looked around. "Don't tell me my lazy-ass brother bothered to . . . " The rest of the words were swallowed by his surprise. He only managed to mouth her name. Mandy. *Mandy.*

Five feet away, she stood, three pink bakery boxes stacked in her arms. Her honey hair was longer, her face thinner, but a smile curved her beautiful lips. With slow movements, he slipped the strap of his duffel bag from over his shoulder and let it fall to the ground. Then he took a step forward, freezing again as tears filled her eyes. They were a startling blue, made only brighter by those unnerving tears.

Josh's mother poked his back, a little too reminiscent of those months he'd taken dance lessons at Mr. Xavier's Academy with the rest of his fifth grade classmates. The moms always had been forced to prod their sons to request a dance. "I can handle this, Mom," he murmured to her now. This was nothing like asking Tanya with the training bra to fox trot around the room to *Moon River.*

This was Mandy, and what he wanted from her was so much more than just one dance.

This time it was she who took a forward step. "You're here," she said, gesturing with the boxes, then looked down as if she'd forgotten them. "I've been baking for you," she explained with a rueful laugh. "For weeks."

For weeks. When he'd supposed she'd been spending that same time forgetting about him. He felt his smile crease the sunburned skin of his cheeks. "That so?"

"Let me get those for you," Josh's mom said, bustling over to take the boxes from Mandy.

Josh didn't look away from the face of the woman he wanted with all his soul. "Those are mine, Dad," he called. "No sneaking any."

"Just one," his dad grumbled. "C'mon, it's Christmas."

Mandy laughed, and Josh took that as the signal that she was ready to be in his arms. He hugged her tight, closing his eyes as he swung her around, overcome with how she just . . . just fit. It had been like that since the instant he found her in her uncle's basement. At his first glimpse of those blue eyes he'd been swamped by a wave of tenderness. Possessiveness. As a man trained to make quick decisions, wanting her for his own hadn't come as a great shock.

"What are you doing here?" he whispered against her mouth. Because he shouldn't take anything for granted. What he did was tough on girlfriends, spouses, and families. He understood that. He understood that his lonely Mandy might want someone who could make the kind of promises he was unable to pledge right now.

"I couldn't stay away. I missed you."

She lifted her mouth and they kissed, long and sweet, and God, it felt like its own vow.

"I want to be with you," she said.

It was as if a taut line inside him finally snapped free. He yanked her close again, pressing her to his thudding heart. "Are you sure? Maybe you should take some time . . . think about it." Then he glanced down at her, grinning. "I'll give you until tomorrow."

Mandy pulled back to grab his wrist and check the time. "It *is* tomorrow. And I'm sure."

His head dropped back as he took a moment to revel in the words. Then he refocused on her, lifting her chin. "What made you change your mind?"

She smiled. "Lots of things."

"You'll get my family, you know. They'll be here for you, whether I'm home every day or not."

She nodded.

"The SEAL wives are a tight group, too. You'll have them as well."

Her eyes sparkled and one brow rose. "Is that what I'm going to be? A SEAL wife?"

"If I have my way."

Mandy patted his chest. "You should know that it's the SEAL motto that really convinced me."

"'The Only Easy Day Was Yesterday'?" he said, puzzled. "How so?"

"Because the easy days are the yesterdays I had with you. I want as many of those as I can get."

It sounded like some sort of twisted female logic to him, and he was sure of it when he heard his mom release a sentimental sigh behind him. Of course she was listening. Josh also heard the contented sound of his dad munching a cookie. He looked down at his love, the beginning of a new part of his life. "I think my dad is eating all the stuff you baked for me."

She had the cutest dimple in her right cheek. "There's more where that came from."

"There's more everything," Josh promised. "I love you."

Mandy nodded, and reached into her pocket to pull out a fat, loopy gift bow that she balanced on the top her head. "I love you, too. Merry Christmas, Josh. I'm yours."

The words sounded like music to him, and then he realized they were. Holding her close again, he whispered into her ear. "Right back at you, sweetheart. Signed, SEALed, and delivered."

DOG HEART

Barbara Samuel

Jessie spied the truck through the window—nothing ostentatious, just a solid, late-model truck that any number of men might drive. Like the man who stepped out of the cab now, his dark hair shorn close to his head. He was leaner than he had been five years ago, and as he rounded the truck to the other side, he limped noticeably. Her heart did a little flip-flop of . . . nervousness? Anticipation?

Marcus Stone had been the love of her life from the time they were in seventh grade until the day she finally broke it off five years before, when they were twenty-two. She had, finally, started dating other men. Once in a while.

If he had called for any other reason, she would not have agreed to see him. But as he came forward, that reason came into view. Staff Sergeant Thor.

Thor had been a combat dog, attached to a SEAL unit engaged in a top secret mission in Afghanistan that had gone wrong. One SEAL had been killed, five more badly injured. Thor was one of them.

So was Marcus. Jessie put a careful box around that knowledge, set it aside. She would not be drawn in.

Instead she focused on the dog. He was a brown and gold German shepherd, mixed with a little something else because he had long hair, which had gone a little raggedy. He was the kind of dog people always wanted to approach, to pat on the head, the long dark nose and soft-looking fur drawing on some ancient need in the human spirit.

Sgt. Thor was in no mood for the hungry pats of children. He wore a harness attached to a leash gripped tightly in Marcus's powerful hand. The dog's shoulders were hunched warily as they began to cross the parking lot. Thor, too, limped visibly. When coaxed, he moved forward a few steps, then halted again. Marcus didn't yank on him, just waited patiently, standing alongside, then tried to urge the canine along a little more. Thor crept forward, his entire body apprehensive—belly close to the ground, head low.

"Poor baby," Jessie said aloud. She grabbed a bag of chicken breast tidbits off the counter, and headed outside to meet the pair. "It's all right," she called, coming outside. "Don't force it. I'll come to him."

Marcus nodded, raising a hand in acknowledgement. "Come easy. He can get pretty aggressive if you approach too fast."

"Got it." Jessie knelt to bring herself to a less intimidating height. From a few feet away, she said, "Hello, Staff Sergeant Thor. Would you like a treat?" She held out her hand, palm down and offered it to the dog. He balefully looked her, then up to his handler.

Jessie steeled herself to look at him, too. Marcus was not quite six feet tall, and lean. Always the leanest, strongest guy in school. He wore jeans and a t-shirt that revealed arms that were tattooed—and scarred. White marks riddled the tanned flesh of his left forearm in arcs. His laser-blue eyes zapped her, and against her will, she felt the same old burst of love/yearning/fury.

"Thanks for doing this, Jess," he said.

"It wasn't for you," she returned, then took a breath. High emotion would do the dog no good at all.

"Still. Thanks."

"Yep." She focused back on Thor, watching him, looking at his body language, his face. "It's all right, boy," Jessie said. "Take your time." She stayed where she was, body relaxed. "Tell me about him, Marcus. His handler was killed?"

"Yes." The word was gruff. "Sniper got him in the attack. I always promised Sean that I'd look after Thor if anything happened to him. Not doing the best job so far."

Jessie eased a little closer, and Thor lifted his head slightly, nostrils quivering. She paused, turned her hand over. "Thor was also injured?"

"Both of us where. Thor took a bullet to the shoulder. We almost lost him, but I got him out in time."

"I see." That would account for the limp. Dog and man.

Thor abruptly settled on the ground, his body relaxing. She reached in and offered the treat. He took it gingerly. "Good boy," she said. He sniffed her hand and wrist, and Jessie sat down next to him, keeping her body slightly angled away. "Is he afraid of everything, or certain things in particular?"

Marcus started to kneel, but a stiff leg stopped him and he straightened again. With a slight burst of shame, Jessie said, "I'm sorry we can go inside soon, but I want to make him comfortable first."

"That's all right." He rubbed his thigh, an absent gesture. "I keep forgetting. Just doesn't bend the way it did."

Jessie offered Thor another cube of chicken. He accepted it delicately, then moved his nose along her wrist and up her arm, snuffling, gathering information, eyes trained on her face. She saw vast intelligence there, and exhaustion. Her heart surged toward him, the same hunger she always felt toward wounded dogs—to heal them, love them, protect them. "I can help you," she promised quietly, offering another treat. "If you let me."

He gazed at her steadily. Warily, but with curiosity, too. Dogs usually could sense that she had their well-being in mind.

Marcus said, "He's afraid of going inside buildings for the most part. I can get him into a house, but not a building like this. He's afraid of crowds. And lightning. And the smell of gasoline."

"Poor guy." She grazed the side of his shoulder with the back of her wrist. He looked at her with all the sorrow in the world. "Let's see if you'll go inside, shall we?"

She stood, putting herself on a level with Marcus. His eyes were more guarded than Thor's, but still troubled. "How is your relationship with him?"

He shrugged, looking away. His jaw and cheekbone were hard chipped, the angles sharp. Jessie wanted to ease the tension across his mouth, and suddenly remembered all too clearly how it felt to kiss those lips. "He wishes it was me who died, instead of Sean."

"And you? How do you feel toward him?" She inclined her head. "Truth. I can't help if I don't know the real story."

"Maybe I wish it had been Thor instead of Sean."

"I guess you're starting even, then," she said.

His jaw tightened. "I guess we are."

Jessie crossed her arms. "Can you love him? Can you be good to him even if you don't?"

"Yes. I made a promise," he said. "I will give him the home he deserves."

"Do you blame him for Sean's death?"

"No," he said, and faced her clearly. "Thor's a good soldier. An honorable soldier. He did his best."

"And you?"

A beat. A flash of something across his brow. "I could have done better."

She doubted that most earnestly—in football, in love, in raising horses on his father's ranch, he always gave one hundred percent. She softened toward him ever-so-slightly. "Well, let's get started." She gave Marcus a few treats. With anyone else, she would have explained how to reward the dog for each step, but Marcus already knew. They had been drawn together over their love of animals. All animals. "Let's see if we can get him to come inside."

Marcus eyed the building. "This is a bad structure, for the dog. "

"Why?"

"It's all cinderblock. It's like a building he would have entered on patrol."

"We won't push it, then, but I would like to see how he reacts." Jessie also wanted to observe the relationship between man and dog. "Offer him a treat and let's move toward the door."

"Yes, ma'am." Marcus tugged on the leash. "Come on, buddy," he said, offering the treat. "Let's take a walk."

Thor looked at his handler apprehensively, but stood up, taking the treat. They walked a few feet, and Thor stopped, panting. He sat down.

"That's a warning," Marcus said. "There's danger ahead."

"What's the command to release him?"

"All clear."

Thor disagreed. He looked up at Marcus, then at the cinderblock building, and shifted slightly but kept his dark nose pointed at Trouble Ahead. His ears were up, alert. "Such a beautiful dog," she murmured. "Needs grooming."

"Yeah, good luck with that. He's bitten everybody who tried."

"Ah." For a moment, she imagined the scenes the dog had experienced, protecting his master and the team. She knelt and touched his back. "You are a brave dog, a loyal dog," she said, smoothing his fur. He accepted chicken from her palm. "You don't have to do anything anymore. I promise there's nothing in there. Would you come with me?"

He met her eyes, searching. "That's it, baby." Jessie stood, walking backward, a treat extended. "Come on, Thor. It's safe." When he moved a few feet forward, she let him have a treat. He took a few more steps, had another.

Suddenly, from the alley came a trio of skateboarders, rocking down the concrete slope, whooping, coming straight toward them. Thor leapt to snarling attack mode, barking, lunging, nearly snapping the ankle of one of the boys before Marcus subdued him with an arm around his chest. "No, Thor. All clear! All clear!"

"Dude!" one of the boys cried, "get control of your dog, why don'tcha?"

"Boys," Jessie called, in a voice as non-threatening as she could muster, "you know it's illegal for you to skateboard here. If you don't want a ticket, you'd best get out of here."

Without remorse, they skated away, jostling and shouting. Just being kids.

She turned to the dog and man, huddled on the ground. Thor shivered violently and was panting as if he'd run a hundred miles. Marcus had a bite mark on his hand that leaked blood in a steady stream. "How bad is the bite?"

"It's fine," he said gruffly. "I've had worse."

Jessie eyed the scars on his arm. Dog bites. Savage, deep bites. She only nodded. "That was a disaster. I'm sorry."

"Not your fault."

"We'll stop for now, but I'd like to end on a high note, if you don't mind."

"You're the boss."

"I'm going to have you bring him to my house tomorrow. We'll work in my backyard. It's protected and maybe it won't feel so threatening to him."

"Sounds good." Marcus rubbed Thor's chest with a the uninjured hand. "You all right, bud?"

Thor licked his chin, apologetically.

"I know." He gave the dog's ears a rough scrub. "It's all right."

Enough love there, Jessie thought. *Plenty*.

As Marcus stood, she saw that his legs were shaking. Alarmed, she asked, "Are you okay?"

"I'll be all right in a minute," he said roughly.

The dog was not the only one with PTSD, Jessie thought, and unbidden, tears welled up in her throat. To hide them, she scuffed a foot on the ground. "We need to bandage that hand."

"No, it's nothing serious. I'll take care of it when I get home." He pulled a handkerchief out of his back pocket and wrapped it up. The tremors in his hands were violent, and it took two tries to get the handkerchief around his wound.

Jessie reached out and took the leash. She would need more information, but for now, man and dog both needed normal. "Let's walk," she said. "There's a pond over there. Almost no one ever goes there."

Marcus was ashamed. His hand shook, his heart pounded. Sweat poured down his back. Next to him, Thor crept close to the ground, one shaky step after the next. Jessie simply walked next to them, offering a treat to Thor every few steps, murmuring encouragement.

She had always been a dog charmer.

The roar of adrenaline slowed, then stopped. He could hear some little birds hidden in a tree. A breeze swept over the water, making it ripple. He took a breath. Thor eased, too, beginning to walk naturally even if he was still hypervigilant, waiting for the snipers to come again, from somewhere.

Anywhere.

At any moment.

"Give him a treat," Jessie said. She was wiry and small, like a gymnast or a triathlete, with a cloud of brown hair. No beauty but her wide, clear eyes. And yet, he had never loved another woman in his life. Just looking at her now made him ache in a hundred places— aches of memory, aches of hunger, aches of regret and love. A wisp of hair blew over her neck and Marcus acutely wanted to kiss the smooth skin there.

He'd lost that right, by making the only choice possible for himself. And he'd paid the price. Big time.

"Tell him how proud of him you are," Jessie added.

"Good boy, Thor," Marcus said. The dog's slick tongue slipped the treat from between his fingers.

"This is good," she said. "Let's just make a couple of turns around the pond."

He nodded. "Have you worked with other dogs with PTSD?"

"A few. It's a military town."

"Is Thor pretty bad?"

She raised those big direct eyes and met his gaze. Blue, like the lake, like the mountains rising behind her. "I think you know the answer to that question."

"Yeah." He cleared his throat. "Can you help him?"

When she smiled, it was the first time he'd seen Jessie, *his* Jessie, since they'd arrived. It smashed into his solar plexus like a metal beam and nearly buckled his knees.

"You know the answer to that question, too," she said, that impish dimple arriving and disappearing.

Maybe this had been a big mistake, he thought. But he really thought he might be over her, five years later. Five hard years. Five satisfying years. She had never understood why he wanted to serve. She didn't believe in war, said it was a stupid way to solve problems, flinging men at each other until they died. It was the only thing they'd ever fought about—that all he'd ever wanted, ever expected to do, was be a soldier. His pride in making the SEAL team had been the most powerful emotion of his life.

Jessie had given him an ultimatum—SEALs or her. He had not so much chosen as been called, which he'd never been able to make her understand. She gave him back the ring he had saved to buy, a diamond still carefully tucked into the back of a drawer.

"So, what does an ex-SEAL do for work?" she asked.

"I bought a ranch," he said gruffly. "Appaloosas."

"You'll be good at that."

"I was a good SEAL, too."

She looked up sharply. "I'm sure you were. I never doubted that."

"Yeah."

"Let's not go over old ground, okay?" Jessie said. "I—I made mistakes. So did you. Let's leave it at that."

Gruffly he said, "Fair enough."

Thor suddenly moved forward, snuffling hard into a clump of long grass. He lifted his head, sneezed, wagged his tail ever so faintly. Stuck his nose into the grass again, and scrapped the earth with his paws.

Jessie put her hand on Marcus's arm. "Let's let him be a dog."

Her fingertips touched his skin, right over the scars Thor had left. Electricity moved through his skin, through his belly. Idiotic, and yet, there it was. As if she felt it too, she looked up, and for a long moment, it honestly seemed as if she might not mind if he bent down and kissed her.

Abruptly, she pulled her hand away.

Marcus focused on Thor, who sniffed along the grass, followed the scent to the edge of the pond, and then scraped his paws on the earth, flinging dirt far and wide, his chest puffed out. "That's as relaxed as I've seen him," Marcus said, and unaccountably, his throat was tight. What? Would he freaking cry now? For God's sake.

Thor wandered over and Marcus gave him a treat. "Good job."

Jessie stuck her hands in her back pockets. The move pulled her shirt tight over her breasts and he suddenly, shockingly, remembered how plump and pretty they were.

No, not going there. He rubbed his eyes. "Are we done for today?"

"Yes. You can take him back to the truck and I'll write down my address. Can you come tomorrow?"

Jessie told herself that she was not dressing up for Marcus, just that she needed to look her best in order to be able to work with him. Mascara gave a woman confidence—everyone knew that.

She had already taken her two dogs, Alex and Wendell, to the training studio for the morning. Jessie's assistant, Michelle, would look after the border collies, using them as helpers and examples, and Thor could come into the environment that smelled of other dogs, but not have to deal with them. She also walked the perimeter of the backyard, looking for problems, trouble, anything that might spook the nervous canine. Nothing. A Ponderosa pine in one corner, shrubs and a wide border planted with flowers along the fences. There were no dogs in the other yards to bark and make Thor feel the need to defend his area.

Overnight, she'd done a lot of reading, to increase her confidence in dealing with PTSD specific to combat dogs. Since Thor had so many issues, they would have to handle them one at a time. The first thing was to restore his sense of safety and trust. Thor had to learn to trust Marcus.

And Marcus had to learn to believe in himself.

Even with all the preparation, when the doorbell rang, she nearly jumped right out of her skin. Her heart skittered into overdrive, banging so hard in her rib cage that she had to put a hand to her side. She flew to the door, then halted when she spied him through the window, his face in profile as he looked toward the street. It was still his face. Marcus's face. The face she had spied the first time at lunch in the seventh grade; the face that she had cheered for through dozens of seasons of sports—football and track and soccer; the face she had hardened her heart toward when he insisted on joining the Navy after college graduation.

Signing up to get yourself killed, she cried.

Signing up to help people who don't have anyone else, he countered.

Signing up to be an absent husband!

Signing up to serve the country I love!

Now here he stood, older and weary, still serving the same way he always had. The least she could do was to help him heal the broken heart of a dog who needed a second chance. Putting on a professional demeanor, she opened the door. And laughed.

Staff Sergeant Thor stood perfectly still on the square concrete porch, gazing up at her like a calendar dog, a single rose encased in a rolled up newspaper in his mouth.

"Give it to her, Thor," Marcus said.

Thor stood, walked over to Jessie, and put the flower against her hand. When she took it, Thor made a very pretty bow.

Delighted, Jessie laughed, then squatted to dog-eye level and said, "You are one amazing creature, aren't you?"

Thor gave Marcus a sidelong look, practically a wink, and Marcus laughed. The sound boomed out of him, that deep rich enjoyment that infected everybody around him, and Jessie felt it course through her entire body—elbows, palms, lips.

Oh, to just kiss him one more time!

She looked up at him at the same moment he looked down. She saw him look at her mouth, and his hand lifted, as if to touch her arm.

Thor nudged her leg, and Jessie was shaken from her swoon. "Sorry, sweetheart! You are the greatest dog in the world. So smart! So wise!" He lifted his chin and she scratched his chest. He made a low groan, lifted a paw to her arm, and shot a glance toward Marcus.

Jessie said, "He is really, really smart."

"He is that."

Remembering what they were here to do, she stepped back and opened the door. "Do you want to come in, baby?"

He leaned to see around her legs, then settled back into a sit.

"Not sure?" She shifted the rose to her other hand and reached into the treat bag attached to her belt. "How about this?" She gave it to him and he accepted it politely.

She opened the door wider, and had Marcus hold it open. She walked backward into the house, offering a treat, talking quietly.

No go.

"Does he go inside at your house?"

Marcus nodded. "I had to blindfold him the first time."

"Was the attack in a building?"

His face went blank. "Yeah."

Jessie put her hands on her hips. "What's your goal, Marcus?

What do you want to accomplish with him?"

He looked at Thor, sitting politely on the step. "I want him to feel okay again, like the world isn't dangerous at every turn."

"He's going to have to trust you. What might be standing in the way?"

Marcus turned down the corners of his mouth. He was silent for a long moment, and Jessie watched as he rubbed a palm over the deep, ropy pink scars on his forearm. Finally, he looked up at her. "Me, I guess."

She nodded. "Trade places with me."

He offered her the leash, and stepped into her living room.

"Now back up a few steps and call him. Offer a treat."

Thor moved ever so slightly, a foot at a time. After awhile, he followed Marcus all the way into the kitchen, and at that point, Jessie gave the dog a rest. "Good dog, Thor," she said quietly, and offered a bowl of water. To Marcus she said, "You did a great job. He is going to transfer his loyalty to you. It's just going to take some time."

He nodded, looking gravely at Thor, who now snuffled the edge of the area rug, and cautiously looked around. "Sean taught him that trick, with the rose. He loved that man so much, it was—" he paused. Cleared his throat.

Jessie filled a glass with water and gave it to him.

"Thanks," he said roughly, and drank deeply.

Eyeing the scars on his arms, she reached out and absently touched them. He shied away as if he'd been burned. Embarrassed, Jessie said, "I'm so sorry! I don't know what made me do that!"

He took her hand, sandwiched it between her own. "Shhh. It's okay. Complete strangers do it, too. Damnedest thing."

Every molecule of her body seemed to suddenly overheat, as if his touch were some kind of chemistry experiment, and Jessie trembled very slightly, looking up at him. She was struck dumb, her brain awash in the same cloud of heat that boiled her vocabulary right out of her head. She could only feel, only see: his beautiful laser blue eyes, peering right through her, into her heart, her foolish, foolish heart; his mouth, sensual and severe at once; his hands, sandwiching her own.

The moment seemed to stretch, exaggerating everything. The steadiness of his regard, the shape of his shoulders under the simple t-shirt he wore. "I missed you so much it was like somebody burned a hole in the middle of my gut," he said quietly. "It wasn't fair, what you did."

"Marcus, I—"

Abruptly, he pulled his hands free and walked away. Thor scrambled behind him, hurrying to catch up as Marcus headed outside into the backyard.

Standing alone and bewildered by her kitchen counter, Jessie thought, *well, at least we're getting somewhere with the dog.*

Marcus paced the perimeter of the back yard, trying to calm his raging emotions. A thousand things welled up—fury and hope and anger and disappointment.

And love.

Damn it.

It took a moment, but he saw Thor out of the corner of his eye, pacing behind him, his hips low, ears high. On alert. Protecting him, looking out for danger.

"Sergeant Thor, at ease," he called out.

Thor paused, midstep, head cocked, ears at the ready. One paw was lifted. He looked exactly like Rin Tin Tin.

"All clear, Thor," he said. Firmly, clearly.

The dog sat, his body at ease. After a second, his long pink tongue fell out of his mouth. "Good dog," Marcus said, and maneuvered himself into position to give Thor a good knuckle scrub, down his back and haunches, as Sean used to do. It was awkward for Marcus to do a puppy bow, but he came as close as he could, slapping his hand down on the ground. Thor leapt up, smiling, and bowed, then danced sideways.

Marcus chased him, then let himself be chased, playing that he was terrified. Thor leapt and lightly bumped hips with Marcus, then dashed away. Neither man nor dog were the graceful creatures they once had been, but they'd been through it together.

They knew.

At last, Marcus fell on the grass, breathing hard, and closed his eyes. Thor came over and fell against him, his back against Marcus's side. Idly, Marcus flung an arm around the front of the dog, and after a moment, he felt the slippery dog tongue gently washing his forearm. Caressing the scars.

Marcus turned his head. Thor paused, his whiskey brown eyes earnest, and met his gaze, steadily. He lifted one wheat-colored paw and put it on Marcus's chest, the pad directly over the man's heart.

"I love you, too," Marcus said. "I know you didn't mean it."

Jessie quietly, easily sat beside them. "What happened to your arm, Marcus?"

"Both Sean and Thor were shot by the snipers. Sean was dead instantly." He closed his eyes, telling the story in a steady monotone, trying to keep it at a distance, maybe. "Thor covered Sean's body with his own, and wouldn't let anybody near. He was bleeding badly, and the mission was falling to pieces, and I had to get him out of there, but every time I got close, he snapped at me. No one could get anywhere close to him." He swallowed, his nostrils filled with the acrid smell of smoke and dust, the coppery scent of blood. And there was Thor, about to die for love if Marcus didn't save him. "So I just grabbed him and hauled him away, and he bit the hell out of me, trying to get back to Sean until I could get him muzzled and subdued."

He sensed her hand hovering over the scars and opened his eyes. Looked at her. "It's all right," he said. "You can touch them."

Her fingers brushed over the marks, lightly, just as Thor had done moments before. Tears flowed down her face. "I was so unfair to you, Marcus," she said.

"Yes, you were."

"I'm so sorry." With misery, she looked down at him. "I never stopped missing you. Seeing you like this feels like the world is suddenly alive again. Like it was black and white and now it's color."

He lifted a hand to her cheek, feeling the tears beneath her hair. Fiercely she pressed his hand closer, turning her face into his palm. She kissed the center.

"Come here," he said, and she flowed over him, into the hollow on the other side of his body, so that he was sandwiched by dog and woman. Sunlight poured down over them, and the air smelled of freshly mown grass, and maybe things could work out. "If my leg heals well enough, I'll go back into the military," he said.

"I asked something of you that I never should have," Jessie said, and lifted up on one elbow. She touched his face. "You are honorable and driven to serve. Asking you to give that up was wrong, and I'm sorry. Do you think you might give me another chance? Give us another chance?"

Thor's paw still rested across his chest, reminding him of second chances, of the possibilities that might still be available if you could choose to live in this moment, not the past or the future. They had a long, long road back—Thor, and Marcus, and Jessie and Marcus, too, but it was a road worth walking.

"I think that's possible," he said. "But you probably need to kiss me so I can decide."

With a little cry, she bent over him, pressing her mouth into his. He was flooded with the fresh apple delight of her, the familiar and perfect way they fit and as they tumbled sideways, bodies wrapping naturally and easily into the other's, he thought he heard a faint voice say, "All clear, men. All clear."

Thor woofed softly.

WHIRLWIND

Roxanne St. Claire

Billie waited until the last possible moment to delay the inevitable. With the wind rocking the rusted corrugated metal of the trailer and fat drops splattering like a thousand hammers against the roof, she watched a soundless, ancient television set. Over the past two hours, the hurricane's path had changed dramatically, shifting east over the Gulf of Mexico. Instead of passing by as a rainy, windy night, the storm was bearing down on Florida's west coast barrier islands, ready to do some major damage to the vulnerable shores of Barefoot Bay.

Clutching Nutmeg, Billie soothed her nervous little terrier with loving strokes, sharing sips of bottled water with her four-legged companion to buy every extra second before evacuating.

Billie Jo Taylor was scared, but she wasn't stupid enough to try and ride out a hurricane in a two-room mobile home. She had to go to the school shelter, where they'd probably demand an ID she didn't want to show them, and all the Mimosa Key locals would stare at her, wondering who the hell was the crazy blonde lady with the ratty looking dog. Everybody knew everybody on this island . . . except nobody knew *her*. And that was how she'd planned to keep it until this damn storm blew in.

Still, the longer Billie waited, the easier it would be to slip into the shelter and hide in the bathroom, possibly undetected until morning.

The lights flickered, drenching her in darkness, making Nutmeg bark. But the power came back after a second, something which probably wouldn't happen the next time. An outage was inevitable, and the least of what she'd have to endure if she stayed.

"It's time, Nutsie." She settled the dog on the bed next to the overnight bag that held most everything that mattered in the world— including the package that had landed in her P.O. Box yesterday. She hadn't had time to get to the library computer and log on to her eBay account to post auctions, and with the storm, who knew if there'd even be a library tomorrow?

She pulled out the soft leather box just to look at the contents one more time, touching the large military watch that made her pulse jump when she'd found it online. The seller had been a fool, taking only twelve hundred dollars. Billie's years of owning an antique store had given her a flawless eye, and a Laco in this condition was worth almost five times that much.

This watch was her ticket to her next destination . . . wherever that may be. She'd been on this island, hiding in the rented trailer for almost four months, slipping in and out of town for what she needed in a beat-up old truck she'd bought for next to nothing. Four months was enough time for Frank Perlow to use his considerable resources to find her. It was time to move on, except now she had to go to the damn shelter and risk exposure.

A gust of wind whistled through the cracks of the drafty windows, startling Nutmeg.

"Shhh." She petted the dog's head with one hand, but fingered the timepiece with the other. This would get her enough money to run, hide, and survive another four months. Maybe by then Frank Perlow would be dead. It was her only hope.

She turned the watch over and read the inscription she'd already memorized.

I am what you will be. I was what you are. R.M.S.

"Back in the old days," she whispered to Nutmeg. "I would have created a whole World War II display around this. I'd have one of my historian friends write up a story about this RMS person. Robert Martin Smith, a hero who died in action. Or Raymond Michael Simmons, a seasoned vet." Whoever bought this would truly appreciate a fine piece like this and the deep history behind it. "Back in the old days, this would have been a showpiece in my store."

But the old days were gone, along with her precious antique shop and well-ordered life. With a sigh, she stuffed the box back in her duffle bag, refusing to think of how much being in the wrong place at the wrong time had cost her.

"All right, baby. We'll go now and . . . " She stopped talking, a distant sound humming louder than the wind. Was that a car engine? All the way up here in the deserted, forested tip of Barefoot Bay? Nutmeg heard it, too, lifting her furry little head and cocking her ear.

The rumble grew louder, more distinct, then bright beams of headlights streamed in through the corners of the blinds she kept pulled tight. Instinctively, she dropped to her knees.

Who could it be?

A neighbor from the more populated end of Barefoot Bay coming to warn her to leave? That lady who lived in that beat up old house on the beach being a good Samaritan in a storm? Or maybe the Mimosa Key sheriff had to alert every resident to evacuate.

Or maybe . . . Frank had found her.

"I bet it's the sheriff," she said softly, more to reassure herself than her terrified dog. Still, she reached under the bed for the last item she'd been planning to take, even if it would spend the night under the front seat of her truck because they'd never let her bring it in the shelter.

The Winchester Model 12 might be over a hundred years old and therefore a bona fide antique, but the rifle could shoot, and it had been locked and loaded since the day Billie'd moved into this tin box.

A car door slammed. Nutmeg jumped up and barked sharply.

"Shhh, quiet." Chill bumps crawled up her arms, despite the sickening summer heat in the trailer. Nutmeg obeyed the order, but dipped her head to launch a low, slow growl that could easily escalate into a loud bark.

Holding the rifle, Billie stayed down and inched to the window to sneak a peek at a compact car. The door opened with the headlights still on, blinding her to whoever got out of the driver's side. But as the figure emerged into the light and walked toward the door of the trailer, she hissed a breath of horror.

"Son of a bitch. He sent someone to kill me."

Someone who obviously could do the job. The man must have been six two and damn near two hundred pounds of rock solid muscle covered in a rain-soaked T-shirt and worn camos. His hair was shorn to highlight sharp features, an angular jaw, and a mean slash of black brow.

But it was his hands that stole her breath. Hands the size of a small country, with long fingers and wide palms. Hands designed to do two things: make a woman scream in pleasure or squeeze the life out of another human.

Billie had no doubt which one this beast had come to do.

Nutmeg's growl grew louder and Billie shook her head furiously. "Hush, Nutsie, please!"

As if she understood her owner's fear, Nutmeg obliged, sinking back into the pillow. But it wouldn't last; the second Conan the

Barbarian reached the door—the only door in or out of this damn place—nothing could keep that dog quiet.

Think, Billie Jo, think. Just as she turned to grab the dog, the man pounded on the metal door, the sound reverberating back to the bedroom where Billie stayed.

"Anybody home?"

As expected, Nutmeg vaulted from the bed, staccato barks echoing as she ran into the trailer's only other room.

A hit man who knocked?

Still, Billie directed the barrel of her rifle toward the door that led to the living room, while she considered her options. If Frank had hired him, this man wouldn't leave with her alive. She'd have to escape somehow. There was only one way out—through the front door that she couldn't even see from where she stood in the bedroom. If he got in here, she'd have to somehow get past him to the door.

Without Nutmeg? It was unthinkable.

But, then, so was dying. So she'd shoot the guy. The callousness of that thought made her swallow. Okay, maybe not a mortal wound but enough to immobilize him, say a shot in both legs. Then he'd be stuck here and the hurricane would . . . do what hurricanes do.

Would that be murder? Not . . . *technically.*

She snapped her fingers three times, usually enough to get Nutmeg to come, but the dog didn't hear or respond, and Billie didn't want to give herself away by calling out.

"Hey!" the man called again, a bellowing baritone louder than the wind and rain and far more terrifying. "Is anybody in there?"

Would a trained killer ask to come in first? Maybe this was a concerned neighbor or—

He rattled the door, shaking hard enough that the whole trailer moved.

A looter? Some creep looking to make a quick buck in places evacuated for the storm? On instinct, she scooped up the bag and threw it into the bathroom. Maybe she wouldn't have to shoot him if she convinced him she had nothing of value. Maybe she could—

The shatter of wood splintering and metal tearing echoed from the living room, drawing a tiny shriek of shock from her lips. He'd kicked the door open! A heavy footstep landed in the living room and she braced her legs, ready to fire, lowering her rifle so she'd hit his legs and not his heart.

"Hey, pooch, you get left behind?"

She blinked in surprise at the sudden change in the intruder's voice. Who was he? Whoever, he knew how to subdue dogs, because Nutmeg instantly quieted to a breathy pant.

"What the hell kind of dickhead evacuates and leaves their dog behind?"

Oh, a looter with *opinions*. Resentment sparked through her and she had to clamp her mouth shut to keep from responding. Nutmeg whined, the happy sound she made when someone picked her up. Damn it. *I really should have gotten a Rottweiler.*

Another footstep, bringing him that much closer to the only other room in the trailer. Billie squared her shoulders, curled her finger around the trigger, and took a deep, calming breath just as her bedroom doorway filled with the silhouette of a man holding her dog.

When he stepped into the light, their gazes locked instantly. Surprise widened his steely blue eyes and unlocked a square, whisker-shaded jaw. And disgust rolled off him as he angled broad shoulders and tightened his hold on Nutmeg.

"Don't shoot the dog."

She almost choked. "Get the hell out of my trailer or I'll kill you," she said through gritted teeth, hoping she sounded tougher than she suddenly felt.

"I'm not leaving till I get what I want, ma'am." The threat was quick and easy, scary and sure, accompanied by a few steps and punctuated by a sputter of lights. And then complete darkness.

Nutmeg barked.

Billie gasped.

And the man just kept walking toward her.

She tightened on the trigger, squeezed her eyes shut, and—the whole rifle went flying out of her hand, the force of the blow making her teeth crack together. Before it hit the floor, a shot echoed through the trailer, making Nutmeg yowl as the man cornered Billie against the wall.

He peered down at her, still holding her dog, close enough that even in the darkness she could see the ice in his eyes. They were shockingly blue, fringed with black lashes, somehow threatening and inviting at the same time.

"Look, lady, I don't want to hurt you. I don't want to hurt this cute little dog. I don't even want to be here. But someone named William Josephs, who rents this hellhole of a house, has a Laco B-Uhr Type Two Pilot Watch. I'm not leaving until it's in my hands. Is that clear?"

Holy hell. He wanted the watch.

The tiniest glimmer of recognition flickered in the hazel eyes that peered up at Rick, wiped away so fast that a lesser trained man would never have noticed. But Lieutenant Rick Stone was trained by the U.S. Navy, and SEALs didn't miss a tell. Annie Oakley in her double-wide with an old-school rifle had just given herself away.

"I don't know what you're talking about," she said, her jaw still tight in a mix of fear and fury.

"The watch that was delivered to a P.O. Box owned by William Josephs, who rents this fine piece of property. Know him?"

"No."

Squeezed between them, the ratty little terrier whimpered softly. It probably knew she was lying, too.

"Is he your husband?"

"If you hurt my dog, I'll kill you."

He'd already disarmed her with one fairly light touch, so he doubted she could manage to carry off that threat. Still, he knew she had the watch and he had no reason to piss her off even more.

Very slowly, he inched back and eased the dog to the floor. A noisy gust of wind rattled the whole place, hard enough to make the cheap, raised floor rock underneath them and terrify the dog, who took off to the front of the trailer, barking insanely.

"Nutmeg!" the woman called, jerking away, but Rick slammed his hands on narrow shoulders to hold her in place.

"The watch."

She looked up at him, searching his face, her expression well guarded. Her hair was wild, fried by a bad home bleach job, and she didn't wear a speck of makeup. Still, for trailer trash, she wasn't bad looking. Pretty, even, but for the raw terror on her face. Maybe thirty, with wide-set eyes and southern belle skin. She looked like Hollywood had miscast a starlet for the role of a redneck.

"What's it worth to you?" she demanded.

Everything. "Double whatever you're asking."

Another flicker of response. "How do you know I have it?"

"I know."

This time there was definite interest in her look. Interest in money, not him.

"Are you seriously offering . . . " Suddenly, she frowned, jerking away, her attention shifting. "Where's Nutmeg?"

The dog had stopped barking.

She pushed him with far more force than he expected, wresting out of his grip and running into the darkness of the trailer. "She got out!"

He followed, jolted by the unexpected crack in her voice, and reached the other room in four long strides. She stood at the front door he'd bashed open, the rain falling hard and steady in the headlights he'd left on to help navigate his way.

"Nutmeg!" She screamed into the storm, then turned to him, fire in her eyes. "God damn you, she's all I have in the whole world! She'll never survive this!"

Something inside him squeezed tight in his chest. The same pressure he'd felt when he'd gotten the word that Granddad had passed. A punch of helpless guilt, a kick of loss. And he'd been ten thousand miles away from home on a trawler taking down Somalian pirates and couldn't do a damn thing except kill pirates. Which he did, a lot.

She took a bold step into the downpour to call for the dog again, just as a furious gust ripped a branch off a tree twenty feet away, the wood splintering, the branch blowing inches from her face.

"She can't be far," he said, putting two hands on her shoulders, not as a threat this time, but to ease her back into the shelter of the trailer. "I'll get her. What's her name? Nutcase?"

She almost smiled, but tears filled her eyes. "Nutmeg. Please. *Please* find her."

So blondie could disappear with his watch?

No, scratch that. He'd just offered to double the price, and he'd go four times higher than that if he had to.

She gripped his arms in a death squeeze, her fingers strong, warm, desperate. "Oh my God, I'll die without her." Wind buffeted the trailer, making her momentarily lose her balance and tumble into him, the pressure of her body surprisingly pleasant before she jerked away as if he'd burned her.

"Where does she usually walk?" he asked.

"She doesn't. I mean, she never goes outside without a leash, and I just take her out back a couple times a day. She doesn't know her way around here. She'll be lost in minutes."

"Get back inside." He nudged her further out of the rain and stepped down into the mud. "I'll find her."

"I should go with you. She might come if she hears my voice."

"Then stand here and call." He took a few steps away, peering into the downpour and wind. The outer bands of this hurricane had made landfall and another tree branch could snap at any time. "I have a flashlight. Just wait here and stay under the roof. If it gets too bad, get in the bathroom, away from any windows."

Without waiting for her response, he jogged to the car, opened the passenger side, and dug into the bag he'd brought for his brief mission. Which, except for a dumb dog, could be accomplished now.

"Nutmeg!" The woman had come back outside, the rain flattening that mess of her hair and soaking the thin T-shirt she wore. The headlights beamed right on her wet body, pulling his attention to feminine curves that, like the pretty face, seemed completely out of place in this trailer hiding in the woods.

Or maybe the trailer wasn't hiding . . . maybe she was.

"Go back in," he hollered over the wind. "I'll find her."

But would he get what he came for, or would this little enigma keep pretending she didn't have it? "And you'll give me my grandfather's watch when I come back," he added, as insurance.

Her eyes flashed wide open and she swiped water out of her eyes. "If you find my dog."

He flipped on the flashlight to scan the scrub and brush. Nutmeg. Damn it, he'd find her if it killed him.

"Wait!" she called out, making him turn to look at her soaked silhouette again. "What's your name?"

"Lieutenant Richard M. Stone, United States Navy SEAL, ma'am."

She practically buckled with something that could only be called relief. "Oh. That's . . . good."

Usually, it was. "And you?"

"I'm . . . Billie Jo."

Billie Jo. As in *William Josephs*, owner of the P.O. Box where Rick's watch had just been shipped. "I'll be back, Billie Jo," he promised. "And I'll have your dog."

She disappeared in the house, hopefully to retrieve his watch. He couldn't help noticing that she didn't make any promises, though.

Inside, Billie took just one minute to catch her breath and count her blessings. He wasn't hired by Frank, that would be her first blessing. He wanted that watch badly enough to pay good money, and that was another blessing because she could leave right away without waiting for a sale online. And if Nutmeg had to run away in a storm, who better to rescue her than a big, burly, Navy SEAL? The third blessing was the most intriguing, no doubt about it.

She headed back into the bedroom, disregarding the pools of muddy water left by her soaking wet clothes and the pounding rain that blew in the open door. Another gust made the cheap aluminum roof scream as it fought to stay on, reminding her that nothing was safe in this trailer, but she couldn't leave now. She couldn't leave Nutmeg or the Navy SEAL who was risking his life to save her dog.

Slipping into the bathroom, she dug through the duffle bag and pulled out the watch. The piece was in its original box, too, which added to the value. Sitting on the edge of the bed, she snapped the box open and took the watch off soft satin casing, turning it.

I am what you will be. I was what you are. R.M.S.

His voice echoed in her heart.

Richard M. Stone, United States Navy SEAL, ma'am.

An inexplicable thrill danced through her, making her crackle like a live wire had touched her wet skin. Of course, she needed the money, but what she wanted most was to see Richard M. Stone's raw-boned face soften, because she just knew it would.

RMS . . . this belonged to *him.*

Footsteps pounded hard enough to wobble the whole trailer. She jumped, and the box fell off her lap, but she ran toward the front, stuffing the watch into her pocket because the minute he handed her Nutmeg, she'd hand him his treasure. Not for money, but because . . . he *owned* this.

And because he was a good man. A Navy SEAL, a hero, no doubt related to the original RMS. He was a man unlike—

"I knew you were too stupid to evacuate during a hurricane."

Frank Perlow.

She didn't even think, just launched herself right past him so fast she was practically airborne on her way out the door. He spun, but she heard him thud to the floor and swear, sliding in the puddles on the linoleum floor.

Billie didn't bother to look back, she just took off as fast as she could go, directly into the storm, directly into the brush that scraped and tore at her skin and clothes. Nothing mattered but to run as far and as fast from Frank Perlow as she could. It was the only way to stay alive.

Nutmeg was a squirmy thing, but Rick held tight to his captive and muscled his way through the blinding rain toward the little trailer. It hadn't taken that long to find the freaked out little pup, hidden under a thicket of mangroves, crying like a banshee. But in the time he'd searched, the next, more serious band of the storm had moved in. The flying leaves and small branches were blinding and dangerous.

He'd have to get both Billie and Nutmeg out of there, and fast, before the next gust took the place apart.

He powered on, waiting to get closer so she'd hear his victorious hoot. She'd be happy. Why that mattered to him, he had no clue. All he wanted was the watch that had been on his father's wrist when he died.

Well, not *all* he wanted, he admitted to himself. In the last half hour, he'd wanted something else, too. He wanted to get to know Nutmeg's owner a little better. Something about her intrigued him. What was she doing in the middle of nowhere, hiding in a rusty trailer?

"Let's go see your pretty mistress, Nutcase. She's got something I want." As he came around the last grouping of thick scrub and oak, he slowed his step, frowning at the door he'd kicked open. Why was it open again?

Shaking off as much water as he could, he stepped inside. "Billie Jo?"

Nutmeg practically launched out of his hands with excitement, but there was no other response.

"Billie?" He closed the front door before putting the dog down and heading to the back. She must be hiding in the bathroom, maybe in the tub with a mattress over her head, which would be smart.

The wind was screaming now, loud as a freight train, and compounded by the noisy drumbeat of the downpour on the roof. This place wouldn't last another hour, that was for sure.

"Billie!" he called one more time as he walked into the bedroom. Nutmeg barked loud and furious, so she must have known he'd rescued the dog. So where . . .

His gaze landed on the box on the floor next to the bed. Reaching down, he picked up the familiar case, the leather as soft and worn as he remembered, the inside still creamy satin. And empty.

Damn it, Rick. How could you be so fucking naïve?

For a moment, he just stared at the box, memories pouring over him like the rain on this tin trailer, flooding his senses. He'd held this case as a child, when his father first showed him the watch and promised if he went into the Navy, the watch would be handed down to him someday. He'd held the case when he sat with Granddad, after Dad had been shot down and Rick became next in line for the watch. He'd held the case when he left for BUD/S training, asking Granddad to keep the watch for him.

Then Granddad died while Rick was in Somalia, and his shit-for-brains cousin Dan sold everything he could get his hands on. For the past six months, Rick had a friend up in Boston tracking this thing, and it finally showed up on eBay, shipped here.

To William Josephs . . . or *Billie Jo*, the scam artist who had no last name, who had taken his watch and run.

Despite the roar of the wind and the smack of a good size branch against the mobile home, he stood there for a moment, frowning. What was wrong with this picture? She'd left on foot? The poor excuse for a truck was still parked in the back; he'd just seen it on his way in with the dog. So, unless someone came and picked her up, she was out there on her own.

Looking for the dog? Hiding the watch? Running . . . from him? Hadn't he proved he was legit?

The shatter of glass and crunch of metal spurred him into action, the sound of a tree smashing that junky truck. Dropping the box, he snagged the dog and took off. This place was about to get eaten by Hurricane Damien.

He tossed the ball of fur onto his passenger seat before he climbed in to drive away. Just as he did, a powerful gust buffeted the car, so strong he swore the vehicle lifted up on two tires for a second, and so massive that the whole roof of the trailer ripped away and curled like the top of a sardine can.

If she'd hidden the watch inside somewhere, then he'd never find it when this storm was over. If she'd run off with it . . . well, she might not make it until morning. At which point, he'd deal with the coroner or law enforcement.

Billie Jo With No Last Name wasn't his fucking problem.

Nutcase barked.

"Neither are you," Rick muttered, turning the ignition on. "But you're stuck with me now."

Billie could barely drag her legs forward, her feet were so stuck in mud and her body was so soaked through to the bone. Still, she forced herself deeper into the mangroves and pepper trees that formed the forest of scrub.

She thought about running to the beach, but, for one thing, she couldn't fight the wind. For another, the beach would be too out in the open. The nearest house was way down on the bay, but that's where Frank would look for her. She couldn't bring that lady and her teenage daughter into this if they were still there, riding out the storm. Frank would kill them, too.

A burst of body-flattening wind exploded through the scrub, ripping leaves and branches and throwing Billie backwards on her rear end. She cried out, but that just got her a mouthful of dirty, sandy water. She spit it out, peering into the blackness, laying on the bramble, not sure which death was scarier: the one inflicted by Frank or the one from mother nature.

Either way, she wasn't going to make it through the night.

And what about Nutmeg? Another wave of misery, as strong as the wind, blew over her. Even if the Navy SEAL had rescued her, Frank would kill him *and* Nutmeg when they got back.

Maybe not. Maybe *he'd* kill Frank.

A flicker of hope sparked in her chest, enough to push her up, despite the impossible wind trying to grind her back down. A tree next to her cracked and sailed into the air, a whirlwind of leaves whipping wildly around her head. She sank again, using her arms to cover her face, rolling into a ball, sliding along the mud.

She didn't even react to the thump on her back, so many stones and branches had hit her.

But she saw stars when a man's hand snagged her wet hair and snapped her head backwards. And through the rain and swirling leaves, she saw the face of Frank Perlow.

"You little bitch," he spat at her. "You thought you could hide?"

She jerked to the side, just wet enough to slip out of his hand, scrambling away. He caught up in two strides, the wind at his back, propelling him toward her.

"Leave me alone!" she managed to scream.

"I have been, Billie."

He was so close now she could smell him. Despite the musky scent of wet earth and salt water in the air, every breath was full of the filthy, foul stench of a murderer. She managed a few more steps, just out of his reach.

"I've been waiting for the perfect opportunity," he said, his words caught in the wind. "Now I can kill you and this storm will wipe away every bit of evidence."

Of course. That's what he was good at—killing without leaving a trace. Except that one time *she* had been the trace. *She* was the witness.

He lunged toward her, a knife flashing wet from the rain. She rolled further away, branches slicing her face, making her cry out in pain.

"This is gonna hurt more, Billie." He brandished the knife, momentarily frozen by a gust of wind circling the other way. She used the delay to cling to a tree trunk to keep from blowing right into him and his knife.

He smiled. "I'm going to slide this blade across your throat."

She tried to swallow, just imagining the horror and knowing he could and would make good on the threat.

He leaped forward, grabbing her shoulder and tearing her from the tree, tossing her to the ground. In an instant, he was above her, his knee jammed into her chest.

She fought wildly, turning so she could scream, kicking, pushing, opening her mouth to chomp on his wrist but getting nothing but a downpour that choked her.

He was stronger and had the wind at his back now, leaning over her, lifting the knife, his steely gray eyes full of hate and the determination to silence the witness to his heinous crime.

The next gust pushed him closer, her punches useless against his much more substantive size.

"You'll never tell anyone what you saw!" Once more, he lifted the knife, aimed directly at her throat. She twisted, moaned, and tried to jerk so he'd miss her. The knife came down and so did he, his weight landing hard on her while an echo of something sharp and loud and deafening rang in her ears.

A gunshot? Had she just heard a—

The pressure of his body suddenly disappeared as he was lifted by . . . the wind?

No, by a hero who held Frank's bloodied body in one hand and a pistol in the other.

"Did he hurt you?" Rick dropped to his knees next to Billie, tossing Frank aside and reaching for her with hands so gentle and strong it was impossible to believe he'd fired the bullet that went into

Frank's head.

Impossible, but . . . amazing.

"No," she managed to whisper, finally able to see him as he leaned over her protectively. "You killed him."

"I saved you. Big difference."

"You killed him," she repeated, still unable to grasp the simple fact that was about to change her life back to normal.

"If that's a big problem for you—"

She yanked his head closer, kissing him with all the fire and joy and relief and gratitude that rocked her with more force than the hurricane winds. And he kissed her back, opening his mouth, transferring the same tsunami of emotions, the same amount of need.

"I've been hiding from him for months," she whimpered into his kiss.

He eased her up, so close that she could see cuts on his face, evidence of what he'd just battled to save her. "I knew it," he said softly.

"You knew I was hiding from him?"

"I knew you wouldn't run with my watch."

She smiled. "It's in my pocket. Where's my dog?"

"In my car." He pulled her up. "C'mon."

She clung to him as they fought the wind so powerful it could uproot trees, bare branches, and, quite possibly, blow dead bodies out to sea.

Standing in the sunshine surrounded by the remnants of what was once her personal jail, Billie held Nutmeg to her chest and stroked the dog's hair. The trailer was virtually gone, nothing but bits of metal, a refrigerator, and her upside down truck remaining.

"We don't have to hide anymore, Nutsie," she whispered, tears of happiness burning her eyes. "We're free. We can go back to Charleston, we can open a business, we can—"

"Found it!" Rick burst out from behind a truck, his arm raised in victory, his handsome face flush with success. In his hand, the leather box that the watch had arrived in.

"Awesome," she called, letting squirmy little Nutmeg down to scamper over to him. Billie didn't blame the dog. She wanted to get close to Rick, too.

They'd spent the night safely in the school shelter, where they'd found a quiet corner in the boy's locker room. There, two people who'd met under the most extraordinary circumstances finally had an ordinary conversation.

Not that there was anything ordinary about Lieutenant Rick Stone.

"This box is all I want from this place," he said as he reached her. "How about you?"

"There's nothing here I want." She glanced around at the rubble, but her gaze settled on him. "Except I kind of like the guy who saved me."

He grinned, reaching to tunnel his hand under her hair and guide her face up to him. "And I thought you were Annie Oakley trailer trash."

"I don't even have blonde hair," she said with a laugh.

"Good. I like brunettes. And this is one crappy bleach job, by the way."

"I'll have it grown out in six months."

He didn't answer, his beautiful blue eyes searching her face, the way he had all night when they told each other their stories. When she'd told him of witnessing the murder, he'd held her in his arms and let her cry with relief now that it was over. And when he'd told her about the loss of the his father in the first Gulf war and how it had wrecked the life of a seven year old hero worshiper, she'd held him, too.

"Six months?" He pulled her closer, eliminating the space between her body and his. "I'll be home in six months."

"I'll be in Charleston, opening up a new antique shop."

"Can I visit?" he asked with a smile.

"You better."

"Can I stay overnight?"

It was her turn to smile. "If Nutmeg lets you."

He looked down at the dog. "Nutcase loves me."

And, in that single suspended moment of time, Billie had one simple thought: *so could I.* "Then you'll be welcome in my home, in my shop, and in my . . ." *Bed.*

"I'll be there." Rick grinned, a crazy thing of beauty that squeezed air out of Billie's lungs and common sense out of her head.

He lowered his head and kissed her gently, the first time they'd kissed since the furious exchange in the brush. This was softer, sweeter, full of promise and hope and warmth.

They were still holding hands as he navigated his car over the rough roads and fallen trees of Barefoot Bay, heading back to the south end of the island. As they reached the most picturesque part of the inlet, he slowed the car so they could see through the bare trees to the beach.

There, a woman and a lanky young girl slowly walked over rubble and debris of what had to have been one of the first houses built on the island. The girl looked to be sobbing, but the woman was talking animatedly.

Rick lowered the window to call out, "You need help, ma'am?"

The woman lifted her hand and beamed a smile that seemed completely out of place. "We're great. Never been better."

Rick threw a look at Billie. "Is that sarcasm or has she lost her marbles?"

"I haven't gotten to know her." But she could, now. She no longer had to hide or avoid her neighbors. She was free. For the thousandth time in the last ten hours, she looked at Rick Stone with gratitude dampening her eyes.

"Are you sure?" he called again. "Do you need a phone? Water?"

"Honestly, we're great." She gave her daughter a squeeze. "Mother Nature is doling out second chances!"

Billie laughed softly, absently stroking Nutmeg's head where it rested on her lap. "You can say that again."

"Mother nature is doling out second chances," he repeated, turning to give Billie another kiss. "And I think we should take her up on it."

Nutmeg barked in complete agreement while they kissed like the lifelong lovers Billie had a feeling they were going to be.

HOLDING ON

Stephanie Tyler

This is dedicated to all the men and women who've served
—thank you.

A quick note from Stephanie:

This story is set approximately six and a half months from the end of HOLD ON TIGHT. So many readers asked about what was happening with the Navy SEAL brothers from the HOLD series, I thought this was the perfect opportunity to catch everyone up and give back to military men and women at the same time.

Chapter One

> *"The only easy day was yesterday."*
> —US NAVY SEAL saying

Virginia Beach
2 days before Christmas

"We're going to be delivering this baby," she heard Nick say, and his brother's answer was in typical Jake fashion, "You've got to be kidding me with that shit."

Jamie Michaels looked up from the book she'd been halfheartedly reading and smiled. Jake was finally home after being gone a month, and it was nothing he wouldn't say to her face, which was one of the many things she loved about him and Nick both.

"No offense, but I do not want to be the midwife," Jake continued. "Dude, that's Chris's job, legally bound and all that crap."

She shifted to catch sight of him. He wore his jungle cammies, evidence of paint still on his face and neck.

He'd rushed, and she was grateful. She'd be more so if she heard from Chris at all over the past month. Under normal circumstances, she'd be optimistically concerned, her FBI past clouded by the fact that she was waiting on the man she loved.

The nine months pregnant part of her was a hormonal mess she barely recognized, waiting for her Navy SEAL husband to come home.

Nick, also a Navy SEAL, as was Jake, had been home with her for the past week, treating her like a live grenade.

If one pregnant woman could bring terror to a SEAL, why weren't they put to better use during wartime?

She contemplated this as she heard Jake continue to mutter to himself as he walked through the house.

Earlier, she'd spoken with Jake's wife, Isabelle, who was headed back to Virginia from visiting her mother in DC. Nick's girlfriend, Kaylee would be there shortly as well, along with Jamie's sister, PJ and Kenny, who was the father of the three SEALs. They would all be together for Christmas—the baby's due date—except for the possibility of Saint and one other extremely important person.

Her husband. Her midwife. *Legally bound and all that crap.*

She was getting cranky again. As if Nick's radar was in tune with her mood, he called from the kitchen, "Do you want more of that soothing tea stuff?"

"No," she snapped. Never wanted tea again in her life.

"Ice cream?"

"It's ten in the morning."

"Never stopped you before," he murmured.

"I heard that."

"Meant you to."

"Whoa." Jake stopped in the doorway and gaped at her. "You're goddamned huge."

"Not smart," Nick told him over his shoulder.

"It's the truth," she groaned. Her belly stuck out precariously from her slim frame. "Have you heard anything?"

Jake stared at her, his gray eyes stormy. Even if he had, he technically couldn't share. Wouldn't. She had to trust that everything was good and that she was in the more than capable hands of Chris's brothers and the rest of the crew.

Since marrying Chris months earlier, she'd moved into the big house that had once been Kenny's, where the men had grown up. There was plenty of space and it was rare that more than two of them were home at the same time.

That would change in a few hours.

"We all set for the storm?" Jake asked Nick now.

"Put in the generator last week," Nick said.

"Going to be worse than they thought," Jake continued.

"Hadn't told her about that yet," Nick muttered.

"Is that why you wouldn't let me turn on the TV?" she asked him.

"Reading's good for the baby," Nick said.

She threw the book at his head and both men ducked.

"Not so good for you, brother," Jake said. "Jamie, let's go for a walk."

She struggled up, refusing the men's offers of help. Maybe Jake would tell her something about Chris outside.

He kept a hand on her lower back as they walked. The streets were clear, the air cold—snow was a given.

They talked for a few minutes about the storm. Isabelle. Anything and everything but the topic she wanted to know most about.

"Somalia's really a hot zone again," Jake said and she froze for a second, but Jake's hand pressed her and she kept moving.

Somalia. Of all places.

But somewhere inside, she'd known, had watched the beginnings of the new uprising on the news with dread in her throat, had been aware of Nick steering the conversation—and the television stations— to happier things. Chick flicks.

She should've been suspicious when he didn't bitch and moan about watching reruns of bad reality TV on a continuous loop over the past few days. But when it came right down to it, she was grateful for Chris's brothers. She'd hold herself together—for Chris and for the baby.

Now, she paused against to look up at the sky, Jake at her side. She put her hands on the swell of her belly, remembering how Chris knelt and kissed it before he left that morning, two months earlier. How she'd prayed it was a training mission but knowing in her heart it wasn't.

"It's okay, baby boy. Daddy's going to be here in time," she whispered to the bump. "You just hang in there."

Somali Republic, East Africa

Chief Petty Officer Chris Waldron waited, belly down on the top of a low lying building in a decidedly unsafe zone. Keeping his eye on the goddamned prize. The doorway of the windowless dwelling where one of east Africa's most wanted al Qaeda militants the SEALs had been sent to take out had hunkered down to wait out the latest U.S. Troop invasion.

They'd been in country for sixty-seven days and thirty-six hours on this particular op at last count. His CO, John 'Saint' St. James was next to him, taking his rest. They'd been spelling each other the entire time. Chris was the sniper, Saint his spotter, although either man was fully prepped to take this shot.

But Chris was a master sniper—the best of the best, they called him.

The men's only movements had been head up, head down, even when the skies opened angrily to produce a warm rain that left the air sticky and full of godforsaken mosquitoes and tsetse flies.

"Son of bitch," he muttered as a fly bit the shit out of his neck through the netting he wore. He was sweating, jonseing for a cigarette but keeping the rest of his mind purposely blank.

You'd go crazy if you didn't, and he was already halfway there.

Chris checked his scope and then he froze, not from anything in his vision but from that familiar feeling that had been a part of him for as long as he could remember—some called it sixth sense, his father called it *the sight* and Jake called it *that psychic Cajun bullshit* and no matter what it was, it had saved Chris's ass more time that he could count.

Now, it would do so again. Next to him, Saint's head jerked up like he'd sensed the problem as well.

"Incoming," Chris told him quietly. It wasn't surprising—they'd learned of the Al Qaeda militant's location from a Somalian warlord who was paid for his cooperation. Now, the warlord would no doubt start an attack so it wouldn't look like he sold the operative out.

Everything in this part of the world was tricky, touch and go and no one could be trusted for very long. This trust lasted longer than most.

A short moment later, the series of explosions started, came from both sides of their building without actually harming it, tearing down the walls of one structure next to them and upending an old Land Rover on the other side.

It hadn't been meant for them, but they weren't the only ones with a bounty on the militant's head. Still, if they didn't pull out now, they'd be headed back to their makeshift base and command center under the line of direct fire.

If they pulled out now, Chris would lose the shot.

It took a second of eye contact between the men and the decision was made.

"Get the shot and we're gone," Saint said, and since it was his direct order, Chris would follow it. He settled back in behind the scope to wait for the militant to evacuate.

With the heat sensor, he could make out shapes through the covered window and the stone and mud mixed walls. But he'd prefer not to expect a bullet to go through stone. And they'd been told to get a clean shot and Chris wanted nothing less.

"He's not coming out the front," Saint mused.

"Front or back, doesn't matter—I'll still get him," Chris muttered. His finger curled around the trigger as that hazy sense of *right now* shot through his brain and he fired seconds before the target turned to face the street for a brief moment. But those seconds of clarity for Chris were like an early warning system, much like the lag in a digital camera, which gave the bullet the precise path it needed.

The bullet landed cleanly, probably nearly silently, between the militant's eyes.

Chris barely had a second to feel the satisfaction of a job well done when the explosions started, no doubt the US's way of counteracting the warlord's attack.

He took out two of the militant's bodyguards cleanly while Saint, covering him, took out six more a little less so. In seconds, he and Saint were off the building that had been their home sweet home for two straight days and ran down side streets, weapons at the ready, stretching muscles screaming from hours of underuse.

His feet were all pins and needle for the first half mile but finally his entire body cooperated as the shelling and the blasts from overhead began. Caught between friendly and not so friendly fire, plus impending darkness made it imperative that they get the hell out of the danger zone.

Far more dangerous to find themselves cornered at night with barely any ammo and no supplies.

He'd done this more times than he cared to count, his body on autopilot while his brain measured every ounce of risk and danger.

Made split second decisions imperative to his and Saint's safety.

Not that Saint wasn't doing the exact same thing.

He fired a few rounds from his M-14, even as pain shot through his side, adrenaline keeping it tamped down so he could take the next shot. Took down two rebels and heard Saint firing from behind him.

They were partially surrounded with no extraction team. Running and stealth were the best options. They were getting blasted, even as they ran for cover, Saint shoving him down as they came to a low wall.

"Stay here, just a second," Saint told him as they crouched down and let the chaos rein behind them. "How hard were you hit?"

Chris looked down at his side—the blood came through his cammy jacket, ran down his side although he was pretty sure the bullet hadn't hit anything major. "I'll live."

"Good to fucking know. We'll make a run down the alleys toward the base. If we can get close, they'll pick us up."

No choice. Like his old Master Chief used to say, *pain is just weakness leaving the body.* And Chris hoped it would leave really goddamned soon.

Chapter Two

Saint muttered in Cajun French the entire time the doc stitched up his shoulder. Chris, who understood every word his CO said, lay on his side with a way bigger piece of him taken out, but he wasn't telling Saint that without a running start.

"Any word?" Chris asked as the man checked his phone for the thousandth time.

"Just the same sit around and wait."

He stared at the ceiling, the way he'd been for the last two hours since they'd arrived after being picked up a couple of miles from base by a truckload of Marines.

The wait would kill him this time if he let it, especially because he was so close to being homeward bound.

Except no helo was coming this way again for days. Normally, the prospect of spending Christmas OUTCONUS was perfect—had been since his mother died.

But not this year. He didn't want to do that to Jamie.

She'd deal with it, he knew, but that wasn't the point. She'd dealt with way too much in her life not to have this go right. She deserved it.

But the little boy was breech—he could feel it. Happened sometime last week, and Jamie would find out about it today during the doctor's appointment.

He'd insisted she visit traditional docs, would have whether or not he'd been home the entire pregnancy. He knew his brothers were back stateside, which was a comfort. Although they were adopted, they couldn't be any closer if they were blood. Together from the age of fourteen, along with Chris's mom and dad, they'd moved to Virginia and attempted to settle down.

Until his mom, Maggie, was diagnosed with ovarian cancer and died nine months later. All of them still felt that loss acutely.

Finally, the doc finished with Saint and headed toward Chris, who pulled the blood stained packing gauze from the wound and turned to give the doc a better angle with the stitches.

"I could do this myself—" Chris started.

"Yeah, but then I'd be in the middle of this godforsaken country for nothing," Doc drawled. He was from Mobile, Alabama, in for fifteen years—and probably until they forced him out.

Chris knew he wasn't a lifer, but the teams had been good both to and for him.

The hospital was old with ancient looking equipment compared to what they had in Virginia and Germany. The sandstorm had blown through just after they'd arrived, trapping them there for hours. It was over now, but neither he nor Saint was crazy enough to drive around here in the dark unless it was absolutely necessary.

And unless there was a tank involved. He could definitely hot-wire a tank if he could find one.

"You all right?' Saint's Cajun drawl cut through the tension.

"Fucking fantastic," Chris muttered.

There was silence for a long moment and then, "There's a helo set to pick up some Deltas at 0400, about twenty miles from here. It's our best bet."

Chris glanced up at him. "Do they know we're coming?"

"Reid says he'll wait as long as they can." Saint looked out the window. "A couple of Land Rovers out there look like they might make the trip."

They would have to. Chris would make sure of it. "We'll take it as far as it goes."

The nightmare grabbed Jamie by the throat and refused to let go. It was six months ago and she was back outside the school, and PJ and Kevin were trapped inside by the man who'd made her life hell since she was little . . . they were trapped and she couldn't help them. And Chris was nowhere to be found and she was completely panicked.

She woke with a start and grabbed her belly, as if to reassure herself that things on that front were fine. She hated that dream, more so because it was all real except for Chris being missing. He'd been the one to save them all that day and rescue her and PJ from a man who'd been trying to kill them their entire lives.

The man who'd adopted her and PJ, Kevin, had admitted that he'd been to blame for some of what had happened, indirectly, and while she and her sister had forgiven him, he still kept his distance, his guilt too great to overcome at the present time.

He'd come around eventually, she knew that. And she'd stop having nightly reminders of the past, too.

"You don't need to be saved," she said firmly, out loud, trying to convince herself. "Baby boy, we'll be fine if you come out now. Daddy will be home soon."

The baby gave a resounding kick and then promptly fell asleep.

"Great. Stubborn." Why she should be surprised at that, she had no idea. She also wondered how long Chris had known about the fact that their baby was now in breech position and unlikely to move back at this late date, considering how big he was.

Which meant C-section. But she knew Chris could do miraculous things with babies—she'd seen some evidence of it firsthand, had listened to stories from Jake and Nick about how Chris worked magic, like he was channeling his midwife mother, Maggie or something.

"Help me out here, Maggie." She put her hands on her belly, tried to imagine the baby turning, but the little one seemed determined to sleep.

It was two days until Christmas. For the first time since Maggie died, there was a tree in the house. Nick had dragged it inside by himself, grumbling the entire time but it was a perfect fit.

It remained undecorated—that would be up to her and Izzy and Kaylee, Nick informed her darkly. But didn't seem all that displeased overall.

Now, she got up, the baby sleeping and her still restless and unsettled from seeing her past played out in her nightly dreams. She wished she could blame the nightmares on not knowing where Chris was, but really, it was more her problem than any deployment or mission he was on.

Every deployed spouse or family member had the same worries, no matter the brave face they put on. Jamie had come into a ready-made family with four military personnel to worry about.

Her sister, PJ, was engaged to Chris's CO, Saint. Isabelle and Jake married months earlier and Kaylee and Nick would no doubt just show up one day married. For now, they were happily discussing adoption and Chris told her he'd never seen either brother so happy.

PJ took a job piloting private jets for private contractors—it kept her in just enough danger to satisfy her and not enough to make Saint drag her home and chain her to the couch.

Jamie smiled, because she was guessing Chris felt the same about her. Desk work wasn't exciting, but she could still help people by getting them comfortable with the process of witness protection before they were turned over to the US Marshals. After the baby was born, she'd continue that way because Chris's job was enough danger for one small baby.

Chris had been away for a lot of her pregnancy. They Skyped whenever possible but she'd known the nature of his job as a SEAL even before she'd met him. She was part of the FBI and had spent the majority of her life in Witness Protection as well, up until several months earlier. She wasn't a wuss by any means.

They'd fought about that very thing right before he'd gone away this last time, about how they both couldn't be in the line of fire. She knew he was right. Having grown up in danger, she knew that better than anyone. But being told what to do was never her style. It made her bristle. She thought Chris knew that, but since all of this happened, it had been tough settling back into normal for all of them.

None of them had ever really had it. PJ seemed to be handling it the best of all of them, relishing in having a place of her own. Well, Saint's own, but he didn't care what PJ did as long as she remained happy.

And it appeared she reciprocated the favor to Saint, because according to Chris, the big, Louisiana born and bred CO hadn't been this happy ever.

Neither had she, but it was hard not to be when surrounded by love and heroes.

Chapter Three

There was no radio in the car but that didn't stop Chris from singing "Rock of Ages" not as loudly as he would've liked to out of respect for Saint and the fact that they couldn't afford to draw any extra attention to themselves.

He was so tense that his entire body ached and he wouldn't relax until he touched down in Virginia.

You're gonna have a kid—no more relaxing for you, anyway.

They'd made it twenty miles along precarious roads before the car started breaking down.

"Come on, come on," he muttered, ran his hands along the steering wheel like he could cajole it into staying alive.

Didn't work. After another several miles and a sputtering, smoking engine, the Land Rover finally gave up the ghost.

"Not like we didn't expect it," Saint said. "On foot."

The two of them were out of the jacked up Land Rover and moving stealthily and fast along the side of the road, just out of view.

They could attempt to hitch, but in these early morning hours before the light of day, trusting any random vehicle along the way to get them there faster would be risky as hell.

The hit of his boots against the soft dust was the rhythm in his head for the next four miles. He'd had harder runs, with heavier gear and more danger but none of them meant anything close to what this one did.

He didn't care about the sweat or the fact that his stitches stopped holding somewhere along mile two. Saint pushed him along at one point when Chris got lightheaded and then he got a second wind.

But they both stopped dead in their tracks when they heard the familiar rat-tat-tat of AK fire.

"That's near the LZ," Saint cursed, checked the SAT phone. "Battery's dead."

Chris listened for any other sounds over the din. "Which way would Reid go if this started?"

And then he answered his own question like he knew it to be the truth. "North. There's room for the helo."

"The soldiers being there is just dumb luck."

"For our sake, hope there's a lot of that going around." As he finished, Saint was already headed back out to the road.

"Come on, man!" he called and in seconds, Chris was scrambling into the back of a truck that barely slowed to let them on board.

Didn't matter—they were traveling in the right direction and away from the gunfire.

Didn't matter even when he heard the squawking as the sounds of shots receded, turned to discover they were riding with the chicken cages. It was crowded and it stank and Chris didn't care. Saint did, muttered the entire next few miles that Chris and his child were going to owe him. That Jake and Nick already did, owed him more than any human could possibly hope to payback but Saint would make sure they did.

"We're not stopping on this next stretch of road," the passenger called back to them a little while later.

"We've got to get off here," Saint said after they'd gone a decently quick five miles. Hell, they'd jumped from higher into worse and Chris followed Saint as they jumped and rolled away before they could be spotted by other cars.

"Six klicks," Saint confirmed and they went down the hill and into the jungle until they finally hit a clearing big enough for a helo to land, which it had. The big bird sat silently and Chris sighed thankfully as he and Saint made their way toward it, signaling the pilot they were the men he'd been waiting for.

They boarded and the pilot started the engines. Take off would be quick and dirty and they headed toward the back before they were thrown.

"Maybe we have to start giving the SEALs more credit," Reid called, his drawl apparent even as he yelled over the roar of the helo.

Chris shot him the finger and hunkered down on the floor to check out how much blood he was losing. It was freezing but he stripped down and let Delta's medic deal with it while he slept or passed out or some combination of the two.

When he opened his eyes, it was time to refuel.

"Phone?" he croaked.

"Dude, you have an infection," the medic told him.

"Dude, I need the phone."

Saint handed him one as the medic frowned and Chris dialed Jake's number.

"Dude, where the hell are you? Because your wife pregnant is scarier than Saint," Jake said in lieu of hello.

"Tell him I heard that," Saint barked. "Comparing me to a pregnant woman."

"Is she all right?" Chris asked, ignoring them both. "I'm six hours out."

"She's hanging in. Worried. A storm's coming through." Jake paused. "You hurt?"

"A little. I'll be fine by the time I get there. Just keep her calm."

"We're all here for her, man. Just get your ass home safely."

"Tell her—"

"I know what to tell her. Don't get all goddamned sappy with me," Jake said before hanging up, right on time, too, because the roar of the engine started a second later.

Chris handed Saint back the phone and let the medic do his thing with IVs and antibiotics. Slept a little and woke himself up when he realized he was dreaming about that night at the school when he killed a man to save PJ—and ultimately, Jamie. Because although he harbored no guilt over taking out a criminal, the scars Jamie would bear from the entire ordeal would never leave her. He could only hope to lessen them with time.

Chapter Four

Jake hung up with Chris and paced until Isabelle's car pulled into the driveway maybe ten minutes later. He was out the door in seconds, because that smile, that fucking smile of hers lit him up from the inside.

She hugged him tight, like she was saying, I'll never let you go.

She wouldn't, he was sure of it. And neither would he.

"Missed you," she murmured against his neck. "Traffic was horrible."

"I offered to come get you."

"You couldn't land."

"Climbing the rope's not that hard. I would've helped," he chided lightly.

"The scary part is, I know you're completely serious." She threaded her hand in his. "How's Jamie?"

"Freaked out and trying not to show it." He let go of her so he could grab her bags. "Come on, let's get you inside."

"Wait. I have something to tell you—about Africa." The memories that country brought back flooded his mind, some good, some painful. She'd been back to Africa for Doctors Without Borders once since they'd married. And it had been with him.

She'd agreed, since they really didn't want to spend any more time apart than his job allowed, and they were going back again next year. Together.

He kept his voice neutral "What's up?"

"We might have to cancel."

"Why? What's wrong?" he demanded, his hands on her like he could feel what the problem was. But she took his wrists and put his palms on her belly.

It took him about five seconds to catch on. He breathed in sharply and then again because he felt a little dizzy. And then he met her eyes and Isabelle's floodgates opened.

"I had no idea. I'm three months along and it's twins. Girls. Never had them in my family and your know I'm on the pill . . . "

"Hold up." Jake stared at her, one hand reaching up to brush away a few stray tears. And this was a woman who rarely cried. "Twin *girls?*"

"Yes."

"Are they sure?"

"Pretty sure, yes."

"God help me," he muttered as the earth shifted beneath his feet.

"Jake, I'm really freaked out."

Join the club, baby. But before he could stop it, a huge smile spread over his face. "We're going to be fine. We've handled so much worse than this. This is the good stuff—and we deserve it."

He hugged her and her arms threaded around his shoulders—she was laughing, relief evident in her voice. "You're not upset—really?"

"Not at all." He kissed her as the snow started to fall around them, until all he wanted to do was get her alone. Picked her up as she protested, carried her through the house and up to the second floor, because he could tell his brothers and Jamie later.

But right now, it was just for the two of them.

"Storm's coming," Kenny murmured to himself as he looked up at the night sky and tried not to connect with Chris. It was too hard on both of them, especially when his son was deployed.

The psychic Cajun bullshit, as Jake deemed it years ago, came in handy at times. This was not one of them.

All the missions Chris went on were important, but this one . . . it made Kenny's heart heavy. He wasn't sure if it was the time of year or the impending birth but dammit, his son needed to be here, for so many reasons.

"Maggie, you've got to help them," he said quietly. "Have to help me, too."

The wound of her loss was still so fresh. Watching his sons find the loves of their lives brought him more comfort than he'd ever hoped to have.

"The baby's breech," Jamie said softly from behind him. "I just came from an ultrasound. Maybe I should—"

"Give him time," Kenny told her, turning to put his arm around her shoulder. "Nothing's going to happen to that bebe."

She smiled when he slipped into Cajun cadence.

"Chris was breech—shouldn't be surprised," Kenny continued. "Maggie and her momma, they fixed it all good."

He didn't tell her that Maggie nearly died giving birth. Obviously, Chris had wisely chosen to spare Jamie that information as well.

But Jamie was insistent on a home birth, wanted Chris to deliver the baby. He'd tried to steer her toward a hospital birth without scaring her, but she would not be deterred.

Of course, that was before the baby was breech. Now, he knew he would have to convince her to get to the hospital at the first signs of labor if his son didn't arrive in time.

Jamie and Kenny ended up sitting in the kitchen for a while—he heated her up some of the gumbo he'd made earlier, which she loved, and being connected to Chris like this made everything all right for that little while.

"Hey, anyone here?" PJ called after letting herself into the house.

"Kitchen!" Jamie called back.

Her sister walked in and dumped her bag before hugging both her and Kenny. "I brought extra clothes, because I don't think I should leave you during the storm."

"Good idea," Kenny told her. "We have plenty of room."

"Hopefully you have a lot of food, too," Kaylee said as she walked into the room, Nick behind her, holding onto her hand.

"Always," Kenny said as he hugged her too. And then Jake came in, with Izzy by his side and yes, the house was filling up. It wasn't exactly a typical Christmas, but hers growing up had always been fairly quiet.

PJ looked at Jake. "Have you heard anything?"

"They're on their way home, I think."

"What does that mean?"

"He and Saint left the hospital -"

"Why were they in the hospital?" Jamie and PJ demanded in unison.

"And they're fine," Jake finished.

"Because you say so?" Jamie asked.

"Yes," Jake said coolly.

"Can we get back to the hospital thing?" PJ prompted.

"No. I've said too much already."

"Now what?"

"You were in the military, so you should recognize this part. We wait."

PJ snorted. Jamie felt her belly tighten into what she hoped was only one of those Braxton Hicks contractions. "I'm going to go lay down for a while."

"You okay?" PJ asked and Jamie nodded, avoiding Kenny's face. She didn't want to upset him any more than he already was, and so she went into the rooms she and Chris had been using on the first floor, more like a private suite with a living area and separate bedroom. She sat on the edge of the bed and lifted her legs a little so she could stare at her swollen feet.

She'd done research on the Internet about how to turn the baby naturally—there were several techniques, including acupuncture—and she'd try any of them.

They're on their way home, I think.

Chapter Five

Jamie couldn't sleep hours later, found herself pacing restlessly as if on guard. It had started to snow hours before and it was a heavy, blanketing blizzard with diagonal icy hail that scratched the windows and rattled the house with its fierce winds.

She rubbed her hand on the glass door that led out to the back terrace as if that could help her see through the snow. She started a little, blinked, then stared a little harder as she spotted something—someone—moving through the blowing snow.

A mirage. A fantastic, tall mirage, his jungle print cammies cutting a path through the white stuff. As he got closer, she saw the blood and dirt and once he came close enough, paint on his face.

She was the one who remained frozen because was so sure this was a dream. The best kind.

And then, after what seemed like hours, he was at the glass door. He saw her, cocked his head as if waiting for her to realize this was all very real and finally—*finally*—he opened the door and stepped inside.

She took several steps back to let him in. Cold air enveloped her, refreshing, like some kind of renewal. And then he shut the door behind him and said, "Hey."

"You look—"

"Wet," he finished and she laughed softly, not wanting to break the spell. She reached up instead and uncovered his head first, the wool cap giving way to reveal the ever present green bandanna he wrapped his hair in every time he was on a mission. "I walked ten miles in the snow, uphill. And don't think this kid will ever hear the end of it."

His different color eyes stood out in stark contrast to his very tanned skin. She reached out and stroked his cheek, just to make sure he was real. "You just got in?"

"About an hour ago. Roads are impassable."

"Not for you."

"Not for *you*," he countered as her fingers skittered over the buttons on his jacket before skimming the icy material off him, letting it falls to the floor.

He stood patiently, this familiar act becoming something of a ritual between them. It was like she had to catalogue everything when he came back—every smile, every scratch—and he let her, without complaint.

Her pace quickened as she touched the cold skin on his biceps. She needed to get him warm, wanted him skin to skin with her. At this moment, that was her only mission and the only one that mattered.

She pulled the shirt over his head next, his dogtags clinking and coming to rest on his bare chest, and saw where the blood had come from. The gauze that covered his size was large, but clean.

"It's nothing," he told her and she didn't press even as she continued to memorize the other, numerous bruises and scrapes littering his upper body. He wore them as if they *were* nothing. He bent and took off his boots, but only because she couldn't. And then she helped him off with his pants next—he eased them off and laid them on a chair carefully because they were heavy with some of his gear.

"Rough trip home?"

"Not so bad," he said.

"Why are there chicken feathers coming out of your pocket?"

"Just be grateful the walk home in the storm washed away the smell."

"Most of it," she teased.

"Fuck, you look beautiful," he murmured, a hand on her swollen belly.

"Big."

"Gorgeous," he corrected, and he meant it.

"Let me clean you off," she murmured. "Come on."

He followed her to the bathroom, sat on the edge of the bathtub while she wet a washcloth and wiped the paint and dirt from his face gently, like she was uncovering the real him again, like she did every time he came back.

It would never be that easy—coming home rarely was for these men, she'd learned—but this helped connect them again.

He let her finish with his face and neck, both knowing he needed more than a washcloth, but he wasn't complaining. He'd stripped completely before he sat down and it was warm enough to where he'd stopped shivering.

"Thanks," he said when she was done, and she cupped his clean face in her hands as time dropped away and it was their first time together on the plane or the second in Africa before things went bad and it all blended together in a wonderful way. Their history.

He made her sentimental; she'd never been that way before. "Why don't you take a nice, hot shower and then—"

"Later," he said, the way she'd hoped he would before standing and pulling her close.

And then she couldn't wait—had never wanted anyone more. No words were necessary—he was on her the way he'd been from day one. Logistics were of course trickier but the man and his body seemed to bend in ways that were superhuman. Chris's hands were weapons all their own—the fact that they roamed her body with such gentle and purposeful need made it all the better. And when he took her, all was right in the world again. His mouth covered her skin, his kisses hot against her neck as he trailed his tongue in a way that made her squirm with pleasure. She exploded, then melted and he was far from done.

She hadn't known how badly she'd needed this. Beyond the sex, she'd simply needed to be in his arms.

Jamie held him the way she always did, an embrace that had a meaning all its own. Her touch had always said more than she'd allowed herself to verbalize, especially in the beginning. She was different now, but he still relied on the old ways to reconnect.

Coming back was hard. He felt different—*was* different—but this was the same, with Jamie's soft skin and the scents that were uniquely hers, the way she moaned under his touch. The way she let go like she never had with anyone, that was all his. Her nails scored his shoulders as he shuddered against her, finally letting himself go after making sure she was more than satisfied.

You're home, he told himself. In more ways than one, in Jamie's arms, he was.

Chris massaged Jamie's belly as they lay there, naked, sated. It was Christmas morning now, but she didn't mention that, or his birthday, because neither were particularly happy memories.

Today, with them all together, they'd try to change that. But his mind was somewhere else, his hand splayed out now like he was feeling the shape of the baby inside of her.

"Can you turn him?" she asked.

"It's going to hurt you if I try, *Chere*. What about just going to the hospital?"

"You would try with any other random woman, but not me?" she asked and then narrowed her eyes. "And why aren't I in labor?" Why doesn't your crazy labor mojo work on me?"

"Hush, *bebe*," he told her with a smile, bent his head to her belly and began to sing—it was a lullaby in Cajun French he'd sung to her belly before, but this time it was all for the little boy. He held his hands so they hovered just above her bared skin in a Rieke formation, like he'd told her his momma taught him when she was a midwife.

She closed her eyes and listened to his voice as everything flashed in her mind. Their first meeting, the downed plane where this baby boy was conceived, against all odds, and they'd survived despite all of it. The hospital in Djibouti where she'd been scared to see him again. The school in Brooklyn where he'd saved her and PJ in a standoff with a killer, ending the nightmare they'd been living with since they were young.

Everything had worked out so well, despite the many times she'd thought they never, ever would. She had to believe now, too, because everything Chris did seemed to be touched by a certain kind of magic she'd never known existed.

All she needed to do was believe. Concentrate. Felt Chris begin the actual manipulating of her belly as the life inside of her began to shift.

It hurt. The pain was almost to the point of unbearable. But she squeezed her eyes tight and she dealt with the pain and she just breathed. Because, in the end, that's what life was really all about—breathing and holding on.

She was doing both.

"Jamie, it's okay—you can open your eyes."

"Did it work?" she asked.

"I think so. His head is here." He put her hand on her exposed skin and she felt the bump, where it was supposed to be. Except now, there was a lot of pressure she felt. "That's normal."

"Normal, but not exactly fun."

"It's going to happen any time now, Jamie."

"Let's try to get through Christmas first. Your dad cooked so much and Nick brought in the tree," she said. "I hope that's okay. I just thought -"

"It's more than okay."

There was a knock at the outer door, and Jamie slid a shirt on as Chris pulled on sweats and padded to answer it. She was surprised they'd waited this long to check—and she heard Saint's voice in the background as well.

Chris hadn't walked here alone.

"Wait a minute, you mean the one woman not affected by your baby mojo crap is your own wife?" Jake was demanding as she walked into the other room. He pointed to her. "She's like a hundred years pregnant for Christsakes. Help her."

"Jake, leave him alone," Isabelle told him, took his hand. "And as long as we're not in any rush to labor, I have some news."

"Oh my God," Jamie said before Isabelle could speak again and she and Kaylee were hugging her, because they just simply knew.

"'Bout time," Chris told Jake, who snorted, but the pride was evident in his brother's face. Nick's eyes were wet, his voice rough when he said, "That's good stuff, man. Really good."

Kenny's voice boomed out, "And I, for one, can't wait for payback. Because, my boys, you are going to be her bitch for many, many years to come."

Chapter Six

It was the nightmare again, but even though it was as scary as ever, it soon turned around. Because Chris was there, *right there* next to her, with his rifle and his sniping magic and he was saving the day . . . saving her . . .

"Can you please breathe?"

A voice—Chris's voice, in her dream. She turned and saw him, and that's when the contraction hit.

"You've been in labor for half an hour," he said.

"I guess this is some kind of delayed reaction," she grumbled after the worst of the pain hit her.

Chris wasn't listening, instead rummaged through the black doctor's bag his team had brought him as a gag gift. Of course, that was before they'd realized that his delivering of babies was more than a one-time thing.

It was Christmas Day and Chris's birthday, too. She'd come in here to rest before dinner and was now in full-blown labor if the look on Chris's face was any indication after he did a quick check.

"I'm ready," she said.

"Jake said he'd get us to the hospital if we need to go—he's got a truck with chains and he and Nick are plowing now, just in case."

"Good. That will help with the karma," she murmured.

"You've also got me."

She opened her eyes and saw the man the brothers called doc standing by the bedside.

"I owed him one." He nodded in Chris's direction. As she watched, he set up a portable fetal monitor and ultrasound.

"So far, it's all looking good. He's not in any distress, and he stayed turned," doc said. "Are you going to deliver your baby now?"

Chris cocked his head at her and she smiled. "Go ahead. Don't break your record now."

In the end, Chris wouldn't be able to say he remembered much. As usual, it was a blur of making sure mom and baby were both okay during what became an almost frighteningly fast birth. Jamie had some choice words for him as she couldn't take much in the way of pain meds since she was so close, but for the most part, she was stoic.

He and Isabelle and Doc worked together to make it as stress free as they could. And when the time came, he called Jake and Nick in, because, in cases like this, they were typically his wingmen, the ones who would hold and clean the baby while Chris attended to the mom.

He didn't see a reason to change things now. And when his boy was delivered and took his first breath and then howled, he put him on Jamie's chest for a few moments and passed the baby to Jake first. Watched for a few seconds as his brother cradled his nephew gently, cleaned him and checked him with a quick, silent efficiency Chris had always admired, but never more so than now.

"He's pretty damned perfect," Jake said, his voice rough with emotion. He passed the baby to Nick who teared up but didn't say a word, just kissed the baby on the forehead and smiled before bringing him back to Jamie.

Yeah, things were exactly the way they should be.

"She looks good," Doc told Chris when all was said and done, and everyone left them alone for a few minutes.

"You have to bring your dad in," she told him.

"You won't see that baby again tonight."

She laughed softly as the baby snored against her. "Love you."

"Love you," he murmured back.

"Guess you have to share your birthday with Christmas and your son," she pointed out.

"Not a bad deal. Not a bad deal at all.

Kenny held his grandson, looking at the snow, grateful for the full circles life brought him.

"Lucien, you're a lucky boy," he said softly, and at the sound of the good Cajun name, the baby's eyes fluttered and opened, stared at him like they both shared some deep, dark secret.

The men in his family passed down the sight to the males only. Luc or Lucky, as they would no doubt end up calling the boy, would no doubt have it, the way Kenny's own great-grandfather, also called Lucky, did.

Lucky would also have family. Lots of it. And that had gotten all of them to hell and back.

He enjoyed watching Isabelle and Jake together, knowing their girls would soon be coming, and Kaylee and Nick, committed and content. Kenny had no doubt they'd come home one day and causally announce they'd married in a quick civil ceremony on impulse. That suited them—they both had that impatience and dislike of conventions and rules.

As for him, he held the next great love of his life in his hands.

They had a new reason to celebrate Christmas, and he was so sure Maggie would be pleased as anything.

LETTERS TO ELLIE

Loreth Anne White

"I'm Ellie Winters, your host every Friday night at eleven, and you're listening to *Your Call* on CKNW 97 AM." Ellie reached for the console, cueing the music. "This last request is for Marcia whose son's plane was shot down over Iraq in 1991. Captain Nick Morgan is still missing."

Through the soundproof studio window Ellie could see Mitchell, her producer, vetting last minute callers. The show computer on her desk showed several still in the line-up. She glanced at the studio clock—they were not all going to get on tonight.

She began to gradually fade-in the song as she spoke. "While the goal is to leave no man behind, the reality of war is that sometimes our heroes don't come home. Sometimes our soldiers go Missing in Action, become Prisoners of War. Their fate unknown. But we dare not forget them." She paused, struggling to keep the huskiness of out of her voice. "We dare not stop trying to bring them home.

"I want to thank everyone who called into our show tonight, on this last hour of National POW/MIA Recognition Day, and for sharing the ways in which you remember your missing sons, brothers, fathers, mothers, daughters, sisters—those who make the ultimate sacrifices to guard our very existence."

She increased the volume, removed her headset and scrubbed her hands hard over her face. Almost fifteen years and still, it got to her. Some wounds cut deep, healed thin—or never healed at all. Because without closure, without knowing what happened, there would always remain a little kernel buried deep inside her heart—maybe he was alive, maybe he'd still come home. That quiet, insistent doubt had shaped Ellie's entire adult life, whether she'd liked it or not.

From behind the window Mitchell made a sign asking if she wanted to take one last caller. Ellie nodded, reached for her water bottle and took a swig. As the song came to an end, she re-adjusted her headset, pulled the mike closer.

"This is *Your Call*. I'm Ellie Winters, and we have time to take one last call." She glanced at her monitor. Next in the queue was Max from Fort Orchard, but the prefix of the number from which he was calling was not local. The subject line read: Navy SEAL, vet.

Something inside her stilled.

She hit *Enter*.

"Our last caller for the night is Max, a Navy vet from Fort Orchard, our own special little corner of Pacific Northwest. Is there someone you want to honor tonight, Max?"

There was a moment of static silence.

"Go ahead, Max, you're on air."

Another beat of silence. Then, "Ellie . . . is that you? Ellie James?" His voice was rough, low, with a hint of North Carolina, and the mention of her maiden name brought her past crashing down over her shoulders. Her pulse began to race.

On the other side of the glass, Mitchell made a quick sign across his throat. But Ellie held up her palm, compelled by something she couldn't begin to articulate.

"Go ahead, Max, is there something you want our listeners to know?"

He cleared his throat, but when he spoke, his voice was still thick, gravelly, his words very slightly slurred. "I went MIA—captured in hostile territory almost fifteen years ago. I'd like your listeners to know that when you're out there, being held in some enemy shithole, the simple belief that someone back home has not forgotten you, is still waiting, *still* loves you . . . " he was quiet for a long moment. "It can keep you alive. It can bring you home."

She stared dead ahead, hands pressing down on the top of her desk, her chest filling with an emotion so powerful, so painful, she barely registered Mitchell gesticulating on the other side of the window for her to axe the call, start wrapping the show.

"I set a table for two," she said, her voice going thick with emotion. "With a white linen cloth and a single red rose. I drape the POW/MIA flag over the back of his chair. I cook a special meal." Her vision blurred. She pressed her hands down harder, struggling to go on.

The phone on the left side of her desk lit up red—showing Mitchell wanted to speak to her.

"Then I light a candle," she said. "And I sit and eat with him . . .

so he doesn't have to dine alone. I . . . " Tears leaked down her cheeks and she was unable to speak.

Mitchell quickly took over from his computer, fading in the pure, solitary notes of a lone trumpeter's rendition of Amazing Grace, and as the music played, Ellie sat in her soundproof studio staring into nothing, tears sliding down her face.

Naked apart from undershorts, he leaned back against the motel room headboard and closed his eyes, listening to the clear notes of a trumpeter playing Amazing Grace. She remembered.

He wondered how long she'd waited before marrying, moving on.

He swigged back the last of his whisky. The room was too hot, thermostat not working. But he was used to the heat, used to dark, confined spaces. And the slight whisky buzz took the edge off the constant pain.

How long was it reasonable to wait, anyway? Fifteen years? Ten? Five? Forever? Death was easier. It gave you closure. But the never knowing, always wondering—that had to be the worst kind of curse, a damnation to limbo.

He opened his eyes. Across the room on the dresser was the box. The reason he'd come to Fort Orchard.

He'd wanted to give it to her today, on this day of all days. It meant a lot to him. But his flight had come in late so he'd checked into the motel, intending to look her up tomorrow.

Then he'd turned on the radio, heard her voice—smooth, husky. It reminded him of jazz, smoky bars, lounge singers and Scotch. And the more she spoke, the more convinced he became that it was her, Ellie James. He hadn't known she hosted her own show.

He'd been unable to stop himself from calling, connecting with her, on this day.

Closing his eyes again he began to drift into blackness, and instantly he was slam back in that hell hole of a jungle, the smell of piss and vomit assailing his nostrils, the burn of pain. The scream of monkeys in the dark trees. His pulse jackhammered. Perspiration dampened his body. He began to see things in the morel room shadows. Then he forced an image into his mind—Ellie at nineteen. Her chestnut hair soft as silk. Her honey-brown eyes liquid and deep with mystery. Her body smooth and naked under his hands. His pulse calmed. His chest filled with warmth, goodness.

My dearest Ellie, I fell asleep with your head on my chest that last night we spent together, the night you promised yourself to me. It felt familiar, so warm, so right, and it scared the hell out of me. For a brief moment I didn't want to leave. Maybe it was a premonition. But I didn't want to lose you . . .

The studio door swung open.

"Ellie?" Mitchell's eyes were wide with concern. "Are you alright—what happened in here?"

She removed her headset, reached for the box of tissues on the desk, blew her nose hard, then cleared her throat. "I'm sorry, Mitch. I lost it for a moment. My fiancée went MIA almost fifteen years ago. That last caller . . . he . . . " Something inside her crumpled and tears welled again. "I thought it was him. For a goddamn bizarre moment I thought he was alive, come home. After all this time. I can't believe that just happened to me."

Mitchell placed his hand on her shoulder, solid, calming. "I'm so sorry. I didn't know."

She shook her head. "It's okay. I don't like to talk about it, but it's why I wanted to do this show tonight—I know how it feels. I was 19 when I got the news. He was a Navy SEAL, twenty-three years old when his chopper went down in a routine training accident in the Gulf of Aden. They found the bodies of eight SEALs. The other four were declared MIA. His name was Flynn Traeborn. We'd been dating since high school, but my parents never knew. My father was a minister—he had some weird ideas, so I kept it quiet. Flynn enlisted at 17, with the consent of his grandfather who was his guardian." She inhaled deeply. "We were going to marry when he came back from that last deployment."

"But he never did."

She shook her head.

"That last caller asked if you were Ellie James."

"My maiden name. I haven't used it for seven years." She laughed, attempting to shake off the eerie sensation that had overcome her. "Probably just some freak who Googled me. I'm not that hard to find."

Mitchell did not return her smile. "Be careful, Ellie."

Ellie stepped out into September darkness. It was cold, well past midnight and a thick Pacific northwest fog rolled in off the ocean. The distant cry of a ship's horn sounded out at sea.

She drew her coat close, moisture misting her hair and face as she made for her car.

Inside her vehicle she sat, waiting for it to warm, cell phone clutched in her hand, along with the piece of paper on which she'd written the last caller's number.

Be careful, Ellie.

Mitchell was right—she needed to think of security. Late night radio shows got their fair share of crackpot callers, Friday nights especially. And hosts got their share of stalkers.

She fingered the piece of paper, remembering why she'd wanted the late Friday slot in the first place. When Flynn first went MIA, Friday nights were the worst. She'd so desperately wanted to connect she'd called a talk show herself. She knew how it felt to have others out there, listening, feeling their own kinds of loneliness. And she'd wanted to give back, to be there for someone else.

She dialled the number.

It rang four times.

"Hello?"

She killed the call, shaking, all the old emotions suddenly rearing up like a tsunami—the last night she'd spent with Flynn, sleeping in his arms. He'd proposed to her that night. Then a week later she was told he was MIA.

Just gone.

She'd waited, unable to believe her Flynn had gone down with the others. She'd started seeing Flynn's features in the faces of others, on the subway, walking down the road. Thinking it was him, she'd sometimes run after the person, before stopping herself. Her mind had started playing conspiracy theory tricks. Navy SEALs operated in shadows—perhaps he was on some covert op, and he'd come home soon. But he never did come home.

How do you remember, Ellie James?

Jesus. What was she doing here? That voice was not Flynn. She swore, again, tossed her phone onto passenger seat, and put her car in gear. But as she drove, wipers clacking, wet autumn leaves plastering a road as shiny wet as black oil, she knew, deep down, something had changed.

Upstairs Ellie opened the door to Jessica's room. Her daughter was asleep. Ellie tiptoed in, kissed her head lightly. But Jessica stirred and sat up. Light from the porch light outside made shadows from trees blowing in the wind move on the walls and across her daughter's face. The porch light was always on—there was once a time Ellie didn't want Flynn to arrive to a house in darkness. She'd thought somehow a light would guide his way back to her. Old habits died hard.

"What happened mom?" Jessica said groggily. "You didn't sign off properly, you didn't tell your listeners that it was me on the trumpet."

Ellie seated herself carefully on the edge of the bed. Rain was coming down harder, ticking against the windows. The heavy wet branches of a conifer scraped on the roof as wind gusted.

"I'm sorry Jess. I—" *Why hide it?* "I got emotional. After listening to all those stories, I . . . "

"You thought of dad?"

"Yes," she whispered. "I thought of your dad." She stroked her daughter's hair. It was soft and dark like Flynn's. "Sometimes . . . just sometimes, I wonder if he could still be out there. He'd be so proud of you."

Wind rattled at the windows, and a fog horn called in the distance, the sound haunting, so alone.

He woke in gray silence. Confusion pressed down. Fear drummed. Sweat dampened his torso. He moved his head on the pillow. The shapes of the motel room came into focus. He heard rain. He was stateside. Pacific Northwest.

Jesus.

He got up, crossed the room, leaned his hands hard on the dresser, his head bent into his chest. He waited for the pain to ease in his leg.

He showered, dressed, and found himself outside Ellie James's house, the box tucked under his arm. It was a nice bungalow, block up from the ocean. Rain dripped from a giant maple at the bottom of the driveway. Leaves as big as his hands, orange and brown, rotted on the lawn. His breath misted white on the chill air and cloud socked low over the distant mountains.

The name on her mailbox read 'Winters'. Only one vehicle in the carport. *Would Mr. Winters be home? Gone to work?*

He tensed, almost ducking back into the shadows of a spruce hedge as the front door swung open. A young teen wearing a knitted toque skittered down the porch stairs, a school backpack slung over her shoulder. She waved to a window upstairs then disappeared down a path round the side of the house.

His gaze sifted to the upstairs window. He saw her shape. Then a drape dropped back. He stood immobile under the branches of the maple tree, water dripping down the back of his neck.

He couldn't do this.

But he had to. Not for himself. But for someone *he* could never forget.

I imagine coming home to you, Ellie. I imagine what you'll look like. How your arms will feel as you fling them around me. I imagine the smell and shape of your body under my hands. I want you to know that I love you . . . .

Maybe giving her the box of letters would rock her suburban life, just a little. For a while. But he was a SEAL. He'd made a vow to a fellow serviceman, a brother in arms.

A friend whose letters to Ellie had kept them both alive for fourteen years.

But it was something deeper that held him back, something he wasn't fully able to articulate to himself—he felt like Ellie belonged to him, too. For years he'd ached to see her, touch her even. Part of him wanted her to know that indirectly, she had brought *him* home, even though Flynn never made it.

As he stood there, wavering, the front door on the porch opened suddenly.

It was her.

Staring right at him.

Time hung, stretched taut, like an elastic band. She stepped out, wrapping her arms over her stomach. Wind gusted, flipping chestnut strands across her face as she crossed the porch towards him. He saw she had a cell phone clutched in one hand.

He began to advance slowly across the lawn. Her eyes flicked past him and he could see her doing the math—no car.

Adrenaline spiked through Ellie. It was him, Max, the caller. Had to be.

He was tall, maybe 6' 3", dark-blonde military buzz cut, powerful jaw, high-cheekbones—dangerous looking. Under his calf-length black coat his shoulders were broad. And in spite of limp, his stride was slow, purposeful.

Her gaze went to the box under his arm. Fear whispered.

"What do you want?" she called out.

"I just need a minute of your time." He came up the porch stairs as he spoke, the sound of his boots heavy on old wood. Up close Ellie could see the color of his eyes; intense, very dark blue. His face was scarred. His knuckles, too. A fighter, a broken one. She judged him to be in his late thirties, although it was hard to tell. His coat hung open to reveal a black T-shirt stretched taut over muscled pecs.

The small hairs at the nape of her neck began to tingle. She wrapped her arms tighter around her stomach.

"You're Max," she said quietly.

"Maddox McDonough," he said. "Max for short." A wry smile curved his lips. "Or Mad Dog. But that was another time, another place." His eyes went to the ring on her finger.

Her spine straightened and her fingers tightened around the cell phone clutched at her waist, her thumb hovering near the keypad.

"I shouldn't have called the show. I'm sorry if I upset you, Ellie."

"You've got one minute to tell me what you want before I call the cops."

He inhaled slowly, something tightening in his features. It took several beats before he spoke.

"I was with Lieutenant Flynn Traeborn when he died."

Blood drained from her face.

She didn't move. Couldn't. Her eyes locked defiantly onto his. "You're lying," she whispered. "You're some sick fuck who's come to mess with my head. Get off my porch before I call 9-1-1."

"I came to give you these." He held out the box to her. It was covered in deep purple fabric, embossed with the pattern of leaves.

Ellie swallowed, afraid of hearing more, of knowing what was in that box. She *needed* to believe Flynn could still come back. She *needed* to keep loving him. Her entire life was predicated on that. She thought of Jessica. Of telling her that her father had died.

"Please—" she said, feeling desperate.

"They're letters, Ellie. From Flynn."

Max saw the sudden stillness in her hands, how she fought to keep her spine straight, how she refused to look at the box. Time hung.

Wind licked again at her hair. For an instant she looked proud, then her eyes turned bright and he watched as her features slowly collapsed. She took a step back, her shoulders rolling inward, as if she'd been punched in the stomach. She grasped for the doorknob behind her, seeking balance, and she looked up at him with those honey brown eyes, liquid and deep with mystery. Max felt he was stepping through time and reality.

"When . . . where?" Her voice caught. "What happened to him?"

"May I come in, Ellie?"

They sat in her small living room, a fire crackling in a black cast iron stove. The coppery glow of flames shimmered on her hair and the color reminded Max of Autumn in the deciduous forests back home.

"Our helo took enemy fire off the northwest coast of Africa—"

"I was told it was a training accident, Gulf of Aden," she interrupted. The box rested on her lap, her hands pressing down flat onto the lid. Her knuckles were white with tension. Max focused on the smooth gold band around her left finger and his stomach tightened. Part of him was glad Flynn hadn't made it home to see that his fiancée was married. It would've killed him.

"Our assignment was classified, Ellie," he said quietly. "It will likely remain classified. I shouldn't even be telling you this," he paused. "But I made a vow to Flynn. I'm going to tell you just enough to honor that vow."

Her eyes held his, her features pale, tight. "They lied to me," she said.

"For security reasons. You can't talk about any of this. I'll have to deny it."

"Go on," she said quietly.

"Flynn and I were the only ones to survive the crash into the ocean. We were captured almost immediately—"

"They said four SEALs went MIA."

"Correct—four bodies were unaccounted for. But to my knowledge, Flynn and I were the only two left floating alive in the Atlantic. We were picked up by enemy craft, taken ashore."

"What enemy?"

He held her eyes. "Ellie, I'm telling you what I can."

Her lips pressed into a tight line as she struggled with the information and Max had to tamp down a raw and sudden urge to get up, sit beside her. Hold, comfort her. Feel that chestnut hair against his cheek.

Your hair is like silk, Ellie. I can feel in now, between my fingers when I think of that last night we had together—it changed everything for me, you know, that night . . .

He inhaled deeply. "For the next thirteen years or so, we were marched from one equatorial jungle camp to another, handed over from one team to another, forgotten, rotting in captivity."

Ellie didn't move, but a small muscle began to quiver along the left side of her lip.

"Then we got a break, we managed to escape." He searched for words that would convey only the basics. "We spent maybe six, seven months in the jungle, hiding at first, then trying to move towards the border. We got sick, survived on what we could. We ran into rebels and Flynn took a machete swipe for me, across his thigh." Max swallowed. "It was the beginning of the end. Got infected. The infection started to spread—stuff breeds like a nightmare in equatorial moisture and heat."

Max looked down at his scarred hands, memories like vultures circling.

"We got to the border. It was marked by a river. Big brown mother fu . . . river in flood," he corrected himself. "Halfway across we took fire from rebels along the banks. We stayed in the water until dark, drifting down current.

Max rubbed his knees, Ellie's silence making him uncomfortable. "Flynn . . . went down shortly before dawn. I dived, brought him back up, performed CPR in the water, and he came round. But after another hour or so, I lost him. He died in my arms, Ellie."

She made a small sound and he couldn't meet her eyes.

"The current took him right out of my hands in the dark dawn hours."

"Maybe he didn't die. Maybe he came around again, and—"

"He died in my arms, Ellie." Max hesitated, fighting the emotion that burned hot and unbidden into his chest.

"Before he went, he made me vow I would make it home, and find you. He made me promise I would tell you what happened." Again, another surge of emotion assailed him. He paused, gathering himself. Flames cracked, popped in the beats of silence.

"He wanted you to know that he tried to come back for you, that he loved you, right to the very end. Flynn wanted me to tell you that he survived as long as he did, because he knew you were waiting for him."

Her face was sheet white. Her whole top lip quivered against her control now, and her eyes glistened.

"But *you* came back."

"I wouldn't have made it without that promise to him. I wouldn't be here today, Ellie, without you, without Flynn's love for you."

She stared at him, silver trails tracking silently down her cheeks, and there was anger in her brown eyes, deep anger. At him.

He glanced again at her ring. She noticed him looking and her hand moved reflexively atop the box. Unspoken words shimmered into the air between them, hovering, like something alive.

You're married, Ellie. You have at least one child. Flynn would have come back to that.

"It took me a while to get to Fort Orchard," he said. "There was debriefing, hospitalization, discharge. And those." He nodded at the box sitting unopened in her lap. "Flynn's letters to you. I needed time to get them down."

She looked down at the box. "I don't understand—he wrote to me? How did you—"

"He spoke those letters out loud, to me. It started after three years of hell, when we got so low we lost all hope. One night, after we'd been left alone, in a new camp, shackled together and bleeding in a tiny shack, in the kind of darkness that is so impenetrable you wonder if there will ever be light, I asked him to tell me about you.

"He did. And we got through that night alive. The next night, I asked again, and that's when Flynn started the first verbal letter to you." Max was silent for several long beats. When he spoke again his voice was rough.

"The letter format gave us a connection to home. It made us believe we would not be forgotten, that we *would* get out. And with each letter, our drive to survive grew stronger, and more focused."

She smoothed her hand over the box in her lap, her attention riveted on him. But the anger in her eyes had not dissipated.

"As I listened to Flynn's words, Ellie, you came alive for me. I began to see you in my mind. You became a part of me, too—I felt that you belonged to both of us. Talking to you became like crack. When Flynn ran out of words, I asked him to repeat old letters. Sometimes his words changed a little, but they became burned into my brain. I could call them up at will, and when I got into a bad headspace, I could read them to myself, and it would make me strong again. After I came home, when I was in hospital, I wrote them down. For you. For him. Word for word."

"That's not poss—"

"You know what's not possible, Ellie? Imagining what it's like to be a PoW. For over fourteen goddamn years. You have no mirror—no functioning society to bounce yourself off. No norms. You don't know what's sane, what's not . . . you do what comes, what you can to survive. And, yeah, maybe you go mad. But Flynn was my rock and I was his. You became our lighthouse, the symbol of home, of why were out there in the first place—to guard our shores. You brought me home, Ellie."

She looked up at him, really looked, into his eyes, as if searching there for sights he'd seen, for an image of Flynn, for a sense of the pain they'd endured, both physical and mental, lost and forgotten. And Max could see compassion eating away at her anger, her denial.

"I still don't have proof, Max."

"I'm it, Ellie. Those letters are it. You're not going to get more than this. Technically he's still MIA. And the assignment remains classified. Read them."

Her gaze went to the box.

Slowly she took the lid off.

Ellie stared at the words on the cover page. *Letters to Ellie.*

She lifted the page.

My Dearest Ellie . . .

She almost choked on a raw surge of emotion. "That's how he started?"

"Each night."

She turned another page.

My dearest Ellie, I fell asleep with your head on my chest that last night we spent together, the night you promised yourself to me. It felt familiar, so warm, so right, and it scared the hell out of me . . .

A tear plopped onto the page, softening ink around the edges. Her vision blurred.

She turned the page. Then flipped faster. With trembling fingertips she touched the words. *"I dreamed of you again last night, Ellie, of coming home. You had the porch light on . . .*

She choked on raw sob of emotion, then her shoulders heaved quietly as she bent her head, filled to capacity with an overwhelming sense of loss, grief, pain. Max got up, came across the room. He placed his hand on her shoulder. It was large, heavy, comforting—a human connection, and she fought the urge to lean into his touch.

"I thought you were him," she said quietly, "when you called the show. I thought he'd come home . . . I dared hope he . . . "

"I'm sorry."

"I wanted you to be him, Max. I wanted you to be Flynn."

Why? she wanted to say. *Why didn't you die instead of him—why can't you be Flynn, here, touching me . . .*

The front door burst open suddenly and Max jerked round in shock.

"Mom! I forgot my lunch!" A young teen burst into the living room, palming off her hat, eyes shining, cheeks pinked from cold. She stilled as she saw Max, and her gaze shot to her mother.

Max's attention remained riveted on the teen.

Her hair was a mass of wild curls, black as a raven's feathers, her eyes soft gray. Long lashes. Narrow features.

His heart slammed against his chest. It was like looking at an echo of someone else.

Slowly, he stepped forward. Ellie got to her feet, her movements nervous.

"This is Jessica, my daughter—"

"I'm Max," he said, his attention fixed on her.

Jessica's eyes went to the open box of letters on the ottoman, shifted back to her mother.

"Will you give us a moment, Jess?" Ellie said. "Max and I have something discuss."

Uncertainly crept into Jessica's features. She looked at Max. "You going to be okay, mom?"

"Of course. Why don't you get your lunch and get back to school. I'll explain later."

"She's Flynn's daughter," Ellie said after Jessica had left.

"He never told me." His voice came out hoarse.

"He didn't know."

Max's gaze went to a photograph on the bookshelf. It was of Ellie, Jessica and some guy who had his arm around them both. It had been taken on what looked like a family ski vacation—they were in snow, holding skis, laughing.

"It happened the night Flynn left," she was saying.

That night changed everything . . .

"A week later I got news he was MIA. It was much later I learned I was pregnant with his baby."

His gaze shot to her, and his heart hurt. "Does Jessica know?"

"That her father is a hero? Yes, she does."

His attention went back to the photo on the shelf, to the smiling family.

"I . . . should go."

She said nothing—didn't ask him to stay, and it cut like a blade. He hobbled to the door. Hand resting on knob he hesitated, then said quietly. "I'm at the Three Pines Motel, room 206. I'll be leaving tomorrow."

She made as if to move forward. Her hand rose slightly, then it fell back to her side.

And he left quickly.

Outside, thank God, it was raining—no one could see that a PoW of more than fourteen years, a soldier, could cry. Max limped back to his motel feeling as if his guts had been ripped out. He'd been living towards this moment. This moment had kept him alive. Now it was over. He'd fulfilled his vow, he'd transcribed and given Ellie the letters. And it was done.

What in hell's name was left for him now?

He stopped at a store, bought a fifth of Scotch, went back to his room, sloshed three fingers into a glass, swigged it back, and followed with another. When he felt the beginnings of a slight buzz, the edge dulled a little, and he began to pack the few possessions he'd brought into his bag.

She was as beautiful as Flynn's words had described, and while the last fifteen years had ravaged him, killed Flynn, time had been good to Ellie Winters.

I imagine coming home to you, Ellie. I imagine what you'll look like. How your arms will feel as you fling them around me. I imagine the smell and shape of your body under my hands . . . .

Max stilled, then cursed. What in heaven's name had he even been thinking? She was married—untouchable. And fuck, it hurt. He hadn't realized just how deeply he'd loved the idea of her, how much she'd become to him, until now. Seeing her was like seeing a woman he'd known half his life.

Christ, there was no manual for this. No twelve-step how-to. He and Flynn had done what they could to survive. They'd endured things no man should, while seemingly forgotten, left to die in some hell hole jungle. How did one convey any of that?

How did one come back from that? Would he always walk an outsider along the edges of existence now?

Could he ever be normal again?

That night, after explaining to Jessica that Max McDonough had been with her father when he died, after comforting her daughter when she cried, Ellie climbed into her own bed with the box of letters.

Rain ticked against her windows and the conifers outside twisted in the wind. She pulled her duvet close, switched on her reading light, and opened the box. When she saw Max's handwriting again, guilt swamped her.

Until she'd started reading these letters, she'd been nervous of him, unsure whether she could trust him, unsure of the feelings he'd stirred in her. She'd let him walk out into the rain without a word, and she hated herself for it.

She'd gone to the window, watched him limp down the street, his posture still proud. A broken soldier. And she'd let him go, even as something inside screamed inside her to run out after him, stop him.

Ellie started to read. At 2 AM, she was still reading, a pile of crumpled Kleenex at her side, her eyes thick and raw, her chest aching with unfathomable emotion.

My dearest Ellie, today is you birthday, I think. It's hard to tell so near to the equator what time of year it is. Nightfall and daybreak come like clockwork every twelve hours, year round. We guess we've been in captivity five years now. Sometimes I don't know who I am, or even if our captors remember why they have us, why they move us from jungle camp to camp. Max tries to count days. It was him who said it was time to do you birthday letter. He helps keep you alive in my mind. He makes me believe I'll come home to you.

Last year on your birthday—I won't lie, they take pleasure torturing us—my face was beat up so bad and I'd lost so many teeth, I couldn't talk to you. So when our captors had passed out shitfaced, the night thick as hot velvet, the crickets, and jungle noises drowning our whispers, Max began to recite your birthday letter for me. I think he loves you now, Ellie, as much as I do . . . She heard Jessica get up and go to the bathroom. A few moments later her bedroom door inched open.

"Mom? I saw your light. You okay?"

"Come here." Ellie patted the empty side of the double bed.

"They're making you sad," she said about the pile of letters.

"And happy." Tears welled again. "Just knowing how much he cared, that in a way I was there for him until the end." She blew her nose. "God . . . it's so hard to bear, all in one go."

Jessica curled up beside her. "Can I read them?"

"Let me finish them first, okay?"

"And that guy, Max, wrote them all down, for my father?"

Ellie nodded.

"That's incredible."

"It is," Ellie whispered. "I think he must be an incredible man."

Jessica fell asleep curled next to her. Ellie touched her hair. Dark, almost blue-black like her father's. Same eyes. In a way, she thought, Max had brought them all closer. He'd given Jessica a gift, too.

Leaning back against the headboard, Ellie closed her eyes

She lay there thinking about the man who *had* come back. Flynn had shared his love for her with Max. It's what had brought Max to her door. He'd brought closure in these words, these letters. Ellie inhaled deeply, feelings she didn't know still existed reawakening in her, like someone thawing after years of being suspended in ice.

Did you not have someone waiting at home for you, Max? Did you not share your own stories with Flynn?

She shook her daughter's shoulder softly. "Jess, you need to go to your bed. You've got school tomorrow."

Jessica pushed her thick curls back from her face, her eyes sleepy. "You going to be okay, Mom?"

Ellie smiled. "Yeah. I'm going to be fine, sweetie, thank you."

But she wasn't sure about Max.

At 4 a.m. she dialed Max's number, torn by fear he'd leave before she could speak to him, and that she'd never see him again, desperate to connect with him after reading these letters. To thank him. The call went straight to voicemail. Ellie listened to his message, his voice deep, rough like gravel, flavoured with a hint of North Carolina, of home.

She killed the call, glanced at the clock. Panic kicked her pulse into sudden overdrive.

Ellie yanked on her clothes, shrugged into her coat, and drove to the Three Pines Motel. She got out her car and stood on sidewalk, rain coming down on her, impossible things pulling at her.

Max had brought an end to the wondering, the never knowing. But he'd also made it real, raw again. He'd thrust her back in time, started a process of profound grief. He'd stirred passions, needs, in Ellie that she'd put on ice for over a decade. She began to shake, her hair plastering wet against her cheeks.

A dull yellow glow came from behind blinds in room 206. It was the only light in the strip of darkened rooms. Ellie stared at the glow, unsure of herself, of why she was really standing out here. She almost turned to leave, but something deep and burning compelled her to take the steps up to 206. She knocked.

He opened the door. She stood there, the corridor lights bleaching her complexion, her hair plastered wet against her face, her eyes dark with a need and confusion he recognized. A silver sheen of rain drummed down behind her, splattering in the parking lot.

Max's hand tightened on the doorknob, his heart pounding against his ribs. He knew what he looked like—he was shirtless, his torso sliced with scars, and he'd been drinking. He didn't trust himself. "Ellie?" his voice felt thick.

She stepped closer, crowding him. Max kept his hand firm on the door, blocking access, not ceding ground. She raised her hand, lightly touching a scar on his chest. He quivered at the coolness of her fingertips against his hot skin, and his mouth went dry.

"They tortured you," she whispered.

"And Flynn."

"I read about it, in the letters."

Her hand moved to another scar, below his pecs. Max felt his groin harden. "Ellie," his voice was coarse, his need so raw it scared the hell out of him. "You should go."

"I came to say thank you, Max. I was terrified you'd leave before I could, and that I'd never find you again."

He stared her mouth, trying to avoid what he could read in her eyes. She came a little closer and he could smell the shampoo in her hair. Perspiration beaded along his lip. He grabbed her wrist, held. She flinched, a flutter of fear touching her face, then something darker took over. Her lips parted and her breathing became light.

He moved her hand away from his chest. "You're married," he said.

Her eyes widened. Slowly she extracted her wrist from his grasp. Gaze holding his, she removed her gold band and held it out to him.

"Read the inscription, Max."

He took the ring from her fingers, stepped back into the room, and held it up to the light. Engraved around the inside circumference were the words, *Forever, I will wait.*

His gaze flashed to hers. Rain drummed. Small drops glittered like jewels on her lashes.

"I'm not married, Max. Lord knows I tried, but I could never stop waiting. It wasn't fair to continue. I wear that ring for Flynn."

Emotion punched through his stomach—relief, a hot thrill, things he couldn't even begin to understand raced through his chest.

"What about Winters? The man in the photo on your shelf? The name on your mailbox?"

"Are you going to ask me in? I need to explain it to you. After those letters... I need to tell you everything. I want you to understand."

He stepped back.

Ellie entered the small motel room. It was hot inside. She began to remove her coat.

"Thermostat doesn't work," he explained, closing the door and helping her with her coat. He hung it over the bathroom door, gave her ring back.

Their fingers brushed and Ellie's pulse jackhammered. Time seemed to stand still, the room too small, too warm, too confined. Slowly she looked up, met his eyes, and she swallowed at the rough edginess she saw there, the sense of danger and physicality.

Gingerly Ellie seated herself of the edge of the bed—it was the only place to sit. She pushed the wet hair back off her face. "You went low budget accommodation, huh?" She tried to smile, but it felt wrong.

He said nothing, just stared at her, almost devouring her, perspiration gleaming on his scarred and honed torso. Heat rose in Ellie's cheeks. Half naked he looked even more ruggedly powerful to her than clothed. And she knew how he felt about her, from the letters.

In turn, Ellie felt she knew aspects of Max McDonough intimately. All she wanted to do was hold him, feel that hard, scarred body in her arms, have him hold her back. She wanted to connect with the beautiful mind she knew lived inside him. Her eyes began to burn.

Slowly, she reached up, took his hand in hers. "Sit beside me, Max."

He did, not too close, but close enough that she could feel the warmth rolling off his body. His scent was male—a hint of aftershave, of whiskey. Something stirred low and hot in her belly.

"I waited, Max," she said, her voice going husky. "For seven years I waited for Flynn to come home. People tried to help me move forward, tried to get me to believe he was gone, but there was this hole in my heart, this feeling he was still out there, alive."

"He was."

Ellie nodded. "You showed me I was right. But I was young, and I had a small daughter, and . . . Greg Winters was there for me. He gave me my first job at a radio station. He's a good guy, Max. He loved me, asked me to marry him. He said Jessica needed a father, a family. I did it for her, I think. I tried to love Greg back, and in a way, maybe I did. But he knew he was sharing his life with the ghost of Flynn. He thought I'd get over it. I didn't. Our marriage just fizzled. Lasted all of two years. I thought it best to let him go—it wasn't fair on him."

Ellie looked down at her hands.

"I kept the name Winters," she said softly, "because I'd started to build a brand in the industry. The ring—it was a signal I was unavailable, I suppose. I didn't need anyone, Max, not after the screw-up with Greg. I had Jessica, the rest of me was . . . dead."

Max saw her shoulders sag, her energy suddenly wane. "Until now," she whispered. "Waiting for Flynn defined me. Now that I know he's gone, I don't know who I am."

He cupped the side of her face. Her eyes lifted, met his.

"Hey," he said, his voice thick with lust, with compassion. "I get it. I don't know who I am, either. I don't know where I fit."

Tears pooled in her eyes and Max felt her lean into his touch. Time stilled, stretched, thick. He could hear a refrigerator humming down the corridor, tires crackling outside on wet streets. A fog horn sounded, lonely on the ocean.

"I feel like I know you Maddox McDonough," she whispered, her gaze holding his. "I'm sorry for what I said—I'm glad you came home."

Emotion arrowed through him. The need between them swelled, shimmered, like a hot and electric thing in the room.

She touched his chest again. "Be with me Max," she whispered, her voice low, thick, her eyes dark.

He swallowed, need burning fierce and dangerous in him, too powerful for him to control.

"Ellie—"

She brought her mouth up to his, silencing his words. Her lips were soft, sweet, so full of promise. Her scent, her arms, wrapped around him and her tongue entered his mouth.

Lust exploded in his gut and his control snapped, a raw and primal need coursing violently through his blood. It stole thought, stole logic. Everything narrowed to this moment. He pulled her close, her breasts pressing hard up against his bare chest as he forced her mouth open wide under his, his tongue tangling with hers, slick, hot.

Her hands slid down his waist, found the waistband of his shorts. He pulled back suddenly, chest heaving, his groin pulsing, hot.

"Ellie? Are you sure?"

"More sure than anything."

"I'll get the lights—"

"No," she whispered. "I want them on." Under the harsh motel room lights there was no hiding, no mistaking the cruelty of the marks on his body. She wanted to see, embrace—all of him. And she craved exposing herself, every imperfection, she didn't care.

"I'm not nineteen, Max," Ellie whispered. "The person in those letters, in your mind, she doesn't exist anymore. I want you to see who I am, all of me, every flaw."

He kissed her, hard, fierce, and fire speared through her belly. She fumbled with the buttons on her blouse, the zipper on her jeans, as she kissed him back. He cupped her breast, scoring her tight nipple with his thumb, a low groan in his throat. He slid his hand into her panties. Ellie gasped as he thrust a finger into her. Her world tilted, her breathing came fast.

And it was like the room couldn't hold them anymore—too small, too hot, clothes everywhere. Hair damp, bodies slick with sweat. They slammed against the headboard, against the wall. Old emotions burning, new ones searing, past memories colliding into present. Then he had her up against the wall, a dark hard look on his face that excited her, and he was inside her again. Her legs found his waist, wrapping around him, giving him deeper access. He kissed her so hard she tasted blood, didn't care.

He thrust deeper, his fingers digging into her butt as he yanked her against him. She threw her head back, arms around his neck, as she arched into him, pleasure, pain, need, driving her higher, a scream building in her chest as every nerve in her body began to quiver. Ellie thrust her pelvis harder against his, faster, her world becoming a swirling kaleidoscope of reds and blacks.

He held her still for a moment, her breasts pressing hard against his scarred, hard chest, and she could feel from the way he quivered inside her that he was close. He looked into her eyes, and then he suddenly thrust again to the hilt. She released with a cry, head thrown back as rolling waves of contractions took hold of her.

Banging sounded on the wall. They were waking the place up, but Ellie didn't care. He came inside her, pressing her hard against the wall, and she laughed, breathless as she held onto him. She felt all of nineteen again.

They lay on the bed, she in his arms. He stroked her hair, still damp from rain, damp from sweat, her lips swollen and bleeding a little.

It felt familiar, so warm, so right, and it scared the hell out of me . . . for a brief moment I didn't want to leave . . . I didn't want to lose you . . .

He traced his finger over the curve of her breast, her dusky nipple.

"He made me love you, Ellie."

She stilled, something suddenly shifting in her, and Max saw fear touch her face, like the quick beat of a moth's wing.

She inhaled, sat up, began to gather her clothes. He felt fear himself now.

"I need to go," she said, pulling on her jeans. "I need to see Jessica off to school."

"You're a good mother, Ellie."

She looked up from buttoning her blouse, something unreadable in her features. She turned round quickly, grabbed her coat, shrugged into it.

Max felt the bottom drop out of his heart. She was leaving. This was it. Over.

"I'm sorry, Ellie."

She stilled, her brown eyes showing a vulnerability he'd not seen yet.

"I'm sorry it was me who made it, and not Flynn."

She inhaled, sat on side of bed. "What are you going to do, Max?"

"I've been offered contract work. East Coast based."

"You going to take it?"

"Yeah," he lied. Truth was, he wasn't sure. He had a few options.

"Your leg going to be okay?" There was compassion in her eyes. He didn't want compassion, pity.

He got up, wrapped a towel around his waist. "Yeah, fine. My flight leaves in a couple of hours." Her eyes met his. "How 'bout you? You going to be okay, Ellie?"

"I will. Thank you, Max, for . . . everything."

She got up, went towards the door. Then stilled, hand on the knob. She turned suddenly. "It's Jessica's birthday tomorrow—she turns fifteen. We're having a small dinner party, just close friends." Ellie hesitated. "I'd like you to meet her, Max, properly. I'd like her to hear about her father from you. Would you come?"

Emotion raw, ripped through Max's chest. He didn't trust himself to speak.

He knew what she was doing—opening a door. She didn't want to end it right here. They shared something subliminal, deep, something few might understand, and she wasn't going to throw it away.

"Please?" she said.

When Max knocked on the bungalow door the next evening he had a different box tucked under his arm—a present for Jessica, something he imagined Flynn might buy for his daughter. And he held a single dark-red rose in tissue paper.

Ellie opened the door to him. Warmth layered with the scents of cooking spilled into cold air.

Her eyes went to the rose. "There's no manual for this, is there?" she said softly.

"No," he said. "There isn't."

She leaned up, kissed him lightly on the lips. "Then we'll have to write our own." She took his hand. "Come inside, Max, there are some people I want you to meet."

Max stepped into the warm glow and he knew, finally, truly, he'd come home.

About the Authors

Jami Alden is a multi-published author of dark, sexy, romantic suspense and hot steamy contemporary romance. She lives near San Francisco with her socially well-adjusted alpha male husband, two sons, and a German shepherd of questionable lineage. Learn more about Jami and her books at www.jamialden.com.

———

Kylie Brant is the author of over thirty books for Berkley and Harlequin. A three-time Rita nominee, she's the recipient of two Daphne du Maurier awards for excellence in mystery and suspense and a *Romantic Times* Career Achievement Award. Her most recent full-length novel, *Deadly Sins*, is available now. Her hometown is Charles City, IA. Visit her at www.kyliebrant.com.

"My father is a World War II veteran," says Brant. "When we began talking about donating the proceeds to a veteran's group, I immediately said, 'I'm in.'"

———

Helen Brenna is the author of the popular *Mirabelle Island* series set off Wisconsin's Lake Superior shore. Since her first book was published in 2007, she's won numerous awards, including two Romance Writers of America's RITAs, two RT Book Reviews Reviewer's Choice awards, and the National Readers' Choice award.

She lives with her family and a menagerie of pets, in Minneapolis. For information on upcoming releases or to contact her, please visit her website at www.helenbrenna.com.

———

Stephanie Bond was born on the U.S. Army base in Fort Riley, Kansas. Her father, Willis Bond, served in the First Infantry in the Vietnam War. (Go Big Red One!) The author of over sixty romance and mystery novels, Stephanie is honored to contribute to the *SEAL of*

My Dreams anthology. She lives in Atlanta, GA.

———

Robyn Carr is married to a former Air Force helicopter and jet pilot and her son is an Army orthopedic surgeon who served in Iraq. She takes her military-based heroes very personally. Robyn is the New York *Times* bestselling author of over forty novels, including the Virgin River Series.

———

Best-selling and award-winning romance author **HelenKay Dimon** has an undying respect for the military. Not only does she live in a military town—San Diego—her husband is an attorney for the Navy, and her father-in-law is a retired Army Colonel.

Dimon is a former divorce attorney who is thrilled to write romance full time. Two of her novels have been designated as "Red-Hot Reads" by *Cosmopolitan Magazine* and excerpted in its issues. Her books have been featured at numerous venues, including *E! Online* and *The Chicago Tribune,* and translated into more than a dozen languages. HelenKay lives with her Navy husband in San Diego. You can visit her at www.helenkaydimon.com

———

Cindy Gerard is a New York *Times, Publisher's Weekly* and *USA Today* Bestseller. She's a six-time RITA finalist and is proud to display two RITAs in her office. Cindy writes fast, sexy, action-adventure romantic suspense featuring former Spec Ops warriors and is proud to count many military families among her readers. LAST MAN STANDING, book 7 of her award winning Black Ops series, is available in February, 2012. Find all of Cindy's books at www.cindygerard.com.

———

Tara Janzen is the author of the *Steele Street* Series, eleven books about a crew of juvenile car thieves and chop-shop boys who become one of America's most elite black ops military teams, Special Defense Force. The series began with *Crazy Hot* and *Crazy Cool* and ended with the New York *Times* bestselling *Loose Ends.*
Visit her at www.tarajanzen.com

Leslie Kelly has written dozens of light, sexy romances for Harlequin Temptation, Blaze and HQN. She also writes dark romantic thrillers under the pseudonym Leslie Parrish. A three-time nominee for the highest award in romance, the RWA RITA Award, she was also honored with Career Achievement Award in Series Romance from *Romantic Times* Magazine in 2010. Visit her online at www.lesliekelly.com.

A RITA-award nominated author, **Elle Kennedy** began pursuing writing at a young age and holds a bachelor's degree in English. She currently resides in Toronto, where she writes full time. Visit her at www.ellekennedy.com.

The daughter of an Air Force veteran and daughter-in-law of an Army veteran, both of whom served during the Korean Conflict, **Alison Kent** currently writes about the cowboys of the Great State of Texas. She lives near Houston with her petroleum-geologist husband and three rescue dogs, one a Hurricane Katrina survivor. Visit her at www.alisonkent.com.

Jo Leigh has written over fifty books for Harlequin, is a triple RITA finalist, and teaches writing whenever she can. She lives in a tiny Utah town with her many rescue pets, and sends care packages regularly to her nephew, who is currently serving in Kabul, Afghanistan. Visit her at www.joleigh.com.

Gennita Low writes sexy military and techno spy-fi romance. She's also a roofer and knows six hundred ways to kill with roofing tools. A three-time Golden Heart finalist, her first book, *Into Danger*, about a SEAL out-of-water, won the *Romantic Times* Reviewers Choice Award for Best Romantic Intrigue. Besides her love for SEALs, she works with an Airborne Ranger who taught her all about mental toughness and physical endurance. Gennita lives in Florida with her mutant poms and one chubby squirrel. Visit her at www.Gennita-Low.com and www.facebook.com/gennita

Marliss Melton is the author of the bestselling *Team Twelve* Navy SEALs series. Wife of a retired Navy veteran, she relies on her experience as a military spouse and on her many contacts in the Spec Ops and Intelligence communities to pen realistic and heartfelt stories about America's most elite warrior, the U.S. Navy SEAL. As the daughter of a foreign services officer, Melton grew up in various countries overseas before settling permanently in Williamsburg, Virginia.

Christie Ridgway is a five-time RITA finalist and the *USA Today* bestselling author of over thirty-five contemporary romances. She lives in San Diego, California, where Navy SEAL teams are based and can be seen training on local beaches. If that isn't inspiration enough, she is the daughter-in-law of a former fighter pilot and now-retired Navy captain. Visit her at www.christieridgway.com.

Barbara Samuel, a native of Colorado Springs, is the proud mother-in-law of an Air Force staff sergeant at the Air Force Academy. She's the winner of six RITAs, with more than 38 books to her credit in a variety of genres. She has written historical and contemporary romances, also a number of fantasy novellas with the likes of Susan Wiggs, Jo Beverley and Mary Jo Putney. She now writes women's fiction as Barbara O'Neal for Bantam, including *How to Bake a Perfect Life,* which features a soldier at the heart. Visit her at www.barbarasamuel.com

---

Roxanne St. Claire is a New York *Times* bestselling author of twenty-seven novels of suspense and romance, also a five-time RITA nominee and one-time RITA winner. The author of the popular *Bullet Catchers* and *Guardian Angelino* series featuring many military heroes, she will also be launching a contemporary romance series soon, called *Barefoot Bay,* and a her first young-adult novel, *Don't You Wish,* in 2012.

She can be reached via her website, www.roxannestclaire.com or through her fan page at www.facebook.com/roxannestclaire.

New York *Times* bestselling author **Stephanie Tyler** writes what she loves to read—romantic suspense novels starring military heroes, and paranormal romance novels, all complete with happy endings. She also co-writes as Sydney Croft. Visit her at www.stephanietyler.com

———

Loreth Anne White was born and raised in South Africa, but now lives in a ski resort in the moody Coast Range, a place of vast, wild and often dangerous mountains, larger-than-life characters, epic adventure, and romance.

It was here she was inspired to abandon a sixteen-year career as a journalist to escape into a world of romantic fiction filled with dangerous men and adventurous women. Her real-life hero, her husband of twenty-six years, is an ex-naval serviceman whose veteran father was a pilot in two wars.

Loreth has won the *Romantic Times* Reviewers' Choice award, is a double *Romantic Times* Reviewers' Choice award finalist, a RITA finalist, a double Daphne Du Maurier finalist, and multiple Cata Romance Reviewers' Choice winner. Her website is www.lorethannewhite.com. She loves to hear from readers.

———

Debra Dixon and Deborah Smith, partners and co-publishers in Bell Bridge Books, are well-known, award-winning romance novelists with more than fifty published novels between them, including Smith's New York *Times* bestseller, *A Place To Call Home*. They are very proud to be trusted with the honor of publishing *SEAL of My Dreams*, donating all proceeds to veterans' medical research.

Dixon and Smith, along with partners Sandra Chastain, Nancy Knight and Virginia Ellis, started Bell Bridge Books (original name: BelleBooks) in 2000, publishing their regional (Southern) short stories. Now Bell Bridge has published over 100 titles by dozens of authors, with fifty more coming in 2012. Bell Bridge will be a sponsor of the 2012 Romance Writers of America national conference and recently was a sponsor for the 2011 Dragon*Con, the world's largest fan-based sci-fi and fantasy conference.

About the Veterans Research Corporation

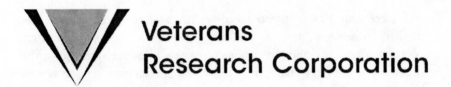

All of the men and woman who have courageously served our country deserve the finest health care available—the kind that requires a substantial and sustained level of funding for medical research. Only through formally organized research can we create and verify new best standards to advance patient care for our brave veterans. The need for veteran-based medical research is great due to emerging health challenges that particularly pertain to veterans such as Traumatic Brain Injury (TBI) and Post Traumatic Stress Disorder (PTSD), as well as the healthcare concerns of an aging veteran population, including heart disease, osteoarthritis, diabetes and a host of other common medical issues. The Veterans Research Corporation, a non-profit organization based in San Diego, CA, was founded with the specific purpose of raising funds to support veteran based medical research to improve the lives of veterans and benefit society at large.

The Veterans Research Corporation works with the Veterans Medical Research Foundation, which administers cutting edge research studies at the VA San Diego Healthcare System. Many of these studies are national in scope, and their findings help elevate the level of healthcare for veterans everywhere. While the Veterans Medical Research Foundation works closely with the VA to serve VA patients, it is solely funded by external sources and does not receive VA funding. Thus, the goal of the Veterans Research Corporation is to secure funding by seeking alternative and private sources to support the growing need, and to foster a new generation of researchers for tomorrow's veterans' medical and health care challenges. Your purchase of this book will help us to continuously improve the standard of care for our veterans, who so richly deserve the best we can provide for them. Thank you!

For more information on the Veterans Research Corporation, and a link to specific research administered through the Veterans Medical Research Foundation, or other innovative programs available to help veterans, please visit:

http://www.veteransresearchcorp.org/

or

http://www.facebook.com/VeteransResearchCorporation

The Veterans Research Corporation is a tax exempt 501(c)(3) public benefit nonprofit organization. Its Taxpayer Identification Number (EIN) is 26-3695803.

CPSIA information can be obtained at www.ICGtesting.com
Printed in the USA
LVOW090245210412

278583LV00002B/12/P